Fame

*Also by Karen Kingsbury
in Large Print:*

Oceans Apart
One Tuesday Morning
Beyond Tuesday Morning
A Thousand Tomorrows
A Time to Embrace
A Treasury of Miracles for Women:
  True Stories of God's Presence Today

*Also by Karen Kingsbury and
Gary Smalley in Large Print:*

Redemption
Remember
Return
Rejoice
Reunion

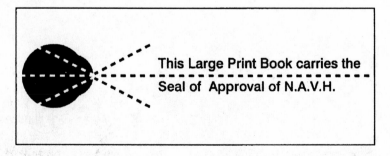
This Large Print Book carries the
Seal of Approval of N.A.V.H.

Fame

Karen Kingsbury

Thorndike Press • Waterville, Maine

Published in 2006 by arrangement with Tyndale House Publishers, Inc.

Thorndike Press® Large Print Christian Fiction.

The tree indicium is a trademark of Thorndike Press.

The text of this Large Print edition is unabridged.
Other aspects of the book may vary from the original edition.

Set in 16 pt. Plantin by Elena Picard.

Printed in the United States on permanent paper.

Library of Congress Cataloging-in-Publication Data

Kingsbury, Karen.
    Fame / by Karen Kingsbury.
      p. cm. — (Thorndike Press large print Christian fiction)
    ISBN 0-7862-8213-4 (lg. print : hc : alk. paper)
    ISBN 1-59415-114-8 (lg. print : sc : alk. paper)
    1. Motion picture actors and actresses — Fiction.
  2. Motion picture industry — Fiction. 3. Large type books.
  I. Title. II. Thorndike Press large print Christian fiction series.
PS3561.I4873F36 2005b
  813'.54—dc22   2005027641

Fame

National Association for Visually Handicapped
----------------------- serving the partially seeing

As the Founder/CEO of NAVH, the only national health agency solely devoted to those who, although not totally blind, have an eye disease which could lead to serious visual impairment, I am pleased to recognize Thorndike Press* as one of the leading publishers in the large print field.

Founded in 1954 in San Francisco to prepare large print textbooks for partially seeing children, NAVH became the pioneer and standard setting agency in the preparation of large type.

Today, those publishers who meet our standards carry the prestigious "Seal of Approval" indicating high quality large print. We are delighted that Thorndike Press is one of the publishers whose titles meet these standards. We are also pleased to recognize the significant contribution Thorndike Press is making in this important and growing field.

Lorraine H. Marchi, L.H.D.
Founder/CEO
NAVH

*Thorndike Press encompasses the following imprints: Thorndike, Wheeler, Walker and Large Print Press.

To Donald, my forever prince.
Can it be seventeen years ago that you swept me off my feet and showed me what true love was? How it puts our loving God first and how it waits as a way of honoring Him? People ask me if there are really guys like my characters Landon Blake and Ryan Taylor, and I always tell them yes. Of course guys like that exist. I should know; I'm married to one. We stand on the brink of a new season in life. I love you, and I can't wait to see what God's going to do next.

To Kelsey, my precious laughter.
You are in the becoming years, my sweet daughter. And it delights my soul to see you becoming everything I prayed you would be — a young woman dedicated to the Lord and to family and to whatever plans God lays out for you in the years ahead. The other day you told me you loved high school, but that it was a little sad because we had so much less time together. That's true, but what we do share is golden, sweetheart. Thanks for our late-night talks. I love you, and I'll always have a light on for you.

To Tyler, my beautiful song.

Your voice, your music is the sound track of our lives, dear oldest son. Having you home this year, homeschooling you, has given me more hours to enjoy the melody, to watch you go for your dreams. Keep God at the center, Ty, and I know He will give you the desires of your heart. When He does, your father and I will be in the front row. I love you always and forever.

To Sean, my happy boy.

Of all the ways you've blessed our family since coming to us from Haiti, most of all I love how you make us smile. The other day the smile came when you rubbed my back as we all read Dr. Seuss and giggled at the silly rhymes. But my favorite smiles come each morning when you rush up to me with our devotion book, thrilled to the point of squealing that this day, like every other, we might get a chance to learn a little more about Jesus. Good for you, Sean! I love you, honey.

To Josh, my softhearted leader boy.

You define perfectionism, and still you have time to laugh once in a while. We gave you a flashlight for Christmas, and now — as a treat for doing so well in school — you get to read the Bible every night when the lights are off. Remember that, Josh. A decade from now when the NBA and NFL fight over which one wants you more, at the end of the day the best treat of all is God's Word. I'm grateful for you in our lives, and I love you so.

To EJ, my chosen one.
Always that will be you, little son, the one chosen first. When God put it on our hearts to adopt, there was never a question after He led us to you. Something in your eyes told us that this terrifying idea of bringing new children into our family might just work out after all. I'm breathless at the ways you are growing and maturing, finding your way with the talents and gifts God has given you. I love you, EJ. Keep making Him proud!

To Austin, my tenderhearted boy.
I'm amazed every time I watch you scoring circles around the competition on the basketball court or the soccer field. Often the image blurs and I see you as you were seven years ago — an infant facing emergency heart surgery. When you pulled through, I knew you would always have a special heart. But watching you put your arm

9

around a buddy who's being picked on or seeing you get teary-eyed when Daddy sings praise songs tells me just how special your heart really is. You'll always be my little MJ, my Brett Favre, fist in the air, running across the field. I love you, and I thank God for every day we have together.

And to God Almighty, the author of life, who has — for now — blessed me with these.

Acknowledgments

As always, a novel like *Fame* doesn't come together without the help of many people. The list is long, but so very important. First, thanks to my husband and family for putting up with my sometimes hectic schedule and helping me survive my deadlines. When I'm at the computer wearing headphones connected to nothing, you all know better than to ask me where your homework is. You're the best! Thanks for understanding.

Also thanks to my friends at Tyndale House Publishers. Becky Nesbitt, you had a vision for this series and my place as a fiction author at Tyndale, and I will always be grateful for that! This book and this series wouldn't have come together without Becky, Mark Taylor, Ron Beers, Travis Thrasher, and so many others. A special thanks to Jeremy Taylor and my editor, Lorie Popp.

I couldn't do what I'm doing in the world of fiction without my amazing agent, Rick Christian. Rick, I look to you on so many levels — as a strategist, a negotiator, and a prayer warrior. My family and I thank God for you in our lives. Thank you is never enough.

Also thanks to my mother, Anne Kingsbury. You are the most diligent and careful assistant I could ever dream to have. I look forward to spending the next decades working together in this wonderful world God has given me. And thanks to my father, Ted Kingsbury, for being my greatest encourager. I always know where to turn when I need a smile.

A hearty thanks to the people who have helped with my children when life gets a little busy. Those include Cindy and Al Weil, Barb and Bill Shaffer, the Head family, and all my friends at CYT. Also Kira Elam, Paige Grenning and the Juventes soccer gang, and the Schmidt family.

Thanks also goes to my extended support group who continue to love and pray for me, those special people who have stayed by me through the twists and turns of this writing ministry. Among them are my sisters Susan, Tricia, and Lynne, and my brother, David. The Russells, the Cummins, and also my niece, Shannon, and my mother-in-law, Betty.

In addition, thanks to my precious

friends Kathy and Ken Santschi, Bobbi and Erika Terret, Randy and Vicki and Lola Graves, John and Melinda Chapman, Stan and De-Ette Kaputska, Aaron Hisel, Theresa Thacker, Ann Hudson, Sylvia and Walt Walgren, Richard Camp and the entire Camp family, the Dillons, and dozens of friends at the high school.

Also a heartfelt thanks to the hundreds of retailers who carry my books. You are a vital part of what God is doing in changing lives through this Life-Changing Fiction, and I pray you will be inspired to keep on! Books make a difference! I'm honored to be partnering with you.

In that same light, thanks to the readers across the world who connect with God through reading these books. I hear from hundreds of you every week, and I'm touched to the center of my being. My soul rejoices at the news you report. Please know that you remain in my prayers as I write.

And of course, thanks most of all to God, who is allowing me to chase this wonderful dream, and I know without a doubt that all of it is for Him, because of Him, and through Him. To God be the glory always.

Forever in Fiction

A special thanks to my Forever in Fiction winners whose characters are represented in this book — Krissy Schick, Chris and Amy Helmes, Kelly and Becky Helmes, and Tani Zarelli.

Krissy Schick, a thirty-six-year-old mother of four, won the Northshore Christian School auction in Bothel, Washington, and chose to have a character named after herself. She loves being a mom and is grateful for her family. She has a zest for life that makes her a favorite among her friends.

Chris and Amy Helmes, and Kelly and Becky Helmes each won Forever in Fiction at the Firm Foundation Christian School auction in Vancouver, Washington. The two couples chose to have their characters named after Chris's and Kelly's parents, Alvar and Nancy Helmes. Alvar and Nancy have been married more than fifty years and stand as the pillars of the Helmes family. They have a deep and abiding love for Christ, for each other, and for their eight children. They spent most of their lives in Ironwood, Michigan, but since moving to Washington they have become very involved in medical missions to the people of India. Al loves books and music — especially old hymns — and spending time with his family. The couple's youngest daughter, Cara, has Down syndrome and is a special source of love for them. Nancy is a wonderfully loving mother and grandmother whose passion for her family is unequaled. She loves hot coffee and Cinnabon rolls, and her family always expects a fresh and witty saying whenever she's around.

Finally, Tani Zarelli won Forever in Fiction at the Salmon Creek Soccer Association auction and chose to name her character after her seventeen-year-old daughter, Ashley. Ashley is the adopted daughter of Tani and Senator Joseph Zarelli of Washington State. Ashley's passion is horseback riding and anything to do with horses. She loves spending an evening baking cookies and watching movies with her family. Her favorite color is blue, and she enjoys a strong understanding of God's providence in her life. Ashley, your parents want you to know you are very loved.

May God bless all of you who have given so generously to the charities of your choice in an effort to place your name or the name of a loved one Forever in Fiction. Thousands of dollars have been raised for wonderful causes through Forever in Fiction, and I am humbly grateful for the opportunity to allow this as a way for God to bless both the giver and receiver in this endeavor.

Chapter One

The part should've been easy to cast.

Dream On, the romantic comedy that would star Dayne Matthews, called for a small-town girl, an upbeat, outgoing type, with dreams of the big city and a genuine innocence that overshadowed everything about her.

Dayne had spent the morning watching half a dozen top Hollywood actresses file through the room for an interview and a quick read, and so far none of them fit the bill. They were talented actresses, friendly, beautiful. Two he'd starred with in other films, two he'd dated, and two he'd hung out with at some party or another.

He'd shared the night with three of the six.

They were girls whose faces decked the covers of every gossip rag in town, and in theory, any one of them could play the part of a small-town girl. How hard could it be?

The actresses Dayne had seen today could be upbeat and outgoing, and they could certainly pull off the role of a dreamer.

But something was missing, and by three that afternoon Dayne knew what it was.

The innocence.

Dayne leaned back in his chair and crossed his arms as the last of the six read through her lines. A person couldn't fake innocence — not even with an Academy Award performance. Innocence was something that grew in the heart and shone through the eyes. And it was the innocence that was lacking with each of them.

Mitch Henry, casting director, was pacing near the back of the room. He finished with the final actress and bid her good-bye.

On her way out she looked at Dayne and gave him a teasing smile. "See ya." She was one of the ones he'd dated. Actually, he'd lived with her off and on for a month or so. Long enough that their pictures made the tabs a couple of times. Her eyes locked onto his. "Call me."

"Yeah." Dayne pretended to tip an invisible hat, but his grin faded before she left the room. He turned to Mitch. "Who's next?"

"Who's next?" Deep lines appeared between Mitch's eyes, his tone frustrated. "Do you know how hard it was to get *six* A-list actresses in here on the same day? The part doesn't even require the kind of talent we had in here, Dayne. Any one of them would knock it out of the park."

"They're good. They're all good." Dayne uncrossed his arms and tapped his fingers on the table. "But something's missing." He paused. "I'm not seeing innocent, Henry. Sophisticated, flirty, take me to bed, yes. But not innocent."

"Fine." Mitch tossed his clipboard on the table and yelled at a passing intern to shut the door. On the table were the files belonging to the six actresses, and when the door was shut, Mitch took a few steps closer. "We're on a schedule here, Matthews." He gripped the edge of the table and leaned in. "Hollywood isn't exactly a stable of innocence."

"Okay." Dayne pushed his chair back, stood, and walked to the window, his back to Mitch. He stared out through the hazy blue, and a face came to mind. A face he hadn't forgotten in nearly a year. He held the image, mesmerized by it, and an idea started to form. It was possible, wasn't it? She worked in theater. She must've dreamed of the silver screen somewhere along the way, right?

Dayne felt Mitch's eyes on him, and he turned around. "I have an idea."

"An idea?" Mitch scratched the back of his head and strode to the door and back. "We don't need an idea; we need an actress. Filming starts in four months. This film is too big to wait until the last minute."

"I know." The idea was taking root. It was definitely possible. What girl wouldn't want a chance like this? Dayne sucked in a slow breath. He couldn't get ahead of himself. "Listen, Mitch, give me a week. I have someone in mind, but she's out of state." He leaned against the windowsill. "I think I can have her here in a week, by next Monday."

Mitch folded his arms, his expression hard. "Some girl you met at a club, Matthews? Someone you made drunken promises to? Is that what you want me to wait for?"

"No." Dayne held up his hand. "She's the real deal. Give me a chance."

A moment passed when Dayne wasn't sure which way the casting director was leaning. Then Mitch swept up the six files and the clipboard and shot him a look. "One week." He was halfway out the door when he turned once more and met Dayne's eyes. "She better be good."

Dayne waited until he was alone to look out the window again. What had he just done? Buying a week meant putting the other talent on hold. It meant playing with a budget of tens of millions of dollars so he could find a girl he'd seen just once and ask her to read for a starring role opposite him in a major motion picture.

All when she might not have the interest or ability to act at all.

The idea was crazy, except for one thing. In the past year the only time he'd seen genuine innocence was when he'd watched this same girl light up the stage at a small theater in Bloomington, Indiana, directing the chaos of a couple dozen kids in costumes at the close of what was apparently the theater troupe's first show.

He remembered most of what he'd seen that day, but still the details were sketchy. The location of the theater was easy, something he could definitely find again. But he had almost no information on the girl except her name.

Dayne gripped the windowsill and leaned his forehead against the cool glass. He could fly out and try to find her, but that would bring the paparazzi out of the woodwork for sure, make them crazy with questions about why Dayne Matthews was in Bloomington, Indiana.

Again.

He turned and grabbed his keys and cell phone. There had to be a way to reach her, to ask her out to Hollywood for an audition without the story making every tabloid in town. Dayne shoved the phone in his pocket and headed down the hall toward the elevator.

A coffee, that's what he needed. A double-shot espresso. Most of his friends in the industry had found offbeat coffee shops, places where they were less recognized. Not Dayne. He was a Starbucks man; nothing else would do. If the paparazzi wanted to take his picture coming and going with his double espresso — and they almost always did — that was fine with him. Maybe he'd get an endorsement deal and he could stand out front and pose for them. Dayne chuckled. That would send them packing. Take all the fun out of it.

He opened the back door of the office building and felt a blast of warmth as the sunshine hit his face. The weather was perfect, not the usual June fog. He crossed the studio's private parking lot to his black

Escalade near the bushes and high privacy fence. Usually the studio back lots were free of the press hounds. Sometimes a lone photographer would climb the trees or sit on adjacent hillsides with high-power cameras trained on the office door. But only when a big deal was coming together or someone was in need of rehab — something like that.

Today things looked calm. This time of the day there wouldn't be too many camera hounds on the hunt. Besides, his SUV was new. Only a few of them would know it was him behind the tinted windows. He pulled out of the studio lot and turned left on La Cienaga Boulevard.

Two blocks down he looked in his rearview mirror and saw a familiar Volkswagen. Paparazzi. Even now, even with his new vehicle. He shrugged. *Whatever. They can't crawl into my mind.*

Once in a while he liked to lead them on. He glanced in his rearview mirror again and shrugged. He could use a little amusement. He turned into the Starbucks strip mall, but instead of stopping in front of the coffee shop, he parked near the Rite Aid, three doors down. He grabbed his baseball cap, slipped it low over his brow, and headed inside. There wasn't another person in the store. Dayne dashed to the magazine rack and found the current editions of each of the four national gossip rags — the colorful, busy magazines that reported all manner of information regarding celebrities.

Bloodsuckers, he and his friends called them.

The old, white-haired man at the register didn't recognize him. "That'll be nine fifty-eight." The guy hummed "Moon River" as he slipped the stack of magazines into a bag and handed it to Dayne. "Nice day, huh?"

"Yeah, beautiful." Dayne gave the man a ten-dollar bill. "June's not usually this sunny."

"God's smiling on the Dodgers." The man winked. "Five wins in a row, I tell you. This is the year."

"Could be." Dayne grinned. He relished the moment. A sales clerk — probably a retiree — making casual conversation with him. Moments like this were sometimes all the normalcy he had anymore. "See you later."

"Yep." The man shook his fist. "Go Dodgers."

Dayne walked outside, scanned the parking lot, and found the Volkswagen and the camera aimed straight at him. Then, with broad, dramatic gestures, he jerked one of the magazines from the bag and appeared to stare, shocked, at the cover. He covered his mouth and pretended to be absorbed in some scandalous story.

After a minute he saw a group of teenage girls headed his way. They hadn't recognized him yet, but they would. He slipped the magazine back in the bag, saluted the photographer, and slid back into his SUV. The fun was over. Enough of the cameraman. He hit the Lock button on his key chain, made sure his windows were rolled up tight, then pulled into the Starbucks drive-thru lane.

By the time he hit Pacific Coast Highway the double espresso was gone, and he'd forgotten about the photographer or whether the guy was still behind him. The girl from Bloomington. That's all he could think about now. How was he going to find her without flying to Indiana? And how crazy was he to tell Mitch he could get her into the studio for a reading in a single week?

Dayne passed the usual landmarks — the Malibu Surfer Motel and the Whole Foods Market. His home was just past that, sandwiched between others belonging to people in the entertainment industry. A director and his singer wife on one side and an aging actress and her much younger husband on the other. Nice people. All drawn to the ocean, the watery view of endless calm and serenity. The picture of everything their lives lacked.

Dayne took his bag of magazines inside and made himself another cup of coffee. Black, no sugar. Then he slipped on a pair of sunglasses and went outside onto his second-story deck. No photographer could see him up here, not with the steep walls built around the deck's edges. He sat down, just barely able to see over the edge out to the Pacific Ocean.

One at a time he took out the magazines. Of the four, his face or name was on the cover of two. Dayne studied the first one: "Dayne Matthews: Hollywood's Most Eligible Bachelor Hits the Party Scene."

"I did?" he muttered and turned to the article. There were many more photos on the two-page spread, each one showing him with a different woman. One he was kissing. One was a waitress and no matter what the photo showed, he wasn't making moves on her. The bar had been loud, so he'd moved in a little closer when he ordered. Beneath that photo the caption read "Even barmaids are fair game."

"Nice." Dayne frowned. What would the waitress think? She was only doing her job, and now she had her picture splashed all over grocery checkouts throughout the country.

He flipped through the pages. There had to be other pictures of him; there always were. A few pages in he saw a short article in the section titled "Police Blotter." The small heading read "Is Dayne Matthews Being Stalked by a Woman? Police Find More Clues."

Dayne rolled his eyes. Often there was a nugget of truth to the articles in the gossip magazines. Police had notified him three times in the past month about a stalker, someone who was mailing strange letters to the police department threatening violence against Dayne Matthews.

So far Dayne hadn't seen any sign of a stalker. The matter wasn't something he thought about for more than a few minutes when he was talking to the police. But leave it to the rags to have the latest scoop. He read the article, looking for anything truthful.

Police say they've received another letter from the person writing threatening letters about Hollywood heart-

throb Dayne Matthews. This time handwriting specialists say the letter is from a woman.

One source close to the story said he was fairly certain the person writing the letters was a deranged fan, someone intent on harming Matthews. "She could be a phony, someone looking for attention, but still," the source said, "we can't be too careful."

Exact details of the letters were not available, but a source told our reporter that the person writing the letters is demanding a day with Dayne Matthews or his death.

Police will keep us posted on the story.

Dayne blinked and a chill ran down his arms — more because of the breeze off the Pacific than any fear the article might've stirred up. A day with him or his death? Were people really that crazy? He scanned the story again and dismissed it. Anytime information came from the ever-popular and oft-quoted "source," Dayne and his friends knew to ignore it.

Real truth came from real people — not imaginary sources.

He turned the page, looking for additional stories. This was his ritual, his way of staying in touch with the audience and its view of him. Whether the stories were true or not didn't matter. If they were in print, he wanted to know about them. He kept flipping. Near the front was a section titled "Regular People." Sure enough. There he was coming out of Starbucks with his double espresso. The caption read "Dayne Matthews loads up at his favorite haunt."

Ten pages later was a photo of him and J-Tee Ramiro, a hot Cuban singer he'd dated a month ago. Okay, maybe they never went on an actual date. But they spent the better part of a week together, and the paparazzi hadn't missed a moment. The shot was of the two of them sharing a salad at a small café near Zuma Beach. The point of the story was that J-Tee was seeing someone new and that she had better rebound abilities than half the guys on the LA Lakers.

Dayne thumbed through the rest of the magazine. For the most part the thing was made up of pictures. It was why the photographers followed him, why they followed anyone with celebrity status. Whatever the rags paid the paparazzi, it was enough to keep them coming back for more.

And some of the pictures were ridiculous.

A section near the middle of the magazine showed half a dozen actresses and the undersides of their arms. "Who's Flabby and Who's Not?" the banner headline shouted. The photos were close-ups of actresses caught pointing or raising their arms in a way that showed less-than-perfect triceps muscles.

Dayne rolled his eyes and turned the page. In the past few years the rags had gotten even uglier. One of his friends — an A-list actress named Kelly Parker — was definitely feeling the effects of the pressure. She used to go out dancing or shopping with friends. Now she rarely left her house, and the last time he talked to her the spark was missing from her voice.

He flipped another ten pages, and something at the bottom of one of the layouts caught his eye. A breeze off the ocean rustled the pages as Dayne squinted. It was a small article with two photos — one of Marc David, Dayne's friend and fellow actor, and the other of a bedraggled man behind bars.

Beneath the photos it said *"Hollywood's*

People sent a reporter to investigate Marc David's recent trip to Leavenworth and guess what we found???" Dayne inched himself up in his chair. His heart raced, and he felt blood rush to his face. What was this? Marc was his friend, but the guy had never mentioned anything about Leavenworth. Dayne kept reading.

Marc says he was raised by his mom with no whereabouts of his father. Not true, *Hollywood's People* found out. Not true at all. Marc's dad isn't missing. He's Joseph L. David, a two-time felon, rapist, and drug addict serving time in Leavenworth. Our reporter followed Marc to the prison. Sources say Marc's known about his father all along. Now you know the whole story and so do we!

Dayne felt his stomach turn. He slammed the magazine down on the table, reached into his pocket for his cell phone, flipped it open, and dialed Marc's number.

His friend picked up on the third ring. "Hello?"

"Marc, it's Dayne." He stood up and moved to the balcony wall, staring at the surf. "Hey, I just picked up *Hollywood's*

People. It came out today." He paused. "Is it true?"

There was the sound of a long breath on the other end. "About my dad?" Marc sounded tired. "Yeah, it's true."

"But you never . . . I thought he was missing."

"That's what I told everyone." Marc moaned. "Man, this stinks. My parents split when I was young, and after that my dad made some mistakes. Got into coke and speed and ran out of money. Robbed a few liquor stores. My mom tried to keep it from me, said it was too ugly. I was at New York University when I figured out how to reach him. He got some help. Then I started getting big, and we decided to keep it a secret."

"He's at Leavenworth?"

"Yeah."

"Man . . ." Dayne closed his eyes and shielded his face with his free hand. He didn't mention the part about Marc's dad being a rapist. "I'm sorry."

"It was bound to happen someday. The press . . . they're sharks."

"How's your dad now?"

A sad chuckle came from the other end of the line. "That's just it. He's been clean for five years. Found Jesus, made a change.

He gets out in two years. My mom and him are even talking."

The pieces were coming together. No wonder Marc hadn't wanted anyone to know about his father. The tabloids would print all the dirt and miss the part about how the man was doing today, how he'd changed for the better.

And that's exactly what happened.

"The picture?" Dayne glanced back at the magazine on the table, still open to that page. "He doesn't look too good."

"Yeah, I know. They found his booking pictures. They must've doctored it up. He wasn't behind bars when the police took those."

"Nice. So today the guy's clean shaven with sober eyes, but they run that one."

"Exactly." Marc was quiet a moment. "Dayne . . . I called an attorney. It's gone far enough."

Dayne felt a surge of adrenaline, the way he used to feel back at boarding school when he and the guys would get in a tight game of soccer. "Serious?"

"Yeah." Marc inhaled slowly. "My dad's never raped anyone. The rag threw that in, just made it up."

The hot feeling was back in Dayne's face. "Go for it, Marc. Make it hurt."

"That's the plan." Marc's voice was strained. "I talked to my dad. He's okay. We'll get through this."

"You will." Dayne clenched his jaw. He watched a seagull dive into the water and come back out with a fish. Every now and then a celebrity would sue one of the magazines and win. It didn't happen often, and the rags didn't care because they made enough money to defend an occasional lawsuit. But it still felt good.

Marc David taking on *Hollywood's People* magazine. Dayne straightened and scanned the beach for cameramen. There were none. "Listen, Marc, you'll have my support all the way."

"Thanks, man. That means a lot." His tone grew softer. "Hey, Dayne, I gotta go. One quick thing." He paused. "What do you hear from Kelly Parker?"

"Kelly?" Dayne returned to his chair and put his feet up on the railing of the balcony wall. "She never goes anywhere. The paparazzi are freaking her out."

"That's what I thought. Tell her to call me, will you?"

"Definitely."

When the call was over, Dayne tossed his phone on the table, pulled the magazine closer again, and stared at the picture.

Suddenly the image changed in his mind, and it was no longer Marc and his father. Instead it became a family. His family. The biological family who didn't know he existed. He pictured them the way they'd looked that day in Bloomington. Eight or ten people with a few small children walking together through the parking lot of the local hospital, the same weekend he'd seen the girl at the theater. One of the little girls with them was in a wheelchair.

Even with the sun hot on his face, a chill made its way through him. He shut the magazine and threw it back on the table. What would the press do to the people he'd seen that day in the parking lot? What skeletons lay in the closet of the Baxter family? For starters, John and Elizabeth had given him up for adoption and apparently never told their other kids.

But what about the wheelchair? Was there a birth defect or an accident that put the child there? Whatever it was, the rags would find out and gleefully splash it across a centerfold given the chance.

Dayne stood and filled his lungs with the damp, salty air. He leaned his forearms on the railing and stared far out to sea this time. What were the Baxters doing now? No doubt they were still grieving the loss of Elizabeth. The private detective his agent used had found out the information almost immediately. Elizabeth Baxter died of breast cancer just hours after he had visited her briefly.

Down the beach a way, a young couple was holding hands and flying a bright yellow-striped kite. Dayne studied them, the way they easily kept their faces out in the open. Did they know how wonderful it was, being out of the limelight? Or did they long for fame the way so many did in Los Angeles?

He shifted his eyes upward. At least he'd found Elizabeth before she died. The conversation they'd shared was enough to answer his hardest questions — who was his birth mother and why did she give him up.

Elizabeth had loved him and longed for him. She had searched for him at one time and wondered about him all of her married life. In her dying days, her single prayer had been to find him, hold him once more the way she'd held him as a newborn, and tell him she loved him.

Those bits of truth were enough.

As for the others, his biological father and siblings, he'd made the right choice by leaving them alone. Dayne leaned hard against the railing. He'd only seen them for a handful of minutes as they walked from the hospital to their cars. They looked like nice people, loving and close. The sort of family he would've been proud to call his own.

But he could hardly land on their doorstep announcing the fact that he was their parents' firstborn. The paparazzi would capture the moment from the bushes for their next cover story. No, he could never contact the Baxters, never tell them the truth about who he was. They deserved their privacy. Dayne narrowed his eyes. He could see the headlines: "Dayne Matthews' Secret Family Revealed." He couldn't let that happen.

Even if he spent the rest of his life thinking about them.

He took his cell phone from the table, slipped back inside the house, and closed the screen door. Suddenly he knew how he was going to find the girl, the one from the Bloomington theater. He dialed his agent's number.

"Matthews, how you doing?"

"Great." Dayne didn't pause long. "Hey, I need a favor."

"Oh yeah?" There was an edge to his agent's voice, but it was a humorous one.

"Mitch Henry tells me you need an actress."

"That too." Dayne managed a weak laugh. "That's the favor. I need you to find an actress in Bloomington."

"Matthews." The humor was gone. "Not Bloomington. I thought we agreed."

"No, this isn't about my family. It's about a girl, an actress I saw there. At the community theater."

Silence shouted at him from the other end. Then he heard his agent draw a long breath. "You saw a play at the community theater when you were in Bloomington?"

"Yes. Well, no." Dayne walked the length of his kitchen and stopped near the sink. The view from the window was the same as the one from the deck. "I mean, the girl wasn't in the play; she was the director."

"The director?"

"Yeah. She's perfect. Everything the part calls for." Dayne felt a grin tugging at the corners of his lips.

"How do you know she can act?" His agent sounded tired.

"Call it a hunch." Dayne took a glass from the cupboard and filled it with water. "Come on, man; do it for me. She's perfect; I'm telling you."

"I have a question." There was resignation in his agent's voice. "You didn't sleep with her, right?"

"Come on!" Dayne threw his free hand in the air. "Don't believe everything you read in the papers, friend."

"Okay, but did you?"

"Of course not." Dayne pictured the girl, the way she'd looked onstage surrounded by kids. "I never even talked to her."

"Great." His agent let loose a long sigh. "So I send the investigator to Bloomington to find a girl who's perfect for the part, even though you're not sure she can act and you've never spoken to her."

"Right." Dayne felt himself relax. His agent liked toying with him, but in the end he'd do whatever was asked of him. It was why Dayne had stayed with him for so long.

"Do you have anything else? A name? Something?"

Dayne didn't hesitate. Her name had been on his tongue all afternoon. "Her name's Hart. Katy Hart."

Chapter Two

More than a hundred kids and their parents were lined up at the door of Bloomington Community Church — Christian Kids Theater's practice facility — when Katy Hart pulled her faded red two-door Nissan into the parking lot for the second time that Monday afternoon.

The first time had been half an hour earlier. That time, she'd driven the speed limit, casually noting the thunderheads in the distance as she passed through the downtown area and pulled into the parking lot ten minutes early, the way she'd planned. Not until she was at the church door did she realize she didn't have the key.

That set off a race back through Bloomington and into Clear Creek, where she lived with the Flanigan family. A frantic search through her bedroom finally turned up the key, but now she was fifteen minutes late, and if the line waiting outside was any indication, she needed to move fast.

Auditions for *Tom Sawyer* were set to start at 4 p.m.

Katy and her creative team had just three hours to get the kids through the audition process and another hour to make a decision about who would get called back for a second audition. At eight o'clock the church staff needed the building for a meeting, and she'd promised that everyone from Christian Kids Theater would be out by then.

Katy bit her lip, grabbed her canvas bag, and darted out of the car. As long as CKT didn't have a permanent home, schedules like the one they had today were part of life. At least Bloomington Community Church was willing to open their doors every Monday and Thursday and twice on the weekends so CKT could hold classes and practices. A facility of their own would've been nice, but Katy didn't dwell on the fact. She picked up her pace. *I'm thankful, God. Really, I am.*

The minute they saw her, the kids began waving and grinning. "Katy . . . Katy!"

She ran along the line to the side door and spouted apologies as she opened it. A burst of stuffy hot air met her. Katy frowned and stared up at the dark ceiling. The church staff had promised to leave on the air conditioner. She'd have to check it once the registration started.

Katy hit the light switch as the parent volunteers hurried to a few tables set up in the lobby. The children moved in behind them.

"You know the routine." Katy waved at the kids, calming their voices long enough to be heard. "Have a photograph of yourself and your tryout form completed and signed by your parents. Get in line and someone will give you a number. Anyone without a photograph can line up in front of —" Katy peered around a group of kids to see which parent was manning the Polaroid camera — "Mrs. Jennings. I'll take the first ten in five minutes inside the sanctuary."

Three people would join her on the panel. Rhonda Sanders, the choreographer and Katy's closest friend, and Al and Nancy Helmes, a couple whose passion for music and helping kids made them pillars of the CKT community. Al and Nancy would act as music directors for *Tom Sawyer*, and they'd be in on the audition process as well. The couple had an amazing love for each other and for their eight children — three of whom were part of CKT.

Once in a while Katy would catch the couple, their heads bowed in prayer before a meal or eyes locked on each other even in a room of people, and she'd wonder. Would she ever have that sort of love? A love that rolled up its sleeves and worked together, played together, and raised a family together, all while looking happier and more enamored with each other all the time?

Katy hoped so.

She gave a few more directions to the moms working the check-in table, and then she spotted Cara Helmes, one of Al and Nancy's daughters.

"Hi, Katy! Another audition!" Cara grinned, her eyes dancing the way they always did.

"Best one yet!" Katy gave the girl a hug. "I'll see you down there."

Cara nodded and headed down the aisle with her parents toward her spot in the second row, where she would sit ready and waiting for the auditions to begin. Cara was twenty-two and had Down syndrome. She had an open invitation to attend any of CKT's performances or auditions, something she looked forward to more than anything in her life. Cara was quick with a hug or a smile for the kids. No matter how poor a practice they might have, Cara would clap as if it were a Tony Award–winning performance. She never had a bad thing to say about anyone, and the kids and families of CKT loved her. Katy and Rhonda had agreed that in some ways Cara was CKT's guardian angel.

"Katy, Katy . . ." A chorus of frantic voices brought Katy back to the urgency of the moment. She looked down and saw three fourth-grade girls. One of them was out of breath. "I forgot my music!" Tears welled in her eyes. "My mom wants to know if there's time to go back and get it."

Katy put her hand on the girl's shoulder. "Calm down — everything's okay." She smiled. "You have plenty of time."

More kids called for her attention, and one after another she addressed their needs. Yes, they needed a photo in order to try out. No, they couldn't sing without accompaniment. Yes, they could sing a song from church.

Normally she would chat with the kids, ask them about school and their families. But today would be all business. CKT might be a children's theater troupe, but it was Katy's passion, her purpose. *Tom Sawyer* could be their best show ever. Yes, it was CKT's first production of the summer. Never mind the stuffy church or the long lines or the fact that she was late or even the threatening thunderstorms that could very easily knock out the electricity. This audition would be as professional as the others. Katy held her bag tight to her side and headed for the double doors leading to the sanctuary.

"More kids than ever." Heath Hudson came up alongside her and handed her two pencils. Heath was a twenty-seven-year-old salesman with an uncanny ability to run a soundboard and a strong fascination for theater. The talk among CKT families was that he had a fascination for Katy too. "You look hot."

"Oh." Katy stopped short and looked at Heath. "Is that a compliment?"

"Uh . . ." He was only an inch taller than her, so she could see his forehead was damp with sweat. "Not hot that way, but . . . well . . . I mean, you are hot that way, of course, but . . ."

"I'm teasing." Katy stifled a laugh. She had every reason to like Heath Hudson. They'd gone to the movies a few times, and kids were always giggling and winking at them whenever they were together. But she couldn't quite convince her heart. She took the pencils, then patted Heath on the shoulder. "It's okay. I know what you mean. I *am* hot; we're all hot." She gestured toward the ceiling. "The air-conditioning isn't working." She wrinkled her nose and took a step back. "Maybe you could check that for me, Heath. Whadya say?"

"Sure thing." Heath straightened and cleared his throat, more composed. "I'm on my way."

She was halfway down the center aisle toward the front of the church when the rest of her creative team caught up with her. Nancy Helmes started with the updates while they were still walking. "Adam Franklin threw up in the lobby."

"What?" Katy set her things down on the first pew and stared at Nancy. "You're kidding."

"Nope." Nancy moved to the piano a few feet away and opened the lid. "His father said he's been nervous all day. Ate a burger and fries for lunch and, well . . ."

Her husband, Al, made a face. "It wasn't pretty."

Rhonda opened a card table and set it in front of the first pew. "Sarah Jo Stryker's here too. Her mother says they barely made it. Straight from a commercial audition in Indianapolis." Rhonda raised an eyebrow. "She pulled me aside and asked me if we knew what we were getting with Sarah Jo."

"Huh?" Katy let her hands fall to her sides. "What did she mean?"

"She told me Sarah Jo was going to be a star one day. We're lucky to get her while she's young and inexpensive."

Katy exhaled hard and set her yellow notepad and pencils on the card table. Most CKT families were levelheaded people, thrilled with a chance to have found a drama troupe where moral standards were high and faith was at the foundation of all they did. Teamwork was stressed, and after eight weeks of practice and rehearsal, everyone involved felt equally important on opening night.

But in the year since the group's start in Bloomington, every now and then someone would miss the point. They'd come thinking CKT was a launching pad to something bigger, better. Something paid. Katy hadn't met Sarah Jo or her mother, but her phone calls with the woman had told her there was trouble ahead.

Katy blinked. "She really said that?"

"Yep." Rhonda glanced at her watch. "I think she's in the fourth group."

What were people thinking? "If she talks to you again, tell Mrs. Stryker —" Katy grabbed her notepad and a pencil and pretended to write something down — "I've got it noted about Sarah Jo and how lucky we are." She paused. "The rules are the same as always, by the way. In an audition like this, props and elaborate dance steps only take away from the singer. The kids know that."

A clap of thunder shook the building, and Katy turned toward the back of the room. Krissy Schick, the CKT area coordinator, was there waiting for the signal. "Ready?"

Katy took a deep breath and nodded to Nancy, Al, and Rhonda. They were all seated at the table. A few feet away, one of the moms was at the CD player, seated and holding a stopwatch. Katy looked back at Krissy. "Send them in."

In a flurry of motion, dozens of parents and kids with numbers pinned to their shirts hurried into the sanctuary and immediately took their seats and quieted themselves. Rules were that anyone could watch auditions, but people could only come and go between the groups of ten.

The first group of children auditioning for parts separated themselves from the spectators and took the front row adjacent to where Katy was seated.

Another clap of thunder filled the auditorium. Katy held her pencil tight. The temperature was still smoldering inside, and she glanced over her shoulder for Heath. If he'd found the air conditioner, it wasn't working. Maybe rain would cool things down.

Katy looked at the assortment of kids seated in the first row. "Number one?"

Tim Reed stood, walked to the mom at the CD player, and gave her his music. There were a few seconds while he explained to the woman in hushed tones which song he was singing. Then he took the center of the stage, faced Katy, and smiled. "Hi, my name's Tim Reed. I'm sixteen years old, and I'll be singing 'King of New York' from *Newsies*."

Katy nodded and sat back.

Tim Reed was one of the nicest kids she'd ever met. In past plays, he was the first to help the younger boys with their makeup, first to clean up the greenroom, and quick to pull out his guitar and sing praise songs with the rest of the cast between Saturday shows. He was home-schooled and had recently earned Eagle rank from the Boy Scouts. On top of that he had a natural ability to sing and act. Tim had played Charlie Brown in CKT's first production and had earned a lead part in every play since.

Katy smiled as the music began. This one would be easy.

The song built and grew, and Tim nailed it, hitting the highs just right and letting his vibrato show on the lows. Each person auditioning would have one minute before their music would be cut. Tim finished at just under, thanked the panel, and returned to his seat.

Katy pulled her notepad closer and wrote: *Tim Reed — Tom Sawyer?*

Next up was a rail-thin boy with short, wavy hair making his first attempt at a CKT production. He had a life preserver around his waist and a green swimming mask on his face. In his hand was a yellow rubber duck. After he set up his music and took the stage, he nodded to Katy.

She sucked the inside of her lip to keep from laughing. "Go ahead."

"Okay." His voice was nasally because of the mask. He pulled himself up some. "Hi. I'm Eric Wade. I'm twelve years old and —"

"Eric?" Katy shook her head. The boy

might as well have been underwater for how garbled he sounded. "Do you have a cold?"

"No." His shoulders fell a little.

"Then take off the mask, honey. We can't understand you."

Eric slipped the mask off and dropped it to the floor. "Is that better?"

"Yes. Let's try it again."

It was no surprise that Eric's song was "Rubber Duckie." He sang it while feigning first a freestyle stroke and then a backstroke up and down the length of the stage. It was impossible to tell whether he was on key or not. Katy could only guess what the rest of her creative team was writing.

She jotted down *Eric Wade — maybe next time.*

The stream of kids continued until the first ten were finished. Katy stood and stretched and spoke loud enough for everyone in the sanctuary to hear her. "We'll take two minutes, and then we'll need the next ten."

During the break, Heath found her. "Good news and bad news. Which do you want first?"

Katy folded her arms and angled her head. Audition days were always like this. "The good."

"Okay, I found the air-conditioning controls and turned it on." Heath puffed out his chest. His breath had the faint smell of garlic and onions. "Because your wish is my command."

"Wow. How'd I get so lucky?" A weak laugh sounded from Katy's lips. "The bad?"

"The bad news is it'll probably take an hour to cool down, and right now it's hailing outside."

"Oh." Katy nodded. "That's not bad news." She hurried up the aisle, her eyes still on Heath. "We'll just open the doors."

In a blur, she rushed into the lobby, flung open the double doors, and was instantly slapped in the face by a sheet of hail. "Oh, brother." She shut the doors again and spun around.

The parents and kids in the lobby were all staring at her, trying not to laugh.

"That's why we had the doors closed." One of the dads grinned.

"I see that." Katy brushed her clothes off and shook the hail from her arms.

Tim's little sister Mary came up and tugged on Katy's blouse. "You have snow on your head."

"Yes, thank you, Mary. I thought I might." She ran her fingers through her hair and dashed back into the sanctuary. "Okay," she shouted. "Group two, get ready."

Katy was running back down the aisle when she spotted one of the college girls who would help with the show. She was seated at the back of the sanctuary next to her boyfriend. He had his arm around her, his eyes lost in hers, their heads tilted toward each other.

The picture filled Katy's senses and drew her back. Suddenly the ache in her heart returned, raw and painful and lonely the way it still felt even two years after leaving Chicago. She glanced once more at the couple. They were laughing about something and holding hands, lost in a world of their own.

Katy hesitated. That was her not so many years ago, wasn't it? The college girl sitting with her first love — her only love — in the back of an auditorium while their class rehearsed near the front. Back then she had dreams of marriage and babies and living in Chicago forever. But it hadn't worked out that way, and here, now, she missed that time with an intensity that took her breath away.

She turned her attention back to the front of the church and picked up her pace. Tears stung her eyes. The pain hit her at the strangest times, smack in the midst of an entire building full of people who loved and adored her. She cupped her hands around her mouth. "Let's go! Group two, get your music ready."

A single breath and Katy felt control coming over her. The life she had in Chicago was gone; she would never go back. Her eyes were dry again, and she forced herself to focus on the whispery jitters and rustling lyrics sheets and excitement brimming all around her. This was her home, where she belonged.

And it was enough.

Katy sat at the table and stared at her notepad. *This is all I need, isn't it, God? Isn't that what You told me? Being a part of three dozen families with a hundred kids calling my name? These are the plans You have for me, right?*

There was no answer, not even in the quiet places of her heart.

"Katy, you with us?" Rhonda tapped Katy's foot under the table. "Let's get these kids through here."

"Right." Katy looked at the first row, where the next ten kids were waiting. "Number eleven, take the stage."

Katy didn't lose focus again.

After the first thirty auditions, a woman came up to Katy and touched her shoulder. "You're Katy, right? The director?"

Katy turned in her seat. "Yes, hello." They'd only talked on the phone, but Katy had no doubt this was Sarah Jo's mother.

Alice Stryker moved in closer and lowered her voice. "Sarah Jo's been practicing the part of Becky for some time now." Mrs. Stryker pinched her lips together and gave Katy's shoulder a light push. "I already made her a Becky Thatcher dress."

"Mrs. Stryker —" Katy tried to keep the shock from her tone — "the team won't be choosing kids for the roles until after tomorrow's callback."

Her expression changed and she uttered a polite laugh. "Of course, dear. I'm just planting seeds for tomorrow, since parents can't watch the callbacks and I'm convinced Sarah Jo can play the part."

Mrs. Stryker was gone before Katy could catch her breath. It would take everything in her to call Sarah Jo back after her mother's unfair expectations.

Katy was still replaying the woman's words when Sarah Jo approached her. Katy watched the girl's tentative steps, her wide, hesitant eyes. For the first time she considered that maybe Sarah Jo was nothing like her mother.

"Miss Katy?" The girl glanced over her shoulder as she ran her tongue along her lower lip. Her face was downcast when her eyes met Katy's again. "I'm Sarah Jo." She held out her hand. "Whatever my mama said, I'm sorry. She —" the girl swallowed, her expression tense — "she has her ideas about me."

Katy's heart melted. "Oh, honey, it's okay." She took hold of Sarah Jo's hand. "Don't worry. Everyone's a little excited at auditions."

"Yeah, I guess." The hint of a sparkle appeared in Sarah Jo's eyes. "Thanks."

Katy watched Sarah Jo blend back in with the other kids and noticed the two oldest Flanigan children, fifteen-year-old Bailey and twelve-year-old Connor, near the back of the room. Connor had earned a part in each of the first three shows, but Bailey was an unknown. Since Katy lived with the Flanigans and felt like part of their family, she had worried for a week about whether Bailey would have what it takes to get a part and whether it would be uncomfortable with Jim and Jenny, their parents, if either of the kids wasn't cast in the play.

During the break before their auditions, Jenny Flanigan came up to the table and took hold of Katy's hand. "No favors, Katy. Treat them like anyone else."

They were just the words Katy needed to hear. "Thanks." Her heart swelled and she squeezed Jenny's fingers. "I needed that."

Bailey was first up when they got started again. Her audition was upbeat and right on key. Everything about it proved that Katy had nothing to worry about. The Flanigan girl was a natural, a willowy beauty with a sweet voice. She moved easily onstage, and Katy guessed she would be a wonderful dancer. Katy made a note next to Bailey's name to call her back, maybe for the part of Becky Thatcher. She could always ask Alice Stryker to have the dress adjusted.

Sarah Jo was next, and Katy held her breath. *Okay, let's see what she's got.* Sarah Jo sang "Part of Your World" from *The Little Mermaid*, and after the first line, Katy understood Mrs. Stryker's determination. The girl looked unremarkable — thin with wispy brown hair — but she sang with her entire being, letting the song flow through to her fingertips as she stretched out her hands during the chorus.

Very simply, Sarah Jo Stryker lit up the

room. Her voice was amazing, beautiful and full, mature in a way that sent chills down Katy's spine. She was composed and self-assured, presenting the song in a way that made everyone in the room see her as Ariel, the conflicted mermaid.

No wonder her mother expected Sarah Jo to be famous. If the girl wanted a career on the stage, she definitely had the voice and stage presence for it.

When she finished, a burst of applause came from the group seated in the sanctuary. Sarah Jo gave Katy a weak smile and a slight shrug.

Katy's heart went out to her. It was clear Sarah Jo expected to be penalized because of her mother's behavior. Katy returned the smile with a nod. She stared down at her notepad and pursed her lips. Apparently she'd have to find a way to work with Mrs. Stryker. She poised her pencil over the paper and wrote *Sarah Jo Stryker — callback.*

Next up was Ashley Zarelli, a sweet, dark-haired seventeen-year-old who had overcome a troubled past. As an infant, Ash had been left in a dresser drawer for the first two months of her life. A local senator and his wife took her for the next eleven months, but then the state stepped in and placed her back with her biological mother. Life spiraled downward quickly, but not until Ash was four years old did the state take her from her biological mother for good and return her to the couple. She'd been part of the Zarelli family ever since.

Tani Zarelli, Ash's adoptive mother, once told Katy that as difficult as her daughter's life had been, she was certain the Lord had given her a message regarding Ashley. That one day she would be a teacher of His Word. It was a promise Tani and her husband held on to when Ash was younger and suffered from low self-esteem and nightmares.

As the Zarelli girl took the stage, Katy was struck by the faithfulness of God. Here was a precious teenager who had been left for dead by her biological mother, now glowing with the light of Christ. Ash's involvement in the theater was a living picture of God's promises alive and at work. In the last CKT performance — *Charlotte's Web* — Ashley had worked with Tim Reed to lead the cast in Scripture reading or prayers.

She sang a song from *The Sound of Music* and did well enough to earn a callback.

The auditions continued right up until seven o'clock, with one hundred thirty-six children from both ends of the CKT age range — eight-year-olds auditioning for the first time to eighteen-year-olds taking their last chance at a part.

Once the kids and their parents were out of the building, Heath Hudson approached Katy. "Want me to wait for you?"

Katy's mind went blank. "Do we have plans?"

"No, I just, uh . . ." Heath's cheeks grew a shade darker. "I thought maybe I'd wait in the other room and we could get coffee when you're done."

"Heath, that's so sweet." Katy took his hands in hers. "But we'll be a while, and when we're done I need to get home." She paused. "Okay?"

"Sure." Heath gave her hands a squeeze and separated himself, taking a few steps back. "I'll see you Friday at practice."

"Right." Katy gave a friendly wave. "See you then."

When she turned back to her creative team, both Nancy and Rhonda had knowing looks on their faces. Katy held up one hand. "Stop. Don't even start." Being single around so many families meant someone was always trying to set her up.

But that night they had more to talk about than Heath Hudson.

"I won't give you a hard time, Katy." Al crossed his arms and gave his wife a teasing poke in the ribs. "You girls are terrible around each other. Can't she say hello to Heath without you setting a wedding date?"

They all laughed, but the silliness faded quickly. The creative team huddled for the next hour and decided on forty-three kids for callbacks. There would be some sixty kids in the play, but not everyone needed a callback to get a part. The second day of auditions was only to cast the speaking parts. Some children would earn smaller ensemble parts merely on the strength of their first audition.

Katy's stomach was in knots by the time she drove back to Clear Creek and pulled into the Flanigans' driveway. The knots were normal. Auditions were the hardest of all. In a perfect world, every child wanting a part in the play would get one, but Katy had parts for less than half the kids who tried out.

And something about the way she felt was different this time.

The lights in the house were off, which was good. She didn't want the distraction of conversation, not tonight. Not only because of the task that lay ahead the next day, while she and her creative team held callbacks and cast the show, but because of something else, something that made the knots in her stomach worse than usual tonight.

Katy lay awake trying to figure out what it was, and she kept coming back to the same thing — the memory of the college girl and her boyfriend at the back of the sanctuary. Even after three hours of auditions and another hour of discussion, Katy couldn't get the picture out of her head.

The longer she thought about it, the more it made sense. Because for all the richness of CKT and all the ways she felt part of the biggest family anyone could ever hope for, there was no denying the basic truth. Katy had no one to call her own, no boyfriend or special someone as a prospect for the future.

As she fell asleep she was convinced that the thing causing knots in her stomach was more than anxiety over casting *Tom Sawyer*, something more than worrying about what part Bailey Flanigan or Sarah Jo Stryker or Tim Reed or Ashley Zarelli might earn at callbacks. It was something no one else could see or understand, something so big it threatened to send her packing her bags straight back to Chicago.

A deep and crushing loneliness.

Chapter Three

꧁꧂

Ashley Baxter Blake was sitting at her easel putting the finishing touches on a lakeside painting and missing her mother when she heard the front door open.

"We're home!" Landon's voice rang through the house, and the sound of a child's footsteps followed.

"Mommy, we caught the greenest frog on the whole shoreline!" Cole was six now, kindergarten behind him. He had mud smudges on his cheeks and lake scum stuck in his blond hair. "I couldn't get him 'cause he was lickety fast, but then Daddy creeped up real quiet and —" Cole made a sweeping motion with his hand — "he snatched him just like that."

Landon entered the room, the knees of his jeans caked with dirt. He looked at Ashley, his eyes shining, speaking volumes before he ever said a word.

"Actually —" Cole scratched at the

green slime stuck in his hair — "Daddy caught *three* frogs. He's the bestest catcher."

"Three?" Ashley raised her eyebrows in Landon's direction, teasing him. "My big, strapping, firefighter husband catching not one but three frogs on a sunny summer morning? I'm so impressed."

"Yeah, me too." Cole's eyes were big and excited. "But the last one was the greenest one." He looked up at Landon. "It even had bright green feet, right?"

Ashley lowered her chin in Cole's direction. "And where's the bright green froggy right now?"

"Oh, we let him go." Cole gave a serious nod. "He lives at the lake." His eyes lit up. "But we can catch him again next time, right, Daddy?"

"Right." Landon dropped down to Cole's level and worked his thumb across one of the smudges. "Hey, how about that shower?"

"Oh yeah." Cole grinned at Ashley; then he bent halfway over and shook his hair. "No lunch until we get the dirt out of our hair." He straightened; then with a quick wave at both of them, he dashed out of the room and down the hallway toward the bathroom.

Ashley set her paintbrush down. She used the back of her hand to brush a lock of hair off her forehead; then she moved away from the easel and into Landon's arms. "Sounds like a successful morning."

"Mmmm." He nuzzled her face. "A hike along the lake with my favorite boy . . . bright green frogs . . ." He kissed her, a kiss of smoldering passion and desire that had only grown stronger in the year they'd been married. "And now this." He drew back and looked into her eyes. "Mornings don't get much better than this."

From down the hall, they heard the sound of the shower.

Ashley drew Landon closer and kissed him again, longer this time. When she stopped for a breath, she giggled, brushing her nose against his. "Know what I love?"

Landon ran his hands down the length of her arms and searched her eyes. "What?"

"I love hearing Cole call you Daddy."

Light and love mixed together and shone from Landon's eyes. "Not as much as I love having him as my son."

Ashley moved into his arms again and laid her head on his chest. "All those years I fought you. How could I have been so stubborn?"

He kissed the top of her head. "It

doesn't matter. Look at what we've got."

Landon was right. Never mind her escapades in Paris, the fact that she'd come home pregnant and alone and feeling like the Baxter family black sheep. Landon had always been there, coaxing her toward him, making her believe she was worth something even when she couldn't believe it herself. They survived the years when he was in New York City and she was dealing with fears about her health. Years when she never would've dreamed they'd find a life together.

But here they were.

He pulled back and studied her painting. "You haven't done one of the lake from that angle before. I like it." He cocked his head, his voice tender. "Reminds me of the last Baxter picnic."

"Before Mom died." Ashley took a step closer and ran her fingers along the edge of the canvas. "I thought so too."

"Will there be people in it?"

"I think so." She looked at him. "I'd like to put an older couple on a bench looking out at the water. We'd only see the backs of their heads."

Landon shifted his attention to the painting and then back to her. "Your parents?"

69

Tears stung Ashley's eyes. "Mmm-hmm." She let her gaze drift to the image of the lake. "It's like if I put her in my paintings, I can keep her memory alive longer."

"Ash." He held his arms out to her. "Come here."

In the background the shower stopped, and they heard Cole moving about in the bathroom.

Ashley closed her eyes and let herself get lost in Landon's embrace. "I can't believe it's been almost a year."

"I can still hear her voice."

"Me too." Ashley sniffed and looked up at Landon. "Every time we visit Dad it's like I sense her there, working in the kitchen or having tea at the dining-room table. Reading a magazine in the living room." She hesitated. "I miss her so much."

Landon didn't say anything, and Ashley was glad. He didn't have to have an answer every time she missed her mother. It was enough that he held her and let her talk about her feelings.

"Know what I've been thinking?" She moved back to her easel and sat on the stool, facing him.

"What?"

"We need to get involved in some I

70

don't know, some community work. Something in Mom's memory."

Landon leaned against the wall and looked out the window. "Your work at Sunset Hills was like that."

He was right. The work she'd done with Alzheimer's patients at Sunset Hills was something that would've honored her mother's memory. But she had left the job after getting married and never returned. The owner of the house had hired a new manager, and now she only stopped by on occasion to visit her favorite residents.

Ashley sat a little straighter. "Kari was telling me about this new theater group in town — Christian Kids Theater — something like that." She and her sister Kari had grown much closer in the past year, comforting each other in the wake of losing their mother. Now she tried to remember the details of their conversation.

"That's right." Landon squinted. "One of Ryan's coaching buddies is involved, isn't he? Jim Flanigan?"

Ashley snapped her fingers. "That's it. Jim Flanigan. He and his wife have kids in the theater group, I think."

"So . . ." Landon moved closer, smiling. "What's my little do-gooder wife thinking up?"

71

"Well . . ." Ashley felt a surge of hope rise within her. It was one more thing she loved about Landon, that even when she was missing her mother the most, he could help her find a reason to smile. "Maybe they need help making sets, you know, painting backdrops, that kind of thing."

"Hmmm." He scratched his chin. "I thought you said you wanted us both to get involved."

"I do." She hopped off the stool and reached out, taking hold of his hands. "You can paint, Landon. Just because you're a big macho fireman doesn't mean you can't paint."

"I can paint a house maybe." He gave her a skeptical look, but the way his eyes danced told her he was considering the possibility. "Theater sets?"

"Yes." She tugged on his hands and angled her head. "Mom loved the theater. We could work at it together and do it in her memory."

Landon gave her a crooked grin. "I hope they have a lot of plain brown walls to paint."

Ashley let her head tip back as she laughed at the image — her painting landscapes on theatrical backdrops and her husband painting brown walls. "Oh,

Landon." She caught her breath and looked at him. "It feels so good to laugh."

They heard Cole running down the hall to his bedroom.

Landon leaned in and kissed her again. "It feels good to hear it." He crossed his arms and made a silly expression. "Okay, call Kari and get the Flanigans' number. Tell the theater people they have two more volunteers if they need them."

"Yay! I'll call her right now." Ashley squeezed his hands and looked straight to his soul. "Thanks for understanding. I think helping out would make Mom proud."

The teasing faded from his eyes. "Me too." He hesitated, and his expression changed. "Hey, there's something else I want to talk to you about." Landon caught her gently and searched her eyes. "Remember that honeymoon we were going to take?"

Ashley bit her lip and nodded. "The timing never seemed quite right."

"Losing your mom, then school starting up for Cole." He paused, a new glow coming from his soul straight through his eyes. "But it's summer again, Ash." He pulled an envelope from his back pocket and held it out to her.

"What's this?" Ashley's heart fluttered. It had been so long since their wedding, she figured Landon had forgotten about the honeymoon they never took. Not that it mattered. With Landon, every day was a honeymoon. She opened the envelope, and inside were two ticket folders. A piece of paper wrapped around them had a heading across the top: "Congratulations on the purchase of two Caribbean cruise tickets!"

Ashley felt her arms grow weak. She looked at Landon. "Are you serious?"

"They're the real deal." His grin took up his face. "We'll be gone the week of July 12, our first anniversary."

"Really?"

"Really. Kari and Ryan said they'd watch Cole."

Ashley pictured Landon and her on a cruise ship, vast blue skies and endless warm seas, sailing the Caribbean. The idea felt like something from a dream. "Landon, I'm in shock!" She held up his hand and danced a pirouette beneath it. "Yippee!"

Cole darted into the room, his hair clean and combed as best he could comb it. "What's yippee, Mommy?" He looked from Landon back to her. "Did you and Daddy find another froggy?"

"No, silly." She grinned at the crooked part in his hair. "Mommy and Daddy are taking a trip! On a big boat!"

"Can I come?" Cole jumped in place a few times. "I love boats!"

Ashley smiled to herself. The only boat Cole had ever been on was his uncle Ryan's ski boat. "This boat's a little bigger, and nope, sweetie. This time it's just Mommy and Daddy."

"You, Coley —" Landon winked at him — "will stay with Aunt Kari and Uncle Ryan. Maybe they'll take you out on *their* boat."

"Yeah! Then I can kneeboard again!" Cole dashed out, calling as he ran, "I have to find my swimming suit if we're going out on the boat."

Ashley pulled Landon into her arms one more time. "A cruise, Landon Blake. So romantic . . ."

"You know me." He batted his eyelashes at her. "Mr. Romantic."

"I can't wait." Her tone was more serious now, the desire from a few minutes earlier back again. "I wish we were leaving today."

"No, you don't." He tapped her nose and chuckled. "Because today you're calling Kari and finding out about painting sets for Christian Kids Theater, remember?"

Ashley gasped. "That's right. I thought I'd spend the summer missing Mom. Instead it looks like we'll spend it celebrating life."

"Yes." Landon led her from the room toward the sound of Cole rummaging through his closet. "And that's exactly what your mother would've wanted us to do."

Chapter Four

The information on Katy Hart was better than Dayne had hoped. She'd graduated from the University of Illinois with a theater degree and an emphasis on film. Three times she starred in university plays and tried her hand at a few community plays outside Chicago.

But that wasn't the best of it.

Straight out of college Katy had earned a starring role in a television pilot. A two-hour TV movie about a Midwest family struggling to stay together. She played the family's oldest daughter opposite a cast of unknowns, all of whom were said to have considerable talent. Rumors linked her to her cast mate, her love interest in the film.

Despite good reviews for the pilot, the series was canceled before the first episode was filmed. After that Katy appeared in two commercials before she dropped off the entertainment radar screen and got involved with Christian Kids Theater in Chicago. A few years later she moved to Bloomington, Indiana.

Dayne didn't care about the reasons why she left the film industry. All that mattered was that she was capable. Very capable.

Once again, the private investigator had done an amazing job. The report came in Wednesday afternoon, just two days after Dayne's agent hired him. It included more details than Dayne needed and best of all a VHS tape recording of Katy's television pilot. Dayne sat on his back deck and read everything in the report before snatching the tape and heading into his soundproof viewing room.

It was a glorified home theater, really, painted black with two rows of black leather recliners. This room was the place Dayne would watch first-cut versions of his movies, the place where he studied and scrutinized and made sure he was still gaining ground as an actor.

Now he slipped the tape into his VCR, sat on the edge of one of the recliners, grabbed the remote, and started the movie. He fast-forwarded past the credits to the opening scene in the kitchen of a house. The next shot was outdoors and showed a girl heading through tall grass toward a tree and a boy waiting near it.

Dayne hit the Play button.

The girl was Katy, no doubt. She was everything he remembered her to be. She wore a fitted navy turtleneck and jeans, her long blonde hair straight down her back. In the scene she was supposed to be upset about something, sneaking out of her house away from her family to meet the boy she was dating.

The details didn't matter. What did matter was the way Katy Hart lit up the screen, her eyes a brilliant cornflower blue that seemed to take up half her face. She met the boy and the two hugged. Dayne studied him for a minute. He looked familiar, and then he made the connection. The guy was a soap star now, heavy in the Hollywood party scene for a few years before he moved to Manhattan.

Dayne returned his attention to Katy. Her character was listening intently to the guy, and then whatever he said made her laugh. Dayne hit the Volume button and listened. The sound of Katy's laughter filled the room. It was the most real and wonderful sound Dayne had heard all day. Not only because Katy was so engaging, so pretty, and able to dominate the screen. But because her laughter and her eyes held the very thing he knew he'd find if he ever got hold of her.

They held innocence, the sort of innocence his world knew nothing about.

Katy Hart wasn't a Hollywood imitation. She was the real deal; otherwise why did she give up a budding career in the movies for director work with a kids' theater company? That last question hung in the rafters of Dayne's mind until he had to have an answer. He flicked the Pause button and trotted back to the kitchen where he'd set Katy's file.

It had to be there somewhere, the reason why Katy stopped making films. But all he could remember reading was about the series being dropped before it even got started. After that there were the commercials and eventually her work with the children's theater.

Dayne scanned the sheets of paper until he found what he was looking for. The page was titled "Unsuccessful Attempts at Films." Beneath it was a list of auditions both in Chicago and Los Angeles. Four in a row, without so much as a callback. Dayne frowned at the information. Hollywood directors didn't know what they were missing, but who cared? Their loss was about to be his gain.

If the information was correct, Katy had wanted a break into the industry but never got the chance. He hesitated and tapped the sheet of paper. If she'd wanted a break that badly, why'd she give up after four auditions? She'd already shot a pilot. Lots of actresses go years without anything half that big.

Dayne looked through the rest of the information, but still the question remained. If Katy had walked away so quickly, how badly could she have wanted the break? And how inclined would she be to attend an audition now, given the chance?

There was only one way to find out.

He pulled his cell phone from his pocket and dialed Mitch Henry, the casting director who'd put everything on hold for him.

Mitch answered after two rings. "I'm making dinner, Dayne. What've you got? You ready to go with the A-list?"

Mitch was always like this, hurried and to the point. He defined multitasking, and Dayne guessed he was probably laying out a cast list, creating a film schedule, and making dinner all at the same time.

Dayne cleared his throat. "I found her."

"Huh?" There was a hesitation. "Found who?"

81

"The girl, Mitch. The one I told you about." Dayne snagged an apple from his fruit bowl. His housekeeper was good to him, always keeping fresh food around in case he had time to eat it.

"Your wild idea, you mean?" A crash of pans clanking against each other sounded in the background. "Stupid spaghetti sauce doesn't fit in the usual pan. I must've made too much." Another loud series of sounds filled the line. "There. Sorry. Go ahead. What'd you find?"

"Not what . . . who. I found her, the girl I was telling you about. The real deal, remember? The one from out of state?"

Silence. "So what's your point, Dayne? I have three people coming for dinner."

"So . . ." Dayne took a bite of his apple. "I want you to call her. Tell her she's being invited in for an audition."

"You call her. She's your girl."

"Nah, I never said that." Dayne leaned against his counter, facing out the window at the ocean. Fog was rolling in, dancing low over the gray surf.

"Come on. Of course she's your girl."

"No, really. Never even talked to her." Dayne paused. "In fact, don't mention my name. Just call her and get her out here. She's the one; I'm telling you."

Mitch exhaled hard into the phone. "We don't have time for games, Matthews. We start filming in —"

"I know, I know." Dayne chuckled. "Four months. That's why you better call her tonight."

The director made a series of exasperated sounds and a few pans clanked together again. "Fine. I'll play your games, Dayne, but if she can't get here by Monday, you're choosing from the A-list. You're the only reason they're willing to wait a week. The ladies can't get enough of you, man. Maybe you should call the girl."

"No." Dayne took another bite of the apple. "It has to come from you." He turned his back to the ocean view and stared into the living room of his three-story beach house. He wasn't sure if Katy Hart had seen him in her theater that day a year ago, but the offer had to sound legitimate. If she got a call from him asking her to fly to Los Angeles and read for a part, she might doubt the whole thing. But if the call came from the casting director . . . "Call her, okay, Mitch?"

"All right. I'll do it as soon as I hang up." He hesitated. "I've got paper. What's the number?"

The PI had found every number that might possibly be associated with Katy Hart. The list started with the most current information, then went backward for a three-year history, just in case she was more easily reached by an older number. Dayne rattled off the information for her home, business office, and cell phone.

"You have all that and you don't know her? Come on, Dayne. What're you hiding?"

"Nothing." Dayne laughed. What would she think if she knew that her private information was so available? Dayne guessed she wouldn't like it. But that wasn't his problem; it was hers. He was only glad the PI had been able to find her. "I looked her up. It wasn't hard."

"Fine." He made a grunting sound and then cursed into the phone. "My sauce is burning, Matthews. I gotta go."

The conversation ended. Dayne wasn't worried. Mitch would call her. He could complain and sound frustrated, but *Dream On* was Dayne's film. The final call on the female lead would be his. He finished the apple and was about to head back into the screening room to watch the rest of Katy's movie when the phone rang.

Dayne reached for it and clicked the On

button without checking the caller ID. He held the phone to his ear. "That was fast."

"What was fast?" The voice was familiar, but it belonged to a woman — not Mitch Henry.

"Sorry." Dayne went into his family room and plopped down on an overstuffed leather recliner. "Who is this?" He grabbed a remote. With a single click, the fireplace sprang to life.

"It's me. Kelly." Her voice sounded hushed and frightened. "I'm not doing too good."

"Kelly . . . what's wrong?" Dayne sat a little straighter. The last few times he'd talked to Kelly Parker their conversations had been the same, based around the fact that she was falling apart, afraid to leave her house because of the paparazzi. Now something in her voice told him things were worse.

"I need you, Dayne. Can you come?"

"Of course. Where are you?"

"Ruby's. Just off Hollywood Boulevard."

"Where in Ruby's? The private room, the one in the back?"

"Yeah. They opened it early for me." A few sobs sounded over the phone line. "Come quick, Dayne. I need you."

"I'm on my way." He hung up, snatched

his car keys, and stuffed his cell phone back into his pocket. If Kelly needed him, he'd go. No questions.

Kelly Parker was one of the most popular leading ladies in Hollywood. Four years ago she'd starred opposite Dayne, and the two hooked up during filming. They'd dated twice since then, but their schedules always kept things from staying serious. In the past six months she'd been linked with another of her leading men, but she'd kept her friendship with Dayne.

Now he felt his heart rate pick up. About a year ago he'd read something about Kelly getting mixed up with drugs. At the time he figured it was only Hollywood gossip, the sort of detail the rags needed in order to stay in business. But tonight . . . something in her voice sounded desperate.

The sun was just starting to set as Dayne drove his Escalade beyond the speed limit, south on Pacific Coast Highway to Santa Monica Boulevard. His mind was so set on Kelly he forgot to watch for photographers trailing him.

When he reached Ruby's, he hopped out, handed his keys to a valet attendant, and nodded toward the nightclub. "I might not be long."

The attendant was wide-eyed. "Certainly, Mr. Matthews. We'll keep your vehicle close by."

"Thanks." He slipped the young man a five-dollar bill and walked inside. The manager's permission was needed to get into the back room. It was a private room with a second bar, not too different from the one off the main lobby, a dark-lit drink station with high-top marble tables and leather barstools and a dance floor in the middle of the room. Beyond that was a DJ hired just for the private back-room crowd. Dinner was served in the early evening by request only.

Dayne approached the manager. "I'm meeting Kelly Parker."

"Yes, Mr. Matthews." The tuxedoed man slid a key into the door and opened it for Dayne. "She's by herself." He bowed. "Enjoy your evening."

Dayne made his way into the room and looked around. He'd never been here during dinner, only during the late evening, the nightclub hours. His eyes searched the back of the room, and he saw her sitting in a booth by herself.

She was crying.

"Kelly . . ." He whispered her name as he jogged the remaining distance to her table. Without waiting for her to acknowledge him, he slid in beside her and put his arm around her. "Honey, what's wrong?"

She looked at him, and something about her was different. So different he almost didn't recognize her. Gone were the confident look, the dimpled smile that had won her millions of dollars for every film. Now her face was tearstained, her mascara running down her cheeks. "Dayne . . ."

He pulled her into a long hug and rocked gently. "It's okay, baby. It's okay."

She wept on his shoulder for a few minutes before lifting her head and searching his eyes. "I can't do it. I can't take it."

Dayne nodded. "Okay, Kelly, tell me about it."

She took a tissue from her purse and wiped her nose. "I'm sorry."

"It's all right. What happened?"

"I was . . ." She took three quick breaths, still finding her composure. "I was having dinner with a friend, one of the makeup artists I met on my last film." She pointed toward the main dining room on the other side of the door. "It was early. I figured I wouldn't get recognized." She gestured to her white T-shirt and denim miniskirt. "I don't exactly stand out dressed like this."

Dayne kept his opinion to himself. Kelly Parker could stop traffic in a potato sack.

"So what happened?"

"We were . . . we were eating when someone from another booth walked up and handed my friend a copy of *Special Event.*"

Dayne felt his stomach tighten. Of all the Hollywood magazines, *Special Event* was most known for exaggerating the facts and sometimes fully making them up. "Do you have it?" He held out his hand. "Give it to me, Kelly. Let me see what it says."

She hung her head, but after a few seconds she pulled the magazine up from the seat beside her and handed it to him. "How can they print this, Dayne?" Her voice was a strained whisper. "Do they think we're not real people? That we don't feel things?"

The magazine was turned to a layout with pictures of Kelly. One showed her with her most recent leading man, Ari Aspen, the guy she'd been seeing until lately. The other showed her sitting at a restaurant with her friend the makeup artist. Above the pictures the headline read "Did Kelly Parker Leave Ari Aspen for a Woman?"

Dayne let the magazine fall to the table. "That's ridiculous." He pushed the air from his lungs and then tightened his grip on the rag. In a rush of frustration he picked it up and used it to hit the side of the table. "It's insane, Kelly. No one who knows you would ever believe that."

"That's just it." The tears were gone, but her hands shook. "Most of the world doesn't know me, Dayne. They're the ones who'll be reading it."

A painful mix of feelings churned in Dayne's gut. Anger at the magazine for having the nerve to print such a story and a helpless ache for his friend. "Ah, Kelly . . ." He stilled her hands with his. "I'm sorry. Know what they're saying about me?"

She managed a smile, despite her puffy cheeks. "That you're an alien woman in disguise?"

"Practically." He gave her fingers a gentle squeeze. "They say some crazy woman is stalking me, that she wants a day with me or my death." He held both hands out and made a funny face. "See what I mean? Crazy stuff."

Kelly's expression changed, and fear settled in around the corners of her eyes. "What if it's true?"

"It's not true." He covered her hands again. "I know when the paparazzi are on my tail; I'd certainly know if some deranged fan was following me." He paused. "See? It's all nonsense."

"What is it with those people?" She leaned her head back against the top of the leather booth. "They build you up until you're so . . . so big you can't leave your house. Then they tear you down."

"Yes." Dayne remembered his conversation earlier in the week with Marc David. "Piece by piece."

"I can't stand it." Kelly sniffed and sat up straighter. "Take me home, will you?"

"Isn't your car here?"

"No." She collected her purse and stuffed the magazine deep inside. "My friend gave me a ride. It's easier going out in someone else's car." She nodded toward the magazine in her purse. "At least it was before that hit the streets."

Dayne took her hand and led her from the booth. Before they entered the public part of the restaurant, he stopped and faced her. "Keep your chin up, Kelly." He used his thumb to clean the mascara smudges from her face. "Don't let 'em see you crying."

She worked her fingertips into the roots of her hair and straightened the wrinkles in her T-shirt. "That's what I keep telling myself." For a moment she locked eyes with

Dayne. "Sometimes I'm not sure it's worth the trouble."

"What?" An alarm went off in Dayne's mind. "The acting?"

"No." The fear in Kelly's eyes was so deep, it was impossible to see past it. "The living."

"Hey." He pulled her into his arms and rubbed his hand along her back. "Don't talk like that. You scare me."

"I'm sorry." Her words were mumbled against his chest. She drew back. "I don't know how to get away from it."

Dayne reached into her purse, grabbed the magazine, and ripped out the pages with the pictures of her. He crumpled them into a ball, strode across the room, and dropped them into the closest trash can. Then he ripped out the rest of the pages, grabbing big handfuls of them, crushing them in his fists and dropping them into the trash.

From across the room, Kelly let loose a few small giggles.

Finally all that was left was the cover. Dayne held it up, aimed a pointed grin in her direction, then ripped the glossy layout into a few dozen pieces. He let them drift from his hands into the trash can, and when there was nothing left of the magazine, he returned to his place facing Kelly.

"That's how you get away from it." He moved in closer to her and took her shoulders in his hands. "Don't read them, Kelly. They're not real, and the people who read them aren't real either. You'll never know those people, and they'll never know you. Who cares what they think?"

A desperate look filled Kelly's eyes and she reached up, holding on to his forearms. "I want to think that way, really." She gave a small nod. "You're right. I need to stay away from them." She wrinkled her nose. "Is that how you live with it?"

"No." He chuckled and fell in alongside her, leading her to the door once more. "I read every word because it makes me laugh. By the time I reach the end of the rag, my sides hurt."

"Wow." She looped her arm through his, her tone lighter than before. "That's why you're my hero, Dayne. Really."

Having Kelly so close sent a familiar desire through Dayne's body. He wove his fingers between hers and opened the door. Before taking another step, he scanned the room. It was almost empty, the dinner crowd light that evening. A few couples, nothing more. Certainly no photographers.

He turned to her. "Come on. The coast is clear."

Together they moved quickly through the club, out the door, and to the valet. They were in his SUV headed back to her Hollywood Hills home in a matter of minutes. Dayne kept the conversation light as they drove, but he wondered if she might invite him in. They had never figured out how to have a relationship, but the time they did share was unforgettable.

Once they were in front of her house, he rolled down his windows and cut the engine.

She turned toward him, and a shy smile lifted the corners of her lips. "Thanks. I feel better."

"Good." He took her hands, and as he did, his fingers brushed against her bare knees. Crickets sang in the background, and a breeze rustled the leaves of the trees that lined her driveway. "Hey . . . it's been a while since we were like this."

"I was thinking that." She glanced at her front door, then back at him. "You dating anyone these days?"

"No." He thought about the month he spent with his last leading lady and Sarah Whitley before her. Both were old news. It'd been a month since he'd been with anyone. He shrugged. "Trying to keep things simple."

"What about Sarah Whitley?"

"Nah, she's seeing a producer. Someone more serious than me." He leaned back against the driver's door and grinned. "I guess I was too wild for her."

Kelly tipped her face and looked deeper. "You're not wild, Dayne." She squeezed his fingers. "It's all a big act. You're just waiting for the right one."

"Oh, really?" His chuckle helped keep the moment light. But in that instant, the image of Katy Hart came to mind. Katy with her long blonde hair and innocent eyes and dedication to kids' theater. He coughed, shaking the picture. "What makes you so sure?"

"I know you, remember?" The air between them changed, and the electricity that had been there earlier that evening was back. She lifted his fingers to her lips and kissed them. "Wanna come in?" Her eyes held a hint of shame but not enough to hide her desire. "I could use the company."

"Are you sure?" Dayne felt his body respond to her offer. He had hoped things might go this way, but he wouldn't have pushed it.

"I'm sure." She leaned closer and kissed

him on the lips, a kiss that left no doubt as to her intentions. "I need you, Dayne. Please."

"Okay." He kissed her, dizzy with anticipation of the pleasure that lay ahead. He didn't want a relationship, not with Kelly Parker. The two of them had already explored that possibility. But every now and then a night together was something they both enjoyed. He swallowed and shifted in his seat.

She was still inches from him, her breathing fast, heavy. "I'll go first. In case they're watching." Her lips met his again. "Could you drive around the block, maybe park down the street and walk up?"

"Sure." Anything to keep her mind off the paparazzi. Tonight it would be just the two of them, sharing the night, savoring each other. He framed her face with his hands and kissed her with an abandon he hadn't felt since the last time they were together. "You better go in."

"I will." A giggle surfaced from between her lips. "Soon." She moved closer, nuzzling her face against his. "This is going to be fun. Catching up on old times."

Dayne was thinking the same thing. He kissed her again, the intensity between them building. He was about to tell her they should leave, get themselves inside before someone saw them making out in the SUV. Only just then he heard a series of clicks. Crickets, maybe. Yes, it had to be crickets.

"Let's get inside." He whispered into her ear, "I missed you." His lips made a trail of kisses down her neck. "We've waited too long for this."

At that instant the clicks sounded again, too quiet, too distant to make him pull away.

But she must have heard them too, because she sat straight up. "What was that?" She ran her tongue along her lower lip and shot furtive glances out the window, squinting at the dusky shadows around his SUV. "Did you hear something?"

"Relax, Kelly." He drew her close again and kissed her once more. "Just the crickets."

But even as he tried to convince her, even as he leaned over, opened her car door, and told her to hurry inside where their catching up would certainly continue into the early morning hours, he heard the sound again. A series of rapid clicks. This time he couldn't convince himself it was crickets or rustling leaves or anything but the obvious.

The sound of a camera.

Chapter Five

⁂

The inside of the old yellow Honda Civic was stuffy, but that didn't matter.

Her windows were already cracked an inch, and that's all she would allow. Anything more and he'd see her, hear her. Sense her heart beating across the street from Ruby's. And that was something that absolutely couldn't happen.

Otherwise the whole plan would fall apart.

As it was, she was having trouble following him. He stayed at the studio long hours lately and spent way too much time at his beach house in Malibu. It was better when he went clubbing. Then she could dress up and work her way inside. Sometimes she'd sit at the bar for hours, sipping the same glass of Sutter Home burgundy.

The conversation there would keep her interested, and she would never take her eyes off him. Sure, she'd look in other directions so people wouldn't catch on. But even when her back was to him, she could see him, sense him. He could be twenty feet away surrounded by women, but still she could feel his breath against her face. The breath of the man she was married to.

Dayne Matthews.

"Are you sure you should wait here?" Anna tapped her on the shoulder and stared at her. "If he's your husband, he'll come out and find you and the two of you can go home."

"He *is* my husband, okay!" Chloe hissed the words at her sister. "He's my husband, and I'll sit here as long as I like."

Anna laughed, a long, cackling laugh. The laugh of a witch. "Hey, there he is. Your dream boy." She pointed. "Take a look."

Chloe spun around and glanced out the window. Anna was right. Dayne was leaving Ruby's with that prostitute on his arm, that no-good Kelly Parker. She tightened her hands into fists and slammed them against the steering wheel. A string of expletives fired through her lips at the image they made, two of Hollywood's biggest and brightest stars, sneaking out of Ruby's, believing that for a single moment maybe people weren't watching.

"Stupid people," Chloe spat. "Of course we're watching."

"You might be watching." Anna laughed again. "But I don't believe he's your husband. Not for a minute."

Chloe jerked herself around and glared at her sister. "He is my husband. I told you that before."

"Then where do you keep him? Why haven't I seen you together?" She flicked her finger at Chloe's arm. "It's because you're a liar, Chloe. A crazy liar."

Her mouth felt dry, so Chloe ran her tongue along her lower lip. "Where do I keep him?" Inside her, a pounding started up, loud and strong and steady. A familiar pounding, one that made her want to reach out and —

"There they go, the lovebirds!" Anna's laugh grew more wicked than before. "You're a nutcase, Sister. Anyone ever tell you that? A nutcase."

Chloe turned once more and watched Dayne and Kelly Parker disappear around the corner. "I know where he's going. I could be there before him." She started the engine of her car and pushed the gas pedal. Again and again she pushed it, but the Civic didn't move a bit.

"Wine," she said. "Anna, give me a glass of wine."

"Not till you tell me where you keep him. Where does this husband of yours live? I mean —" she brushed a piece of lint off her shoulder — "I'm always with you, Chloe. And I've never seen your husband spend so much as a day with you."

"You just don't look careful enough." Chloe stared at her sister, and then in a sudden motion she slapped her hard against her cheek. "I . . . I keep him in the glove box."

Anna's eyes were blazing now. "He's not in your glove box — he's with Kelly Parker." She leaned closer, sneering at Chloe. "Spend a day with him; then I'll believe you."

For a moment, Chloe held her breath. Two decades of hatred and anger and poisonous venom had built in her heart. This time she slapped Anna across the other cheek, harder than she'd ever slapped her before. "I'll spend a day with him; you'll see. Dayne Matthews is my husband. I'll prove it to you."

"You're a crazy spinster, Chloe. You'd have to be beautiful like me to have Dayne Matthews as your husband."

Chloe felt in her pocket for the knife, the

one she kept with her all the time. In case she needed to defend Dayne or force him into the car with her. Her hand wrapped snug around the handle, her eyes tearing into her sister's. "Don't tell me what I have to —"

There was a sharp knock on the window, and Chloe froze. *Casual, act casual.* She angled her body so she was facing the driver's-side window. Outside stood a police officer, a scowl on his face.

She had to roll down her window — he wouldn't settle for anything less. And Dayne was far enough away now that it wouldn't matter. He wouldn't hear her heartbeat, not even with it screaming in her temples and echoing through the inside of the Honda.

Smile, she told herself. *You have to smile.* She felt the corners of her lips lift as she cranked the window all the way down. "Uh, hello, Officer. Can I help you?"

He frowned at her and stooped down, looking past her toward the passenger seat and the back of the car. "We had reports you were yelling at someone." He straightened back up and pulled a notepad from his pocket. "Were you in some sort of trouble, ma'am?"

"Not at all, Officer. Just chatting with my sister."

The man took a step back and raised his brow a bit. "Okay." He looked inside her car again. "Can I get your driver's license, please? I need to make a report."

"My license?" Her mouth was dry again. That, and Dayne Matthews was getting away. He couldn't leave Ruby's with Kelly Parker. What would happen if the two of them got together again? It could be weeks before he came back to his senses and went home to her. She glanced toward the side street, the one where Dayne and Kelly would come out from if they were headed back to his house.

"Ma'am, can you please hurry?" The officer poised his pen above the notepad. "I need your license."

"Oh." She felt her composure returning. "Right. I'm sorry. I was thinking about my sister." Chloe pulled her designer purse from the seat beside her and began rummaging through it. After several seconds, she smiled up at the officer and batted her eyelashes. "Wouldn't you know it? I left it in my other purse." She tilted her head, doing her best to look demure and alluring. "I'm so sorry, Officer. Would you like to follow me home so I can show it to you?" She gestured down the road. "I live just a few miles from here — up in the hills."

The officer hesitated for a minute. "What's your name?"

"Margie. Margie Madden."

"Well, the report was that you were maybe in trouble, screaming at someone."

Chloe gave a light laugh, reached out, and patted the officer's arm. "Sir, now do I look upset about anything? Like I said, I was chatting with my sister."

"Where is she?"

Chloe's heart beat louder, faster. Why, she was sitting right beside her, wasn't she? But a quick turn toward the passenger seat told her the answer. Maybe she'd already left. Maybe she really had been looking for her and not Dayne Matthews. She smiled at the police officer again. "She's doing some shopping. That's why I'm here, just waiting for her."

The officer narrowed his eyes and moved closer. Then he stooped down and stared at her cheek. "Ma'am, has someone hurt you recently?"

"No, sir." She smoothed her shirt and set her purse back on the seat beside her. Her heartbeat fell silent and slow. "I told you, everything's fine."

"Have you seen your face lately?" The man moved in closer still, scrutinizing her cheeks. "Looks like someone slapped you pretty hard."

Chloe felt the blood drain from her face. Someone had slapped her? Was it Anna or was it Dayne? Maybe it was Kelly Parker. She swallowed hard. "Must be the heat, Officer."

After a few seconds the officer nodded. He didn't look quite convinced, but he put the pad of paper away. "All right." He looked down the street as if he expected to see her sister returning to the Civic. He studied Chloe one last time. "If everything's okay, I won't make a report. Let us know if you need assistance. And if you're too hot, I'd keep the windows down from now on. It's in the nineties today."

"Right. Very good, Officer." She nodded at him. "Thank you, sir." She watched him go, felt her body react with every step he took away from her, the beat of her heart speeding up, pounding loud the way it had before.

She had to get out of here, had to find Dayne before he did something stupid. The press would catch wind of it, and she'd never hear the end of it from Anna.

Someone was laughing at her again, and she turned toward the passenger seat. Anna was back. "See, you're nothing but a crazy liar. Dayne's gone off with Kelly

Parker. You've never even met the man."

"Stop it!" Chloe yelled, then reached out to slap her sister one last time. But her hand caught only air and the dashboard. She rubbed her stinging fingertips on her jeans and lifted her eyes to Anna again. "Now look what you've made me do, you —"

Her sister was gone.

The entire car shook with the sound of her heartbeat, and Chloe held her breath to make it go away. She was alone and she needed to leave, needed to find Dayne now. She stepped on the gas again, but the car stayed where it was, unmoving. It was only then that she caught a glimpse of herself in the rearview mirror.

The police officer was right. Across her cheeks were bright red marks in a very distinct pattern. Sometime in the past half hour someone had slapped her. She looked down and realized why she wasn't going anywhere.

The car was still in park.

She slipped it into gear, checked her mirror again, and pulled out into traffic. Dayne's house, that's where she needed to be. Maybe he could tell her what happened to her face and who would have had the nerve to slap her not once across the face.

But twice.

Chapter Six

The dinner was Jenny Flanigan's idea.

She and her husband, Jim, were in charge of the sets for CKT's upcoming *Tom Sawyer* production, and until a day earlier they were the only people on the committee. But yesterday she took a call from her good friend Kari Taylor, who said that her artist sister, Ashley, wanted to help paint sets.

Jenny was thrilled at the news. She contacted Ashley and the two hit it off.

"My husband wants to help also." Ashley's tone held a trace of humor. "He told me to tell you he could paint brown walls." She lowered her voice, as if the next part were top secret. "Landon's a firefighter. He's used to tearing down plywood, not painting it."

"I understand." Jenny laughed. "My husband's a football coach. Same thing, but that's all right. We'll show them what to do." She thought a minute. "Hey, why don't you and Landon come for a barbecue tomorrow night? We can talk about sets and what's involved, get to know each other a little."

Ashley talked the idea over with her husband and called back later that afternoon accepting the offer. Now she and Landon and their son, Cole, would be here in fifteen minutes.

Some country song played from the computer in the study as Jenny seasoned a tray of raw hamburger patties. Next she fanned the sliced cheese on a plate, easy to grab, just the way Jim liked it. The salad was chopped and covered, the watermelon sliced and in the refrigerator.

She looked out the window as she washed her hands. All six kids were outside splashing and laughing and playing a game of tag in the pool. It was the perfect day for a barbecue, eighty-five and nothing but sunshine.

Jenny took a few steps toward the entryway and the stairs that led to the bedrooms. "Jim, time to start the fire."

"Be right down." His voice filled the house with a rich warmth.

Jenny smiled as she headed back to the kitchen. The barbecue would be a welcome distraction from the roller coaster of emotions that had hit the Flanigan household since auditions for the play. Monday night had been pure jubilation, with both Connor and Bailey getting callbacks for the second day of auditions. But after Tuesday's limited tryout, the cast list was posted that night on CKT's Web site, and the results sent emotions spiraling in opposite directions.

Connor was happy. He had earned the part of Joe Harper, Tom Sawyer's sidekick. It was a major role with multiple speaking lines and solo parts in three songs. But Bailey's part was something much smaller. She was a townsperson, a nondescript ensemble member who would help make up the background during full-cast scenes, town picnics, and a few song-and-dance numbers.

Tim Reed was Tom Sawyer, Sarah Jo Stryker was Becky Thatcher, and Ashley Zarelli won the part of Aunt Polly.

Jenny took the ketchup and mustard from the fridge and placed them on a blue-and-white plastic tray. It had hurt so much to watch Bailey check the cast list that day. She'd sat in the computer chair, Connor looking over her shoulder, as she navigated the mouse to the right page.

"Well, find it!" Connor had hopped in place, his eyes wide. "Hurry, Bailey, it's gotta be there."

"I'm trying." Her eyes had darted down the list not once but twice. Then, without bursting into tears or even complaining, she slowly pushed the chair back, stood, and hugged Connor. "Congratulations, buddy. You deserve it."

Then she trudged up the stairs, one slow step at a time.

Jenny let her go and spent the next five minutes calling Jim and the other Flanigan kids into the room to celebrate Connor's part. Finally Connor grabbed the phone and raised one eyebrow. "I have to call Tim."

Jenny remembered everything about what happened next. She had dismissed the four younger boys back to the kickball game they'd been playing outside. Then she headed up the stairs after Bailey. With quiet steps she made her way down the hall to Bailey's room, praying for the right words.

She knocked a couple of times on her daughter's door. "Bailey?"

"Yes?" Her voice had been thick, muffled. "Come in."

Jenny went inside and found her place

on the edge of Bailey's bed, the place where they often held late-night talks, sometimes into the early morning hours. Bailey stared straight ahead, silent tears sliding down her cheeks onto her pillow.

"I'm sorry, honey." Jenny had brushed a lock of hair off her daughter's forehead.

"What I can't figure out is why they called me back." She propped herself up, searching Jenny's eyes. "I danced better than anyone there, Mom. I promise." She rolled her eyes. "And that Mrs. Stryker, she sent her daughter in this . . . this yellow dress. Almost like she'd made it just for the *Tom Sawyer* play." She uttered a single laugh, but it held not a bit of humor. "I thought Katy didn't like pushy people."

Jenny winced. "Sweetheart, it's not Sarah Jo's fault if her mother's pushy. You wouldn't expect Katy to take that out on a child."

"No, but . . ." Tears filled Bailey's eyes again. "I sang just as well as Sarah Jo." She sat up and crossed her legs, her eyes on Jenny. "And I know I can dance better." She let her head fall toward her knees. "I wanted it so bad, Mom."

"I know." Jenny had taken care with her next words. "Remember your Bible verse? Jeremiah 29:11?"

Bailey lifted her head a bit and sniffed. "Of course."

"You believe it, right?" Jenny had brushed her hand over her daughter's forehead once more. "The part about God knowing the plans He has for you?"

"I guess." Bailey dragged her hands beneath her eyes. "It's hard sometimes." She knit her brows and looked hard at Jenny. "How come His plans for me didn't include a part opposite Tim Reed?" She frowned. "When'll I have that chance again?"

Jenny continued to prepare for their guests. She walked to the garage and the outside refrigerator where she kept the hamburger buns. She grabbed three bags, then returned to the kitchen.

It was no surprise that Bailey's frustration ultimately came down to Tim Reed. In the drama that was Bailey's life, half her time was spent with her friends in her class at Clear Creek High School and the other half was spent with the mostly home-schooled kids involved with CKT.

Bailey was on the cheerleading squad at Clear Creek, a commitment that had kept her out of the first two CKT shows this past school year. *Tom Sawyer* was the only production she could be a part of, and even then her participation meant giving up summer cheer camp.

Jenny opened the buns and set them out on another tray. Good thing that day was behind them. Bailey was doing better now, talking to her CKT friends and getting excited about being in the show — however small her part. Meanwhile her school friends were frustrated that she was in the play at all. Heather and Sami and Spencer had all weighed in with their opinion on CKT.

"It's for artsy kids," Heather had told her. "You're not like that, Bailey. Spend your time with us."

Then there was Tanner Williams, quarterback of the freshman football team and Bailey's longtime friend. Most of the time he was confident about his place in Bailey's life, but when she took part in a show, as she'd done twice her eighth-grade year, he saw her much less often. When he did come around he would flip through the most recent CKT program and ask questions about Tim Reed.

Jenny chuckled to herself.

Four years ago when Jim and Jenny adopted three boys from Haiti, Jenny sometimes wondered if they were crazy to take on such a feat. But more than once her mother would stop in to visit and pull her aside. "Don't worry about all those little boys. Bailey's almost a teenager." She'd raise an eyebrow toward whatever part of the house Bailey happened to be in. "You'll spend more energy on that girl than you do on all the boys combined."

Her mother had been right.

It wasn't that Bailey was any trouble — other than her struggles with keeping her room clean and getting her homework done on time. She was a delight, a morally driven girl with a contagious laugh and more friends than she could count. The time-consuming aspect came with the hours of analyzing and agonizing over whatever development the day brought.

There was a knock at the front door. Jenny dusted the crumbs off her hands and headed for the door. A glance through the living-room window told her it was Cody Coleman, the sixteen-year-old boy from down the street.

She swung the door open and smiled. "Hello, Cody. Come on in."

"Thanks." Cody gave her a quick hug and motioned toward the kitchen. "Can I grab a sandwich?"

"Cody, you're always hungry." Jenny laughed and led the way to the refrigerator.

"We'll be eating in less than an hour."

He grinned at her as he reached for a package of lunch meat and a loaf of bread. "Good. That's just about when I'll be ready for more."

At that moment, Jim bounded into the kitchen, raised his fists in the air, and sucked in a deep breath. "I love summer." He winked at Cody and continued across the kitchen to Jenny. He kissed her lightly on her lips. "Have I ever told you that?"

"Every June." She smiled and gave him a playful shove, creating enough space between them so she could hand him the tray of raw meat. "Cody's having his predinner meal."

"Good man!" Jim pointed a finger at him and adjusted his tone to the one he used for coaching. "Six meals a day if you wanna pack on the muscle this summer."

Cody raised his sandwich in the air, his mouth too full to answer. He took the plate of cheese and followed Jim out back toward the barbecue.

Jenny watched for a moment, and her heart soared at the sight of her husband working alongside Cody Coleman. All last year — while Cody ran with the wrong crowd and nearly got kicked out of school

115

for bringing liquor on campus — she and Jim doubted whether they'd ever see him again.

About a month ago, Jim had taken him to lunch, and Cody had been dropping in for dinner or a conversation or a swim in the pool ever since. He'd also started attending church with them and asking questions about the Bible. Once in a while he even hinted at living with them, the way he'd lived on their sofa for three weeks at the end of his freshman year.

Jenny didn't mind. Both she and Jim were certainly open to the possibility if Cody's mother agreed. She was single and worked two jobs — one of them at a strip club. Over the years she'd been verbally abusive to Cody, and when he was still in middle school she introduced him to the world of drinking.

"I can make the meanest gin and tonic in all of Bloomington," Cody had told them a couple years back, the first time he came down the street and introduced himself.

Jenny and Jim had entertained the thought of contacting social services, but they were torn. As much as the woman wasn't a good mother, she was all Cody had. Instead they watched the situation closely and decided against seeking inter-vention.

There was only one problem with Cody's latest involvement in their lives.

Bailey had noticed him.

Jenny positioned herself near the sink so she could watch her daughter's reaction to Cody's arrival. Sure enough, Bailey climbed out of the pool, smoothed her hair back, and grabbed a towel. She knew the game of interacting with boys better than to appear too interested. She spent another few minutes talking with her brothers; then she pulled away and made her way across the deck to Jim.

The two smiled and chatted about something, but almost as quickly Bailey shifted the conversation to Cody. The pass-through window was open, and Jenny could hear voices, but she couldn't make out the exact conversation. What-ever story Bailey was telling, she bent over and made a silly face; then she gave Cody a light touch on his elbow and threw her head back, laughing hard. Cody laughed too and said something in return. But after that he turned his attention back to Jim. If body language was any indication, Cody wasn't interested in Bailey. Not at this point.

Jenny prayed often that things would stay that way.

Cody was a year older than Bailey and very good-looking. Together he and Bailey made a striking pair. But Cody was an alcoholic, one who could go months drinking every day to the point of blacking out. The idea of his being interested in Bailey sent terrible shivers down Jenny's spine.

Another knock came from the front of the house.

"Coming!" Jenny took quick, light steps into the foyer and opened the front door. Standing on the porch was a beautiful young woman in her late twenties and next to her a strapping dark-haired man. On his other side was a towheaded little boy. "Hi!" Jenny held the door open and stepped back. "You must be the Blakes. Come on in!"

The woman held her hand out. "I'm Ashley." She put her hand on the man's shoulder. "This is my husband, Landon —" her gaze shifted to the child — "and our son, Cole."

Jenny stooped down. "I'm Mrs. Flanigan. Nice to meet you, Cole."

He shook her hand and looked her straight in the eyes. "Nice to meet you, Mrs. Flanigan."

They moved through the foyer into the kitchen, and Ashley said, "Jenny, your house is beautiful."

"Thanks." Jenny never got over feeling a little embarrassed about the size of their house. It was seven thousand square feet with six bedrooms and an apartment over the garage. She shrugged and gave Ashley a lopsided grin. "God provided it. Now it's our job to use it for Him."

"Well, it's very lovely." Ashley folded her hands. Her eyes sparkled as she took in the stone tile and cherrywood detail around the perimeter of the kitchen. "Maybe later you could give me a tour?"

"Definitely." Jenny looked at the three of them. "Can I get you some water, something to drink?"

Cole hopped in place a few times. "Yes, please. Ice water, please."

Ashley rolled her eyes. "Ice water's his new thing." Her voice dropped to a whisper. "Makes him feel like a big boy."

"Well, then, ice water it is." Jenny found a ceramic pitcher in a lower cupboard and began filling it. She looked over her shoulder at Ashley and Landon. "One of Jim's players is with us tonight too. His name's Cody. He's sort of like a sixth son, I guess."

"And Katy Hart, right? She lives here too?" Ashley accepted a glass of water and leaned back against the kitchen island.

"Yes, she has the apartment." The mention of Katy's name caused a strange feeling in Jenny. Ever since auditions, Katy had been gone more often. And when she was around, she was less talkative than usual. Or maybe it was only Jenny's imagination. The truth was, she'd been upset with Katy after the cast list was posted. Bailey had already given a lot to CKT. The part of Becky Thatcher would've been perfect for her.

But those thoughts had cleared by the following morning. Casting a show couldn't be an easy task, and Katy put great thought into her decisions. Besides, she'd told Katy not to play favorites. She couldn't stay frustrated at Katy over the way Bailey had been cast. It was like she had told Bailey in her room that night. If God had wanted her to have the part of Becky Thatcher, she would've gotten it.

The small talk in the kitchen continued. Ashley was sweet and excited about working on the sets committee. After just five minutes with the couple, one thing was very clear: Ashley and Landon were crazy about each other.

After Cole had his water, he joined the other kids out back where they were drying off near the pool. Ashley mentioned that Cole was a very strong swimmer, but she still wanted to stay outside as long as he was near the pool.

That's when Jenny remembered Kari's and Ashley's sister Brooke and how her youngest daughter had nearly died in a drowning incident a few years back. "Tell you what." Jenny led Ashley and Landon out to the covered patio. She walked to one of the side walls of their covered patio and turned a key. An electric cover began making its way across the pool. "With all the kids out, it's better to keep the water covered."

"Yes." Ashley held Landon's hand as they followed Jenny to where Jim and Cody were barbecuing. "You can never be too careful."

Jenny introduced the Blakes to everyone, and she stifled a smile at Cody's reaction to Ashley. As Jim chatted with Landon and finished cooking the burgers, Cody didn't take his eyes off Ashley. The kids changed into their shorts and T-shirts and hovered near the barbecue.

Cole fit right in with their four younger boys, and Bailey worked herself into a conversation with Ashley about the music in *Tom Sawyer.* The group was about to move inside for dinner when the phone rang.

"I'll get it." Jenny jogged back to the kitchen and caught the phone on the fourth ring. "Hello?"

"Yes, hi." It was a man's voice, and the connection wasn't great. "This is Mitch Henry. I'm a casting director in Los Angeles."

Jenny held the phone away from her face and studied the caller ID. Probably one of the CKT kids playing a trick. She returned the receiver to her ear. "I'm sorry. Could you say that again?"

"Yes." The static grew worse. "Does Katy Hart live there?"

"She does." Jenny pressed the phone to her ear, trying everything possible to hear the man. She moved to the built-in desk, pulled a notepad toward her, and grabbed a pen. "Can I take a message?"

"Please. Tell her Mitch Henry called." Every few words, the signal cut out. Jenny struggled to make sense of the man. "I'm a casting director . . . Los Angeles. Please have her call me." He rattled off a phone number, and Jenny had him repeat it. She promised to pass on the message.

They were halfway through the meal when Katy came in through the side door and peeked her head into the dining room. She waved. "Hi, everyone."

Jenny lifted her napkin and wiped her mouth. "Katy, come in. I want you to meet our new sets committee members."

"I heard you're a real live actual artist." Katy entered the room and stood near the head of the table, her eyes on Ashley.

"Yes." Landon answered for her. "Real, live, and actual."

"Mommy's a good painter." Cole nodded, the beans on his fork falling to his plate in his excitement.

"Well, good." Katy grinned at Cole. She took a step back. "I have to finish blocking the script, so . . ." She waved again. "Have a good dinner."

She was halfway toward the side stairs that would take her up to her apartment when Jenny remembered the message. "Wait! Someone called for you." She excused herself from the table and went to the kitchen desk.

"Someone from CKT?" Katy turned back and came closer.

"No." After a few seconds Jenny found the note she'd written. She held it out to Katy and gave her a curious look.

"Someone from Los Angeles. Says he's a casting director."

"Great." Katy made a face. "Probably Sarah Jo Stryker's agent."

They both laughed, then turned and went their separate ways, Katy to her apartment, where she stayed the rest of the night, and Jenny back to the table and company. Cody was asking Ashley if she'd ever sold a painting, and Landon was gushing about the numbers she had indeed sold.

The rest of the evening was comfortable, easy conversation and a few rounds of the ABC dinner game — a favorite of the Flanigan family. They talked about Ashley losing her mother and the declining health of Jenny's mother.

"She's in a retirement village, but she's going downhill." Jenny had a catch in her voice. "We might need another level of care — maybe assisted living."

"If you get to that point, let me know." Ashley's voice was kind, understanding. "I worked at Sunset Hills Adult Care Home. It's a wonderful option when it comes time."

They talked about the sorrow of watching parents age and fall ill. After that the conversation switched to the Flanigans' home and the busy lives they all led.

Finally they discussed the upcoming theater production.

By the time the Blakes left, they'd agreed that *Tom Sawyer* needed a full-size backdrop, a landscape that would lend the feeling of the small Missouri town where the play was set. Also they would need buildings, a house for Aunt Polly, and a fence for the famous whitewashing scene.

"I can take care of that part," Landon chimed in, and they all laughed.

It wasn't until she was getting ready for bed that Jenny thought back to Katy's brief appearance that night. Until that moment, Jenny had almost convinced herself that the strange tension she felt around Katy lately was all in her mind.

But something hadn't felt right about their conversation, even the part when Jenny gave her the strange message from the casting director in Los Angeles. And as she was brushing her teeth, Jenny realized she'd been right. Things really did feel strained between them. She knew for sure it was not because of something Katy did — her tone had been friendly enough. No, it was something Katy didn't do. Something she hadn't done since the auditions, not with Jenny or with Bailey.

Katy never once made eye contact.

Chapter Seven

The first day of practice for any CKT show was always the most chaotic. That Friday night, excitement ran at a record high as kids milled about the Bloomington Community Church sanctuary, moving in hurried, boisterous circles, congratulating each other, and guessing at costumes and solo numbers.

Katy was glad for the distraction.

Things around the Flanigan house had been tense since she'd posted the cast list, and she understood why. Bailey had gotten the short end of the deal — there was no way around it. Everything about the Flanigan girl was perfect for the part of Becky Thatcher, except one thing.

No one at CKT could sing like Sarah Jo Stryker.

With all her heart, Katy wanted to relegate Sarah Jo to the role of a townsperson. Not because of anything the girl had done — in fact Sarah Jo proved to be even more polite and talented on the second day of auditions than she'd been on the first. But Katy hated the fact that the girl's mother had known her daughter would get the part, hated the fact that she'd already made Sarah Jo a Becky Thatcher dress.

Of all things.

Before the second day of auditions, Katy convinced herself that Sarah Jo hadn't been that good, that no one but Bailey Flanigan could play the part of Becky. Bailey had earned it with her patience and with the effort she'd given to every minor role she'd played.

Besides, Sarah Jo wasn't a Christian. Her mother told Katy as much the morning of the second day of auditions.

"We don't believe in God." Alice Stryker set her purse down on the table where Katy was stationed. "I just want to get that out in the open before it becomes an issue."

Katy did what she was supposed to do in that situation. She assured the woman that faith was not a requirement for participation in CKT, and it wasn't. Still, a girl like Bailey Flanigan — a teenager with a love for Christ and an ability to share God's truth with the younger kids in CKT — was a much better choice for a lead part, right? Same as Tim Reed was a wonderful choice for the male lead.

After Bailey sang Becky Thatcher's solo on the second day of auditions, Katy was sure she had the cast all figured out. But all of Katy's reasoning flew out the window the minute Sarah Jo Stryker took her turn singing the part. The girl's voice was golden, no question. And even though it meant letting Alice Stryker think she'd called the shots, Katy had no choice.

Sarah Jo had to be Becky Thatcher.

But ever since then she'd doubted her decision. Even worse, she felt tension between the Flanigans and herself, as if maybe they were holding it against her that Bailey didn't win a major role.

Katy organized her stack of scripts on the table in the lobby and motioned for her creative team — Al and Nancy Helmes and Rhonda — to join her. Whatever the Flanigans were thinking, she couldn't let it bother her today. She wouldn't live to be thirty if she didn't stop feeling so stressed about her casting decisions for each show.

Besides, if ever she had to be on her game it was now, trying to rein in sixty kids and block the show's opening number, all while assigning scripts and solos to the various leads.

She huddled with the others for ten minutes; then she stood on one of the chairs. At five foot five, dressed in jeans and a sweatshirt, Katy easily blended in with the kids. When she wanted to be heard, she stood on a chair and did her series of signature hand claps. No whistling or shouting at CKT practices. Katy had her special clap, and as the kids heard it they instinctively turned to her, quieting their voices. When Katy stopped, the kids clapped out the same rhythm in response, and as they finished, the talking had stopped, all eyes on Katy.

"Congratulations to everyone who earned a part in *Tom Sawyer.*" The palms of her hands were damp, and she rubbed them on her jeans. She looked around the room at the clusters of kids and made eye contact with Tim Reed and Ashley Zarelli, standing next to each other on one side of the room. "Lead parts are a precious thing in CKT." She shifted her attention to Sarah Jo Stryker. "I'll expect you to learn your lines in a week and give me your best effort at every practice."

Nancy Helmes motioned to Katy, and Katy nodded. "Take a seat. Mrs. Helmes has something for you."

"Yes." Nancy had a strong voice, and it carried easily through the sanctuary, where the kids quickly sat down. "Al and I've heard that some of you aren't happy with your roles or your friends think less of you because you won the part of a towns-person." She raised a finger. "We have one cast, ladies and gentlemen. One cast. And we perform for an audience of One." She paused. "There are no small parts. In fact, we'll need each of you doing his or her personal best if this show is to shine for Jesus when we take the stage eight weeks from now."

Katy nodded. "Mrs. Helmes is right." For an instant, she met eyes with Bailey and caught the hint of a smile. Warmth filled Katy's soul as she continued. "Okay, here's the plan. If I read your name, go with Mr. and Mrs. Helmes to the chorus room at the end of the hallway. You'll be working on the solos in the first act." She winked at Nancy. "And if I know Mrs. Helmes, she'll have a box of Cinnabon rolls ready for break time."

She read a list of seven names, and one by one the kids peeled away from the group and followed Al and Nancy. Cara Helmes tagged along at the back of the line, beaming, probably at the thought of hearing the first songs come together. Again Katy noticed Tim Reed and Ashley Zarelli looking friendly as they walked together, their heads bowed close, whispering. Katy looked at Bailey and saw that she was watching the twosome. Katy forced herself to stay focused. She wasn't responsible for Bailey's social life.

With the soloists gone, Katy continued. "If I didn't call your name, I want you to line up shortest to tallest." She looked over the bunches of remaining kids. "Ready . . . go!"

Katy watched from her place on the chair as the kids began running in different directions. Someone took the smallest CKT kid and put her at the far end of the stage. A minute passed while children tried to figure out where they belonged, and at one point Katy winced as one of the big boys collided with a littler one.

She turned to Rhonda. "You sure you wanna teach this group to dance?"

"Yes." Rhonda gave a tired laugh. "But I think we'll be here later than eight o'clock."

"Me too."

It took four minutes for the kids to put themselves in a line that was close to organized. Katy walked over to the smallest one and patted her on the head. "Okay, everyone look at who's in front of you." Katy waited while the kids followed her order. "Now look at who's behind you and remember their face." The kids did as they were told. "Tomorrow morning I want us to make this line in fifteen seconds. Got it?"

A couple of weak "Got it" responses came back at her.

Katy slapped her knee and laughed. "No." She looked back at Rhonda. "They can't answer that way, can they?"

"Not at CKT." Rhonda smiled and came a few steps closer.

"Let's try it again." Katy looked at the faces up and down the line. "Fifteen seconds flat tomorrow, okay, guys?"

This time the line of kids practically shouted, "Yes, Katy!"

"That's better." Katy tried to give them a stern look, but she could feel her eyes dancing. "Now . . . I want four even lines of twelve to thirteen kids, with the tallest kids in back. Ready . . . go!"

The kids moved much quicker and more efficiently this time. They formed four rows in no time.

"Better." Katy looked at Rhonda again.

"I think we might even finish early."

A few of the older kids giggled, and Katy grinned at them. Then she asked Rhonda to move to the nearby piano and play the opening number. She wasn't as strong with music as Al or Nancy, but she could give the cast a melody to work with.

"All right, here's what's going to happen." Katy's voice was animated and upbeat. This was the part she loved, making a story come to life. "This song is the opening number, and it's about the arrival of the *Big Missouri* — a boat that came into the city of Hannibal only once in a while. Everyone in town is thrilled that the big boat's coming, because it carries mail for some people, friends and relatives for others, and sometimes a family that might be relocating to the area. That's the case with this story. The Thatchers are moving to town, arriving on the *Big Missouri*."

One of the smaller kids raised his hand. "Katy, why didn't they just take a U-Haul?"

"Good question." Katy gave a pointed look at the older kids who were snickering in the back. Then her eyes found the young boy again. "Because U-Haul wasn't around back then. For that matter, roads weren't really around back then. Not the way they are today." She took a deep breath. "The point is, the people of Hannibal, Missouri, are very, very excited."

She took a few running steps and did a sideways bell kick. "That's how excited they are."

"So —" Rhonda was at the piano — "the music is strong and steady, like this." She played the opening notes of the song.

"And what Rhonda and I want you to do is pump your arms like this . . ." Katy looked like a mechanical jogger running out of batteries as she pumped her right fist straight forward, paused, and then pumped her left fist straight forward. She repeated that several times. "I want you to pump your arms like that and stomp your feet forward until you're near the front of the stage. Then I want everyone to spin to the left, make a sharp U-turn, and head to the back of the group where you'll form your line once more." She paused in midpumping motion. "Got it?"

"Yes, Katy." Their voices were loud and together.

"Okay, let's see what it looks like."

Rhonda played the music while the first row marched forward without incident, spun to the left, and moved to their spots at the back of the line. Not until the last line, the oldest, tallest kids, did three of them turn the wrong direction and smack straight into the person next to them.

The music stopped.

Six kids were holding their heads, and the others looked nervous. One girl raised her hand and said, "Katy, do we need a medical release for this dance?"

"Yes." Katy crossed her arms and nodded. "I think after tonight we might consider that. Definitely."

The injured dancers were stabilized, and Katy ordered everyone to line up again. "Okay, let's set a goal. Only two injuries this time." She shot a look at Rhonda. "Ready . . . go!"

This time the blocking worked without a hitch. One line after another the kids marched and stomped to the beat, spun around to the left, and returned to the back of the pack. All in unison, and almost all in time with the music.

"Yay!" Katy raised her hands in the air. "Let's do it again!"

By the half-time break, they had most of the song choreographed, and Katy felt her heart dancing along. At this point in putting together a show, God always gave her a glimpse of what was to come. This time the glimpse gave her chills.

She pulled herself away from the craziness and went to her car for her water bottle. On her way back to the sanctuary, she stopped. She'd forgotten to call the California guy. All day she'd been meaning to make the call, but she'd met with Rhonda and they'd become absorbed in blocking out the first number.

Now she checked her watch and saw it was seven o'clock. That meant it was only four in LA, still early enough to call. She stepped inside the church's front doors, found a quiet corner in the vestibule, and pulled the message from the inside of her checkbook, where she'd placed it the night before.

Mitch Henry, the message read. *Casting director.*

She still believed the guy must've had something to do with Sarah Jo Stryker. Who else would have connections with a casting director in Hollywood?

There were five minutes left in the break, so Katy pulled her cell phone from the front pocket of her purse and dialed the number.

A man answered almost immediately. "Mitch Henry."

"Uh . . ." His hurried, clipped tone took Katy by surprise. "Hi, this is Katy Hart."

She hesitated. "You left a message?"

"Katy Hart!" His voice became instantly warm. "I was hoping you'd call."

"Yes, well —" she looked at her watch again — "I just have a few minutes."

"Right." The man cleared his throat. "I'm the casting director for an upcoming romantic comedy called *Dream On*. You may have heard of it."

Katy hadn't. "Okay . . ."

"Anyway, we'd like to fly you out to Los Angeles to read for the female lead in the show."

Her first instinct was to laugh, and she did, but not loud enough for Mitch Henry to hear her. "I'm sure there's some sort of mistake, sir. I'm not an actress, not anymore."

"We, well . . . we think you are." There was the sound of rustling papers. "We can fly you out Sunday afternoon, put you up at the Sheraton Universal, and have a car pick you up and bring you to the studios. The audition is at nine o'clock Monday morning. You could fly home late that afternoon."

Katy's head was spinning. The man sounded serious, but how could he be? "Are you sure you have the right Katy Hart?"

"Very sure." He chuckled. "It would make a big difference to the casting of this film if you'd come, Miss Hart."

She pinched her temples with her thumb and forefinger. "How'd you find out about me?"

"Well . . . I don't have access to that information, honestly. I can only tell you we're holding up decisions on this film until we have your answer."

The entire conversation didn't make sense. If the details weren't so specific she would've sworn it was one of the CKT kids playing a trick. But the man was too serious to be joking. Katy's mind raced. How had they heard of her, and how had they known where to find her? And who in Hollywood was even aware she existed?

"So what can I tell the producer, Miss Hart? Can we make flight arrangements for you? I assume you'd be flying out of Indianapolis."

Katy felt light-headed. She gripped the phone more tightly. "Can I . . . can I call you back in a few hours and let you know? I'm right in the middle of something."

"Definitely." He kept his tone upbeat, warm. "You've got my cell number. I'll wait to hear from you one way or another, okay?"

"Yes. Thank you, Mister —" She thought of something. "Who's producing the film?"

"DreamFilms."

DreamFilms? The major motion picture studio, the birthplace of dozens of box-office hits? The moment seemed even more surreal than before. "Okay." She gulped and looked down. Her knees were trembling. "Very good. I'll call in a few hours."

She hung up and tried to move, but the room swayed and she leaned against the wall. Nothing made sense. By the time she found her balance, returned to the sanctuary, and pulled the rehearsal back together, she doubted everything about the phone call.

But just in case it was real, after the rehearsal was over and all the kids' questions were answered, after every one of them had gone home, and even Al and Nancy had left for the night, she turned to Rhonda Sanders and let her mouth hang open for a moment. "You won't believe this."

"What?" Rhonda was single, twenty-eight, and the person Katy could most relate to in the entire CKT organization. Their friendship had come fast and strong when Katy moved to Bloomington, and the two often talked about life and how it didn't always work out the way it was supposed to.

Like Katy, Rhonda had been raised in a Christian home, believing that God had a special person picked out for her, a man with a strong faith and an ability to lead her in the lifelong journey of following Christ. All of that was supposed to happen by her twenty-fifth birthday — at least in the plan. Kids would come along shortly after that.

Instead here they were in their late twenties, wondering if life had passed them by.

Rhonda pulled up a chair and searched Katy's face. "What won't I believe? You met Prince Charming?"

"No." Katy pulled her cell phone from her purse and held it out. "I got the strangest message yesterday, to call this casting director in Los Angeles." She lifted one shoulder. "Naturally I thought it had something to do with Sarah Jo Stryker."

"Naturally."

Katy felt her eyes grow wide. "But it wasn't about her. Get this." She bit her lower lip and stared at her phone. Her eyes met Rhonda's again. "I called the guy and he tells me . . ." A nervous bit of laughter made it hard for her to finish her sentence. She breathed in slowly through her nose.

"He tells me DreamFilms Studio wants to fly me to Los Angeles Sunday for a Monday morning audition." She hesitated, holding her breath. "An audition for the lead in an upcoming romantic comedy called *Dream On*. I told him I had to think about it for a few hours and call him back."

"What?" Rhonda jumped to her feet. She held her hands out toward Katy and let out a scream. "Are you serious?"

"Yes." Katy squealed. Of all the people she knew in Bloomington, only Rhonda had any idea about her short-term career in film or how badly she'd wanted that break back then. Of course, there were some things even Rhonda didn't know, things Katy had never told anyone.

"So call him back and tell him yes!" Rhonda stood and did a little dance. "I can't believe it, Katy . . . things like this don't just happen to people in Bloomington, Indiana." She stopped moving for a moment. "Well, what're you waiting for?"

"What if it isn't real?" Katy paced a few feet in either direction. "Somehow it feels like a practical joke — you know, something thrown together by the Reed family or the Zarellis."

"Oh." The excitement on Rhonda's face faded. "I didn't think about that."

"Okay, so say it isn't a practical joke." Katy plopped down on the edge of a table. "Say a casting director working for DreamFilms really found out about me and wants to fly me in for an audition." She giggled at the thought. "Then right now he's waiting for me to call him back, this Mitch Henry, whoever he is. So what do I tell him?"

"If it's the real deal?" Rhonda screamed again. "Are you kidding? You jump on that plane, Katy Lynn Hart, and you give the audition of a lifetime!"

Katy was on her feet again, pacing once more. She stopped and tossed her hands in the air. "What about *Tom Sawyer*?"

"He's a made-up person. He can't read for the part."

Katy laughed. "You know what I mean. My obligation is here in Bloomington."

"The guy wants you Sunday and Monday. The next CKT class isn't until Thursday." Rhonda raised one hand and lowered the other, weighing the possibility. "Doesn't sound like a conflict to me."

"All right." Katy found her chair and sat down hard. She exhaled and studied the cell phone in her hand. "I'm going to do it." She raised her eyes to Rhonda's. "If it's a practical joke, I'm getting payback before the week's up."

"Just dial it, Katy." Rhonda fell to the floor in a cross-legged heap. "I'm dying here."

Katy pushed a series of buttons, held the phone to her ear, and waited.

"Mitch Henry here. Is this Miss Hart?"

"It is." Katy closed her eyes. "I thought about it, sir, and I'd like to come. What should I do next?"

"Good. I don't think you'll be sorry. It isn't often we do this with someone, well . . . someone unknown like yourself and —"

"Exactly," Katy cut in. "But you're sure they want me to read for the part?" She opened her eyes and looked at Rhonda. "They asked for Katy Hart of Bloomington?"

Mitch Henry laughed. "You're the one. Can you fly out around noon on Sunday?"

"Yes, I guess so." Katy nodded at Rhonda and mouthed the words *It's for real.* Her heart was racing in a rhythm she didn't recognize. What would she wear? What part was it exactly, anyway? And how in the world had DreamFilms found her?

Mitch Henry was talking about having

143

someone make the arrangements. "I'll call you at your home number to give you the itinerary."

Katy thought about the Flanigans getting a call from Mr. Henry again. If she was going to fly to LA and read for a movie role, she didn't want anyone but Rhonda knowing about it. Otherwise all the kids in CKT would find out, and when she came home without the part she'd never hear the end of it. Better to take the trip quietly. That way when she never heard from the casting director again she'd have less explaining to do.

"Actually, try my cell phone." She gave him the number. "When should I expect your call?"

"Sometime after one o'clock tomorrow."

"Okay." She was shaking again. "Thanks, Mr. Henry. I still can't make sense of this, but I'll come. If it's the real deal I'll be there."

"Oh yes, Miss Hart." Again he laughed. "It's the real deal. No question about that."

Katy ended the phone call and stared at Rhonda. "It's not a joke." Her voice was flat, shocked. Then she jumped to her feet and ran in circles, letting out short screams. "I'm really flying to LA on Sunday!"

Rhonda held out her arms and gave Katy a huge hug. "You're going to be famous, Katy. I just know it. I always thought you had too much talent to stay in Bloomington." She took a quick breath. "Let's go to Branches and get a latte to celebrate!"

"Okay." She stepped back and searched Rhonda's eyes. "But let's do something else first."

"What?" Rhonda's smile took up most of her face.

Katy reached out and took Rhonda's hands. "Let's pray."

Then, with her whole heart turned toward heaven, Katy grew more serious than she'd been in days. She thanked God for the strange and sudden opportunity and asked for His wisdom and guidance and protection on the trip. Then she uttered the rhyming prayer that her parents had prayed over her since she was a little girl, the one that in light of the recent turn of events seemed particularly meaningful.

"God, please now my future see, make it clear where I should be. Open windows, close the doors, not my will, my God, but Yours."

Chapter Eight

Even though she no longer worked there, Ashley stopped in once every month or so to visit her friends at Sunset Hills Adult Care Home. This Saturday morning Landon and Cole had plans to clean the backyard and pull weeds from around the swing set. Ashley had to run a few errands, so she stopped at Sunset Hills on the way home.

Jenny Flanigan had called and asked her to check on availability. Apparently on Friday her mother was diagnosed with dementia, and her doctor thought it better to move her into assisted living now, rather than wait until her condition worsened.

The sun shone through the trees that took up the front yard. Sunset Hills was really a converted family home, and as such it blended in with the other houses in the neighborhood. Ashley stopped and studied the roses that ran beneath the front window. The place harbored so many memories. She breathed in the sweet summer air and smiled. God had used Sunset Hills and its elderly people to restore her ability to love. Everything about her life was different because of the lessons she'd learned here.

She walked up the steps and knocked on the door.

After a few moments, Roberta answered. She was a lovely young Mexican woman with a Spanish lilt and a heart for family and faith. She was the perfect one to replace Ashley when she left a year ago. "Ashley! *Como estás?*" She held the door open and ushered Ashley inside.

"Bien." Ashley gave the woman a hug and grinned at her. "See? I haven't forgotten the Spanish you taught me."

"Sí, muy bien." Roberta laughed. "Come in, friend. Things are good here at Sunset Hills." She dropped her voice to a whisper. "The old people miss you. They still talk about you like you're here."

Ashley allowed a smile. "They still talk about 1975 like it's here too."

Roberta cocked her head. "True." She led the way into the foyer and motioned to the row of recliners. "Morning nap is almost over."

Ashley studied the faces in the chairs.

147

Edith was at the far end, dear, sweet Edith. The former beauty queen had been afraid of her own reflection until Ashley removed the mirrors in her bathroom. Ashley looked at Roberta. "How's she doing?"

"Well . . ." Roberta walked to Edith and patted her hand. Edith snored in return, and Roberta kept her voice low. "Her doctor says it won't be long. She's at the end-stage of heart failure."

"I remember." Ashley turned and saw Helen in the recliner next to Edith. "And what about Helen? Still violent when the eggs aren't hot?"

"Still talking about her daughter, Sue." Roberta's eyes danced. "They visit all the time, and once in a while it happens again, that magical thing that happened when you were here. Helen remembers her, and she and her daughter have a day stolen from yesterday."

Ashley nodded, ignoring the lump in her throat. "I'm glad. She loves Sue very much."

"*Sí, mucho.*" Roberta looked at the third woman sleeping in the recliner at the far end. "Betty is new to us, and Frank . . . you remember Frank?"

"Yes. He took the spot when Laura Jo died."

"Well —" Roberta looked down for a moment — "Frank passed on last week. Doctors think it was a stroke." She glanced down the hall. "He was a very nice man. Big family. They were here all the time." Her eyes grew misty. "I miss him."

Ashley slipped her arm around Roberta's shoulders and gave her a gentle squeeze. That was the hard part about working with older people. She remembered Irvel, the woman she'd been closest to at Sunset Hills. Irvel had taught her that the love between a husband and a wife was stronger than time or illness or even death.

"The friendships formed here are often short-lived, Roberta." Ashley stepped aside and set her purse down on an end table. "But they are deep and colorful, and that makes up for it." She looked down the hallway. "Bert's doing well?"

"Still shining his saddle." Roberta led the way into the kitchen. "A man's got to have a saddle to shine; that's what he tells me every day."

Ashley chuckled. The old saddle maker had been unable to speak until a saddle was brought into his room. Having a saddle — a purpose — had changed everything for Bert. Ashley was glad to hear he was doing well.

Eventually she got around to the real reason she'd come. She explained about Jenny Flanigan's mother and asked about the openings.

"We have a room available." Roberta poured water into the teakettle and set it on the stove. "Frank's death was sudden. The owner's taking applications for the space now."

"Tell her I have the perfect person. Her name's Lindsay Bueller and her family's right here in town." Ashley started unloading the dishwasher. "Her family's been praying for a place like this."

From the front room, they heard Helen call out.

Roberta dried her hands on a towel. "I'll be right back. Helen needs help getting out of the chair these days."

Ashley nodded. She took three teacups from the dishwasher and lined them up on the counter. Next she pulled the tray of tea bags closer and chose peppermint for each of them. Irvel had loved peppermint tea, and even with her gone more than a year, the people at Sunset Hills continued her tradition of a hot cup of tea at lunchtime.

Roberta came back into view, leading Helen toward her place at the dining-room table. Helen shot a suspicious look at

Ashley and motioned to her. "Has she been checked?" Before Roberta could say yes, Helen continued. "This place is falling apart, I tell you." Helen held on to Roberta's arm as she lowered herself into her chair. "Nobody gets checked anymore."

Ashley smiled. Some things never changed. The kettle was boiling, so she poured the tea and took a cup to Helen and another to Roberta. Before the hour was up, they were joined by Bert and Edith. The conversation was disjointed and humorous, but it made Ashley miss working here.

When they were finished with tea and lunch, Ashley said her good-byes. As much as she enjoyed the company of her friends at Sunset Hills, she enjoyed being with Landon and Cole more. She was halfway home when she decided to swing by her parents' house and check on her father.

He'd been quieter than usual lately. Probably thinking the same thing all the Baxters were thinking — that it had been almost a year since their mother died.

She pulled into the driveway and saw Kari's car. Of the five adult Baxter siblings, only she and Kari and their oldest sister, Brooke, lived in Bloomington. Luke and his wife and baby lived in New York, and Erin, the youngest Baxter daughter, lived with her husband and four adopted daughters in Texas.

Physical distance didn't matter. The Baxters were closer now than they'd been growing up, especially in the year since the death of their mother.

Once inside, Ashley found Kari and their father in the family room. In her father's arms was Kari's youngest, seven-month-old Ryan Junior, and next to him on the couch, peering in and patting the baby on the head, was Kari's daughter, three-year-old Jessie.

"I wish I had a camera." Ashley set her purse down and went to her father, kissing him on the cheek. "Or maybe an easel."

"Hi, honey." Her father smiled, and for the first time in a while, it went all the way to his eyes. The baby cooed. Her father crooked his finger and ran it beneath the baby's chin. "Little Ryan's the happiest baby."

Kari pulled a bottle of milk from a nearby diaper bag and handed it to their father. "He won't be happy for long without this." She gave Ashley a side hug. "I was just inviting Dad for dinner. You and Landon and Cole wanna come too?"

"I'd love to, but we've got sets tonight."

"Sets?" Her father looked up. "Theater sets?"

"Yep," Kari answered for her. "Sets for *Tom Sawyer*, CKT's upcoming musical." She sat down next to Jessie and pulled the little girl onto her lap. "You must've met with the Flanigans."

"Yes, they're wonderful. I love their family." Ashley smiled at her father. "They remind me of us a long time ago."

Her father's expression softened. "I'd like to meet them sometime." He raised an eyebrow at Ashley. "What made you want to get involved in theater sets?" He chuckled. "Don't tell me it was Landon's idea."

"Actually . . ." Ashley's tone was thoughtful. "It was something I thought Mom would've done. You know, help out with local theater."

"Yes." Her father held little Ryan's bottle for him. "Especially a Christian kids theater. She loved live stage productions."

Ashley took the chair across from the others. "It was something Landon and I could do together, something that helps me know that Mom's smiling down on us, still somehow a part of what we're doing."

Silence settled over them for a moment.

Jessie was squirming, so Kari let her down. "Can I get a book, Mommy?"

"Yes, sweetie. Then come right back." Kari watched her daughter scamper off; then she turned to Ashley. "Jessie's already forgetting." Sadness darkened her expression. "I showed her Mom's picture the other day, and she held up her hands and asked me who it was."

Their father closed his eyes for a few seconds and then exhaled long and deep before opening them again. "At least she remembers where her grandma's picture books are."

Kari stood up and gave Ashley a sad look, one that said she'd been wrong to bring up the subject with their father sitting there. "Anyway, I better make sure she's not messing up the whole bookcase."

With Kari out of the room, Ashley went to her father and knelt near his feet. She ran her fingers over little Ryan's head. "I remember when Cole was this small."

"Me too." Her father sniffed, and a tear fell onto his cheek. "Your mother loved Cole like he was her own son."

"I know." Ashley uttered a sad laugh. "After I came back from Paris, alone and pregnant, I always thought she loved Cole more than me."

"That was never the case." Her father put his hand on her shoulder. "She understood you, Ashley. She . . ." He struggled, almost as if there was something he wanted to say but wasn't sure he should say it. "Well, she always understood you. You were special to her."

"Dad, what were you going to say?"

"Nothing." His answer was quick this time. "I just don't want you to ever doubt your mother's love for you."

Kari and Jessie were returning from the old bookcase in the living room. Ashley could hear Jessie talking about orange kitty cats and striped tails in a happy singsong.

Ashley searched her father's eyes for a few more seconds. Whatever he'd been about to say, it was lost now. She looked at the baby and then up at her father again. "I miss her so much, Dad."

He nodded; then his chin quivered. He brought the back of his hand first to one eye, then the other. "Sometimes —" He stopped, his voice strained. Most of his face was hidden by his hand, so when he spoke again he was barely audible. "Sometimes I miss her so much . . . I can barely breathe."

Ashley stood up, bent close to her father, and hugged him. There was nothing else to say, nothing else to do. Kari and Jessie were back now, and Ashley gave Kari a familiar look, one that told her their father was hurting, but he'd be okay.

As Ashley bid them both good-bye and drove home to Landon and Cole, she let the tears come. Tears because it was unbearable seeing her strong father, the invincible Dr. Baxter, so broken he could barely speak. Tears because her mother would never sit in the audience and watch *Tom Sawyer*, knowing her formerly rebellious daughter had actually painted the set. Tears because little Jessie didn't remember her grandma anymore. But most of all tears because the look she'd given Kari was true. One day they would all be okay again.

And maybe that was the saddest part of all.

Chapter Nine

Dayne was alone at his Malibu house trying to get into an old Barbra Streisand movie when his phone rang. Mitch Henry promised to call the minute he had news, so Dayne grabbed the phone and clicked the On button.

"Dayne, it's Mitch." He hesitated. "She's coming."

"She is?" Dayne was on his feet. "Are you serious?" He paced to the back patio door, stared at the ocean for a few seconds, and headed back to the sofa. All the while Mitch was giving him details. "Hey, wait." Dayne froze. "You didn't mention my name, did you?"

"Not once."

"You sure? Not once?"

"Dayne, she'd never even heard of the movie." He breathed out a short laugh. "Don't flatter yourself. She's probably never heard of you either."

"Ouch." Dayne set his feet back in motion, walking from the sofa and back to the patio door again. "So she's really coming?"

"Yes, but, Matthews, you sure you got the right girl?" Mitch sounded hesitant. "I sweet-talked her like you said, but she's not like any actress I've ever talked to. She kept asking the same thing."

"What?" Dayne felt tingly and alive. Katy Hart was coming to Hollywood for an audition. How great was that? He tuned back into the conversation. "What'd she keep asking?"

"If it was a mistake, a joke." He laughed, but it sounded more sarcastic than funny. "Real confident girl, Matthews. Oughta be fantastic on film."

Dayne ignored that last comment. He didn't care what Mitch Henry thought. Katy was perfect for the part; they'd all see that soon enough. "She's coming Sunday, right?"

"Sunday, yes." He paused. "We're putting her up at the Sheraton and getting her a ride to the studio in the morning. Her reading's at nine o'clock, okay? You happy, Matthews?"

"I am." He chuckled but kept it quiet so Mitch wouldn't hear him. "I've seen the tape on her, Mitch. She's the real deal."

"Innocent, right?"

"As a baby."

Mitch drew a long breath. "I've done my job. Whatever it takes to keep you happy."

"You're forgetting something."

"What's that?" Mitch sounded tired, bored of the conversation.

"You're forgetting that I'm doing this to keep you happy too." Dayne returned to the sofa and sat back down. "I'm telling you, Mitch, you'll love her."

"I'd love to get the film cast. That's what I'd love."

After another minute, the conversation ended, and Dayne set the phone back down on the coffee table. Wow. Had it been that easy? Learning everything about Katy Hart's background, finding out where she was living, and getting her to agree to an audition?

In two days, Katy Hart — a girl he hadn't been able to forget since his brief, secretive visit to a community theater — would stand before him and read for a role starring opposite him in a major motion picture.

Dayne closed his eyes for a minute. He had to keep her from the paparazzi, and that meant one thing. She couldn't be seen alone with him. A girl coming to

DreamFilms Studio for a reading wasn't enough to get their attention. But a no-name children's theater director from Bloomington, Indiana, coming to Hollywood at the sole request of Dayne Matthews?

That story would make the cover.

No, he couldn't be seen with her, and that was okay. He wasn't interested in her, not really. He just wanted the chance to star in a film with her. Someone raw and talented, untainted by the Hollywood life. Acting with her would take him back to his college days, back when acting was something that grew from the center of his soul and consumed him.

He already knew he'd love her on camera, love the fresh look of her face, the innocence in her eyes. But there was one small problem. He hadn't been completely honest with Mitch Henry. He didn't really know everything about Katy Hart, just most things. The missing part took place in Chicago when Katy suddenly stopped attending auditions and switched careers.

Depending on her reasons and whatever happened to her back in Chicago, the possibility existed that maybe Katy Hart hadn't missed her break into the industry.

Maybe she'd walked away from it on purpose. Dayne opened his eyes, leaned back into the sofa, and stared at the vaulted ceiling. That wasn't possible, was it? Every other girl he'd met in the business had wanted the same thing. A chance to be famous, to see her face and name in lights — wasn't that it? But then, that was the only thing that worried Dayne the rest of the night and throughout the next day while he counted down the hours until Katy's visit.

Katy Hart wasn't any other girl.

Katy changed her outfit three times before taking the elevator down to the lobby where her escort would meet her.

The part was starring opposite the lead in a romantic comedy about a small-town girl with dreams of making it as a big-time magazine writer in New York City. Katy had packed an entire suitcase of possibilities so she wouldn't be limited. By six that morning she was showered and staring at her choices.

She'd been taught in film classes that a person should dress the part as much as possible, so her first thought had been jeans and a scoop-necked T-shirt. But after she was dressed she remembered Mitch

Henry telling her that for most of the film the female lead would be in Manhattan. And that meant a different look altogether. So she switched to black pants and a short blazer.

But by the time she had her blazer buttoned, she felt stiff and overdressed and much too hot for Los Angeles in late June.

In the end she chose something middle of the road — khaki pants and a yellow cotton blouse — an outfit she was comfortable in. Not that it mattered. The whole idea of flying to Los Angeles for a reading was so strange, Katy still expected someone to show up at her hotel room and tell her it was all a joke.

And if that didn't happen, then surely DreamFilms had more experienced actresses lined up for the part. She must've been more of an oddity, someone to compare the others to. Or maybe the call came because she actually lived in a small town. Maybe they wanted their top choice to see what a small-town girl looked like, and that's why they brought her in.

Katy didn't know, but there had to be some reason, something that would come to light at the interview. She took a seat in the lobby and waited until a guy in black jeans and a lightweight black turtleneck approached her. "Miss Hart?"

"Yes."

"I'm Greg, a gopher over at Dream-Films." He smiled and shook her hand. "I've been asked to take you to the studio."

"So, it's not a joke?" Katy fell in step beside Greg as they walked to a silver SUV parked just outside the door.

"Nope, it's not a joke." Greg opened her door, then went around and climbed into the driver's side. "In fact, as breaks go, I'd say this is one of the biggest I've seen."

They made small talk on the way to the studio, and the whole time Katy felt like she was playing a part in a play. Because this wasn't her life, being driven to a major motion picture studio so she could read for a lead part in an upcoming film. It was the life she once dreamed of having, back when she was in Chicago.

But when she left that world, she told herself it was behind her. God had taken her out, and God would have to get her back into it if she was ever to act in another film. And now that's exactly what had happened. God had opened a door, and she was willing to walk tentatively through it.

Even if she felt like she was pretending with every step.

The driver led Katy to an office, where she met Mitch Henry.

"Did you look up the film on the Internet?" Mitch sat on the corner of his desk and studied her. "I figured you would."

"No, sir." Katy had meant to. But the only Internet access she had was at the Flanigan house, and things still felt strange between Jenny and Bailey and her. Instead, she'd spent all her time picking out the right clothes and talking to Rhonda on the phone about how this audition could've possibly come up. She shifted in her seat. "I only know what you told me."

"Well . . ." He crossed his arms and leveled his gaze at Katy. He reached onto his desk and handed her a few script pages stapled together. "You'll be reading from this. I'll give you a few minutes to get familiar with the scene, but then you'll be meeting me and the male lead in the room down the hall."

"The male lead?" Katy had no idea who it was.

"Yes." Mr. Henry paused. "Dayne Matthews. He was cast months ago. He'll be in the room, but only behind a desk. Today's read is all about you, darling." He hesitated again, studying her. "Any questions?"

"No, sir." Katy had a hundred, but her mind was swirling too fast to verbalize any of them.

"Okay, then, I'll be down the hall with Dayne. We'll look for you in a few minutes." Mitch Henry left the room and closed the door behind him.

Katy realized she was trembling, and she exhaled. Dayne Matthews? He was the lead? Mr. Henry probably expected her to be excited — starstruck even. But all she could think about was that strange night a year ago when CKT was putting on its final performance of *Charlie Brown.*

Toward the end of that show, a man in his midthirties had entered the theater by himself and taken a seat in the back row. Katy had been busy watching the play, then organizing the strike party right afterwards. But she definitely saw the guy.

And after the show, Rhonda ran up, breathless with excitement. "Dayne Matthews was here, Katy! Can you believe it? Right here in our own little theater?"

Katy had doubted it at first, because it didn't make sense. What business would Dayne Matthews have at a Christian Kids Theater performance? In Bloomington of all places?

But the more people she talked to that

night, the more she became convinced. Dayne had indeed stopped in to watch part of the show. But his appearance had never been explained, and he left before anyone could talk to him. That night before the strike party began, Katy prayed for Dayne. She prayed that if he had come for a reason, that God would bring him back one day.

Now, with Dayne and Mitch Henry down the hallway waiting for her, she had to believe there was a connection somehow. Had Dayne remembered her and called her in for the audition? The idea was outrageous. He saw her for only a few minutes, onstage talking to the parents. Why would that have given him any idea that she could act?

Katy shook from the questions assaulting her. How was she supposed to read for a part opposite Dayne Matthews without understanding why she was here in the first place? Her mind spun in multiple directions, the script in her hands so unsteady she couldn't read it.

Already five minutes had raced past, and Katy could think of just one thing to do. She closed her eyes, breathed out, and lifted her face. *God, fill me with Your Spirit, Your strength, Your power. I don't need all the answers; I only need You.*

My peace I give you, daughter. . . . I will never leave you nor forsake you.

The pressing thought came from the center of her soul and spread warmth and peace all the way to her fingertips. The words were from Scripture, words she'd memorized as a little girl, back when she was too terrified to stand in front of her middle-school class and give an oral report.

And now here they were again, ready to speak calm into her being the moment she asked. Katy took a slow breath. Why hadn't she asked for help sooner? She opened her eyes and looked at the script. Her hands were steady now, and she set about reading the part.

The scene involved the lead female character explaining to her father why she was leaving home and moving to New York City. Other than a few words, it was a two-minute monologue, the character's mixture of defending herself and her decision and being caught up in the awe and excitement of life outside her small town. No wonder it was the part selected for the cold read. It allowed a range of emotions that would give any casting director all the information he needed.

She ran over the words three more times. They would expect her to use the script on a cold read, but after looking at it even that much, she had most of it memorized. She stood, smoothed the wrinkles in her pants, clutched the script, and headed toward the room where the two men were waiting.

With every breath she reminded herself of the calming words from her heavenly Father: *"I will never leave you nor forsake you."*

That was a good thing. Because without God's help she wouldn't get through the first line. She'd be passed out cold on the floor from the sheer fright of it all.

Chapter Ten

When Katy reached the door at the end of the hall, she thought about turning around and pretending the whole invitation to audition never happened. Instead she took a deep breath and knocked.

"Come in." It was Mitch Henry's voice.

Katy stood a little straighter. *Confident. Be confident. I have nothing to lose . . . they asked me to come.* She opened the door, walked in, and gave a polite smile first to Mr. Henry, then to Dayne Matthews. "Hi. I'm Katy Hart."

"Hello, Katy. Did you get enough time with the script?"

"Yes, sir." Katy tried to concentrate all her attention completely on the casting director, but all she could see was Dayne Matthews. What was that look on his face, the depth in his eyes? And what was Mitch Henry trying to tell her? Something about the script. *Focus, Katy. Come on.* She cleared her throat and held the stapled papers out in front of her. "Okay, I'm ready."

"Katy . . ." Mitch Henry chuckled and leaned back in his chair. "You flew all this way, so maybe you could sit down." He motioned to an empty chair across the table from where he and Dayne were sitting. "We'd like to get to know you a little."

"Sure." This wasn't part of the bargain. Katy inhaled and willed the peace from a few minutes earlier to fill her once again. She took the chair. "Sorry." She gave a nervous laugh. "I figured you were in a hurry."

Dayne leaned forward, resting his forearms on the conference table. "Thanks for coming, Katy. We don't do this all the time, calling in someone like yourself for an audition." He hesitated, but his eyes never left hers. Again he seemed to see right through her, as if he'd known her all her life. "Do you have any questions?"

She hadn't planned to ask any, but her curiosity got the better of her. "Yes." She looked from Dayne to Mr. Henry and back again. "Why me? I mean, how'd I get here?"

Mr. Henry nodded at Dayne. "You wanna handle this one?"

"Sure." Dayne smiled, warm and unassuming as he shifted his weight to one arm of his chair. "Actually, it was my doing."

Katy felt her heartbeat quicken. Dayne Matthews had remembered her from a single visit to the Bloomington Community Theater? Still, she didn't feel it was the right time to mention his visit. "How . . . how did you find me?"

"I saw your pilot." His smile shifted to his eyes. "It was very good, Katy. I liked what I saw."

"Thank you." He'd seen her pilot? Her throat felt dry and thick. This wasn't a chance invitation; Dayne had actually seen her work and liked what he saw. Did that mean he wasn't going to mention stopping into the theater? She waited for him to continue.

Dayne exhaled hard, stood, and took a few steps away before turning and looking at her again. His expression was more serious this time. "See, Katy, the part calls for a small-town girl anxious to make it in the big city. You already know that, right?"

"Right." It was easy to forget he was Hollywood's playboy, the leading man wanted for every major motion picture. In that moment he seemed like someone she might've met in a coffee shop in Bloomington. "I understand the part."

"Well, the thing is, the part calls for someone innocent. Someone whose innocence shines from her eyes." He took a step closer and leaned on the table. "I've had six A-list actresses through this office in the past week, and I can't find innocent." Dayne looked at Mr. Henry. "Sad, isn't it, Mitch?"

The look on Mr. Henry's face was more like frustration, but he nodded. "Very sad."

"So . . . I watched your pilot, and I have a hunch about you, Katy Hart." His grin lit up his face. He sat back down at the table. For a moment he let his eyes search hers. "Can I ask you a question?"

"Sure." She folded her hands on her lap. Her heart wasn't racing as badly now, but the stakes seemed higher than before. Six A-list actresses? She was definitely out of her league.

"Why'd you stop acting after the pilot?"

"Well . . ." She trailed off, buying time. He knew far more about her than she'd expected him to. That knowledge sent her heart speeding along once again. Dayne Matthews doing homework on her? It was more than she could comprehend in so short a time. She found her voice and smiled. "I guess it was personal reasons. A change of direction, that sort of thing."

Dayne considered that for a moment, then gave a thoughtful nod. "I can accept that." He leaned back and stroked his chin. "Tell us a little about yourself."

"Me?" Katy should've been ready. The question wasn't difficult, but Dayne's eyes were mesmerizing, rendering her unable to think or speak. Finally she looked at Mr. Henry. "I direct a children's theater group in Bloomington, Indiana. It's —" her eyes shifted toward Dayne — "very fulfilling."

"Are you single, Katy?"

"Yes, I am." She felt her cheeks grow hot under his gaze. Across from her she noticed Mr. Henry give Dayne a curious look as if to say, *What sort of question was that?*

Dayne's laugh was quick and light-hearted, and he pointed to a folder in front of him on the table. "My research wasn't clear about whether you were married. Sometimes that makes a difference when it comes to considering a lead role. The filming for *Dream On* will take at least six weeks, Katy." He gave Mr. Henry a look clearly intended to set him at ease. "That's why I asked."

Katy smiled. It still didn't make sense that she was sitting here having a conversation with Dayne Matthews and about to audition for a part opposite him in a film. The whole thing was crazy. Better to get the audition over and return to her hotel. She could read the rest of the *Tom Sawyer* script and get her focus back where it belonged. She gripped the chair seat with both hands, ready to stand up. "Was there anything else?"

"No." Mr. Henry sat up a little, positioned a notepad in front of him, and called out for a man named Robert.

In a matter of seconds a middle-aged man with a goatee appeared at the door. "Ready?"

"Yes. She'll read through it twice." Mr. Henry gestured toward a video camera set up near the back of the room. "If you'll tape both reads, please."

Robert gave a thumbs-up. "Sure thing." He walked to the back of the room and set himself behind the camera. "Give me a count."

Mitch looked at Katy and pointed to the front of the room. "Why don't you stand up there and give us your best read, Katy. Don't worry if you need the words. That's fine." He paused. "We're looking for emotion and — as Dayne said — an innocence that shines through on camera." He jotted something down on the paper. "I'll give a

3-2-1 lead-in, and then I'll point to you. That'll be your cue to start, okay?"

"Yes, sir." She'd done this before. The pattern of cold-read auditions hadn't changed much in the years since she'd left the business. "I'm ready."

Dayne studied her in a way that was unnerving. "Relax, Katy. You'll be great."

"Okay." But it was God's words from earlier that morning — not Dayne's — that breathed peace into her as she steadied herself and became the character, as she did the thing she asked of her student actors every time they prepared for a play.

Mr. Henry said, "Katy Hart, cold read, June 21, three . . . two . . . one. Roll it." He pointed at Katy.

In a rush of emotions, Katy was no longer standing in an air-conditioned room at DreamFilms Studio in front of a casting director and the famous Dayne Matthews. She was Tory Temblin, small-town girl standing before her father, bags packed, trying to convince him that what she was about to do was the right thing, the only thing.

"But, Daddy, I *have* thought about it. I've thought about it and prayed and planned for it since I was a little girl." Passion rang from her voice as she found the imaginary place in front of her, the place where she could actually see a man in overalls and short hair begging her to put her things away and stay. Stay forever in the small town where she'd been raised.

She swept her hand out in front of her. "This . . . this farm and this small town are enough for you and Mama, but for me . . ." Her mood changed, and suddenly she could see the skyline of New York City. "For me I come to life when I think about Manhattan. I can feel the beat of that place from here, Daddy, and it's an amazing feeling." She turned partway around and then back again. "I want to be surrounded by millions of people — all of them chasing a dream."

Her voice was breathy, beyond excited. "I want to fall asleep to the sound of traffic and wake up in an apartment thirty floors off the ground." She paused and gave her invisible father a smile to melt his heart. "Please, Daddy. Don't stand in my way. Hug me and be happy for me and give me your blessing, but please . . . let me go. It's all I've ever wanted."

The script had one more paragraph, where the character does her best to convince her father she'll be safe, that she can fend for herself even in a city the size of

New York. She finished the piece, and she heard Mr. Henry say, "Got it. Stop the film."

A slow breath eased from between her lips, and then she was Katy Hart again. She had no idea how she'd done. But one thing was sure: For the few minutes she was reading she'd found her way to the imaginary character. That was all she could ask of herself.

Mr. Henry was writing something down on the notepad, and Dayne had his back to her, talking to the cameraman. After a few seconds he looked at Katy and nodded. "Okay, let's do it again."

Katy swallowed and nodded. She'd forgotten this part — the lack of feedback, the indifferent analysis from casting directors. Mr. Henry counted down again, and she launched into the same monologue. This time she looked at the script only once, and the rhythm of her speech was uninterrupted. She was so lost in the character that she had chills when she got to the last part, the part where she had to convince her father that she'd be safe.

She could feel everything Tory Temblin would feel in that situation, and she could see her father's eyes — full of fear and desperation at the thought of losing his little girl. When she was finished with the piece this time, she wanted to continue, wanted to get lost in the part and play it all the way through in an attempt to assuage the man's fears and show him that indeed she could follow her dreams and still come out whole on the other side.

The room was silent, and Katy looked from Mr. Henry to Dayne. "Is that all?"

"Yes, thanks." The casting director tapped the table. "You can leave the script here with me." He looked at Dayne. "Anything else?"

"No." Dayne was on his feet. "Thanks for coming, Katy."

She tried not to feel disappointed. Had she done something wrong or missed the mark in some way? Feedback was almost never given in these situations, but today she wanted it badly. "Good job" maybe, or "That was perfect." Something. Memory of her past auditions came to mind, and she tried to see past the fuzzy lines.

Mr. Henry stood, came around the table, and shook her hand. "We appreciate your taking the time to do this, Katy." He met her eyes straight on. "We'll be in touch. It's possible we might want you back out for an on-camera audition. Something about five or ten minutes long that would involve

Dayne or one of the other actors in the movie."

"Other people are cast?" Katy crossed her arms. Relief was still making its way through her, relief that the ordeal was over.

"Yes." Mr. Henry gave a sharp look to Dayne. "Every part's cast but this one." He gathered his portfolio, nodded to her. "If you'll excuse me." He went to the back of the room and collected a tape from the cameraman, then left through a side door.

Dayne was still a few feet away. He stood more than a head taller than her. He motioned toward the door where Mr. Henry had exited. "Mr. Personality." He grinned. "Sorry about that."

"It's fine." She took her purse from the table and slid it over her shoulder. "All casting directors are that way." She felt her cheeks growing hot under his gaze. "At least the ones I remember." She took a few steps toward the door. "Anyway, thanks for asking me in." A smile tugged at her lips. "It was fun, even if nothing comes of it."

"You did great." He checked his watch. "Hey, want lunch? The commissary is open." He raised one eyebrow. "They've got great salads."

Lunch? At the studio commissary with Dayne Matthews? The strange and unusual dream continued, the one that had started a few days ago with Mitch Henry's call. As surreal as the moment felt, she had no reason to say no. "Sure."

"Okay." He smiled and fell in step beside her. "We could take the golf cart, but let's walk. It's a nice day."

Indeed. The two of them walked side by side, plenty of space between them. He led her through the studio lot, across a street that ran through the center of the place, and over to the cafeteria. They talked about the film, the other people who had been cast, and the time frame for shooting it.

"I think Mitch is a little frustrated with me."

Katy slowed her pace and looked at him. "Really? I thought it was me, my lack of experience." She felt her eyes dancing, teasing him. "Maybe just a general dislike for small-town girls trying to make it in the big city."

"Nope." Dayne laughed as he held open the commissary door and they headed for the back of the food line. "It's not that. I frustrate him, that's all."

Katy could see why. "Six A-list actresses, Dayne? And you bring me in?"

Dayne didn't answer immediately. He

took a plate and filled it with chicken, vegetables, and rice. She did the same, opting instead for the salmon.

Not until they were seated in a quiet booth did he cross his arms and study her. "You were brilliant in there, Katy." He shrugged one shoulder. "I know we don't usually talk about this sort of thing until a person is guaranteed a callback." He lowered his voice. "But you were amazing."

"Really?" She glanced around the room. It was empty except for two parties of black suits in the far corner. None of them seemed concerned that Dayne Matthews was having lunch with a no-name. She looked at Dayne again. "Do you think Mitch Henry liked it?"

"Liked it?" Dayne pulled his ice water closer and took a drink. His grin moved up past the rim of the glass. "You made him put down his pencil."

Katy giggled and leaned back against the white vinyl seat. "That's a good thing?"

"Yeah, Katy. Very good." Dayne narrowed his eyes and looked up for a moment. "I think I've seen Mitch put his pencil down twice in the time I've known him. Both times it was because the person auditioning was so good he had nothing to say." He rested on his forearms, his face closer to hers than before. "Wanna know what he *did* write when you were finished?"

"What?" Katy winced. Big-band music played in the background, and she had to remind herself she wasn't pretending. She really was having lunch with Dayne Matthews. She took a sip of her water too. "What did he write?"

"He wrote just one word: *perfect*."

Katy let that sink in for a minute. The casting director had written that about her audition? Perfect? A chill worked its way along her arms, and she lifted her eyes to Dayne's. "So what happens next?"

"You'll come to Hollywood again. Probably in a week." He eased back a little, keeping things professional. "I'd like you to do a scene with me. Just so we can check the on-screen chemistry between us." He tilted his head. "Somehow I don't think that'll be a problem."

Katy smiled, but suddenly she wanted to run. Yes, Dayne Matthews was good-looking and charming. No question she was enjoying herself. But he was a playboy and a partier, same as Tad had been back when —

She stopped herself. Those days were over. She would never again fall for an actor. Besides, this attention from Dayne, it was nothing more than he'd give to anyone trying out for the part opposite him in a big film.

Dayne was quiet, and she had the unnerving feeling he could read her mind. He shifted in his seat. "So what do you think, Katy Hart? Do you want to be famous?" He held his hands up and stretched them across an invisible marquis suspended above him. "*Dream On*, the romantic comedy starring Katy Hart . . . how does that sound?"

Katy tried to imagine the possibility. "For a long time —" her voice was softer than before — "for a very long time it was my greatest dream." She lowered her chin, feeling suddenly shy. "But that was so long ago. I gave it up when I changed career paths, and I . . . well, I haven't thought about it much until now."

He held her eyes for a moment and then looked at his plate. "Let's eat."

"Okay." She closed her eyes and uttered a silent prayer, something that wouldn't trip him up but wouldn't compromise her beliefs either. Then she picked up her fork and began working on her salmon.

They chatted about CKT while they ate, and still Katy didn't bring up the fact that

Dayne had been in their theater. Maybe he didn't know that she knew. In that case, he could bring it up first. She didn't want to seem too pushy.

Finally when he was almost finished eating, Dayne set his fork down. "Are you afraid of it, Katy?"

"Of what?"

"Of fame, the life I lead." He searched her eyes.

Katy held her fork suspended above her plate. "I don't know. I guess I never thought much about it." She looked out the window at the pale blue sky and palm trees. A breeze had kicked up, and along the walkway toward the commissary, the fronds swayed. "When I was younger, I dreamed of making it big. I guess I never thought about the life that comes with it."

Dayne rested his arm along the back of the booth. "Some people struggle with it, to be honest." He bit his lower lip. "I've never minded. You can't take yourself too seriously. The paparazzi will do that for you."

Katy's head was spinning again. She'd come on a lark, done the cold read only because she'd been asked, and she was curious. But thinking of her life in light of paparazzi and fame was something she hadn't considered. She let a light laugh slip. "I think maybe we're jumping the gun a little."

"Okay." Dayne took another drink of water. "I want you to be aware; that's all."

Their conversation shifted to his last movie and the location where it had been filmed. They kept the talk casual, and by the end of their lunch Katy was convinced she had nothing to worry about. Dayne wasn't interested in anything other than her acting ability.

It was possible, wasn't it? That he'd seen her pilot and figured her to be perfect for the role of Tory Temblin? He was a professional, after all. He would want the person best suited for the part. If that was her and not one of the A-list actresses, then of course he'd have the casting director contact her and bring her out to Los Angeles for a cold read.

There was nothing more to it.

Still, that evening at the airport, waiting for her flight back to Indiana, she called Rhonda Sanders, the one who had convinced her to take the trip. In a stream of details, Katy told her about the cold read, Mitch Henry's nondescript reaction, and her lunch with Dayne Matthews.

"They want me back, Rhonda. Can you

believe it?" Katy couldn't help but squeal. "It still feels like a dream or a joke. But it's real. Dayne really wants me to come back for another audition."

Rhonda did a high-pitched shout. "I'm so happy for you, Katy. I'm shaking for you, really." She exhaled hard. "I can't believe it. You could actually get the part; have you thought about that?"

"Not really. I mean, not in the actual sense of it happening."

Rhonda calmed down, and silence echoed across the line. "You know what I think, Katy Hart?"

"What?"

"I think your life's about to change," Rhonda said. "And I think it's going to happen in ways neither of us could ever guess."

It was that thought that kept Katy lying awake and staring up at the ceiling of her bedroom at the Flanigan house late that night. The thought was a little frightening. Oh sure, the idea of winning the part was wonderful. But there had been something in Rhonda's voice, something that she couldn't quite define, and that was what kept her from sleep.

Finally just after one o'clock in the morning she realized what it was. The thing she'd heard in Rhonda's voice was the same thing that whispered to her from the depths of her soul. A warning maybe or a caution. Something that told her winning this part could really change her very existence — not just for a season.

But for all the days of her life.

Chapter Eleven

Four days had passed since her audition, and Katy had heard nothing from Mitch Henry. He wasn't calling; she was convinced. Dayne must have been trying to make her feel good by telling her he wanted her for another audition. The truth was clearly something else.

She wasn't good enough.

The Friday night practice was under way, and Katy and Rhonda were working with the "Big Missouri" number again. Katy studied it twice through, then pulled Rhonda aside. "We need the feeling of the big round paddles at the back of the boat."

Rhonda blinked, her expression flat. "The feeling of paddles?"

"Yes." Katy tapped her foot and grabbed the song lyrics from the table. "See here . . . 'big wheels turning, churning up the water.' " She pointed at the line and looked at Rhonda. "We need big wheels turning up the choreography too."

"Katy . . ." Rhonda was shaking her head, looking nervous. "We can't bring paddle wheels onstage."

Katy squinted at the kids lined up before her. Then in a rush she snapped her fingers, caught Rhonda by the elbow, and returned to the cast. "I've got it, guys. Everyone pop a squat."

The kids dropped to the floor, all eyes on Katy.

"We need paddle wheels onstage," she told them. "So here's what we're going to do." She chose six taller boys and one little girl on each side of the stage. Then she directed two of the taller boys to hoist the small girl onto their shoulders. As they did, that child would raise her arms high in gleeful celebration, while the two holding her would turn her in tight circles. At the same time, the remaining four boys would put one hand toward the little girl at the center and walk in circles in the opposite direction.

The effect was amazing, and for about fifteen seconds it was easy to believe that real paddle wheels had sprung to life onstage. The problem came at the sixteenth second, when first one little girl and then the other began to fall. Each girl was caught by the boys surrounding her, but every attempt after that involved a fall of some kind.

Finally Katy rushed onstage, helped one of the little girls to her feet, and bent to her level. "Is there a reason why you can't stay on top of their shoulders, honey?"

The child nodded, her curly black hair bouncing with every shake.

"Okay, why don't you tell me." Katy's voice was far calmer than she felt. They had two scenes to get through tonight, and the "Big Missouri" song was taking far too long. She raised her eyebrows, encouraging the child to answer.

"The turning makes me dizzy." The girl put her finger in her mouth and let it hang over her lip. "When I feel dizzy, I fall."

"Yep!" From across the stage the other young girl nodded. "I feel dizzy too."

"Fine." Katy straightened. She clapped and grinned at both girls. "Let's do this. As soon as you get on the boys' shoulders, how about you close your eyes and hold on. I think that'll work."

It worked brilliantly. The next time through the song, the kids marched out, made their turns at the right time in the right direction. When the human wheels set to motion on either side of the stage, the girls were hoisted into the air, hands outstretched above their heads, smiling big, and eyes closed. Neither girl fell.

"Good!" Katy ran back onstage and gave the two girls and twelve boys all high fives. "We've got the big wheels." She looked at Rhonda. "Could you get Al and Nancy? Tell them it's time to block the first scene."

Rhonda leaned in, her voice low. "First tell me about Dayne Matthews. Has he called?"

"No." Katy waved her off. She didn't want to talk about her crazy trip to Los Angeles. Not now. "He's not calling. It's been too long." She looked at her watch. "Better get Al and Nancy. We're running out of time."

Rhonda hesitated. "He'll call." She didn't wait for Katy's response but rather did as she asked, as Katy began calling the lead kids to the stage.

The opening scene in *Tom Sawyer* involved passengers debarking the *Big Missouri*. Among the passengers was the Thatcher family, including Becky, played by Sarah Jo Stryker. Katy watched the girl as the characters came onstage, holding suitcases and waving at the townspeople gathered on either side.

This would be Katy's first chance to

see if Sarah Jo could act.

The Thatcher family lined up, and when the character Becky was introduced, she gave a demure smile and then angled her body so she could see Tom Sawyer, shooting marbles with the boys off on stage right.

Tim Reed, playing Tom, grabbed his straw hat and stood up, his eyes wide as he surveyed Becky for the first time. He walked up to her and held out his hand. "I'm Tom." He straightened himself a little. "Tom Sawyer. Tell me about yourself, Miss Becky Thatcher."

The next ninety seconds were all Sarah Jo. She knew her lines perfectly, including the spacing and inflection necessary to convey the idea that she was both excited and anxious about meeting Tom Sawyer.

But halfway through her lines, her mother — who had been milling around the back of the sanctuary with the other parents — moved to the front row and began coaching Sarah Jo. "Louder! You need to project or you'll never make it. Do you hear me? Project!"

Katy's mouth fell open. This was the first time she'd seen this behavior — the theater version of the obsessed Little

League parent — in CKT. She was about to say something when Rhonda touched her elbow.

"What's that woman doing?" Rhonda hissed the question close to Katy's ear. "She's ruining the scene."

Mrs. Stryker stood up and positioned herself a few feet from Sarah Jo. "More expression!" She made a frustrated sound. "Don't you remember what the acting instructor told you last year?" At this point the woman wasn't even trying to keep her voice down. Her stream of criticisms had caught the attention of the other kids onstage. She continued undaunted. "You're the lead part, Sarah Jo. Now get into character or get off the stage."

Sarah Jo responded with a louder voice, but the character's charm dissolved in the distraction. She no longer looked like a natural talent giving her first impression of a series of lines, but a nervous child unsure of her next move.

Suddenly Mrs. Stryker seemed to realize that she was making a spectacle of herself, and she dropped her voice to a whisper. Twice more she murmured criticisms, and the last time Sarah Jo broke character and looked at her mother. "What, Mama? I can't hear you."

Finally Katy waved her hand at the cast. "Take five."

Every one of the kids was aware of the conflict taking place between Sarah Jo and her mother. They kept their voices low as they slinked off the stage toward the lobby, where other mothers had prepared a snack for them. A few of them looked back at Sarah Jo as they left, their eyes wide. Bailey Flanigan caught Katy's eye and mouthed, *Poor girl!*

Katy nodded, disgusted.

Sarah Jo didn't join the kids. Instead she walked sheepishly off the stage and sat next to her mother in the front row. Even then Alice Stryker didn't seem to know she was the reason for the break. She bent her head close to Sarah Jo's, her mouth moving just as quickly as before. Whatever she was saying, her expression was tense and angry. Sarah Jo did a series of understanding nods as she listened.

Katy felt sick to her stomach.

She didn't waste another moment as she walked to the first pew and stood in front of Sarah Jo and her mother. "Excuse me."

When Mrs. Stryker looked up, an instant smile replaced her frown. "Hello, Katy." She patted Sarah Jo on the hand. "Just giving my daughter some pointers." She crossed her legs and sat back a little. "You know, things her acting coach or her agent has said time and again." Mrs. Stryker laughed — an attempt to lift the mood, no doubt. "Sarah Jo's very, very talented. I think we can all agree on that."

She smiled at her daughter and looked back at Katy. "But these —" she waved her arm over her head as if she were brushing away a fly — "kids' plays are like drama courses for Sarah Jo. She has to get better with each part she plays or she won't be up to par when her break comes." Mrs. Stryker took hold of her daughter's hand and shrugged. "She has to be ready when fame comes knocking. We know for sure it's coming."

Katy wanted to slap the woman. She gave Sarah Jo a sympathetic look and patted her shoulder. "Honey, why don't you go have a snack with the other kids. Your mom and I need to talk."

"Okay." She glanced at her mother. "Is that all right, Mama?"

Mrs. Stryker exhaled hard but managed a smile. "Yes, dear, go ahead. We can talk after the break."

When Sarah Jo was out of earshot, Katy sat down next to Alice Stryker and looked her straight in the eyes. She could feel her blood boiling. "What just happened here can never happen again, Mrs. Stryker. Is that understood?"

Shock darkened the woman's expression, and her eyes narrowed. "What's that supposed to mean?" She made an indignant sound. "I have a right to talk to my daughter, Miss Hart."

Katy had to work to keep her voice down. "Actually, you have the right to stay in the back with the other parents. When we're blocking a scene, it's my job to make corrections and direct the children." She pictured Sarah Jo's defeated look, the way her shoulders had slumped with every critical word from her mother. "From now on you will stay in the back; is that clear?"

"Sarah Jo needs more than the direction of some —" she waved her hand at Katy — "young girl like yourself. She needs professional direction, and I've seen enough of that to know what advice to give."

"Mrs. Stryker, you demoralized your daughter. She was just finding her way, just discovering her part when you started criticizing her." Katy leaned closer, desperate to make her point. "Sarah Jo will never amount to anything in the business of drama if you don't let her find her way."

Alice Stryker was on her feet. "Don't

196

you dare say that about my daughter! One day she'll be more famous than anyone in this theater. Then everyone will be glad I worked her so hard. If you don't let me do it here, I'll do it from home. Whatever it takes, I'll do it. That's the price for fame, and I'm willing to pay it."

"But . . ." Katy was breathless, and as she stood, she felt dizzy from the strength of the woman's venom. "What if Sarah Jo isn't willing to pay it?" Her voice fell, her anger and frustration ringing from every word. "What if she wants to enjoy children's theater today because she's a child?" She reined in her thoughts and emotions. "Do you know how many girls would've liked the part of Becky Thatcher?"

Alice lifted her chin, superiority working its way up to her brow. "Sarah Jo is not any other girl. She's different, special." She clutched her purse to her waist. "She'll be a star one day, and then you'll understand."

Without giving Katy a chance to respond further, Alice Stryker strode to the back of the church, through the double doors, and into the lobby. Probably to give Sarah Jo another dose of correction. Katy watched her go and then looked down at her knees. She was shaking. Was it that important, the idea that every part, every day of practice had to be held at a certain level in order to bring about stardom for Sarah Jo?

Katy was still standing there, stunned, when Rhonda returned. She approached Katy and whispered, "Everyone's talking about it — parents, kids. Everyone."

"If that's what it takes to make it big, why bother?" Katy shuddered. "That woman is determined to take all the fun out of it for Sarah Jo. All that's left is hard work and an obsession for stardom. It's not worth it." Katy looked down at her notes again. She had to get back to the rehearsal. They were already behind. "Let's get going."

The kids were called to the stage, and Katy picked up the scene where they'd left off. This time Alice Stryker kept her distance, but twice Katy looked over her shoulder at the woman and saw a notebook in one hand and a pen in the other. Katy's heart ached. Whatever notes Sarah Jo's mother was taking couldn't be encouraging. Not based on the things they'd all heard her tell her daughter earlier.

Still, with Alice Stryker relegated to the back of the sanctuary, they were able to block the scene without a hitch. Most of the children with speaking parts knew their lines, and no one else was injured during the repeat of the "Big Missouri" dance number at the end of practice.

At just after eight thirty, Katy had the kids sit on the stage. "Acting is many things to many people." She made sure to look at kids seated in all sections of the stage, but she paid particular attention to Sarah Jo Stryker. "For some of you, it's a chance to gain experience for something bigger down the road. Others here treat theater like an after-school club, someplace fun to hang out. No matter why you're here, there are three things I'd like you to remember." She smiled at Sarah Jo. "First, theater is about having fun." She resisted the urge to look at Alice Stryker. "We're putting on something called a play, and it's called that because what we're doing up here —" she raised her hands and did a little jump — "is playing. It's supposed to be fun!"

She settled back down and looked around the stage again. "Second, theater is about sharing." Katy bent down and tapped on the hard surface of the stage. "You don't get up here to tell the world, 'Hey, look how good I am!' " Katy shook her head. "No, you get up here to become someone else, to figure out their world and their character, and to give everything you've got to that part." She scanned the faces before her. "Anyone know how come?"

Bailey Flanigan was one of several older kids to raise their hands. Katy pointed to her. "Bailey?"

"Because it takes every actor onstage to bring the story to life. You have to find your character if the show's going to be any good."

"Exactly." Katy pretended to slip into character and began belting out the words to one of Tom Sawyer's solos. She puffed out her chest, lifted her chin, and exaggerated the pronunciation of each word. Singing was a strength for Katy, so the sound was good. But after two lines, the kids were snickering. She stopped and allowed herself a brief smile. "Okay, someone tell me whether that was a giving performance or a selfish one."

Tim Reed's hand was up first, and Katy pointed at him. "Selfish. Definitely selfish."

"Okay, but why?" Katy loved this, loved the way the kids responded to her. It was part of what she did, not only leading kids through the creation of a play but also teaching them about theater. Especially the kids like Sarah Jo Stryker, whose parents saw children's theater as only a means to an end.

Tim stood so he could be heard better. "It's selfish because when you were singing you were all about yourself. Like you were the only one on the stage and you wanted everyone to know you had a good voice."

"Right." Katy could sense the parents getting antsy in the back of the sanctuary. She had about a minute to wrap things up. "Instead of singing a solo the way you'd sing it at a voice recital, when you're part of a play, you let the character sing it. That way the message is acted out, and it moves the story to another level. That's what we mean by sharing." She held up three fingers. "The third thing is pretty simple. At CKT we do theater to bring glory and honor to Jesus Christ. Anyone want to say a little more about that?"

Ashley Zarelli raised her hand, and Katy nodded in her direction. Ash stood and smiled. If she was nervous she didn't show it. "Well, Jesus gave us our talents. A lot of time people use their talents against God." She did a cute shrug. "Here I think everyone understands that without the Lord we'd be nothing. Each performance is a chance to do our best with the talents

God's given us. Then somewhere up in heaven we can be sure He's giving us a standing ovation."

"Perfect." Katy clapped once and gestured to the kids to gather around her. "Great practice, everyone."

The boys and girls were drawing close when little Mary Reed tugged on Katy's shirtsleeve. "Katy . . ."

"Yes, honey?" She bent down so she could hear Mary over the noise of the other kids.

"I love you, Katy." Mary looked up, her eyes seeing straight to Katy's heart. "Thanks for teaching us."

Katy pulled the little girl into a hug. Warmth and goodness and everything right flooded her soul. So what if Dayne Matthews never called back? She didn't need an acting job, not when she had this. CKT didn't have much money in the budget, and she didn't make enough money to live on her own. But working with these kids was what she loved. The child in her arms was proof.

"Ready for the song?" Katy brushed her nose against Mary's.

"Yep. Ready." Mary stepped back and took Katy's hand.

Then Katy raised her voice so the kids

around her could hear. "Circle up, guys."

Katy ended every practice the same way. The children circled her and she led them in a nonsensical song. "Bang-bang, choo-choo train, wind me up and I'll do my thing. . . ." The song took the kids from their very loudest voices to barely a whisper before they erupted into cheers at the end and headed home with their parents.

When the kids were gone, Katy glanced at her watch. It was nine o'clock, and the next two hours were designated for painting sets. Nancy Helmes brought coffee for everyone, full cups for the others, half a cup for herself.

"I'll never understand the half-cup thing, Nancy." Katy grinned at the woman. "Tell me again?"

"I can't stand drinking cold coffee." Nancy made a funny face. "I take only half a cup because that's the part that stays hot."

"Right. That's what I thought."

"She's a little crazy." Al gave a light-hearted, sarcastic raise of his brow. "That's why I love her."

Heath Hudson was here helping that night, along with Ashley Baxter. Her husband was home with their son. Since this early session was more about creating a design, he figured he could wait and come to one of the later work nights.

The first step was moving the plywood in. Katy placed herself at one corner of the stack of wood and scanned the sanctuary. "Everyone over here for a minute."

Rhonda, Heath, and Ashley hurried over and helped her pick up the corners of three awkward sheets of plywood and carry them to the stage. "Easy does it, everyone. Don't drop your corner." Katy led the way up the stairs.

Rhonda set her corner down and dusted off her hands on her jeans, then picked up the corner again. "If I get another splinter I won't be able to hold a paintbrush."

"Yikes." Katy tightened her grip on the board and helped lift it, moving it toward the back of the stage. Her hands were getting cut up too. "It was supposed to be the finest grain. It shouldn't be splintering like this."

Ashley poked her head around the plywood. "The grain's okay. Even with the splintering, we can still paint on it; I'm pretty sure."

"Good." Katy moved in sync with Rhonda's steps, and in a few seconds they had the board flat on the stage. She smiled at Ashley. "Thanks for doing this. It's just like God to bring you." She looked from Heath to Rhonda. "We prayed for someone with an art background to help with sets." Her eyes returned to Ashley. "And God brings us a professional artist. How great is that?"

When all three boards were lined up side by side, Katy explained what they were for. "These'll make up Aunt Polly's house." She gave the other three a look. "Aunt Polly's on a low budget these days, so no fourth wall." The paint was already sitting a few feet away on a spread of newspapers. Katy pointed to it. "We've got red, blue, green, yellow, and white. Enough to make pretty picture windows and a roofline." She gave Ashley a hesitant look. "That is, if you can take a pencil and sketch out the design so it looks like the roofline's coming down along the top of the three walls."

Ashley laughed and rolled up her sleeves. "No problem."

Heath was still in a white button-down and a tie from work. He slipped an old T-shirt over his head and stood back a little. "Okay, Ms. Baxter, give us something to paint."

Rhonda smiled. "We'll stand here and watch." She positioned herself next to Katy and elbowed her in the ribs. Her next few words were hushed. "I watched her sketch something the other day. She's amazing."

Before Katy could respond, her cell phone rang. Rhonda's eyes lit up as Katy took it from her pocket. Rhonda mouthed the question on both their minds: *Dayne?*

Katy made a face at her, put the phone to her ear, and turned her back to the others. "Hello?"

"Hi, Katy, it's Dayne." He hesitated. "Dayne Matthews. Are you busy?"

The floor beneath Katy felt suddenly molten. She steadied herself. "Hi. No . . . just about to paint some sets." She wasn't sure what else to say, so she waited.

Dayne chuckled on the other end. "That's so great. Painting sets." He drew in a slow breath. "It's been a long time since I did that."

"You should join us sometime." She was regaining her balance, finding her way in the conversation. "Nothing beats an all-night sets party."

"Maybe I'll do that." He laughed again, and then his tone grew more serious. "Hey, I've been meaning to call you, but I had to make sure about the audition time. Mitch and I would like you to come back, do a scene with me this time."

Katy clutched the phone more tightly. This wasn't happening, was it? Dayne Matthews wasn't really chatting at the other end of her cell phone, asking her to come back to Hollywood to do a scene with him, was he? "When . . . when would it be?"

"Tuesday morning. You could fly out Monday if that works for you. The studio already has a flight lined up if you're interested."

If she was interested? "Yeah." She forced herself to take slow breaths. "Tuesday works."

Katy glanced over her shoulder. Heath was watching Ashley, taken by her pencil sketches on the plywood. But Rhonda was only a few feet away, her eyes round. This time she mouthed the words *I knew it.*

Katy waved her fist in a silent cheer and held one finger to her lips. She didn't want Heath or Ashley knowing about her LA auditions — not yet. Dayne was explaining what time her plane would take off and assuring her that someone from the studio would call her with a confirmation and the specifics.

"What should I wear? Is it a city scene or something from her hometown?" She kept her voice quiet, her back to the others.

"You know, Katy —" she could hear the smile in Dayne's voice — "I don't think it really matters."

Then — and only then — did she admit the truth to herself, a truth that built and grew and consumed her even after the phone call with Dayne Matthews ended. After a lifetime of dreaming about making it as an actress — after coming close in Chicago and walking away from it — here, now, the long-ago dream was about to come true. The reason it didn't matter what she wore to the audition was obvious.

Because the truth was, the part of Tory Temblin was practically hers.

Chapter Twelve

Dayne could feel himself falling for Katy Hart.

That didn't surprise him. He'd been taken with her from the moment he saw her at the Bloomington Community Theater a year earlier. What did surprise him was the fact that he couldn't control his feelings.

In his world, women were as plentiful as the grains of sand on the Malibu shoreline. When he came across one he couldn't have — because she was married or seeing someone — he would flirt but never fall. Not hard, anyway. But with Katy things were different. He hadn't met anyone like her since his days of boarding school in Indonesia. She was as genuine as a summer breeze, and no matter how he tried to clear his mind of her, he failed.

Now it was Saturday morning, and Katy would be back in town on Monday. He wanted badly to call her and make plans to take her out, maybe show her around. But it wasn't possible because it wouldn't be fair to Katy. Her innocence even went so far as to her lack of understanding of what might lie ahead for her — the world of Hollywood living.

Dayne was barefoot as he padded across his kitchen and pulled a carton of eggs from his refrigerator. Four egg whites and sautéed mushrooms were on the menu for the day. One of his favorites. He took a bowl from the cupboard and snagged a fork from the drawer.

He liked Saturday mornings in June, liked the fog that hung around his patio, liked the quiet way everything felt when the ocean disappeared from view and his estate became a comfortable cocoon of normalcy.

If just for a few hours.

A pretty instrumental flowed through his house from the sound system. He had a collection of such music, and this one was called *Creek* something or other. Gentle guitar melodies mixed with the cry of an occasional bird or the soft crackling of a babbling brook.

This was peace, these Saturday mornings.

He cracked the eggs, separated the yolks, and whipped the whites with his fork. Katy's face came to mind again as he poured the mixture into a small frying pan.

It wasn't that she was glamorous. He'd been around women like that most of his career. But what she lacked in glamour she made up for in natural beauty. She was gorgeous, pretty in a simple way, with a style that Hollywood had forgotten. It was what made her perfect for the part in *Dream On* and what would catapult her to the top of the Hollywood list if she won it.

And she would win it.

He remembered the conversation he'd had with Mitch Henry about Katy. After her first audition and Dayne's lunch with her at the commissary, Dayne had returned to the studio office and found Mitch at his desk looking at his computer.

Dayne was breathless, energy and enthusiasm flowing through his veins. "Well?"

Mitch took his wire-rimmed glasses from his face, set them on his desk, and focused on Dayne. "You look like a schoolboy, Matthews." He lowered his chin, his expression that of an indignant father. "Don't fall for her." He hesitated and looked at his computer screen again. "She's too good for you."

"I know it." He pulled up a chair and leaned on the edge of the desk that separated them. "But what do you think? The real deal, right?"

Mitch gave an exaggerated sigh and turned toward Dayne again. "You were there."

"Right." Dayne wasn't sure where the casting director was headed.

"In the room watching her audition?"

"Yeah, so?" Dayne sat back a little. "I still wanna know what you thought."

Mitch crossed one leg over the other and gripped the arms of his chair. "I thought she was brilliant. The most natural talent I've seen come through those doors in years." His expression cracked, and a smile softened his eyes. "But you already knew that."

"So . . ." Dayne rose and tossed his hands in the air. "Why aren't you more excited?"

"Because . . ." He faced the window for a moment and then stood. When he turned around, his eyes were serious again. "I don't think she'll take it."

"Of course she'll take it." Dayne had felt the excitement surge through him. He'd wanted to shout to the heavens. Mitch Henry liked her, liked her so much he already expected to offer her the part! Dayne could imagine himself working alongside her, getting to know her better, becoming friends with the girl who had captured his imagination the previous summer. "She wouldn't be flying out here for an audition if she wasn't interested in the part."

"I'm worried." Mitch tapped his fingers on his desk. "Katy Hart doesn't belong here." He waved his hand in the air. "With all the craziness in Hollywood."

"Maybe she wants it." Dayne's answer had been fast — too fast. Even as he said the words, he knew Mitch was right. The lifestyle of the Hollywood elite, the type of actress who would play opposite him in a major film, was something Katy wasn't prepared for. Not at all.

"Be careful with her when she's out for the next audition." He pointed at Dayne, the stern-father look back in his eyes. "I can see it, Dayne. I know how you're feeling about her. Just do everyone a favor and keep your feelings to yourself. I don't want that girl's face on the cover of any magazine, you understand?"

The memory of the conversation lingered as thick as the fog outside.

Was that what he had to do — keep his distance from everyone he wanted to get to know? everyone who might be good for him? The idea brought back another memory, one that was so sad he rarely thought of it. The memory of his birth mother lying in the hospital bed in Bloomington, the feel of her dying arms around his neck as she told him what he'd always wanted to know.

That he'd been loved by her. By her and his birth father. And that if his siblings had gotten the chance to know about him, he would've been loved by them too.

Dayne adjusted the fire beneath the eggs. He gripped the granite countertop and closed his eyes. He could still remember how it felt sitting in that rented SUV, watching the front door of the hospital from the back of the parking lot, and seeing the group come out. The group that he quickly realized was his family, his biological father and siblings and their spouses and children.

Even now he could feel his fingers wrapped around the handle of the driver's door, feel himself opening it and putting one foot on the ground. He would go to them, introduce himself, talk to them. Maybe even hug them. And just like that, in a matter of seconds, he would have the family he'd always wanted. He would never feel disconnected again.

But as he stepped into the light of day, he heard the first series of clicks — paparazzi camera clicks — and in that moment he made the decision. He wouldn't pull the Baxters into the tabloids with him. They were private people, good people from what he knew of them, doctors and lawyers and teachers and artists. People whose lives centered around the comfortable town of Bloomington, Indiana.

So instead of going to them, he stayed in the SUV and let them walk past him to their cars, where they climbed in and drove away. And that was the end of that.

Dayne opened his eyes.

In light of his decision that day, he had promised himself he wouldn't think about them, that he'd put them out of his mind. But the memory of them stayed with him like a favorite song, and it came back whenever it willed. The worried lines on their faces as they clung to each other, obviously concerned about their mother, dying inside the hospital.

It was senseless to think about Elizabeth and the other Baxters. As senseless as it was to think about Katy Hart. His world and theirs were far too different, the distance between them too great to span, and it was up to him to keep it that way. For now, anyway. If Katy took the part, if she received national acclaim for her role the way he figured she would, then she would gain passage into his world.

And maybe they would find something together.

But not now, not Monday when she came into town for her second audition.

He scraped the sautéed mushrooms into the half-cooked egg whites and stirred the mixture. Most of the time the issues his friends had with fame didn't bother him. Who cared what the rags printed? People must lead pretty dull lives to hang on every word in the trash magazines. He could sleep at night without wondering whether a photographer was perched outside in a tree or waiting for him in his driveway. They were harmless, more a nuisance than anything else.

But when he weighed into the mix what he'd lost with the Baxters, the issues became much more complicated.

The eggs were cooked, and he spooned them onto a plate. He poured a glass of orange juice, fresh squeezed from the juice shop across the street. It was his favorite breakfast, compliments of his well-paid housekeeper. She knew what he liked, and she kept the place stocked.

The eggs were good, just the way he liked them. But throughout his meal he continued to see their faces, the Baxters' and Katy Hart's. Maybe it was the music — the soft, melodic sounds like the credits from a sad movie. He was about to get up and switch to something more upbeat when his phone rang.

He snatched it on his way to the stereo system. "Hello?"

"Dayne, it's me. Kelly." Her voice was strained, quiet and desperate at the same time. "I think someone just tried to break into my house."

"What?" Dayne turned back, took his plate, and headed for the kitchen. "Kelly, call the police. Right now."

"No . . . I mean, I think they're gone. I think it just happened. They tried to break in but then they left because I was here and maybe now they —"

"Whoa, Kelly. Slow. You're not making sense." He leaned against his patio door and squinted into the fog. A chill ran down his arms. "Tell me what happened."

"I heard someone tapping on my window, and I ran into the room and looked and there was a lady." She was talking slower now, her words still breathy and filled with fear. "Dayne, I think she had a knife in her hand."

"Hey . . ." Dayne felt his heart lurch into double speed. "Kelly, I'm serious. Call the police."

"No, wait. So I watched her, and all of a sudden she turned and ran to her car and drove away."

His forehead was cold against the glass, and he stood straighter. What sort of freak would do that to Kelly Parker? He focused on what Kelly had said. "What kind of car? Did you get the plate?"

"No, but I saw the car. It had four doors. I'm pretty sure it was an old Honda Civic. A yellow Civic."

"And you're sure it's gone?"

"Yes. I saw it drive away."

"Okay." Dayne crooked his arm up over his head and pressed it against the window. "Let's think this through. Maybe someone was looking for a house, and they stumbled on yours by accident."

"I don't know." Kelly sounded like she was shaking. "Maybe it was a photographer. It just scared me. You know, broad daylight and everything."

Dayne clenched his jaw. Photographers again. He had prided himself on not letting them get him down. He loved acting too much to be bothered by the paparazzi.

Even with what happened in Bloomington, he didn't see the lack of privacy as a prison but rather a price. A price that had to be paid by everyone at the top of the entertainment industry.

Prisons were places from which you couldn't escape. Paparazzi? Give up acting for a couple of years and they'd vanish like fireflies at sunrise, right? Wasn't that what he'd always told himself? Celebrity was a choice, wasn't it?

But now, with Kelly Parker petrified on the other end of the line, Dayne wasn't so sure. "Want me to come?"

"Please, Dayne. I can't leave; I'm too afraid." She sniffed twice. "Besides, I want to talk to you about something else."

Dayne made the drive to Kelly's house without being followed. If the paparazzi knew his pattern, they knew he usually didn't leave his house until well after three o'clock on Saturdays. It was still morning, so they were probably bothering someone else. Kelly Parker, by the sounds of it.

Dayne wrestled with himself as he climbed out of his Escalade and moved fast up the walkway. Whatever Kelly had to ask him, he hoped it didn't involve the other night. He'd been wrong to stay over, wrong to sleep with her. If her head wasn't so messed up, it would be one thing. But she hadn't been well for a while. Being with her that way was bound to confuse her.

She opened the door, pulled him inside, and fell into his arms. "Dayne, I hate this." She drew back, her cheeks tearstained. "This isn't me — hiding inside, afraid of my own shadow. I used to walk around my neighborhood at night by myself."

He'd been thinking about what to tell her, and now he didn't hesitate. He led her by the hand into her living room and sat her down on her couch. He took the seat next to her, gripped her knee, and looked straight in her eyes. "You need help, Kelly. This —" he looked around the room — "staying trapped inside like this isn't normal." For a moment the anger he'd felt earlier rose to the surface again. "You can't let them get to you like this."

She hung her head, her shoulders slumped. "I know I shouldn't read the tabs, but then someone calls or I see it when I'm out and I know what they're saying." Her eyes met his. "This week it's my arms." She motioned to the wall of windows opposite them. "Someone shot me pointing at something, and now I've got flabby arms."

Dayne winced. He'd seen the picture a

few days earlier and laughed at it. Kelly Parker with flabby arms? It was ludicrous. But somehow the photogs had found six pictures of female celebrities whose arms appeared less than perfect. The headline read "Uh-Oh . . . Flabby Arms! Who's Flabby and Who's Not?"

"It's ridiculous. I saw it." He ran his hand from her shoulder to her wrist. "Your arms are perfect, baby. You know that."

"Pictures don't lie." Kelly shook her head. "First I have cellulite, then a lesbian lover, and now flabby arms. Sort of kills the appetite, you know?"

He studied Kelly and realized she was thinner than she'd been a few months ago. "You're eating, right?" There were always a few Hollywood women starving themselves, handling the pressure of looking perfect by letting their weight drop to dangerous lows. A ripple of fear stirred the waters in his soul. "Tell me you're eating, Kelly."

She shrugged. "I eat enough." She hugged herself and kept her eyes downcast. "I wouldn't mind a tabloid saying something about me looking too thin. It would beat the cellulite and flabby arms stories."

"You are thin." He took hold of her chin and lifted it gently so that their eyes locked. "Don't get messed up in all that starving stuff. I mean it, Kelly. Promise me."

She hesitated long enough to indicate a problem. But then he felt her nod against his hand. "Okay." Her fingers met his and eased his hand down from her jaw. But instead of letting go, she wove her fingers between his. "I feel better with you here."

"Good." He settled back against the sofa. "You wanted to talk about something else?"

"Yes." For the first time in weeks, her eyes showed some life. "I want a chance at the part in *Dream On*. The lead female."

Dayne felt his heart lurch. That was Katy's part; it belonged to her. "Tory Temblin?"

"Yep." She gave him a shy smile. "I can play her, Dayne. I hear talk you're having trouble filling the part." She paused. "Call me in and try me."

"You, huh?" He gave her a lazy grin. This was no time to mention an unknown from Middle America. "What makes you think a knockout like you could play a plain girl from the country?"

"You and me." She lifted his fingertips to her lips and kissed them one at a time, slow and sensual, arousing feelings far be-

222

yond his fingers. Her eyes never left his. "On-screen chemistry, of course."

"Okay." He swallowed, regaining his composure. "I'll give you that." He uttered a soft chuckle. "But you're elegant and glamorous, Kelly." He shifted toward her and leaned in. "You're a wonderful actress, but . . . I don't know . . . we're looking for a newcomer."

"Sounds like a challenge." Even in her meek, fearful condition, Kelly's expression was humorous, her trademark confidence back again. "Let me read for it, Dayne. Come on."

Her smile melted his heart. What if Mitch was right? What if Katy was offered the part and refused it? He still had a film to cast, a movie to make in the next few months. "Okay. Come in Tuesday morning." He brushed his knuckles against her cheek. The interview was more because he felt sorry for her than anything else. That and the possibility that Katy might not work out. "Eight o'clock, okay?"

"Why?" Her tone was lighter than before, her eyes playing with him. "Is Miss Newcomer having her audition at nine?"

Katy's face came to mind, but Dayne hid the way his heart reacted to it. Instead he gave Kelly an appreciative nod. "Very good." He wagged his finger at her. "At least you're first."

Their talk shifted to the lives of friends they had in common, how well certain actresses were doing, and how they were able to ignore the paparazzi, take in stride the country's obsession with celebrity.

After an hour, Dayne looked at his watch. "I have a few things to do around the house." He touched her cheek, his eyes lingering on hers. "Are you okay?"

"Yeah." Her expression changed, and something that came close to shame filled her face. She glanced down the hallway toward her bedroom. "You could stay awhile if you want."

Her message was clear. After the way they'd come together the last time he was at her house, it felt natural to him, too, that they might wind up sharing more than a conversation.

"Not this time, okay?" He worked his fingers up along the side of her face and into her hair. "Remember our promise?" His voice was thick, tinged with a desire that he refused to obey. He kept his tone steady. "The promise we made the other night?"

"Yes. Nothing complicated." Kelly brought her lips together in a tight line and let her gaze fall to her lap. When she looked up again, a handful of emotions flashed in her eyes. Regret and rejection, doubt and discouragement. "I don't want complicated, Dayne." She raised one shoulder. "Sometimes I just want you to hold me."

Dayne stood and held his arms out to her. "C'mere, you."

Tears shone in Kelly's eyes as she rose and put her arms around his waist. Again her nearness moved him, but that was all. A physical attraction. In his heart he felt nothing more than friendship for Kelly Parker. When he pulled back, he smiled at her and kissed the tip of her nose. "Go take a shower, baby. Then call your friends and go out tonight. If the chasers take pictures, smile and have fun, anyway."

He thought she might pull him close again, maybe try to kiss him. But she had more self-respect than that. She simply gave him another hug and pulled away. "Thanks for coming, Dayne." She crossed her arms tight against her waist. "See you Tuesday." She paused. "And tell Miss Newcomer she doesn't stand a chance this time. I want the part too bad."

That last part of the conversation played again in his mind as he drove home. What about Miss Newcomer? Would Katy Hart win the role? Would she take it? He thought about Kelly Parker, so frightened she didn't want to leave her own house. What if that happened to Katy?

It was a possibility he hadn't considered before, and he was still thinking about it as he drove down Pacific Coast Highway toward his house. Nearly all the fog had burned off, and the day was warming up. He was only a dozen yards away when he slowed down and studied the driveway next to his. Parked there was an old car with a woman at the wheel — a woman staring straight at his house.

That much didn't surprise him. People were always staring, hoping he'd look out the window or open the garage door or suddenly show up. But most of them had cameras. He squinted, trying to make out more details as he eased his car into the center turn lane. The woman had her hands on the top of the steering wheel. If she had a camera, she wasn't holding it.

At that moment, she looked over her shoulder and saw him. In a sudden rush, she backed straight into oncoming traffic, and a FedEx truck swerved to miss her. Then she straightened her car and zoomed away. She definitely wasn't working for the rags if she chose to run when she saw him.

But that was only one aspect that troubled Dayne as he turned left, hit the door opener, and drove his car into the garage. The other detail was enough to make his blood run cold — the make and color of the woman's car.

It was a four-door, yellow Honda Civic.

Chapter Thirteen

Katy could hardly concentrate on the play.

Her conversation with Dayne Matthews had taken place just twelve hours earlier, and already her entire world seemed to be spinning out of control. Before the morning practice, Rhonda brought her news that a disagreement had come up between the house committee and the souvenir committee.

"The parents were about to duke it out when I got here." Rhonda was sitting next to Katy in the first pew, where they kept their table and directed practice.

Katy frowned. "They're adults, for heaven's sake." She took hold of her yellow notepad and began writing and talking to herself at the same time. "Rule Number 18: Don't let parents arrive at practice early to discuss committee issues."

"Exactly." Rhonda reached for a script and flipped it open. "House wants to be able to seat the lobby of the theater with folding chairs — in case we sell out. But souvenirs said they wouldn't give up the far-right third of that space because they need it to sell buttons and *Tom Sawyer* scrapbooks." She took a quick breath. "Matt Bellonte from house said he'd scoop the souvenirs up and give 'em away before he'd turn down a paying customer who could've sat in that space. Then Melody Thorpe said she'd guard the area herself if she had to, but she wasn't giving up souvenir space for a few more folding chairs."

"Good." Katy felt her tension build. "One big, happy, Christian family."

"Another thing." Rhonda smiled, her voice tentative. "Alice Stryker says we should practice lighting techniques. Apparently Sarah Jo washes out in certain spotlights. Mrs. Stryker doesn't want that happening, because she's hiring a professional videographer to capture the best performance of the play and use the film to promote Sarah Jo to the next level."

"Ugggh!" Katy slid down in her seat and covered her face. She peeked through her fingers. "A professional videographer?"

"Yes." Rhonda checked a page of notes. "Mrs. Stryker tells me we'll never know he's here. But he'll be interviewing Sarah

Jo quite often and maybe me. Definitely you."

"And we'll never know he's here?" Katy pressed her fingers against her temple. "Can they do that? Isn't there something in CKT guidelines against hiring your own videographer?"

"Nope." Rhonda frowned. "I actually checked. As long as the copyright for the play allows videotaping, then it's all fair game."

"Amazing." She still had her eyes sheltered. "Anything else?"

"Sound." Rhonda shook her head, as if even she couldn't believe the next piece of news. "Mrs. Stryker wants a private sound check for the videographer just before the first show."

"Sure." Katy dropped her hands to her sides and sat up straight. "We'll get right on scheduling that. I suppose she wants the nicest mic too?"

"Preferably nothing that crackles." Rhonda allowed a giggle. "She told me, 'Look, I know how these low-budget children's theater groups work. I can't have a microphone cutting out on my daughter. The videographer and I want to hear every word.'"

"You know what I think?" Katy stood,

her enthusiasm all but gone.

"What's that?"

"I think we better get the kids onstage before I go home and cry myself to sleep."

They both smiled at the picture, but Rhonda was off right away, zipping up the aisle to the lobby and directing the kids into the sanctuary and onto the stage.

The practice went from bad to worse. When the lead characters took the stage to block out the second scene, Sarah Jo's voice was all but gone.

Katy walked up and put her hand on the girl's shoulder. "Honey, what happened to your voice?"

"I —" she clutched her throat and massaged it — "practiced too much."

"Practiced what?" The girl had practiced four hours the night before and now was required to be at the church bright and early for another four hours. When would she have had time to practice? "Practiced for CKT?"

"Yes." Sarah Jo shifted her weight from one foot to the other. Her voice was so raspy she was barely understandable. "I practiced my solo. Mama said it had to be better."

"All right —" Katy worked the muscles in her jaw — "here're your new instruc-

231

tions." She looked over her shoulder at the back of the sanctuary. Mrs. Stryker wasn't in the room. She returned her attention to Sarah Jo. "Today I want you to say your lines in your softest voice ever. And when it's time to sing, just mouth the words, so you'll be familiar with the song. Okay?"

"Okay." The seriousness in the girl's eyes lifted a little, and her lips showed the hint of a smile. "Thanks, Katy."

They were fifteen minutes behind schedule by the time Katy was back at her spot near the table, with the scene under way. It was the part in the play where Aunt Polly sits in her rocking chair recounting the trouble with Tom Sawyer when a group of women from church stops in with an invitation. The women's aid society is throwing a picnic for the townsfolk in a few weeks, and the hope is that Aunt Polly will bake her famous pies. Among the women were the Widow Douglas, Mrs. Thatcher, and Becky.

"I do say, that Becky of yours sure is a beauty." Ashley Zarelli, playing Aunt Polly, drew the words out, bringing the perfect mix of Midwestern drawl and anxious gossip to the line. "I daresay my Tom's caught a look at her."

Sarah Jo, meanwhile, was caught in a

conversation with Tom's cousin and wasn't supposed to hear the remark. Her line was next, and she was right on cue. "Your cousin's kinda cute." Her words were barely audible. "Don't you think?"

"Tom?" The cousin gave Sarah Jo a strange look. "Becky Thatcher, you must be wacky in the head to think anything good could ever come from that ol' Tom Sawyer."

The line was supposed to be Tim Reed's cue. By the time he heard the part "wacky in the head," he was supposed to creep along behind what would eventually be part of the set — a white picket fence at the center of the stage. Then he was supposed to run smack into Aunt Polly.

Instead he was nowhere to be seen.

"Tim." Katy allowed frustration in her tone. She glanced around the sanctuary. "Anyone seen Tim?"

The other kids looked around, but no one had an answer.

"Tim?" She shouted his name this time. *Calm down,* she told herself. *They're just kids.* "Tim, you with us?"

At that moment he darted through the back sanctuary doors and flew up the aisle onto the stage, scrambling to a stop just as he crashed into Aunt Polly. The force

233

dropped him onto his bottom and left his eyes wide. "Aunt Polly . . . what a surprise."

A wave of hushed giggles sounded from across the stage and the sanctuary.

Katy stood and walked closer to the action. She looked straight at Tim. "Is that something new you've added?" She waved toward the back of the room. "You know, proving to the audience how bad Tom Sawyer really is?"

Tim stood and dusted off the backside of his jeans. "Sorry, Katy."

"Okay." She gave him a pointed look. "Let's get serious about this. We open in seven weeks."

Rhonda met her eyes as Katy returned to the table. "Want me to take the liberty dancers out in the foyer and work with them?"

"Definitely. That's better than having them sit around giggling at Tim Reed." She looked at the back of the church one more time, and there by the doors where Tim had come running through was Bailey Flanigan. Katy hesitated. Was Bailey the reason Tim was too busy to make it onstage for his line? She raised one eyebrow at Bailey, but it went unnoticed. The girl was too busy watching Tim.

Rhonda made her way out of the sanctuary, eight girls trailing her. Katy made a mental note to talk to Bailey later. Whatever drama was going on behind the scenes would have to take place outside of practice time. She turned back to the actors onstage, every one of them still watching her, waiting for her to resume. "Okay, take it from Tim's entrance."

This time Tim crept across the stage the way he was supposed to and banged softly into Ashley Zarelli. "Aunt Polly . . . what a surprise."

Katy searched the script. That wasn't the line, was it? She found where they were, and not only was Tim off base, but he had more lines. She looked at him, summoning the strictest look she could come up with. "Tim Reed, do you know your lines?"

He straightened and scratched his head, his face lined with resignation. "Not exactly."

"Tim . . ." She gritted her teeth. Somehow she kept from screaming at him. "I expect more from you. You're one of the oldest kids in CKT, and when you have a lead part I need you to know your lines."

"Yes, Katy. I'm sorry." His expression was humble, honest. No question he felt bad about his performance that day.

"Can someone prompt me?"

"Nancy." Katy pointed to the edge of the stage. "Can you sit there and help Tim with whatever he needs?"

"That's what the creative team's for!" Nancy Helmes saluted and did as she was asked.

When Nancy was set up, Katy held up her hands. "Listen, guys, let's take this seriously. Please. This is your show. It's up to you whether you feel proud of the final product or embarrassed for not trying harder." She pointed at Sarah Jo. "All except you, Becky Thatcher. You need to try a little less hard."

The next three hours were as painful and tedious as the first. The only actor who shone onstage was Ashley Zarelli. In fact, her first performance was so strong, Katy worried about another possibility — because she was both talented and prepared, Ash might upstage everyone in the scene.

Sarah Jo was another worry. Though Katy did her best to avoid the girl's mother, Sarah Jo seemed less than enthusiastic as Becky. By the end of practice, Katy began to wonder. Had she made the wrong choice? Maybe she should've given the part to Bailey Flanigan. She never wanted anyone to accuse her of favoritism where the Flanigans were concerned, but maybe in the process of being fair, she'd gone too far.

Katy stared at her tennis shoes. It was too late now. She couldn't take the part away from Sarah Jo. Her only choice was to make the part more fun for the girl, help her see that acting in children's theater was never meant to be a practice ground for bigger and better roles, but rather a place where friendships were forged and the dream of acting could grow and breathe and become.

She crossed her arms and pressed them to her middle. Rhonda and the Helmes had notes to go over as the kids left the theater, and Jenny Flanigan mentioned she had something to talk to Katy about.

Before any of it could take place, Katy went into the women's restroom, took the farthest stall, shut the door, and leaned back against it. Why did everything feel so out of control? Her parent committees were fighting, Mrs. Stryker had a professional videographer, and her most reliable student didn't have a clue about his lines. She was broke until the end of the month with no money to buy a new pair of jeans, and her run-down Nissan had little more than fumes in the gas tank.

Had she left Chicago for this? walked away from acting for a life of lonely chaos and poverty?

Katy knew the answer. Her reason for leaving acting had nothing to do with kids theater or noble causes, not at the beginning. She'd taken the job with Chicago's CKT as a way to run as far away from the other side of acting as possible, to escape the kind of film career that had cost her everything that mattered back then.

She closed her eyes and rested her head against the cool stall door. His name was Tad Thompson, and the two of them had been friends since high school drama class their junior year. Love didn't find them until their first year of college, and by then they were both going to auditions and getting small parts in commercials and films.

His first big part came before hers — a supporting role in a film opposite one of the biggest names in Hollywood.

"Nothing will change," he had promised her. "I'll be gone for a while, but I'll come back. Things will be just like they were."

But the film crew was a wild one, and Tad had been sucked into a lifestyle he wasn't prepared for. Katy did everything she could to keep him grounded, but in the end holding on to him had been like holding the string of a kite caught in a hurricane. In the midst of it all, she got the break she'd dreamed of back then — a series pilot, a two-hour TV movie that would showcase her acting ability and maybe open the door for more auditions, more films.

Tad died the week before her movie aired on CBS.

The loss had knocked her to her knees, sent her reeling, not sure how she would survive one breath to the next. Three months passed in a blur, but every audition felt flat, her dreams ugly and tarnished. Eventually she stopped taking calls from her agent.

Her mother got it right. She found Katy in her room one night a few months after Tad's death and softly closed the door behind her. "It died, didn't it?" She sat on the bed beside Katy and brushed her thumb along her brow.

"What?"

"Your dream of acting. It died just like Tad. And now you're afraid to go anywhere near that world."

Katy's eyes had filled, but she didn't speak, couldn't speak.

"It's okay to be afraid, Katy." Her mother gave her a sad smile. "God's the giver of life. For every dream that dies, a new one takes root."

A lump settled in Katy's throat.

She and Tad were going to marry and buy a condominium in Chicago. They had plans to be onstage, and together they would avoid the mistakes so many other people in show business made. They were going to raise a family, and even though faith had never come easily for Tad, they planned to teach their children about God.

Katy opened her eyes and stared at the bare wall above the toilet. She had missed Tad so much back then, missed him with an ache that for months sent her to bed early. But slowly, like the dawn, the pain lifted enough to allow her to look outside herself. What she found proved that her mother had been right about something else too: Hope lived.

The mere act of breathing, of getting out of bed and facing the day gave her hope, and hope breathed new dreams into existence. The answer was obvious, from the moment she and her mother attended a local CKT performance. Children's theater was the answer, the antidote for her lonely days and nights. She breezed into an assistant position and was named director at the end of her first year.

With the children of CKT, acting no longer represented the world that had taken Tad from her. Instead it was a creative expression of the heart, an extension of the soul, one that could glorify God, the giver of creativity.

Her feelings hadn't veered from that, not once. She believed in CKT and everything it attempted to do. So why was she now standing in a bathroom stall trying not to cry? Why had the parent committees and Alice Stryker and Tim's missed cues sent her running for cover?

Katy had no answers for herself. She drew a full breath and left the cramped space. As she passed the mirror she caught a glimpse of her reflection, and suddenly she knew why things felt so strange and chaotic, why the job she loved so much felt more burden than blessing.

It was because of the audition.

She was headed west to meet with Dayne Matthews, and no matter what she thought of the entertainment industry, no matter how she blamed it for robbing her of Tad Thompson and the life they'd planned together, her reflection told her that it was happening again.

Hope was giving way to new dreams.

Only this time the dream didn't involve

children's theater or directing or anything about CKT. It involved whatever lay ahead of her in Hollywood, California.

Chapter Fourteen

Sun streamed through a handful of puffy white clouds Sunday afternoon as Ashley walked beside Landon and Cole across the church parking lot and looked around one more time. Still no sign of her father, which was strange. He always attended the eleven o'clock service. She took Cole's hand and helped him into their Durango.

When they were all seated inside, she turned to Landon. "Don't you think it's weird?" She buckled her seat belt. "Dad's always here at eleven."

"Maybe he had a meeting at the hospital." Landon started the SUV and pulled it into line behind three others headed for the exit.

"On Sunday?"

"Maybe he went early. You know, something new for a change." He reached out and covered Ashley's hand with his own. "He's okay, Ash. Really."

"Okay." She gave him a weak smile and looked over her right shoulder. "Buckle up, Cole."

"Already did, Mom. I always buckle up, remember?" He grinned at her. Both his front top teeth were missing, and he lisped because of it. "Are we going to the picnic still?"

Ashley shifted her attention to Landon. "Are we?"

"If you want." He motioned to the sky. "Looks like a great day."

"Yeah, Mommy, let's go." Cole put his hand on her shoulder and gave it a squeeze. "And let's stop by Grandpa's and see if he wants to go too!"

"Hmm." Ashley looked at Landon. "I have some paint there I've been meaning to get." She raised her brow. "Could we stop by?"

"Sure." Landon turned left out of the parking lot. "How 'bout I drop you off. Cole and I can stop in at the fire station." He grinned back at Cole. "I have some paperwork to fill out, and Cole can help wash the engines."

"Awesome! I love washing the engines." Cole bounced a few times on his seat. "Can I be in charge of the tires?"

"Sure, Cole. Of all the guys, you're the

best tire washer at the station."

"Yay!"

Ashley ran her thumb over Landon's fingers. "Really? You don't mind?"

"Not at all." He looked at her, to the places of her heart only he understood. "You'll want to do more than stop by, Ash. I know you." He smiled. "The picnic can wait an hour or so."

For a minute, Ashley took in the sight of Landon, strong and tall and loving her the way he did. How had things worked out so well for them? What had she ever done to wind up married to a man like Landon Blake, a man who loved her enough to listen to her when no one else would? a man who knew everything about her past and loved her no less for the painful details?

She leaned close and kissed him on the cheek. "I can't wait for our cruise."

"Me either." He nuzzled his face against hers. "I love you, Ash."

"I know, but guess what?" Her words were barely a whisper.

"What?"

She kissed him again. "I love you more."

From the backseat, Cole giggled. "You guys kiss too much."

"No way." Ashley reached back and

tickled him in the ribs. "You can never kiss too much, Coley."

Landon gave her a sideways glance. "I'd like to test that theory."

"You would, would you?" She moved in close to the side of his face again.

"Maybe on the cruise?" His eyes shone with a brilliance that came from faith and love and knowing how to make the most of a moment.

"Sounds good to me." She settled back in her seat and studied the road ahead of them. Bloomington was beautiful in early summer, the maples green and full, and springtime flowers still holding out for another few weeks.

They reached her father's house in ten minutes, and Landon pulled up to the side door. "Tell him to come with us." He looked at his watch. "We'll be back in an hour to get you, and we can pick up subs. That'll save us some time."

"Okay." She blew him a kiss and then sent another one to Cole. "Be safe."

"Always." Landon grinned at her.

She shut the door and watched them drive away. Cole waved at her until they reached the end of the driveway.

When they were gone, Ashley held her hands straight out to her sides and stared at the vast blue sky. "Thank You, God. . . . You're so good."

She did a simple twirl to emphasize the point, then skipped up the steps and knocked on the door. There was no response, so she went inside and stepped lightly through the mudroom into the kitchen. The temptation to call out to her mother was still there, but she caught herself.

"Dad? You home?"

The house was quiet, and Ashley frowned. He wasn't at church, and he couldn't be in a meeting. Not on a Sunday. Maybe he had a patient in the hospital, someone special who needed a Sunday visit. That was possible, wasn't it?

Whatever the reason, if he wasn't here, she had no need to stay an hour. She reached into her purse for her cell phone and found not one but two. Hers and Landon's. Which meant she couldn't call him until he got to the station, and by then he might as well get his paperwork finished.

She took a look around the house. It was darker than usual, and she realized the reason. Most of the blinds were still shut, even though it was almost one o'clock. Just one more change that had settled over the house since Mom died. When she was alive, she would wake up every morning and make her way through the house, humming one tune or another and opening the blinds.

"Light," she would say. "We have to have light in here."

Ashley felt the familiar ache in her soul. Her mother's love for light always made her feel that somehow they were kindred spirits — despite the tougher years after she returned from Paris. Ashley was an artist, and artists noticed lighting. With her love for light, her mother might've been an artist too if she'd been given the chance.

Sadly, it was fitting that the house was darker now. As if mourning had come to everything her mother had loved, even the rooms of the old Baxter house. Ashley walked across the kitchen to the stove, where her mother had cooked thousands of meals and made a million cups of tea.

With gentle fingers, she gripped the handle of the old copper teakettle. *God, tell her how much we miss her. Tell her I wish she were here so we could share a cup of tea.*

Ashley heard no response, but at the center of her being she felt peace, a peace that didn't have its roots in this world. She filled the kettle, turned on the burner, and waited, studying the kitchen and remembering. Every inch brought with it dozens of memories — laughter and conversation and an intimacy that only a family can share.

When the water was boiling, Ashley took down not one but two teacups. Her favorite and the one her mother had used. From the tray of tea canisters, she took two tea bags and dropped one in each cup. Then she poured water in both, and for a lingering moment she closed her eyes and allowed herself to believe that for just one more day her mother was still alive, still busy in the next room, about to join her in the kitchen.

"Mom . . . the tea's ready." Her words echoed through the empty house, and tears trickled down her cheeks. *God . . . tell her the tea's ready.*

She blinked her eyes open. The shadows were suddenly too sad, too much a reminder of her mother's absence. Here, on this glorious Sunday, Ashley couldn't stand the thought of darkness filling the places where her mother had once welcomed a daily dose of light and warmth.

Ashley left the tea, and starting with the kitchen windows, she worked her way around the downstairs and opened every set of blinds. When she was finished, she climbed the stairs to the room that had once been hers. It was here that she sometimes painted, back before she and Landon married.

Ashley opened the blinds in this room as well. The paints she was looking for were on the bookcase, two shelves from the bottom. She collected them and was heading back toward the stairs when the door to her parents' room caught her attention. She'd forgotten their room, but the blinds should be opened in there too. There of all places.

She set her paints down on a hallway table and opened the door wide enough so she could see inside. It was the darkest room of the house, and Ashley clucked her tongue against the roof of her mouth. What was her father thinking? She moved quickly, first to the window near her father's side of the bed and then to the other one — next to her mother's side.

With light spilling into the room, she stepped back and studied her parents' bed, where her mother had lain sick a year earlier, helping Ashley plan her wedding despite the pain she was in. She looked at the carpeted area next to the bed. It was the place where she had stood in her wedding dress as her mother fastened the tiny pearl-like buttons that ran down the back.

She could hear her mom's voice, feel it in her soul. *Ashley, you look so beautiful.*

God had been gracious, letting her mother live long enough to see her marry Landon. Gracious enough to let her see Erin — Ashley's youngest sister — come home with her four adopted little girls. But no matter what God had given them, Ashley longed for more. One more week or one more day. One more hour, even.

She sniffed and looked at the windows again. Light wasn't enough to chase away the darkness today. Fresh air, that's what the room needed. She opened her mother's window and then rounded the bed and flung open the one next to her father's side of the bed.

A warm, sweet-smelling breeze rustled the blinds and filled the room. There. That was better. As long as the memories of her mother lived, then the places that were most familiar to her should feel alive also. She stepped back again and was about to leave the room when she heard something behind her.

She turned and looked. Her parents' closet door was open. Inside, on the top shelf were two manila envelopes, and next to them was a box overflowing with papers, now moving with the subtle wind. Ashley stared at the spot for a beat. Were they letters, maybe? Things her mother had written to her father?

A look at the clock told her she still had time. Landon wouldn't be back for thirty minutes. She moved across the room and flipped on the closet light. First she pulled down the fullest manila envelope. Inside were old bank records and tax documents.

Ashley returned it to its spot on the shelf. The other manila envelope wasn't nearly as full. Nothing important probably. The box had more promise. She took careful hold of it as she eased it onto the floor. Sure enough, it was full of yellowed envelopes, each addressed to either her father or her mother.

She took one from the box and opened it. A single page held a Christmas message from one of her mother's friends, sent while the friend was on vacation in Italy. Ashley returned it to the envelope and sorted through the stack some more. Partially buried near the back of the box she spotted one that said simply *Elizabeth.*

The house was still quiet, but Ashley peered out of the closet. It felt strange, snooping through her mother's things this way. But her mother had no secrets, nothing she wouldn't have wanted her kids to see. Ashley sat cross-legged on the floor and opened the envelope.

Two pieces of paper held what looked like a handwritten letter from her father to her mother. The paper was old, the writing faded some. She glanced at the top of the first sheet and saw the date: June 17, 1980. The day after Luke was born.

Ashley closed her eyes and tried to imagine the feelings her father would've had that day. By then the Baxter family had four girls but no boys. Luke — their fifth and final child — was the first son. Their father must've been beside himself with joy and gratitude toward God, thrilled that his wife and Luke had come through the delivery without incident.

She opened her eyes and found the first line.

My dearest Elizabeth . . .

Ashley stared at the paper, but her eyes stung and the words blurred. How often had she heard her father call her mother that? *My dearest Elizabeth.* Usually he would come home from work, find her in the kitchen fixing dinner, come up behind her, and wrap his arms around her waist. "My dearest Elizabeth . . . how was your day?"

She blinked, and the words on the page grew clear again.

> My dearest Elizabeth,
> We have a son! A son we can call our very own! Can you believe it, my love? God is so good, that after all we've been through, after four lovely daughters, He has seen fit to complete our family this way — the way it should've been completed from the beginning.

Ashley stopped and uttered a single sad-sounding laugh. "Thanks, Dad." *The way it should've been from the beginning?* She took a quick breath through her nose and got a grip on her feelings. Whatever. If that's how her father felt about Luke's arrival, she couldn't hold it against him now.

She picked up where she left off.

> I am sitting here in our house, anxious for your return, to have you and our son home where you belong. But I can't keep myself from thinking of

your words earlier today. You said that seeing Luke made you remember what you felt when --

"Ashley?"

She screamed and tossed the letter into the air. Her father stood a few feet from her, his expression a mix of surprise and indignation. "Dad . . . you scared me." She stood up and exhaled hard. "I didn't hear you come in."

"You scared me too." Her father looked at the box of letters on the floor and then back at her. "I saw the tea downstairs, so I called out but no one answered." His tone was frustrated. "What on earth are you doing?"

"Well . . ." Ashley glanced around the closet floor and spotted the two pages — one on a pair of her father's shoes, the other in a laundry basket. With a nervous laugh she collected them, folded them, and slipped them back into the envelope. "I was opening the windows and the breeze made the letters in the box rustle a little and —" she laughed again — "next thing I knew I was sitting here looking through Mom's box of letters." Her smile remained. "Anyway . . . I came by because you weren't at church and I was worried."

"Let me see it." Her father took the envelope from her hand, opened it, and pulled out the letter. He seemed put out, frustrated.

Strange, Ashley thought. Okay, so he'd caught her looking at letters in his closet. Still, she would've thought her dad would be more gracious about it. She watched him as he looked over the letter. His expression eased, but there was something new in his eyes. A nervousness, maybe. As if whatever the letter held troubled him.

Suddenly Ashley had the distinct feeling she'd violated something secret or sacred.

Her father folded the letter, slid it back into the envelope, and mixed it into the middle of the letters in the box. Then he lifted the box back onto the shelf and gave Ashley a disapproving look. "The things in there are very special, Ashley. Things only your mother and I have shared."

Guilt hit Ashley hard. She hadn't thought of it that way. "I'm sorry. I guess I didn't think."

His eyes softened, and he pulled Ashley into a hug. "I didn't mean to sound gruff about it." He released her but kept his hands on her shoulders. "I could put together an album, if you'd like. Some of the letters your mother has written over the

years. Maybe it's time to share them with all of you."

She gave him a weak grin. "Just not here on the closet floor?"

"Right." He looked at his watch. "Besides, I need to change clothes for the —"

"Oh." She covered his hands with her own. "That reminds me. Landon's at the fire station with Cole, and he'll be back in a few minutes. Wanna go on a picnic with us?" She gave him a once-over. "You look fine."

"Actually . . ." He began browsing through a stack of lightweight sweatpants. "I already have plans."

Ashley maneuvered around him and backed just outside the closet. "You do?"

"Yes." He pulled a blue pair of sweats from the stack and turned to face her. "I'm going walking with some friends down by Lake Monroe."

Friends? Ashley bristled. "What friends?"

"Some of the friends your mother used to volunteer with at the hospital. You don't know them."

Warning lights flashed in her mind, and Ashley took another step back. "How come you weren't in church this morning?"

"I was." Her father smiled and walked

past her toward his dresser. He looked over his shoulder. "I went to the nine o'clock service."

"You never go that early." Ashley spun around, watching him. She hated the accusation in her voice. But why did she feel like her father was hiding something?

Her father stopped and turned so he could see her straight on. "That's the service your mother's volunteer friends attend." He shrugged. "I thought it'd be nice to sit with them for once."

"Mom's volunteer friends?" Ashley took a few steps closer, but she could do nothing to hide the alarm in her tone. "When did you become chummy with them?"

"Ashley, this is ridiculous." Her father gave a light laugh and turned back to the drawer. He pulled out a pair of white socks and looked at her again. "It's okay if I spend time with people my age once in a while."

His words calmed her, and she felt her shoulders ease back into place. He was right. Maybe she was overreacting a little. Up until a few months ago, he'd done little more than go to work and come home. Her sister Kari had worried that he might never find a life outside that.

She took a quick breath and thought of something. "Elaine Denning isn't part of that group, is she?"

"Elaine?" Her father was sitting on the edge of the bed now, slipping off his black dress socks. "Sure, she's part of it."

"Dad!" Ashley put her hands on her hips and came closer still. "Elaine's a widow." She made the word *widow* sound like an infectious disease. "*She* wasn't at church this morning, was she?"

He pulled one white sock on as his eyes found hers. "Yes, she was. So what, Ashley?" When his second white sock was on, he stood up. "I didn't sit by her, if that's what you want to know. I sat next to Bill and Eddie. For all I know, she's seeing one of them."

A wave of embarrassment washed over her. "Oh. Sorry." She gave him a sheepish smile. "I just . . . you know . . . it's too soon to be . . ."

Compassion filled her father's features. He came to her and brushed his knuckles along her cheek. "I'm not dating anyone, Ash." He looked toward the closet. "Did you see the chair in there?"

"No." Ashley glanced at the spot near the window where her mother's recliner had sat. It was missing. Her eyes found his again. "You put Mom's chair in the walk-in closet?"

"Yes." He stooped down and kissed the end of her nose. "I read my Bible in there every morning, and that's where I sit." He paused. "You know why?"

"Why?" Ashley's voice was thick. She had no idea.

"Because in there, with the clothes she used to wear, it still smells like her. At least in my mind." His voice grew strained. "Sometimes when I can't take missing her another minute, I go in there, sit down, and breathe her in, the smell of her, the memory of her. And I beg God to give me the strength to go on."

Ashley hesitated. Then slowly she embraced her father, burying her face in his chest. Of course her father wasn't dating; the idea was ludicrous. He was still missing Mom as much as they all were. She looked up and hoped he could see the sincerity in her eyes. "I'm sorry." She motioned toward the closet with her head. "Sorry about snooping around too."

"That's okay." He hugged her again. "Why don't you go on out and wait for Landon. Thanks for the offer about the picnic. Maybe next week, all right?"

"All right." Ashley pulled away, and with

a last little wave, she turned and headed down the stairs toward the kitchen. As she passed the living room, she saw the Durango turn into the driveway. Her father probably thought she was crazy, sifting through her mother's personal belongings, sitting on the floor of his closet. And then putting him through an inquisition because he wanted to take a walk at the lake with some friends.

It wasn't like her father had something to hide. What had he said? That he'd be willing to make an album of their mother's old letters, right? That would be perfect, something she could look forward to. And of course he wouldn't be interested in Elaine Denning.

She sighed as she rounded the corner into the kitchen. Good thing she didn't have many plans for the day. She could use a few hours of playing with Landon and Cole in the sunshine.

It wasn't until she spotted the two cold cups of tea on the counter that she was struck by something. Her father was willing to make them an album of their mother's letters, but what about the one she'd been reading when he walked in? She had been right in the middle of it when he called her name. Why hadn't he simply handed it back to her so she could finish it?

When her father did make the album, it would be hard to find that specific letter because he hadn't placed it on top. Rather he had buried it in the middle. Ashley dumped out the tea, grabbed her purse, and looked one last time at the old kettle on the stove.

As she left through the side door and greeted her husband and son, Ashley made a mental note. If the album didn't contain the letter she'd been reading, she'd ask her father for permission to find it. Whatever it said, she had the feeling there was much more to it.

And that she hadn't quite gotten to the good part.

John watched Ashley leave the room, and for the first time in ten minutes he allowed himself a full breath. Of all the letters in that box, how could she have found one of the few that mentioned him — the brother none of the Baxter children knew existed? And what about the other letters on the top shelf of the closet? Had she looked through them?

He stared out the window and felt his heart return to normal. No, she couldn't have looked through them. Ashley was far too outspoken. If she'd come across an envelope with *Firstborn* written across the front of it, she certainly would have asked questions.

The time to do something about the letter was now. Otherwise Ashley would stumble across it some other time, when she was looking for one of her mother's sweaters or putting away laundry. He crossed the room, opened the closet door, and reached up for the manila envelope, the one that contained only three letters — one for him, one for the kids, and one for their firstborn — the son they'd never known.

He took the large envelope and slid it under a stack of folded T-shirts in a bottom cubby near the back of the closet. No one would ever find them there. Then he reached up again and lowered Elizabeth's box of letters down to the floor. He easily found the letter he'd skimmed over earlier.

With greater care than before, he took it from the envelope and opened it. He had no idea how far Ashley had read, but if she'd gotten very far, she would've said so. His written comments about their firstborn son came fairly early on in the letter.

He allowed his eyes to move more slowly this time, savoring every word, every feeling that had been his all those twenty-four years ago.

My dearest Elizabeth,
We have a son! A son we can call our very own! Can you believe it, my love? God is so good, that after all we've been through, after four lovely daughters, He has seen fit to complete our family this way — the way it should've been completed from the beginning.

I am sitting here in our house, anxious for your return, to have you and our son home where you belong. But I can't keep myself from thinking of your words earlier today. You said that seeing Luke made you remember what you felt when you held our firstborn, the child I never met.

Now I understand the pain you must have suffered, the way you still hold on to his memory. Because after seeing Luke, after letting my hands and heart hold him, I can only imagine what it would be like to give him away, how hard it would be to hand him over to a stranger.

John's hands trembled. No matter how many times he thought about it or willed himself to believe it had never happened, it had. Elizabeth had gotten pregnant, her parents had sent her away, and on the saddest day of their lives, she'd been forced to give up the child.

No question Ashley hadn't read most of this letter. Otherwise there would be no more secret to keep. He steadied his fingers and found his place again.

I believe God has given us this boy so that I wouldn't have to wonder any longer what it might've been like to meet our first son. For that, I will be thankful all the days of my life. I'm glad you agree — that we need to put all talk and mention of our firstborn out of our minds as much as possible. We have five beautiful children, Elizabeth. More than I could've asked or imagined. Wherever our firstborn is, he has a family who loves him — we have to believe that.

And so I will close, but please know that as often as I rejoice over this day — the birthday of our little boy — I will take a few minutes and feel your pain: the pain of giving up a child like this one. Thank God that He brought you into my life, Elizabeth. I will cherish you all of my days. I love you.

Forever yours,
John

He stared at the letter a little longer, the pieces of paper Elizabeth had cherished and saved all these years. Then, with a sigh that blended with the afternoon sounds of robins and fluttering leaves, he folded the letter and replaced it in the envelope. For a moment he held it against his heart, a reminder of the man he'd been back then, the life he'd known with Elizabeth when their family was still young.

She'd wanted to meet the boy so badly. In the end it was the only thing she'd prayed for — a chance to hold her firstborn son one more time. Tiny arrows of guilt and regret pierced his heart. Maybe he could've done more to help her find him. Certainly he'd tried harder the first time — ten years earlier — when Elizabeth wanted to locate him. But this time . . . this time he'd been too caught up trying to save her. There hadn't been enough hours to contact private investigators or social workers or any of the people who might've known something about where the boy wound up.

A warm breeze brushed against him and stirred something sad in his soul. Elizabeth's desire to see the boy had been so strong that on the day she died she'd actually convinced herself he'd stopped by, come to her hospital room to see her. What was it she'd said back then?

She'd met their firstborn. His name was Dayne and he was an actor. Something else, something about his parents being dead and him not having siblings. It wasn't until she was a few minutes into her story that she paused and asked if maybe she'd only been dreaming.

That's when John realized what had been happening. The medication had caused her to hallucinate. The person she had talked with must've been Luke, who had sat with her earlier that day. And the mention of Dayne, an actor, must've been Hollywood's very own Dayne Matthews — a client at the New York law firm where Luke worked.

The details must've become jumbled in her final, desperate attempt to believe her prayers had been answered.

It was so sad, really. Their firstborn son was somewhere out there — providing he was still alive — and there was no reason to think otherwise. He would be thirty-six years old now, maybe raising a family in Indiana.

John stared at the contents of the box. Later he'd sort through the letters and pull out anything that even remotely referred to their oldest son. He looked again at the envelope in his hand. For now, he could at least take care of this one. He pulled the manila envelope from the shelf beneath his T-shirts, slipped the letter inside, and hid it once more.

For a fleeting moment he wondered why he was working so hard to hide the truth, anyway. Did it really matter if the kids found out now, if they were faced with the fact that their parents hadn't been perfect? But almost as quickly he remembered having this discussion with Elizabeth a dozen times over the years. He could hear her adamant thoughts on the subject even now.

"We can never tell them, not unless we find him." Her expression would be strained by the seriousness of her statement. "It's enough that we spend a lifetime missing him, wondering about him, without them doing the same thing."

John mulled over her words in light of all that had changed. The kids were old enough now. They wouldn't be devastated or grieve for an older brother the way they might've when they were younger. And it would be easier revealing the truth. That way he wouldn't ever worry about what his kids might find in his closet. But there was one reason he would never tell his children about their oldest brother.

He reached the conclusion in as much time as it took him to set the box of letters back on the closet shelf. The reason was simple: Elizabeth didn't want him to.

And he would protect her wishes as long as he drew breath.

Chapter Fifteen

A series of thunderstorms hit Bloomington Sunday evening, and Katy thought it fitting. Perfect symbolism for her life. She still hadn't connected with Jenny Flanigan, and tensions seemed at an all-time high between them. The CKT cast was off to its slowest start yet, and in twenty-four hours she'd be in Los Angeles, preparing to audition for a part that could change her life.

With so much to think about she didn't want to sit around the Flanigan house. Instead she made dinner plans with Heath Hudson at Sully's Subs, not far from the university.

Katy pulled her car into the parking lot, found a space near the entrance, and put the car in park. What was she doing meeting Heath for dinner? Sharing a meal with him would only lead him on, and what was the point of that? She wasn't interested in him.

She checked her look in the mirror and replayed their conversation in her mind.

"If you're leaving Monday, let me treat you for dinner before you go."

Katy must've looked hesitant, because Heath had chuckled and said, "We need to talk about the sound plans for *Tom Sawyer*, remember?"

He was right, but now as she got out of her car and darted through the door, she wasn't so sure. She took a booth near the front and stared out the window. She was half an hour early, enough time to think over all that was going on in her life.

Still, maybe she should've spent the extra time at home, talking to Jenny, coming clean with her about the trips to California. Only Rhonda knew the reason for her Hollywood visits. But when she mentioned earlier that morning that she'd be leaving for LA, Jim and Jenny had both given her curious looks.

"Two trips so close together?" Jim asked her. The Flanigans had been on their way out the door to church, same as Katy. Jim grinned. "What's going on? You got a secret guy out there?" He was teasing; his eyes danced the way they did when he played with his kids.

She only shook her head and made

something up. "It's research. Nothing more."

As a director for CKT, research was part of the job. Often she needed to fly to a different city to check out a performance by another CKT group. It was up to her to decide which plays CKT performed, what classes would be taught, and what off-season activities they might attempt. Nearly all of her decisions were based on the research she did in other cities.

So the story was believable. But it wasn't truthful, and now, her elbows anchored on the table, that bothered her. It bothered her enough to make her want to head straight home and tell the Flanigans the truth.

If the audition led to a part in the movie, she'd have to tell them, and then what would they think? Even if she didn't get the part, lying wasn't her style. Katy folded her arms and rested them on the table. Her mother had raised her to believe that lying was one of the worst things a person could do.

God, I'm sorry. Lying to the Flanigans, having dinner with Heath when I don't have feelings for him . . . why am I making a mess of everything?

A verse came to mind, one from the

sermon earlier that day. *"You must be holy because I am holy."* It was something Jesus had told His followers, something that had never quite sat right with Katy. How could a person be holy when only God was capable of holiness?

But that morning Pastor Mark had cleared it up. God wanted His people to be holy, not perfect. Holiness for God meant perfection, of course. But holiness for His people meant being set apart. Different.

Katy uttered a sad laugh. Lying to the people she lived with was hardly different. She could tell the Flanigans later tonight, maybe have a little extra time to talk with Jenny about things.

A clock on the wall caught her eye. She was still twenty minutes early. She tapped her fingers on the table and remembered Rhonda. Of course! Inviting Rhonda for dinner would be the perfect solution. That way Heath couldn't possibly mistake it for a date. Rhonda had gone home a few minutes earlier last night, so she'd missed Heath's idea about dinner. But he wouldn't mind if Rhonda joined them.

She flipped out her cell phone and punched in the number. The conversation lasted five minutes, and when it was over, Rhonda promised to come.

Just as she was hanging up, she saw Heath park his car, roll down his window, poke an umbrella through it, and then open the umbrella.

Katy wrinkled her nose. *What's he doing?*

With the open umbrella stuck on the other side of the window, he opened the car door, jumped out, and tried to take a few steps. But the umbrella was too big to fit back through the window, and it caught Heath in his tracks, nearly knocking him off his feet.

A giggle slipped from Katy's lips, and she put her fingers over her mouth. "Come on, Heath," she whispered, "collapse it or push it the rest of the way through and take the handle with your other hand. Something."

For another few seconds, Heath fought with the umbrella, trying valiantly to pull it through the window toward him. When it began bending the wrong way, he stopped and clicked the button on the handle. Once the umbrella was compact again, he finally pulled it through the window. By the time he closed the window, opened the umbrella, and placed it over his head, he was drenched.

"Oh, Heath." Katy exhaled slowly. She

watched him head across the parking lot and into the restaurant. He spotted her right away.

"Hey." He gave her a crooked grin as he took the seat opposite hers. With his head he motioned toward the storm. "That's some wicked rain. Hard to believe that a few hours ago it was bright sunshine."

Water dripped down his face and hung in droplets on his eyebrows and lashes. As goofy as he looked, something about him was endearing.

"Yes." Katy bit her lip so she wouldn't laugh. "And a wicked umbrella."

His expression fell. "You saw?"

"Yeah." She winced. "Next time open the door, not the window."

"Right. Good tip." He shrugged and smiled at her. "You're early."

"Yep." Katy handed him a napkin and pointed at his eyebrows. "You're still dripping."

"Nice." He took the napkin, pursed his lips, and gave a few slow nods. "Just the impression I was trying to make."

She laughed, and the conversation shifted to the progress they were making with *Tom Sawyer*. Katy kept up her end of the conversation, and she found herself enjoying it. Heath told her about a presentation he'd made at a sales conference, a story that was funny and compelling. Outside the world of CKT, without a hundred kids spying on them, she should have had every reason to like Heath Hudson.

Despite the bumbling bit with the umbrella.

Their conversation was light and pleasant, and after a while they ordered. Then Katy remembered Rhonda. "Oh . . . I forgot to tell you —" she took a sip of her water — "I asked Rhonda to join us."

The light in his eyes faded a little. "Okay. Sure."

Katy lowered her chin. After a year of working around Heath, she had only wondered at his feelings. Maybe she should ask now, before things got too far. "Heath?"

"Yeah?" His eyes found hers.

"Was this a date?"

"This?" For a few seconds he looked like he might deny it. But then he lifted his hands and dropped them again. "Okay, yeah. I guess so."

"Heath . . ." Katy reached out and covered his fingers with hers. "I'm so sorry. I didn't know."

"That's okay." He forced a smile. "No big deal. Rhonda's fun too."

Katy slumped slightly. "I'm sorry,

Heath. Really." She hesitated. "But can I tell you something?"

He leaned back and studied her. "I think I can guess."

"Yeah, maybe." She released his hands and sat up a little. "I like being your friend." Her shoulders lifted. "Could that be enough? For now, anyway?"

His eyes softened, and for the first time the strength of his feelings was painfully clear. "That's fine." He looked deep into her eyes. "Can you do me a favor, Katy?"

A warm feeling spread through her heart. The way Heath looked right now, sincere and vulnerable, she could almost imagine feeling something more for him. "Anything."

He held her gaze for a moment. "Could you let me know if you change your mind?"

"Yes, Heath." She allowed the connection she felt with him to last a little longer. "You'll be the first to know."

He looked outside and pointed. "Rhonda's here."

Katy turned and saw her friend jogging toward the front door, a book over her head to keep herself dry. She met Heath's eyes again. "Are we okay?"

A comfortable confidence filled his face,

one that made it clear his heart was no longer exposed. He chuckled low and quiet. "So long as you don't tell Rhonda about the umbrella."

Rhonda approached the table, breathless and damp. "Forecast calls for two inches in the next few hours." She dropped to the spot next to Katy. "Where's the menu? I'm starved."

They ate dinner and discussed the sound setup — which characters would have cordless microphones and which would be positioned near mics hanging from the theater rafters. After a short time, Heath picked up the check and left, explaining that he had errands to run. As he walked away, he gave Katy a last glance, one that lingered a few seconds longer than usual.

When he was gone, Rhonda gave her a pointed look. "What was that all about?"

"What?" Katy picked at the remains of her sandwich.

"Heath. The look there at the end." She raised one eyebrow. "What did I miss?"

Katy laughed. "You never miss anything."

"Exactly." She took a sip of pop. "So tell me."

"It's nothing." A moment passed, but still Katy felt her friend's eyes boring into her. Finally she let out a quiet moan. "Fine. I guess Heath wanted this to be a date."

"I feel stupid." Rhonda leaned back and crossed her arms. "I knew it."

"Knew what? That this was a date?"

"No, that Heath had a thing for you."

"Everyone knows it." Katy pushed her fork around the scoop of coleslaw on the side of her plate. "That's the problem."

"It's not a problem if you're interested."

Now it was Katy's turn to raise her brows. "I'm not." She looked down at her plate. "I told him I just want to be friends."

"I bet that went over well." Rhonda sat still for a moment. "He's not bad, Katy. I think he's kinda cute."

"He is." Katy opened her eyes a little wider. "There you go. Why don't you date him?"

A shadow fell across Rhonda's face. "He doesn't have feelings for me. Anyone can see that."

"How do you know?" Katy's tone wasn't convincing. "What if he's never thought about you like that before?"

"That's not it."

"Okay, but, hey." Katy felt a surge of hope. Maybe this was the answer, Rhonda and Heath. "Never mind him — what about you?"

In all the time they'd known each other, Rhonda had never looked embarrassed. She could walk like a walrus or sing like a chipmunk, turn cartwheels across the stage or wear a purple wig, all in the name of working with the kids at CKT. But at the mention of Heath, Rhonda seemed suddenly shy.

She stared at the straw in her drink. "I told you, I think he's cute."

"Rhonda?" Katy lowered her voice. "You really care about him, don't you? How come you never told me?"

"Katy . . ." Rhonda shook her head and picked at a cold French fry. "The feeling isn't mutual. He doesn't care about me. It's silly to talk about it."

For a while they were both quiet. Katy didn't want to push the issue, but she guessed Rhonda's response had something to do with the way she saw herself. Rhonda was a few pounds heavier than she wanted to be, and her makeup left her skin a little uneven. She wore her blonde hair in a fashionable cut, but she rarely took the time to style it.

Of course, none of that mattered. Rhonda was beautiful; everyone always said so. Maybe Katy could get someone to drop a bug in Heath's ear, let him know Rhonda was interested.

Rhonda broke the silence first. "Sometimes I wonder. . . . You were raised to believe in God, right?"

"Right." Katy blinked. Where was Rhonda headed?

"Weren't you taught that God had a plan for your life, that He wants to give you a hope and a future?"

"Sure. Jeremiah 29:11." Katy dabbed her lips with a napkin. "My mom used to remind me of that verse all the time."

"You know what my mom would do?" Rhonda didn't wait for an answer. "She'd sit down next to me on my bed each night . . . I don't know, from maybe sixth grade on. Then she'd pray with me and almost always she'd pray about my husband."

"The guy you might marry one day?"

"Right." Rhonda folded her hands on the tabletop. "Wherever he was, my mom would ask God to take care of him and raise him up in a good home, believing in the Lord — that sort of thing. Then she'd pray that God would let us meet each other when the time was right."

Katy felt her heart drop. "So where is he; is that it?"

"Yeah." Frustration rang in Rhonda's tone. "I'm ready, you know? I've waited for Mr. Right. I feel like telling God, 'Okay, anytime now.' "

"I know." Katy twirled a section of her hair. "It's supposed to be easier than this."

"Easier . . . sooner . . ." Rhonda tossed her hands. "Anything but this loneliness day after day after day."

Katy was quiet for a minute. "Do you believe it still?"

Rhonda's eyes filled with unshed tears. "Believe what?"

"That God has someone out there for you, that you'll meet him when the time's right?"

"I want to believe it." She sniffed. "What choice do I have? But every day I feel my chances getting smaller." Her voice was calmer than before. "You know what happened the other day? It was seven fifteen and I was leaving my apartment for work, me and about twenty other people. We all wound up squeezed in the elevator at the same time, and somewhere around the third floor the thing stopped, just quit on us." Rhonda looked at her plate. "There was a guy stuck right next to me, shoulder to shoulder. I've seen him a few times before, nice dresser, a little older than me, no wedding ring."

Katy leaned in across the table. "What happened?"

"Okay, so I'm standing there stuck in the elevator. Everyone's complaining and pushing buttons and using the emergency phone to see what's wrong, and half the people are shouting for someone to get the thing moving again. And you know what I was doing?"

Katy shook her head.

"I was breathing in the smell of this guy's cologne, feeling his shoulder against mine, trying to remember the last time I stood that close to a man." She exhaled sadly. "All I could think was, please let it stay stuck like this for an hour."

Katy hung her head for a minute and then looked at Rhonda. "I'm sorry."

"Don't be." She managed a partial laugh. "I mean, think about it, Katy. The closest I've come to a guy in five years is getting stuck in an elevator with one? It's pathetic."

"Well —" Katy gave her a half grin — "did you get his name?"

"Hardly. He was one of the ones trying to get us out, you know, shouting for someone to help us. The elevator started up about a minute later."

"Hmmm." Katy frowned. "Not very promising."

"No." Rhonda drew a long breath. "Anyway, yes. I care about Heath. But I see the way he looks at you, Katy." She took a sip of her water. "I gave up on him a long time ago."

"Heath isn't my type." Katy used her straw to break up the ice in her glass. It was still hard to believe that Rhonda had feelings for Heath. After all this time. "I don't know what my type is."

Rhonda pushed her glass back. Then she leveled a knowing look across the table. Her eyes danced the way they always did when she was teasing. "I think I know."

"What?" Katy smiled. This was why she liked spending time with Rhonda. They could be serious, but they were just as often silly. "You know what type of guy I like?"

"Yeah." She placed her napkin over her plate. "Mysterious guys, guys who drop in on a CKT performance and then disappear, guys who just so happen to be among Hollywood's most famous leading men."

Katy twisted her face. "Dayne Matthews?"

"That's right." Rhonda tapped her chest. "You heard it here first."

"What?" Katy's pulse quickened. She laughed to cover the flustered way she was feeling. "That's crazy, Rhonda. He's a playboy, a movie star. He's the last person on earth I'd fall for."

Rhonda nodded in Katy's direction. "Just remember what I said. You heard it here first."

"I hardly think Dayne Matthews is the sort of guy God would have planned for me." Katy took the bill, stood, and grabbed her purse. "Come on, crazy friend. I have errands to run before tomorrow."

Even after they left in Katy's car and the subject changed to *Tom Sawyer* and the progress the sets committee was making, Katy couldn't get the wild notion out of her head. Dayne Matthews? The idea was insane. The guy had nothing in common with her, and even if he did, he had starlets hanging all over him.

But as Katy dropped off Rhonda at her own car and Katy climbed back into her Nissan, she realized her heart was still beating faster than before. She looked in the rearview mirror and saw something else — her cheeks were red. She held the backs of her hands to her face, doing her best to tone it down.

What was wrong with her? Was her body

betraying secrets even her heart hadn't considered? Did some small part of her agree with Rhonda? That she just might be attracted to Dayne Matthews?

Katy frowned and turned on the radio. Of course she wasn't attracted to him. She would fly to LA, read for the part, and get back home. That was all there was to it. The idea of her and Dayne was laughable, and something more than that.

It was dangerous.

Chapter Sixteen

Chloe was fed up.

She hated the idea of sitting in her Honda all day watching the studio driveway. After all, there was another entrance. Just because Dayne came in through the front didn't mean he'd leave this way. It was hot and stuffy, and the knife in her pocket kept poking her in the ribs.

With any luck, he'd be in and out. An hour or two at the most. Anna had wanted to come along for the ride, but Chloe pulled away before she could grab her shoes. That was the best part about this Tuesday morning. At least she was alone.

She started the day in her usual spot, on the hill overlooking Pacific Coast Highway. It wasn't her favorite place to watch him, but she'd been noticed too often lately. Once outside Ruby's restaurant and once walking around that Kelly Parker's house.

The police had almost figured things out

the first time; at least that's what Anna had told her.

From the hillside, she could see everything she needed to see. Her binoculars worked well, and it was a straight shot down the hill to the place where she could tail Dayne.

She pressed her head against the driver's-side window and stared at the studio entrance. What kind of husband was he, anyway? Living by himself and keeping her locked in her Honda outside the studio? Worst of all, sleeping around with Kelly Parker.

The knife in her pocket pulsed against her rib cage. Kelly Parker wasn't long for this world. Neither was anyone else who messed with her husband. The nerve.

"Go home, you wacko."

Chloe jerked around and looked at the passenger seat. It was empty, nothing there but her binoculars. "Who said that?" She stared out the windshield. "Anna? Are you there?"

"I know what you're thinking." Anna laughed, that same witchy laugh. "You'll wait here for Dayne and follow him to whatever restaurant he'll eat at, and maybe this will be the day he'll claim you as his wife." She laughed again, and the laughter filled the car, seeping into Chloe's mind, filling her head, and pounding through her veins.

"Anna?" Chloe looked on the floorboard beneath her feet and then she remembered. The backseat! She turned all the way around and gasped. Anna was sitting directly behind her. "Have you been there the whole time?"

Her sister sneered. "Don't kid yourself, Chloe. You can't get rid of me." She jerked her thumb toward the studio entrance. "This is stupid, sitting out here. The guy's not your husband."

Anger rose fast and certain, and her heart pounded with the immensity of it. She pointed at Anna. "Don't say another word, you hear? Not another word!"

Anna rolled her eyes and made a zipperlike motion across her lips.

"Good." Chloe liked when this happened, when she got so angry it actually silenced her sister. "Stay that way!"

She looked out the windshield and focused on the studio driveway again. Now the day was definitely shot. Anna would ruin everything. Dayne would never go home with her, never treat her the way a husband should, not while Anna was with her. Dayne had already told her that — although not so much with his words as with the look he gave her that time he saw her parked in his neighbor's driveway.

She had a pretty good idea why Dayne was at the studio today. The magazines said he was trying to find a leading lady for his next movie. Of course, no one would be better to star opposite Dayne Matthews than her. She'd been an extra in three movies so far, and each time she proved herself a better actress.

"I'm right here, Dayne." She rolled down the window halfway and whispered the words into the still summer air. "The woman you're looking for is right here."

"You're delusional, Chloe. You've never acted a day in your life."

Chloe rolled the window back up and gritted her teeth. Anna was going to drive her mad. This time she pulled her knife from her pocket and whirled around in her seat. "I told you to —"

Anna was gone. She wasn't sitting behind her any longer. "Over here, stupid." The voice was harsh and critical.

Chloe jerked back against the car door as she spotted Anna. She was in the seat beside her now. Anna was tricky that way. "I told you to shut up!" Chloe narrowed her eyes and held the knife up near her shoulder, poised, ready to attack if necessary. "I don't want to hurt you, Anna, but I will. I promise I will." Her hand was shaking now, drips of sweat trickling down the sides of her face. "Shut up!"

Anna gave a disgusted look and then turned and faced her window.

Chloe brought the knife down slowly. "That's right — keep looking out the window." She eased the knife back into her pocket. "Don't push me, Anna. I've used this before, you know. No one found out about it then, and no one will this time."

Another drop of sweat fell off her face. What was the problem? Why was it so hot in here? She looked around the perimeter of the car and realized every window was closed. On a summer day she almost had to open the windows. Even if that meant Dayne could hear her beating heart or her murderous threats at Anna.

The windows were the kind you opened by hand, nothing fancy, not for Chloe. Oh, sure, Anna had lived the fancy life once a long time ago. But not Chloe. Her fancy days were ahead of her, once Dayne claimed her as his wife. Then she'd have automatic windows.

She opened her window halfway and barked at Anna to do the same thing. Anna made a grunting sound, but she did what Chloe said. If Anna knew what was good for her, she'd always do what Chloe said. After all, Chloe had the knife.

Cooler air filled the car, and Chloe wiped the moisture off her forehead. That's what she needed. Open windows. She stared at the studio entrance. What had she been thinking about? She waited a beat, and then it came to her.

Dayne's search for a leading lady.

Just then a car pulled into the parking lot, one Chloe would've recognized anywhere. It was a silver Mercedes — Kelly Parker's car. Chloe heard a hissing sound, and for a moment she wondered if she had a leak in one of her tires. She looked at Anna and felt her anger building again. Anna was laughing at her, laughing at the idea of Kelly Parker trying out for the part in Dayne's movie.

"Shut up!"

The hissing stopped.

Chloe leaned her head out the window and yelled, "Not her, Dayne!" He had to hear her. She was so loud she could barely concentrate. "Not Kelly Parker!"

Chloe rattled off a string of expletives. She should've taken care of Kelly while she had the chance. That way Dayne would've asked her to come read for the part — not some floozy phony like Kelly Parker.

Five minutes later the police showed up. As they moved in behind her Honda, Anna came to life again. She turned and faced Chloe, pointing at her and laughing her most evil laugh. "You idiot, now look what you've done."

Chloe's heartbeat skipped around erratically. She couldn't kill Anna, not with the police behind her. With a flick of her wrist she pulled the knife from her pocket and tossed it onto the floorboard. Then she glanced at the rearview mirror and saw there were two officers. Both were getting out of the car.

"Don't say a word, Anna." Chloe spat the words at her sister, and then quickly, before the officers could see, she slapped Anna hard across the face. "Get lost!"

"No." Anna leaned closer. "This is all Kelly Parker's fault. Kill her, not me."

There was the sound of footsteps beside her car door. She turned and smiled at the men. "Hello, Officers. Can I help you?"

One of the men kept his hand on his revolver. The other stepped forward. "Hi." He nodded toward the studio. "We got a call from the studio that someone was parked here. Paparazzi, maybe." He looked around the inside of her car. "You got any cameras?"

"No, sir." *Knives, yes. Cameras, no.* She put her fingers to her chest. "You think the call was about me?"

"Was there a reason why you slapped yourself as we pulled up? A bug maybe?"

"Right." Chloe's mind raced. She hadn't slapped herself. Anna was the one she'd slapped. "Yes, Officer, a mosquito."

"Quite a mark you've got on your face."

"Yes." She laughed. "But no mosquito bite."

The officer stared hard at her. He didn't believe her; that much was written across his face. "Well, ma'am, this is a no-parking area." He crossed his arms. "Why don't you tell me why you're parked here."

"Research." The answer came without warning. Chloe scrambled for a better explanation. "My sister's writing a book about the studio." She tried to look serious. "I'm doing research for her."

He barely paused. "I see. Could I take a look at your driver's license?"

Why were they always wanting that? Chloe thought about grabbing the knife from the floorboard and waving it at the men. That'd make them back off. She looked at the seat beside her.

It was empty. Anna was gone. Typical. She never stayed around for the harder moments.

Finally she gave the officer the sweetest smile she could muster. "I'm afraid I left it at home."

"You know it's against the law to drive without a license?" The man whipped a small pad of paper from his back pocket. "I could haul you in for this, ma'am. Instead, I'll write you a ticket and ask you to leave. If anyone from the studio sees you parked out here again, we'll be back."

The second officer shifted his weight. "We take studio security very seriously. You should tell your sister that any research needs to be done through the studio's publicity office."

Chloe nodded. "I'll do that."

"Okay —" the first officer had his pen poised over the ticket pad — "I need your name."

"Chloe Madden."

The officer nodded. "Date of birth?"

"December 19, 1960."

"Forty-three years old, is that right?"

Forty-three? "Yes, sir."

He walked to the back of her car and scribbled something onto the ticket — her license-plate number probably. The whole time, the second officer stared at her. She could feel him doubting her, doubting everything about her story.

The first officer returned to the window and tore a white slip of paper from the pad. "You have ten days to show proof of a valid license at the courthouse. The address is on the back, along with a phone number." He gave her a concerned look. "Get it taken care of, and get out of here. Understood?"

She gritted her teeth but just for a few seconds. Her smile was back in place almost instantly. "Understood." She gave a nod and a pleasant wave.

The officers returned to their car, but they made no sign of leaving. Chloe groaned. They were waiting for her to go first. She turned the key in the ignition and cursed under her breath. Fine. She would leave, but she'd be back. She'd just have to be more careful next time.

These run-ins with the police had to stop. It was time to do something about all this, time to confront Dayne and order him to come home where he belonged. If anyone tried to stop her — Kelly Parker or some other floozy — Chloe would simply use her knife and do away with her.

She'd used the knife before, without ever

getting caught. She was good at hiding de-tails, very good. A surge of excitement ran through her veins and made her pulse quicken. Using the knife again wouldn't be a problem at all.

It would be a thrill.

Chapter Seventeen

Dayne was standing next to Mitch Henry when Kelly Parker entered the audition area.

The room was oversized, with a warehouse feel — a typical studio soundstage. Half of it was dimly lit, and the other half was raised a few feet, flooded with lights that hung from the black rafters at every angle. The lit area had been set up to look like a sidewalk that led to a few steps, a small porch, and a faux door — meant to duplicate the entry to the female lead's Manhattan apartment.

The point of the scene was to show on-screen chemistry between Dayne and whoever starred opposite him in *Dream On.*

"Okay, Kelly, thanks for coming." Mitch looked up from his clipboard. "You understand what's happening in the scene?"

"The male lead's walking me home at the end of my first week on the job. We come to my apartment door, where we tease and flirt some, and he kisses me." She looked at Dayne, and her eyes spoke volumes. "For a minute I'm tempted to ask him inside, but then I catch myself and remember who I am, my upbringing."

"Very good." Mitch looked impressed. "You've done your homework."

"Of course."

Dayne kept his eyes on her. She was striking, no question. A little too thin, but striking. In her dark jeans and tight white T-shirt she oozed sex appeal. He could feel himself responding to her, and they hadn't even started the scene yet. It was easy to see why the camera loved her, why she'd become such a hot property in Hollywood.

But none of that mattered.

All he could think about was Katy Hart and the fact that he'd see her again in less than an hour. It wasn't fair to Kelly, really. But she'd asked for the audition. He'd only agreed because of their friendship. That and the remote possibility that Katy might not work out, or worse, that she would refuse the part for some reason.

"All right, let's get started." Mitch clapped twice. "Dayne and Kelly, take your spots."

"You want us starting stage left, walking

a few steps, and then up the stairs to the porch, right?" Kelly pointed to the far side of the stage.

"Exactly." Mitch walked alongside Dayne and took his spot near the cameraman. "Let's see what you've got, Kelly."

"Dayne already knows what I've got." She looked over her shoulder, her brow raised.

"Yes." Mitch shot a disapproving look at Dayne. "I'm sure he does."

Dayne ignored the comment. He caught up with Kelly, slipped his hand in hers, and leaned close. "Enough, okay? Mitch is looking for innocent country girl, not sexy siren."

She leveled her famous eyes at him. "I can do innocent." She smiled. "Just watch me."

They weren't quite to the stage yet. "You doing okay? The paparazzi?"

Her eyes darkened. "I'm trying my best. I haven't read a gossip rag since we talked last."

"Good." He took the few steps up to the stage and led her to a place next to him. "You know the lines?"

"Dayne . . . do you have to ask?"

They ran through the scene without missing a beat. Kelly was right — she knew her lines and tried her best to be convincing at the whole innocent thing. When it came time for the kiss, Dayne slid his hand up along the side of her face and put his lips to hers. She responded in a way that was as natural as breathing.

Chemistry wasn't a problem when it came to Kelly Parker.

The scene was finished in less than five minutes, and from the shadows Mitch yelled, "Okay, that'll do it."

Dayne still had his arm around Kelly's waist, and he pulled her close, his lips inches from hers. She smelled of something spicy and exotic, and for a moment he forgot where he was or that Katy Hart would be there in half an hour. "You're good, girl."

"Thank you, sir." She brushed his lips with hers. "You too."

Mitch coughed. "Like I said, that'll do."

Dayne squeezed Kelly's waist once more. "Thanks for coming."

"I want the part, Dayne."

"I know." Images of Katy flashed in his mind. "We'll see what happens."

They held hands as they left the stage and headed for Mitch. He met them halfway and smiled big at Kelly. "That was fantastic. We'll get back to you as soon as we know something."

She thanked him, and Dayne walked her to the studio door. Before she left she looked into his eyes. "Come by tonight?"

"Not tonight." He kissed her forehead and hugged her. "I have plans." He didn't, but he hoped he would. Never mind his first thought that he and Katy shouldn't be seen together. Katy didn't know anyone else. The paparazzi wouldn't bother them, not if they were in her rental car.

"So . . ." Kelly looked around the dark edges of the room. "Is Miss Newcomer here yet?"

Dayne chuckled. "No. Not for a while."

"Too bad." She stepped back and pouted. "I wanted to see my competition."

It wasn't until Kelly said good-bye one more time and took off across the studio lot that Dayne thought twice about her comment. She must've meant competition for the part. But the way she'd looked at him made him wonder. Was he really that transparent? Could she tell that he'd been in a hurry all morning to get through her audition and move on to Katy's? that he'd been looking forward to seeing her again since the moment she'd left?

If so, then he needed to be careful. Otherwise it would be obvious to Katy too.

She wouldn't be impressed that Dayne Matthews couldn't stop thinking about her. He had the feeling she didn't care much for Hollywood or glamour or any of the trappings of his life.

It was why she had stopped going to auditions; at least that was the way he read it. No, Katy Hart wouldn't be excited if she knew what he was feeling for her.

She'd probably run for her life.

Katy didn't know about the kiss until she arrived at the studio.

She should've expected it; the movie was a love story, and the entire point of coming back for a second audition with Dayne was obviously to see how they related to each other on camera. But when Mitch led her to a small room and told her she had fifteen minutes to study the scene, he said nothing about the kiss.

It wasn't until she read through it and got to the end that she realized what was about to happen. In front of Mitch Henry, a cameraman, and whichever other executives from the studio happened to be around, she was about to do an onstage kissing scene with Dayne Matthews.

Rhonda's comment from two days earlier came back again: *"You heard it here first."* Katy dismissed the idea, put it far from her mind. She had lines to memorize. The audition was just that — a chance to act in a movie. Something Katy had dreamed of doing all those years through high school and college, and now she had the chance.

Alone in her hotel room last night, she'd prayed about the opportunity. If it was from God, a way to get into acting long after the loss of Tad Thompson, then she asked Him to give her the part. But if not, if this would take her away from the kids at CKT forever or if it would change her somehow, then she asked for something else.

That God would get her out of Hollywood on the first airplane.

Time and again as she prayed about this day, this moment, she'd asked God for wisdom. And always she felt the same answer: *Wait. Be patient and wait on the Lord.* That was fine with Katy. It meant she didn't have to have all the answers today. She could do the audition, see if they offered her the part, and then talk it over with Rhonda and the Flanigans, who had been out Sunday night so she had no chance to tell the truth about her flights to California.

Wisdom would come one way or another.

She focused on the lines before her. There weren't many, really. Some casual banter about work while they walked toward her front door, then a few awkward lines on the step, and finally his move to kiss her. Her response was supposed to be surprised and then taken. So taken that she considered inviting him in before remembering who she was and what she stood for. The small-town values she was raised with.

Katy had the lines memorized in five minutes. The rest of the time, she pictured the character, the way she might feel — overwhelmed in the big city, walking alongside a handsome colleague, feeling a chemistry with him. If it were her, she'd feel shy and excited and nervous all at the same time.

She checked her look as best she could without a mirror. She had on black dress pants, a fitted tan blouse, and low black heels. She wore her long blonde hair in a simple ponytail. She went over the lines once more, and then Mitch knocked on the door. "We're ready for you, Katy." He gave her a kind smile. "Do you need more time?"

"No, sir." Her heart skipped a beat. This

was it; she was really about to audition with Dayne for the female lead in a film that was bigger than anything she'd ever done or read for. She drew a deep breath and stood up. "I'm ready."

They walked together to the soundstage. With each step Katy reminded herself to breathe, to be calm and feel relaxed and not make more out of the audition than it was. She was an actress — at least she used to be. Auditions had once been commonplace for her.

But all those thoughts fled when she walked through the door and saw Dayne. He was sitting in a chair, one leg crossed over the other, reading something. The script, maybe. He had a pencil tucked behind his ear, and for the first time she didn't see him as a famous actor.

She saw him as a friend, someone she was familiar with.

The moment they walked in, he took the pencil and stack of papers and set them on a nearby table. Then he came to meet them. "Katy." He held out his hand and shook hers. "Thanks for coming. I know all this travel's been sort of hectic for you."

"No, it's fine." Her cheeks felt hot, and she was glad for the shadows. "Thanks for asking me."

Dayne slipped his hands in his pockets, and he looked ten years younger than he was. "Did you get the script?"

"Yes." A light laugh came from her. "I think I've got it. I'm a little nervous."

He touched her shoulder and smiled. "Don't be. You'll do great."

Mitch was talking to another man, and at that moment he turned and approached them. "Let's do it."

Every confident thought Katy had comforted herself with vanished. She was crazy to be here, crazy to think she had the right to read for a major role opposite Dayne Matthews. And even more crazy to think she'd want it. Especially after what had happened with Tad. She didn't belong in this world, didn't have what it took to —

"Katy?" Dayne reached out and took her hand. "Come on. We start stage left."

And just like that the thrill was back again. She wanted this part as badly as she'd ever wanted a part in all her life. Her mind found the place it had created back in the small room, and in a matter of seconds she wasn't only acting the part of the lead character.

She *was* the part.

Dayne's hand in hers felt comfortable and right, the way it would feel if she'd struck up a friendship with him at work and could sense herself falling for him. The surroundings were no longer a hollow soundstage but a New York City street, the air cold around her face.

She breathed it in, and when Mitch shouted, "Okay, action!" the scene was vividly real to her.

"You still glad you came to New York?" Dayne kept his pace slow, comfortable, as they set out on the walkway toward the porch.

"I guess." She looked up at him, and she could feel the city lights reflecting in her eyes. "It's busier than I thought it'd be. Faster."

Dayne chuckled. "Yes." He found her eyes again. "It's definitely fast."

"I don't know." She looked up, and the imaginary buildings towered over her. "I've dreamed of working in the city all my life, but somehow . . ." She shrugged. "I miss my little town, my family."

They headed up the steps, and Dayne let her take the lead. When she was on the porch and he was on the final step, she stopped and looked at him.

"I bet they miss you too." He paused. "I would."

She looked down and then back at him,

her eyes big. "How come you're so nice to me? You're supposed to be my competition, right? Isn't that how we big-time reporters play the game?"

According to the script Mitch had given her, Dayne's character did indeed have motives. He wanted to steal her sources on what he thought was the biggest story of the year. But at this point in the film, against his better judgment, he was starting to fall for her. A flash of guilt passed over his face. "You're easy to be nice to." He stepped up onto the porch beside her. "I'm not sure if I could ever compete with you."

For a moment she searched his eyes, her feelings shifting from coy and grateful to embarrassed. "Well . . . I should probably —"

"I guess I should —"

Their words came out at the same time, just the way the script called for them to. They both laughed, and as the moment faded, Dayne brought his fingers to the side of her face and worked them into her hair. With gentle ease, he removed the rubber band from her ponytail and let her hair fall down around her face and shoulders. "You're beautiful."

Katy stayed in character. What was he

doing? The hair thing wasn't in the script. Not the part about being beautiful either. She swallowed. "I don't know if . . ." Her words died in a breathy blur.

With that, he drew her close and kissed her. His kiss was warm and full, and it swept her away on a wave of emotion and awakening passion. Just the way the script called for. She pulled away, and she could feel the desire in her eyes. "I . . ." She put her hand on the door. "I need to get inside."

His eyes were filled with questions. "Right now?"

This time she brought her lips to his, and he worked his free hand around her waist. The kiss lasted longer than the first one, and Katy knew there was no mistaking the fact that she wanted him to come inside with her. But as she drew back, she remembered who she was and what she was doing. She ran the back of her hand over her mouth and felt her expression change. "I have to go. I'm sorry." And with that she turned and pushed the door open.

"Cut." Mitch Henry sounded happy. "We've got it."

Only then did Katy allow the imaginary world she'd created to fade away. Dayne still had his arm on her waist, and she faced him again. "Well?"

His eyes grew wide. "Katy . . ." He backed up, letting her go. "You were amazing. Wow."

"Really?" She wanted to ask him about the hair thing, but she didn't dare. It was probably only his way of ad-libbing.

Mitch approached them and waved them off the stage. "Very nice, Katy. I'm impressed."

She followed Dayne down the porch steps, then the stage stairs to join Mitch. "Thank you."

"Hey . . ." He shot Dayne a suspicious look. "You sure you've never dated her? That was pretty convincing."

Dayne laughed. "I barely know her." He looked at her. "But it felt pretty convincing."

"Yeah." Katy lowered her gaze and then met Dayne's eyes. "It did, didn't it?"

"You should see what the camera caught." Mitch led them back to the monitor. He directed his attention to the cameraman. "Run it again, will you?"

The man hit a few buttons; then the monitor sprang to life. Katy and Dayne stood side by side, so close she could smell his shampoo, feel the heat from his arm.

Now that the scene was over, the nervousness she'd felt before was gone.

As the action played out on the monitor, she was stunned. She and Dayne looked like they'd been friends forever, walking along the city street, holding hands. And on the stoop, their feelings came across onscreen loud and clear — especially when they kissed.

When it was over, Mitch grinned. "I like it."

"Me too." Dayne gave her a light bump with his shoulder. "You're very good, Katy."

"Thanks." She smiled, and she felt like the character again. "You too."

"Why don't you go with one of the pages, get yourself something to drink." Dayne pointed to a young woman standing near the studio door. "Mitch and I have to talk for a few minutes."

They had to talk? Katy covered up a gulp. This was it, the moment that would make all the difference. There had to be other people reading for the part, and casting directors rarely shared their true feelings at an audition. Mitch Henry's response didn't mean the role was hers. She nodded and gave Dayne a quick look. "I'll be across the hall, I guess."

"I'll meet you over there." Dayne waved and then turned to talk with the casting director.

Katy walked across the floor, and only when she reached the woman at the door did she realize that she hadn't felt a single step. She was floating, happy for more reasons than she could count. The audition was behind her, for one thing, and she'd done the best job she was capable of doing. Not a single mess up.

Then there was her prayer from the night before. She'd asked God to show her if she didn't belong here, and so far He seemed to be flinging doors wide open. But maybe the best part of all was that no one had to wonder if she and Dayne had a connection on camera. Because if the raw footage she'd just seen was any indication, they didn't only have a connection.

They had electricity.

Chapter Eighteen

Katy wasn't even to the door when Dayne turned around and whispered to Mitch Henry, "I want her. She's perfect."

"Hold on." Mitch pulled up a chair and nodded for Dayne to do the same. When they were both seated, Mitch leaned forward. "I'm worried about her."

"Worried?" Dayne raked his fingers through his hair and looked around the soundstage, searching for a reason. "Did you watch the tape? The girl's exactly what we need. Fresh, new, with a look that defines innocent, and you know why?"

"I do." Mitch kept his voice calm. He gave Dayne a knowing look. "Because she is innocent. I get that, Dayne. She's pretty and fresh and she can act. No question the two of you have something on-screen." His enthusiasm fell even further. "But maybe you haven't thought about something else."

"What?" Dayne lifted his hands in the air. "What haven't I thought about?"

"If she's as innocent as she looks, then this might not be the life for her — a starring role in a major motion picture. Ever think about that?"

Dayne waved off the comment. "That's ridiculous. It's one film, Mitch. One lousy film. After that she can go back to her kids theater if she wants to. One film isn't going to change her life. Not forever, anyway."

For a moment, Mitch only stared at him. Then he chuckled in a sad sort of way. "Don't you remember, Dayne? One film changed *your* life. You starred in *Mountain High* and it was all over. The offers were too many to count." He laughed again. "It only takes one film."

Dayne pursed his lips and stared at his shoes. Mitch was right, and he hated the fact. Still determined, he pressed on. "She came here, didn't she? Maybe she doesn't care if her life changes."

Mitch shook his head. "She's an unknown, Dayne. I'm okay with that on a lot of levels, but when it comes to depending on her for a megamillion-dollar film . . . I don't know if we can do it." He paused. "Kelly Parker was fantastic too."

The conversation was over. Dayne stood

and patted Mitch's knee. "I want her. Give me a day with her. I'll get a feel for how badly she wants it, and then I'll offer her the part. If she runs, we'll know it soon enough." He hesitated. "Okay with you?"

Mitch rubbed the back of his neck and then sighed. "All right. Go ahead." He held up a finger. "Don't push her, Matthews. Kelly would handle it just fine."

Dayne felt a surge of excitement. He had the green light. Now all he had to do was convince Katy. Though he might be able to do that in a five-minute conversation, he wanted to take his time, get to know her better. Her plane didn't leave for a couple of days, and she had nothing else on her agenda as far as he knew.

He found her at a break table sipping on a bottle of water. "Hey."

"Hi." Questions filled her eyes. "Well . . . what's the verdict?"

Her eyes were so blue, so pure. He tried to remember where he'd seen eyes like that before, eyes full of light and love and goodness. Then it hit him. Luke Baxter's eyes had been like that, hadn't they? Luke's and Elizabeth's, both. He grinned, regaining his focus. "Let's not talk about verdicts."

"No?" Her expression fell. "Does that mean I take an earlier flight home?"

They'd planned for her to stay through Thursday afternoon in case the director wanted her to take a harder look at the entire script and to give them enough time if they wanted to offer her a contract. He uttered an easy laugh. "No, Miss Katy. There'll be no earlier flight, not today."

Her eyes were big, bewildered. "So, then . . . what's next?"

"Next . . ." He reached for her hand and helped her to her feet. When she was standing, he let her hand go. "You and I find a place for lunch so we can talk."

She twisted her face into a cute frown. "About the movie?"

"About the movie." He wanted to ask her if she knew how adorable she looked. But he kept his thoughts to himself. He would move slowly today, keeping things casual and professional. Whatever else he was feeling would have to wait for another day. Maybe forever. Either way, he wanted her in his movie. He grinned. "Okay with you?"

"Okay. You sure you've got the time?"

"I've got all the time in the world." He thought for a minute. "You've got a rental car, right?"

"Right." She looked curious again.

"Let's take your car." He made a face. "I

don't want anyone getting pictures of you. Not yet, anyway."

Understanding dawned in her eyes. "Paparazzi?"

"Carloads of them."

Katy let Dayne drive, and from the moment they left the studio, the day felt like something from a movie. The sun was high in the sky as they drove toward Santa Monica Boulevard and eventually to Pacific Coast Highway.

"Ever been to Malibu Beach?"

"No. Is it beautiful?" She shifted so she could see him better.

"Not really." He laughed. "Not compared to some of the island beaches I've been to." He shrugged. "But it's nice enough."

"Is that where we're going?"

"Not first." He grinned at her. "First I take you through the infamous KFC drive-thru."

"Really? Wow, I never would've guessed." She felt her eyes dancing. Here she was, driving down Pacific Coast Highway with Dayne Matthews, and nothing could've felt more normal in all the world. He was funny and self-deprecating, calling himself overrated and laughing at his success on more than one occasion.

They ordered a bucket of chicken and mashed potatoes at the drive-thru, and when they pulled up to the window, Dayne kept his face toward Katy. He did the same thing when he collected their meal at the next window, engaging her in conversation until the last moment when the girl at the window had the food in her hands.

"Thanks." He took it from her and immediately turned and handed it over to Katy.

"Hey, wait . . . aren't you — ?"

Dayne was gone before she could finish her sentence. He shrugged in Katy's direction. "Silly kids. They think just because they work in Malibu there're movie stars around every corner."

"Yeah." She laughed and allowed herself to relax a little more. "Silly kids."

They drove another few minutes, and then Dayne made a right turn, away from the water.

"I thought we were going to the beach." Katy looked around. He was taking her into what looked like a college campus.

"Something tells me the beach'll be too crowded."

She was about to disagree. It wasn't

quite noon on a weekday. But then she remembered the scene at the drive-thru. Was he taking her somewhere else so he wouldn't be recognized? It was a sobering thought, how hard he had to work — every day of his life — just to keep from being hounded by fans and photographers.

It was something she understood but hadn't really considered.

They headed up a narrow, neatly manicured hill, past a guard station. "What is this place?"

"Pepperdine University." He leaned close to the steering wheel and stared up the hillside. "It's beautiful, isn't it?"

"Yes." She peered out his window at the ocean in the distance. The higher they climbed, the more breathtaking the view became. "I've heard of this place. One of my friends in high school came here."

They turned left into a parking lot, found a space to park, and carried their lunch down a pathway toward an endless grassy hillside. The area was deserted, and Dayne kept his pace slow and easy. "It's always empty like this." He squinted across the field toward the water. "All this grass and the view, and the students are too busy taking classes to get down here and enjoy it."

"It feels so private."

"That's the best part of all." He led her to one end of a bench; then he sat at the other end and put their food between them. When they'd each taken a plate and served themselves, Dayne stretched out his legs. "So, Katy Hart, tell me about your job in Bloomington."

The question caught her off guard. She'd expected something about the film or the expectations he and Mitch Henry would have for her if they offered her the part. She wondered if he was genuinely interested or if this was part of a casual interview. She held her plate with both hands and watched a pair of geese waddle past them toward a small pond. "I guess you know the name of the group. Christian Kids Theater. We go by CKT."

"Right." He looked up, concentration written into his features. "Theater by kids, for kids, if I remember."

"That's it." She smiled. "We're doing *Tom Sawyer*; I think I told you."

"Ah yes." He took a swig of his Diet Coke. "I was invited to help paint sets."

She laughed. "Exactly." She took a long, slow breath. "I love everything about CKT." Her eyes settled on the blue sky overhead. "The kids, the shows, the parents. It's a ton of work, but to sit in that theater and watch a production come to life, one that you helped create . . ." She looked at him. "There's nothing more satisfying."

He studied her for a moment. "Then why are you here?"

"For the audition?"

"Right." There was no judgment in his eyes. "If it's so fulfilling, why didn't you tell me no?"

"Because . . ." She wasn't sure how much to tell him. But the combination of the warm ocean breeze and the solitude around them made her more willing to talk. "Because a long time ago I wanted this — your world — more than anything in all my life." She smiled. "You know about my pilot."

"And I know you quit going to auditions shortly after." Dayne searched her eyes. "What happened?"

A wave of emotion hit her without warning. She looked down at the dirt path beneath their feet. "It's a long story." When her voice didn't feel quite so thick, she tried to sum it up. "Let's just say I grew disillusioned."

"With the business?"

"With the lifestyle. The nightlife, I guess."

Dayne gave a slow nod. "Yes, that's the rap we get. Wild and crazy partiers, all of us." He leaned his head back and released a low moan. When he looked at her again, there was a pleading in his eyes. "Don't believe everything you hear, Katy." His expression was suddenly serious. "Yes, it's a problem for some people. Too much fame and money, drugs become easily available. But most of us stay away from that stuff."

She didn't know him well enough to call him on his statement, but a few times she'd read one of the Hollywood magazines, and almost always they would catch Dayne at some nightclub or dance place. "You don't do the nightlife game?"

"Once in a while." He set his plate down between them, gripped the edge of the bench, and leaned back, his shoulder muscles bunched up around the base of his neck. "I go out with a few friends, have a couple drinks, and the magazines call me a wild playboy." He cocked his head and found her eyes again. "Most of the time, I spend the night at home watching movies by myself."

Katy studied him. He looked honest, and she had no reason to doubt him. The fact was incredible to her. Dayne Matthews, Hollywood's hunk, sitting home alone watching movies? It was the last thing she expected him to say. It made her like him more, made him easier to connect with.

And it did something else. It shook her view of the Hollywood life.

"So . . ." Dayne interrupted her thoughts. "You didn't stop auditioning because you were afraid of the attention, the fame?"

Katy took her time. "No, I guess not. Something . . . something happened to a friend of mine, but it wasn't the fame that caused the problem. At least not directly."

Dayne waited, and Katy had the feeling he wanted her to tell him the details. But she wasn't ready. She still barely knew him, and the story about Tad was something she hadn't shared with anyone since leaving Chicago. She took a bite of chicken and held her piece up. "It's good. You should try it."

He relaxed his shoulders and picked up his plate again. They ate in a comfortable silence, talking only once in a while about the pretty campus and the wonderfully sunny afternoon and the geese.

"They're actually attack geese." Dayne finished up his mashed potatoes and wiped his mouth with a napkin. He pointed behind them to the pond. "Really. Look."

Katy glanced over her shoulder at a cluster of geese. They were swimming toward the shoreline, climbing out of the water, and heading in a line straight toward them. She let out a light scream and slid toward him a few inches. "Are you serious?"

"Yes —" he reached into the bag and brought out two biscuits — "but that's why we have these." He stood and met the geese head-on. Then he broke the biscuits apart and tossed them ten yards in the other direction. The geese attacked the food, pushing and pecking at each other to get to the big pieces.

"There you go." He dusted off his hands and sat back down beside her. "Once they know the food's gone, they'll leave us alone."

"Good." She shuddered a little. "Keep an eye on them, will you? I'd hate to be attacked by a Pepperdine goose."

Dayne laughed. "I don't think they have teeth."

Their laughter mingled, and for a while neither of them said anything. Then Dayne gave her a thoughtful look. "So, where were we?"

She smiled. "The past, you mean?"

"Mmm-hmm. What are your dreams,

Katy? What makes you tick?"

Her stomach felt suddenly queasy. She couldn't share that either, not exactly. She pursed her lips and thought of an answer that would work. "The tick part's the easiest. I'm a Christian; have I told you that?"

"I figured." He made a funny face, as if he were calculating something. "Let's see, *Christian* Kids Theater?" He grinned. "Yeah, I had a feeling."

"I guess." She laughed, and the feel of it made her heart soar. All the tensions of the play and Heath Hudson and the parent committees felt like they belonged to someone else. She looked at Dayne again. "Anyway, my faith's what drives me. God and I are sort of best friends, I guess."

Something changed in Dayne's expression, but it was too subtle to read. Whatever caused it, Katy had the feeling faith or maybe Christianity had hurt him somehow. He stroked his chin, a smile tugging at his lips. "Okay, so what does your faith say about coming to Hollywood and auditioning for a part in a big film?"

"I've prayed about it." In the distance she saw a couple walk out onto the grassy bluff and sit down. If it was strange before — having lunch with Dayne Matthews on a hillside overlooking Malibu Beach —

now that they'd ventured into her faith, it was downright surreal. She lifted her hands a few inches and let them fall on her knees again. "I've asked God to make it clear. He can either shut the door or open it. I don't want it unless He wants it for me."

"Okay." His smile grew. "Well, then maybe this'll be a sign."

"What?" A pair of noisy seagulls flew overhead and out toward sea. "What sign?"

"Well, to start with, the scene turned out pretty nice. I mean, the chemistry and all." Dayne grinned, and for the first time she had the feeling he was flirting with her. Then, though his eyes were shining, he grew more serious. "The part's yours, Katy. Mitch and I both want you to take it."

"What?" Her head was spinning, her heart racing. She had no idea what to say, no sense of whether it was even really happening or not. He was waiting for her response; she could feel it. But the words wouldn't come. He was offering her the part! It was hers! And suddenly she did the only thing she could do, the thing that felt most bizarre and most natural at the same time: She shouted and threw her arms around Dayne's neck.

Wait until she told Rhonda! And the Flanigans and the other CKT families! They would be happy for her, wouldn't they? If she took the part it would only be one film, one brief commitment. She could return to CKT if she wanted to. But as she hugged Dayne and he hugged her in return, another thought occurred to her. One that was even stronger than every other unbelievable thing that had happened since she arrived at the studio this morning.

If the way she felt now was any indication, she might never go back at all.

Chloe was fuming.

Whoever the new girl was, neither Chloe nor Anna had seen her before. Some sweet-faced blonde with a cute smile. Another floozy, for sure, even if she didn't look like one. Chloe's binoculars let her capture every detail of the little picnic lunch between Dayne and the girl. She was parked just a few spots down from the girl's car. And it had to be hers, because Dayne had never driven a sedan once in the three months they'd been together.

Married, not together.

She would've missed him, but once she returned to her place on the hill overlooking the studio, she decided to check every car that came and went. That way she could see the women vying for a part that should've been Chloe's alone. She hadn't noticed the blonde enter the studio lot, but when the silver four-door sedan pulled out of the parking area, Dayne was driving and the blonde was seated beside him.

The hussy.

Hers wasn't a face Chloe recognized. Probably someone new. And that meant she'd only just met Dayne, but already she was willing to head off with him. Maybe even go home with him.

She felt the knife, ran her finger along the sharpened blade. It wasn't in her pocket anymore. Not when she might need to use it anytime now.

Something wet was on her finger, and she looked down. She was bleeding. The knife must've cut her when she was feeling the blade. She chuckled to herself. Good thing it was sharp. She might get only one chance at a girl like Kelly Parker.

Or the blonde floozy down the hill on the bench.

She'd already made up her mind, and she'd ordered Anna to keep quiet or else. The competition was too stiff, too aggressive. If Dayne was ever going to take his rightful place beside her and live with her as her husband, she had to get rid of the competition.

A golf cart turned into the parking lot, and Chloe studied it. She swore. Security guard, of course. Bring out a pair of binoculars and everyone thought you were a weirdo. Fine. She looked one last time at Dayne and the blonde.

Then she tossed the knife and the binoculars onto the seat beside her and started the engine. She wouldn't get the job done here, in broad daylight on a public campus. But she would get the job done. Once and for all.

The golf cart was approaching. She backed her car up, turned it the opposite direction, and squealed away. The blonde better enjoy her lunch, because if she continued seeing Dayne Matthews, she didn't have many meals left.

Chapter Nineteen

Katy called Rhonda first, but she didn't get the reaction she was looking for.

"That's fantastic, Katy. Really." A hint of sorrow colored her tone. "You're going to take it, right?"

"Rhonda, you're supposed to scream or throw the phone or do a dance. Dayne Matthews wants me to star in a film with him!" Katy squealed. "Can you believe it?"

"I know. That's great." Rhonda hesitated. "Will you move to LA, then?"

"No . . . of course not." Suddenly Rhonda's hesitancy was understandable. She thought she was losing a friend. And there was a possibility of that, wasn't there? If the feelings she'd had at Pepperdine were any indication. She kept her thoughts to herself. "I'll be gone six weeks at the most. You can direct the next show for me, and then I'll be back and everything'll be just like it's been."

"Okay, Katy." Rhonda didn't sound convinced. "If you think so. But, hey, whatever. I'm happy for you. Everyone's going to be thrilled when they find out."

"You didn't tell anyone, did you?"

"Of course not." Indignation rang in Rhonda's voice. "You asked me not to."

"I know." Katy felt bad for bringing it up. "I was just checking."

The conversation stalled after that, and Katy brought it to an end.

Now she paced in her hotel room, a deluxe suite on the eighteenth floor of the Sheraton Universal, wondering who she could tell. Her parents didn't even know she'd gone on the first audition, so she'd have a lot of explaining to do. Besides, it was eleven o'clock in Chicago. She'd have to wait and tell them when she had more time.

She sat on the edge of the bed. The day had been amazing, something from a dream. After lunch, Dayne had taken her for a drive along the beach and then back to the studio. They looked over the first half of the script and picked up dinner at the commissary. Just after seven o'clock, they went their separate ways, and now she had so much nervous energy she could've flown around the room.

Instead she stood and kept pacing.

Her feelings were a jumbled knot, and she wasn't sure where to start unraveling them. Every few minutes she'd catch herself reliving the movie scene — the leisurely walk, hand in hand, his kisses. Always she would stop and chide herself. It was acting, nothing more. Dayne was a professional, and that meant a romantic scene now and then.

She went to the window, opened her blinds, and looked down at the millions of lights. That was okay, right? Performing romantic scenes as an actress, so long as it was fairly low-key?

God, help me know what to do. She allowed herself to be mesmerized by the stream of traffic below on Hollywood Drive. *It's okay, right? What I did today?*

Daughter . . . above all else, guard your heart.

Guard her heart? The words felt so clear she was tempted to look up at the ceiling and see if there was a hidden microphone somewhere. First the reminder about holiness and now this. Guard her heart.

Well, she was guarding it. She wasn't falling for Dayne, at least. Yes, he was attractive and fun to be with. But he wasn't someone she'd fall for, not when faith was everything to her.

"God," she whispered against the cool pane of tinted glass, "is that You?"

Daughter, guard your heart.

A chill ran down both her arms. Once in a while, she was absolutely sure she heard the voice of God respond to her. Not in audible words the way it first seemed and certainly not in a booming tone. But in the quiet recesses of her soul, where she had to be very still to hear Him.

This was one of those times.

If God wanted her to guard her heart, then that meant He wanted her to be careful. But He wasn't shutting the door on the idea of kissing Dayne for a movie scene, was He? And He especially wasn't shutting the door on the idea of her taking the part, right? She gripped the windowsill and stared up. The stars weren't visible, not in contrast to the city lights. Still, she imagined seeing them, the way they looked in Bloomington.

God, I still mean what I said the other day. I don't want this if You don't want it for me. If it would change me or make my life worse or farther from You, please . . . shut the door on it. Show me Your will, Father. That's all I want.

Her cell phone rang just as she finished. She flipped it open. "Hello?"

"Hi. It's Rhonda." Her friend sounded sheepish. "I'm sorry. When you called, I don't know, all I could think about was that everything would be different now." Sorrow and a little fear filled her tone. "You're my best friend, Katy. I don't want to lose you; that's all." She sighed. "Still, I should've acted more excited. Forgive me?"

"Of course." Katy sat on the edge of her bed again. "I understand. It is scary. Who knows where this will go or whether I'll even take the part, but I feel the same thing. Like everything's about to change. And that's not always good. Especially if you like your life pretty well the way it's been going."

"Exactly." Rhonda gave a sad-sounding laugh. "I knew you'd understand. You always do."

Katy smiled. "Thanks for calling. I wasn't mad."

"Well, I'm sorry. I couldn't go to sleep until I told you that."

"You're a good friend, Rhonda." Katy leaned back on the pillow. She pictured Dayne, the way she'd felt when he told her the news. Then just as quickly she pictured her life in Bloomington. "Don't worry; I'm not going anywhere."

There was a pause. "So . . . you didn't tell me the details. You know, the audition with Dayne."

"It was sort of a love scene." Katy giggled. "I wondered when you were going to ask about the good stuff."

"A love scene? Katy Hart, what are you trying to say?" Rhonda sounded intentionally indignant, but she couldn't keep up the act. She laughed. "Say it quick — you're killing me."

"Well, it wasn't that involved, thankfully. Dayne's character is walking me home from work, and both of us are falling for each other and —"

"You are?"

"Rhonda! Not me and Dayne! The characters!"

"Oh, right." She laughed again. "Sorry. Go ahead."

"Okay, so we're walking home and we get to my apartment door and he kisses me."

"He kissed you?" Rhonda screamed. "Dayne Matthews kissed you?"

"Twice." Katy laughed harder this time. It was fun sharing the details with Rhonda. This was the sort of conversation she'd been looking for earlier.

"He kissed you twice? Was that in the script?"

"Of course, silly." She sat up and planted her elbows on her knees. She thought about mentioning the part about her hair and how he'd told her she was beautiful. But that was only Dayne's character talking, his way of going freestyle through a scene that he knew inside and out.

"So . . . you know what I'm going to ask next."

Katy knit her brows. "No, I don't."

"Is he a good kisser?"

"Rhonda!" Katy exhaled hard. "It was acting."

"Please." Rhonda gave a sarcastic moan. "Give me a break, Katy. You spent the morning doing a romantic scene with the man. Can he kiss or what?"

"Well, let's just say he's had a lot of practice."

"So he's good at it, right?"

"The truth?" Katy slid her feet around on the cool bedspread and slipped her free hand beneath her head.

"Of course the truth. The whole truth."

"It was amazing, Rhonda. For about three seconds I completely forgot where I was or what I was doing. Seriously."

"What'd the director say?"

"We got it right on the first take. He didn't think chemistry was going to be a problem for the two of us."

"No wonder they offered you the part." Rhonda's voice took on a dreamlike quality. "I can't believe it, Katy. This is really happening to you."

"I know." Katy's smile faded. She would tell her about Pepperdine and the rest of the day later. When she had a chance to sort through her feelings. "But that doesn't mean things will change, not for me and not for us."

"Okay. Thanks for saying that."

The conversation ended, and Katy got ready for bed. But as she lay there awake she wondered at herself. If she really was desiring God's will, then she'd have to listen carefully. Otherwise she wouldn't hear Him above her own excitement.

And that night proved just how excited she was, because she could hardly sleep. She kept replaying the scene from the movie in her head and imagining six weeks on location with Dayne. She still believed what she'd told Rhonda a few days earlier. He was the last person on earth she'd fall for. She knew nothing about him, except what the public knew.

But he was fun to be with, and that told her two things — first, that the six weeks with him would be a blast. But second, she'd have to be careful.

Very careful.

The next morning Dayne sent a car for Katy, and she met him in the snack room across from the soundstage.

"Ready to look over the second half of the script?"

"Definitely." They had something easy between them now, as if in the past day they'd made a connection that was comfortable for both of them. She pointed to one of the tables. "Should we stay here?"

"No." He grinned. "This place gets too busy." He nodded to her. "Follow me."

He gave her a tour of the studio first. While they walked, their shoulders touched every once in a while. He showed her where various sitcoms and movies had been shot, and he explained that *Dream On* would probably be filmed in two locations — New York City and Thousand Oaks, a suburb of Los Angeles.

"Why?" Their pace was slow and casual, not too different from the way it had been in the scene the day before.

"Thousand Oaks can pass for a small town, especially if you get out into the farmland areas between there and Moorpark."

Suddenly she thought of something. This was her opportunity, her chance to talk to him about his visit to the theater. "Hey, I have an idea."

"What?" They were walking past the most beautiful flower garden. Dayne stopped, picked a petunia, and handed it to her. "What's your idea?"

"Thank you." She took the flower, and for a moment she was too flustered to remember even having an idea, let alone what it was. But then it hit her again. "You should use Bloomington. That way you'd get a real small-town atmosphere. The areas around town are perfect."

He cocked his head thoughtfully. "That's a thought."

"Dayne . . ." She stopped and turned to him, the sun shining on her face. "You've been to Bloomington, haven't you?"

"Me?" For a heartbeat it looked like he might deny it. But then he shrugged. "Yeah, it's a nice place."

"Why?" She narrowed her eyes, trying to see into the deeper places behind the famous smile. "You came to the theater for ten minutes and left. How come?"

"I was passing through." He looked down and started walking again. "It'd been a long time since I'd seen community theater." He looked back at her and grinned. "Come on. It wasn't a big deal."

She didn't believe him, but she caught up and fell in step beside him again. "Is that why you wanted me to read for the part? Because you saw me there?"

Dayne hesitated. He looked like he was choosing his words carefully. "Yeah, it was." He gave a casual toss of his hands. "Happens all the time, Katy. You see someone for a few minutes, and next time there's a casting decision, that person comes to mind." He smiled at her. "Lots of women read for this part, lots of talented actresses. But I kept picturing her the way you looked that night onstage."

"So it wasn't my TV movie?" The information was heady. Dayne had seen her and remembered her, and now she was his top choice to star in the film with him.

"It was a few things." He chuckled. "I had someone check your background, see if you had any acting experience. They found the pilot, and after I watched it I knew you could handle the part." He gave her a lopsided smile. "Nothing more than that."

The pieces were coming together. "But why were you in Bloomington?"

For the first time, a whisper of panic

flashed in Dayne's eyes. He stuck his hands in his pockets and gave an easy kick at a loose rock on the sidewalk. "I told you, just passing through."

"Come on." She lowered her chin and brought the petunia close to her nose, trying hard to keep things light. "From where?"

This time his answer was quick. "The university. I have a friend who teaches drama there." He raised his eyebrows at her, teasing her. "I was a guest speaker for the afternoon classes. I was heading back to Indianapolis for my flight the next morning when I saw your theater."

A low jet rumbled by, and she waited until it passed. His story was believable, and she didn't know him well enough to push him at this point. But something was missing — it had to be. Why wouldn't he have spent the evening with the professor friend? And why had he been driving through downtown? There was easy freeway access from the university.

But he was finished talking about Bloomington; she could tell.

When the plane passed, he motioned ahead of them to a trailer not far from the main studio. "Whenever I'm in town, this is mine." He started walking again. "The studio has me for my next four movies. This was one of the perks."

"Nice." She felt breathless. Reading a script with Dayne alone in his trailer? Her brief time with him told her she could trust him. But how smart was this?

He led the way inside and pointed to a table, a chair, and a sofa. "There's the script. You can get started. I'll make us something to eat."

The trailer was fully stocked with pastries, bagels, and muffins. The refrigerator held juice and a couple dozen eggs among other things. Dayne moved easily around the small kitchen, and Katy remembered what he'd said the day before — that most of his nights were spent home alone watching movies. He probably made most of his own meals. The thought made him seem more down-to-earth, almost like any other guy.

She picked up the script and thumbed to the middle. It was nice to have a chance to look through it. That way if there was anything she wouldn't feel right about filming, she'd know it before agreeing to take the part.

The story line was good, funny and strong with twists no audience would expect. She was caught up in it when Dayne joined her, placing two plates of scrambled eggs and sliced fruit on the table. He took the chair opposite her, and she felt herself relax. He wasn't interested in her, and just because he brought her to his private trailer didn't mean he wanted to reenact the scene they'd done the day before.

She held up the script. "I like it." She gave him a thoughtful look. "It's perfect for this kind of story."

"Yeah." He slid to the edge of his seat and held her eyes for a few seconds. "If you take the part it will be." A file sat on a smaller table next to him, and he reached for it. He took a document from inside it and held it out to her. "This is a contract, Katy. The third paragraph shows what we'll pay you."

She pushed the script away. Her hands were unsteady as she took the contract. She was almost afraid to look, but she did anyway. The amount made her gasp. It was a high six-figure number, a sum she would never earn in a lifetime of directing CKT productions.

She looked at him and shook her head. "Dayne . . . that's unbelievable."

"That's what everyone will say three years from now when you're making five million a film." He leaned back, and a satisfied smile tugged at his lips. "They'll all want to know how we ever got you for such a low price."

Her heart was pounding so hard she wondered if he could hear it from across the table. With everything in her, she wanted to tell him yes. Yes, she'd take this incredible opportunity. Yes, she'd work a few weeks for a lifetime paycheck, working beside him in a film that was both funny and poignant, a movie that was clean enough for her to risk her reputation on.

But a still, small voice inside her was saying something, and Katy calmed herself long enough to listen. *Wait, daughter . . . wait on Me.*

She closed her eyes and took a slow breath through her nose. *Fine, God, I'll wait. But it's yes. I know it is.* She opened her eyes, set the contract on the table next to the script, and grinned at Dayne. "Can I be honest?"

"I hope so." He crossed one leg over the other, his eyes dancing.

"I'd sign it right now, but . . ." She reminded herself to exhale. "I need a week. Just to pray about it and make sure it's the right thing." She winced. "Is that okay?"

"Sure." His answer was quick, and the disappointment in his eyes lasted only an instant. "Mitch'll want an answer no later than that, okay?"

"Definitely." She wanted to run over and hug him again, but she contained herself. There would be plenty of opportunity for hugs in the weeks to come. "I'll probably have an answer sooner."

"Good." He bit his lip, studying her. "So, what about CKT and your life in Bloomington? Are you ready to give it up?"

"No." She gave a polite laugh. "Filming the movie wouldn't take more than a few weeks. I'll miss one of the CKT shows, but that's all. I don't want to leave Bloomington."

Something in his eyes changed. "I guess I never asked you. Is there someone there? I mean, are you seeing someone?"

"No." She felt her cheeks grow hot. Was she embarrassed that at her age there was no one serious in her life, or was she half hoping he was asking for other reasons? She wasn't sure. "No, it's not that. It's just that I like what I do. I don't want to leave it."

"Katy . . ." He stood and went to the kitchen for two glasses of orange juice. He took one and gave the other to her, then sat facing her. "Before you say yes, you have to be willing to give it up. All of it."

She searched his eyes, trying to see if he was serious. He was. "I . . ." She shook her head. "I guess I don't understand. It's my choice, right?"

He chuckled. "You really don't know how good you are." He motioned to the script. "That's just the beginning, Katy. You'll have more offers than you know what to do with." His expression softened. "This was your dream, remember? You said a minute ago that you like what you do with the kids theater. But acting, Katy? That's something you used to love. You told me so yesterday at Pepperdine. Aren't I right? Wasn't acting your dream?"

Her head was spinning. He was right; she'd said that. But what about CKT? From the beginning she'd told herself she could go back, that she could handle a short season of fame and return to the life she'd been living. But now . . .

She looked at him. "Yes. It was my dream for most of my life."

"Well, then, Miss Katy Hart . . . maybe the sign from God you're looking for —" he took the contract and handed it to her one more time — "is right here."

Later, Katy was on her way out of the studio with the same driver who'd picked her up this morning when they nearly collided with another car. The vehicle pulled out right in front of them, so Katy's driver had to swerve into the next lane.

Katy caught a glimpse of the person who nearly caused the wreck, and the woman's look sent chills down her arms. Her eyes were wide and intense, and they looked at Katy straight on. The woman was maybe in her forties, her hair yellow and coarse. She looked like a lunatic.

The driver muttered something under his breath. "No-good paparazzi."

"Paparazzi?" Katy stared straight ahead as her driver pulled up alongside the woman. "She doesn't look like a reporter, really."

"Ah, they come in all sizes. But that one's here just about every day. Parks in a different spot each time." He waved his thumb over his shoulder at the car they were passing. "But it's always that same old yellow Honda."

Katy was barely listening by this point. They hadn't collided; that's all that mattered. Besides, all she could think about was the fact that she'd be having dinner with Dayne tonight at the studio — his idea since she was leaving tomorrow. They'd probably spend more time talking about what he'd told her earlier today.

The fact that maybe the audition and the offer of the part and the contract weren't merely wonderful events that had taken place in recent weeks, but rather the signs from God she'd been praying for all along.

Chapter Twenty

The painting party was Ashley's idea — something fun she and Landon and Kari and Ryan could do. A date night of sorts. She and Landon had been assigned the task of creating the backdrop for *Tom Sawyer* — something with trees and a winding river and distant buildings that might've been seen in the town of Hannibal, Missouri, back in the 1800s. She'd been working since Monday on the design of the enormous canvas. Now it was Wednesday night, and the scene was ready to paint.

They all drove together and picked up cheeseburgers and pop on the way to the Bloomington Community Theater. Each of them was dressed in old work clothes, and Ryan entertained them on the ride over with stories of the first summer football practice.

"Jim Flanigan is so great with the kids." Ryan sat in the backseat, his arm around

350

Kari. "One of these days he should stop dreaming about getting back to coaching in the NFL and come on as head coach at Bloomington High. That way I could be the part-time volunteer and take a break." He tapped Ashley on the shoulder. "After tonight I might become a professional painter."

She grinned over her shoulder at him. "You never know. We might have to hit the road, all four of us." She ran her hand in front of her from left to right. "I can see it now. Painting sets for theaters in small towns across America."

Kari laughed and poked her on the opposite shoulder. "Maybe you should see what we're capable of first."

"True." Ashley looked at Landon. "I know my dear husband can hardly wait to roll up his sleeves and get started." She leaned over and kissed his cheek. "Right, honey?"

"Yeah." He gave Kari and Ryan a sarcastic look in the rearview mirror. "Picasso in the flesh." His gaze shifted to Ashley. "I told you to bring Cole instead of me. That kid's way better at staying in the lines."

Laughter filled the car as they parked and crossed the street to the old theater. Kari stayed next to Ashley, and when they reached the doors she mentioned how happy their father had been to watch the children for the night.

"He had the old spark in his eyes, the one he always had when Mom was alive." Kari wore shorts and a worn T-shirt. The clothes didn't hide her looks, looks that allowed her to still maintain a career in catalog modeling.

"I asked Cole to help out with the little ones." Ashley made a face as she led the way into the theater. "You don't think it'll be too much for Dad, do you?"

"No." Kari stayed beside her, with the guys still talking football a few feet behind. "Little Ryan's tired. Cole and Jessie can play with him for an hour or so, and then he'll sleep."

Ashley flipped on the lights in the seating area and headed up toward the stage. "You guys can start on the burgers. I'll get the stage ready."

Bloomington Community Theater was more than a hundred years old, with detailed architecture that spoke of a different era. It had tall ceilings and a dusky cedar scent, the way an attic might smell in a century-old house. Tall, thick, black velvet curtains separated the stage from the intimate theater seating. At the back, two small balcony sections offered a different view for another sixty people. All said, the theater held maybe four hundred people, perfect for the type of shows CKT put on.

Ashley loved the place.

The theater owners had agreed to let her have access to the stage every evening this week for the purpose of creating sets. During the day the building's upstairs served as a dozen business offices. But at night the facility was open for rental by members of the community.

The wonderful thing about having the painting party at the theater was that the expansive stage was the one place large enough to serve as a workspace for the backdrop.

Ashley tucked a strand of her dark hair behind her ear and jogged up a set of stairs to the stage. It was cool and drafty, a relief from the heat and humidity outside. She turned on the lights, worked the cords to open the curtain, and then spread the canvas out across the stage.

Ryan set his sandwich down and came to the edge of the stage, his eyes wide. "Tell me we're not painting that whole thing." He stuck his hands in his shorts pockets. "I have practice in the morning." He gave

Ashley a teasing look. "We'll be done before then, right?"

"I told her —" Landon strolled up the center aisle and took a spot next to Ryan — "it'd take a crew of people three days to paint this thing. But you know Ashley — where there's a will there's a way."

Ashley gave them a knowing smile and lightly stepped down the stairs back to Kari and the burger they'd saved for her. "We'll start in ten minutes, and you'll see. It'll go faster than you think."

Ashley opened her sandwich and took a moment to thank God for what she had right here — a best friendship with her sister Kari, both of them married to guys who had loved them since high school. It was rare and wonderful, and on nights like this she couldn't be thankful enough.

They ate their meal, the guys continuing their teasing about the task that lay ahead. When they finished their food, they took off their shoes and walked to the middle of the canvas, where Ashley had the paint and brushes set up. They'd work from the center out. She gave out assignments. The guys would use larger brushes and paint the upper area, a row of thick trees and foliage.

"I've already painted the outline of the trees and branches." She pointed to the top half of the backdrop. "All you have to do is stay in the lines. Kari and I will work on the buildings and the river."

Landon took his brush and a can of green paint. "I tell you, you're going to wish you'd asked Cole."

They set to work, painting and chatting about the other Baxters. Ryan asked if anyone had talked to any of the other Baxters lately.

"I've talked to Luke." Ashley was painting the roof of a general store brown. "He and Reagan are coming out for Christmas. At least that's the plan."

"I wish they'd move here." Kari dipped her brush into a pale blue paint and added more color to the river she was working on. "It's hard having him and Reagan so far away. Our kids won't even know each other."

"What about Erin?" Landon was sprawled out, his section of trees growing green at a fast pace. "How're the girls working out now that it's been a year?"

Kari smiled. "I talked to her last week." She sat back on her heels, her brush in her hand. "It hasn't been perfect, but Erin doesn't mind. The two babies have been sick, and the little girls are in preschool, learning their alphabet, that sort of thing. I can't imagine going from no kids to having four daughters in a few weeks like Erin and Sam did." She blew at a wisp of hair and set back to painting. "I think they're doing great."

Landon dipped his brush. "Do the older girls ever talk about their mom?"

"Clarisse did at first." Kari's smile faded. "She wanted to know why Erin didn't yell at her the way her mommy did."

"That's so sad." Ryan stood and stretched, admiring his trees. "Only God could've brought those little girls where they needed to be — with Erin and Sam."

"Yeah, how's Sam doing? Are the girls bonding with him?" Landon didn't look up from his work.

"They are." Kari went to work again. "The babies never had any problem, but the older girls took about eight months. All they'd ever known from men was anger and violence. It's amazing they could bond at all."

Ashley surveyed the canvas. Already it was about a fourth covered with paint. "You guys, see how good you are!" She stood and marveled at their work. "I was right. We need to take this act on the road."

"Yeah, the whole fear-factor thing was just a big act." Kari winked at Ryan. "We've got years of this type of experience, right, Ryan?"

Landon laughed. "You know sometimes I think you and Ashley are twins. You look alike and act alike, and you can both tease with the best of them."

Everyone enjoyed the idea, and again Ashley was reminded of how much they all had. It was hard to imagine that only seven years ago she'd come back from Paris pregnant and alone, the black sheep of the Baxter family. Back then she and Kari might've looked alike, but they had nothing in common. She never could have guessed that one day they'd be as close as they were now.

"I was at practice the other day, and I saw Brooke and Peter, playing at the school park with Maddie and Hayley." Ryan got back down on his knees and started painting again. "I can't believe Maddie's starting second grade in the fall."

"Hayley's doing better; wouldn't you say?" Ashley was working on the door of the general store, taking care with the hinges and handle so they'd appear lifelike. "Brooke's still seeing patients only three days a week, and she and Peter have a therapist coming in Monday through Friday for Hayley."

"I know." Ryan looked up, his eyes shining. "I took a break from the football field and jogged over to tell them hello." His voice sounded thick. "Hayley grinned at me and said, 'Hi, Uncle Ryan!' I almost started crying right there."

They were all quiet for a moment, considering the distance Hayley had come since her near drowning two years earlier. She was still in a wheelchair, but she could crawl from one side of the room to the other and pull herself up. According to Brooke, Hayley's therapists expected her to regain the ability to walk one day.

"No one ever asks this." Ryan lowered his brow, his expression serious. "But do they think she'll get everything back? Her cognitive powers, physical abilities, all of it?"

Kari looked up from the blue river she was still working on. "No one knows. No one but God." She shrugged and shook her head. "That drowning should've killed her. Every bit of progress is another miracle, really."

They all agreed about that, and for a while they painted in comfortable silence.

After a long while, Landon asked Ryan

about his football team, how they looked for the coming fall. As they talked, Ashley remembered the strange scene that had played out between her and their father in his closet the other day.

"Did I tell you about being in Dad's closet?" Ashley moved on to the town post office, the building next to the general store.

Kari twisted her face and giggled. "You were in Dad's closet?"

"Well —" Ashley exhaled hard and stifled a laugh — "I wasn't just standing there." She stuck her tongue out at Kari. "I was opening windows in Mom and Dad's room, and I heard something rustling on the top shelf of their closet. I looked and it was a box of letters."

"Letters?" Kari stopped painting and met Ashley's eyes. "From who?"

"From lots of people. Friends and relatives, Christmas cards, and lots of letters from Dad to Mom, or from her to Dad."

"How come I never knew about that?" Kari fiddled with her paintbrush. "You'd think Mom would've showed them to us."

"The box was pretty far back on the shelf. I don't think she showed anyone." Ashley felt her shoulders fall a little. "Maybe she ran out of time."

"Maybe." Kari took a sad-sounding breath. "Anyway, what happened?"

Ashley dipped the tip of her brush into a can of yellow paint and flicked it against the post office walls, creating texture on what was supposed to look like old wood slats. She finished one section and looked at Kari. "So I take a letter from the box and it's from Dad, something he wrote to Mom after Luke was born."

"Dad's always been thoughtful that way." Kari's hair hung along the side of her face as she used a darker blue to accent the river. "Anyway . . ."

"Anyway, I'm reading it — you know, stuff about how Luke's birth completed the family — and I'm just getting to the sentimental stuff when Dad walks in and sort of freaks out."

Kari gave her a sideways look and tossed her hair off her face. "What do you mean?"

"Well, he gives me this strange look, and it scared me, you know? I mean, I was in the house all alone and I didn't hear him come in. So the letter drops and I pick it up." She soaked a little more yellow into her brush and looked at Kari. "He takes the envelope from me, opens it, glances at it, folds it back up, and puts it back in the envelope."

"I can see that. Those are Mom's precious things. Maybe he was too surprised to find you in there reading the letters, and he didn't think about whether you wanted to finish it or not."

"Maybe." Ashley added texture to the other side of the post office. "But then he goes into this thing about how I shouldn't read Mom's letters, and none of us should read them, and maybe he'll put together an album for us one day, make copies of the best ones, so we can all see them." She raised her brows. "I felt like saying, 'That's okay, just let me finish the one in your hand.' But before I could say anything he took the box and buried the letter somewhere in the middle." She hesitated and met Kari's eyes. "I had the definite feeling he didn't want me reading it."

"Hmmm. Strange." Kari sat up and slid back so she could work on the next section of river. "I wonder what it said."

"That's what I want to know." Ashley finished the trim on the post office and moved a few feet to the side. The town jail was next. "Or maybe it wasn't what was in the letter. Maybe it's like you said, and he just doesn't want us rifling through Mom's things without his knowing about it."

"Could be."

"And something else bugged me that day." She was using a reddish brown to paint the jail walls first. "Dad missed the eleven o'clock service, remember?"

"I remember." Kari's face was close to the canvas, studying the areas where Ashley had penciled in that a different color was needed. "I never did hear what happened."

"Well, what happened was that Dad went to the earlier service with some of Mom's volunteer friends." Ashley got up on her knees and surveyed the row of buildings she'd been working on. Ten feet away, the men were doing a fantastic job on the trees, careful not to cover up the highlights and branches she'd already painted. She looked at Kari. "Mom's volunteer friends. Does that ring a bell?"

"Not really." Kari stopped and propped her paintbrush on the can. "Should it?"

"I don't know. It did for me." Ashley shifted positions and spread her legs out on either side of the building she was painting. "I guess Dad's been doing stuff with a group of them sort of often. Last Sunday it was early church and a walk down at Lake Monroe."

"That's good, I guess." Kari tilted her face. "Who's in the group?"

"A bunch of people, most of them retired. Back in the day when Mom had her first fight with cancer, she would see these people come through with gift packs and encouragement. One on a Monday, another two on a Wednesday, that sort of thing."

"I remember. When she was better, she joined them and helped out once a week or so."

"Right." Ashley switched brushes. "Each of them had lost someone they love to cancer."

"Hope Lives — wasn't that what they called themselves?"

Ashley snapped her fingers. "That's it. I couldn't remember." She leaned closer to the canvas and studied the jail she was working on. "Anyway, guess who's in the group?" She didn't wait for an answer. "Elaine Denning."

"Mom's friend? The one who used to come over for tea once in a while?"

"Yes." Ashley pursed her lips. "I never liked that woman."

"Why not?" Kari didn't look up. "She seemed nice enough."

"She's a widow; that's why." Ashley's voice was louder than before, and she forced herself to bring it down. "She's been a widow for ten years."

"So?"

"So I always thought she was a little too chatty with Dad, you know?"

Kari set her brush down on the can again and sat up on her knees. "You think Dad's interested in her?"

"I asked him." She made a guilty face. "He didn't like that too much. He said he wasn't interested, wasn't dating. Nothing like that."

"Ashley." Kari had the tone of a scolding parent. "You shouldn't have asked. Of course he's not dating. There'd never be anyone for him but Mom."

"I guess." Ashley dipped her brush into a darker paint and began working on the jail bars. "The whole scene just felt weird." She finished that part of the building. "You don't think Dad'll ever remarry, do you?"

"Dad?" Kari picked up her brush and began painting again. "Never. Not in a million years. What he and Mom had was too special."

They painted in quiet for a few minutes. Ashley was just going to tell her about their mother's chair in the closet, but it was too sad. Her eyes blurred with tears, and she had to blink three or four times to see the canvas clearly. Finally she sat back on her heels and sniffed. "I miss her so much."

Kari put her arm around Ashley's shoulders and leaned her head close. "Me too. It's okay to miss her, Ash."

Ryan and Landon stood up then and walked over to Kari, then Ashley. They both had a familiar teasing gleam in their eyes. "Well, it's official." Landon wiggled his sock foot against Ashley's.

"What?" She sniffed again and wiped her fingers beneath her eyes. A smile tugged at the corners of her mouth. It was impossible to stay sad too long when Ryan and Landon got together. "What's official?"

"As of right now —" Ryan puffed his chest out and grinned — "the men have covered more canvas than the women." He put his arm around Landon. "And I think ours is brighter."

"Better," Landon corrected.

"Right." He bowed toward Kari. "Better."

"Really?" Kari moved back to her painting spot and gave the guys a skeptical look.

"Really." They both said it in unison, looking at each other and giving mock checks back at their work. Landon gave a thumbs-up to them. "No doubt about it."

"Let's see." Ashley winked at Kari. She

stood and surveyed the painted sections of the backdrop. Then she threw her hands up and looked at Kari again. "The guys are right. They're faster and better."

"Wow." Kari frowned, trying to play along. "What should we do?"

Ashley set her brush down and dusted off her hands. "We might as well go out for ice cream and let the guys finish. Why compete?"

"True." Kari stood up and set her brush down.

They were walking off the stage when Ashley glanced back over her shoulder. Ryan winced in Landon's direction, at which point Landon jabbed Ryan in the ribs and mouthed the words *Nice going.*

Ryan cleared his throat and took a few fast steps toward them. "Hey, girls . . ." He forced a friendly laugh. "Did we say we were faster and better?" He looked at Landon and back to Ashley and Kari. "What we meant was, we're no match for you, not even on our best day."

"Was that what you meant?" Kari put her hands on her hips.

"Yeah," Landon chimed in. "Not even on our best day."

Kari and Ashley linked arms and laughed. Then they turned and headed back to their spots. "Don't worry." Ashley tossed her hands. "You probably are faster and better." She smiled at Kari. "But our conversation makes up for it."

A ringing sound came from Ashley's purse a few feet away. She darted over to it, grabbed her phone, and opened it. "Hello?"

"Ash, it's Luke." Her brother's voice sounded rich and warm and close enough to be next door. "How are you?"

"Luke! It's so good to hear your voice." She looked around at the others, each of them still standing, enjoying a moment to stretch before getting back to work. "I'm fine. I'm here at the theater painting a backdrop with Landon and Kari and Ryan."

"Sounds like fun." Luke gave a light laugh. "I can never tell what you'll be doing, Ash."

The other three waved and mumbled quiet hellos.

"Can you hear everyone, Luke? We all say hi. How are you?"

"I'm good. Tommy's talking up a storm, and Reagan's feeling great." He paused. "She wanted me to call and tell you our news."

"News?" Ashley's mouth fell open and

stayed that way. She held her breath. Were they . . . ?

"We're adopting!" He hooted loud enough that Landon, Kari, and Ryan all came closer, their expressions wide with curiosity. "The birth mother is due in February."

Ashley screamed and danced in a tight circle. Then she waved the phone at the others. "More Baxter kids!" Suddenly she thought of something. "You can still come for Christmas, right?"

Luke chuckled. "I figured you'd think of that." He caught his breath. "Yes, the mother should still be six weeks away at that point, so we're planning on it."

"Yippee!" Ashley jogged in place for a few seconds. "Luke, I'm so happy for you. Tell Reagan we're thrilled. We wish we could be there to hug you both."

The conversation lasted a few more minutes, and when she hung up she shared all the details with the group. The mood was upbeat and happy, the conversation jumping from their children to the cruise Ashley and Landon were set to take in July.

It was just after nine o'clock when they finished the backdrop. They all agreed it was a work of art, and Ashley could hardly wait for Katy Hart to get a look at it.

It wasn't until that night when Landon was brushing his teeth that Ashley walked into Cole's dark room and sat on the edge of the bed. The conversation with Kari came back again, the one about her father and his closet and the way they all missed their mom.

She slid her fingers through Cole's wispy blond hair. Life moved so fast. Wasn't it just her turn to be pregnant with little Coley? Even more, weren't she and Luke just little kids, closer than any of the other Baxter kids? She sighed.

And now her little brother was about to have a second baby.

Tears welled up in her eyes and spilled onto her cheeks. The night had been so good; it made no sense that she was crying. She leaned down and rubbed her damp cheek against Cole's. He was so big now, reasoning and acting like a schoolboy, not the little tyke he'd been those early years.

He stirred and shifted his head so his opposite cheek was against the pillow.

"Grandma loved you so much, Cole." Her words were a whisper. "I hope she can see you from heaven, what a wonderful boy you're growing up to be."

He sighed and the hint of a smile played on his lips.

Ashley closed her eyes. "Jesus, don't ever let him forget her. Please."

There was a sound behind her and she opened her eyes. Landon stood in the doorway, the light from the hallway hitting his back. She could see the compassion in his eyes even in the shadows.

"Are you okay?" he asked.

"Yes." She patted to the spot beside her.

Landon sat down next to her. He put his arm around her and smoothed his hand against the back of her head. "What's wrong, honey?"

"I don't know." She did a quiet moan. "Just thinking. What with Luke and Reagan adopting and life moving on." She touched Cole's hair again. "Cole's growing up so fast. Just all of it, I guess."

He kissed her cheek. "I heard you and Kari talking earlier. About your mom."

"Yeah." She pressed her face against his. "I guess it's that too." A new wave of tears came. "I want her to see Cole grow up and little Ryan get his first teeth and Hayley able to recognize people." A quiet sob caught in her throat. "And . . . and Luke's new little baby."

"Ah, honey." He held her tighter.

"We still need her, Landon." Another

few sobs slipped out. "Why would God take her?"

"I don't know," he whispered, using his free hand to dry the tears from her face. "We'll never know this side of heaven."

They stayed that way for a while, and then Ashley turned to him. "What would I do without you?" She was calmer now, her tears subsiding. She searched his eyes. "I almost let you get away. I would've lost you forever."

"No, you wouldn't have." He brushed his knuckles against the side of her face and dried the last of her tears. He slowly moved his thumb down until he was tracing the outline of her lips. "God would've found some way to make me stay." A familiar wanting filled his eyes. "At least until you figured out how much you loved me."

She said nothing in response. Instead she brought her lips to his, and as the intensity of the kiss grew, they were both carried on a wave of passion.

He drew back, breathless, his eyes dark with desire. "You know what I'm glad about?"

"What?" She kissed him again, first his upper lip, then his lower lip, then his chin. Cole was sound asleep, but she was careful to be quiet, anyway.

"I'm glad we waited until we were married." He touched his lips to her neck and then looked at her again. "I think that's why loving you gets better every day."

"I'm glad we waited too." She smiled, and even though the sadness remained, it was buried back where it belonged. "But you know what?"

"What?" He kissed the other side of her neck.

She leaned her head back, consumed with him. Her words were throaty, barely a whisper. "We don't have to wait now, Mr. Blake."

His lips found hers again. "No, we don't." And with that, he stood, took her by the hand, and led her down the hallway to their bedroom, where they spent the night celebrating love and life and marriage.

Marriage the way God intended it to be.

Chapter Twenty-one

CKT classes felt wild and out of control that Thursday, and it seemed to Katy that she'd been gone from her Bloomington life for a month. As part of the CKT program, every session involved classes on acting, singing, and dancing, all held at Bloomington Community Church, just like the play rehearsals. Kids had to be enrolled in classes before they could audition for a play. Usually by now the classes would all be working out the details for their showcase night — a compilation of ten-minute performances from each class.

This time, though, three of the ten classes had no idea what to do for the showcase, and in the junior acting class, four kids had dropped out with complaints that it wasn't interesting enough.

By six o'clock when classes got out, Katy had the horrible sense that everything was falling apart. As she was dismissing her class, Rhonda showed up and grabbed her own hair with both hands. "I have parent committees asking me for wooden apples and aprons and fishing poles, Katy." She released her hair. "I'm guessing we're at least a week behind in the practice schedule."

"I don't get it." Katy leaned against the edge of the desk, staring at her feet. "I haven't really missed anything, right? I mean, I've been here for every practice and every class date, and still it's chaos." She looked up. "I can feel it."

Just then, Jenny Flanigan passed by in the hall. She was walking with another mother and didn't stop or look in. Maybe that was it. Maybe if she worked things out with the Flanigans everything would feel better. She held up a finger to Rhonda. "Can you make an announcement? Quick? Before everyone leaves?"

Rhonda put her hands on her hips. "I guess so." She looked over her shoulder. "Hurry, though. Parents are already here to pick up their kids."

"Okay, tell everyone practice starts an hour earlier tomorrow. That way we can catch up."

"Good idea." Rhonda's expression brightened. She turned and ran from the room. "Hey, guys," she shouted. "Every-one, wait. I have something to . . ." Her voice faded as she got farther away.

Katy left her things in the room and sprinted out the door in the direction she had seen Jenny Flanigan walk. She was in luck. Jenny was only a few classrooms up the hallway, still talking to the other mother.

She bounded up to them and gave each of them a quick hug. The other mother waved and headed toward the exit, leaving just the two of them.

"Katy!" Jenny wasn't stiff or distant but happy to see her. "Hey, you're back!"

"I came straight here from the airport."

"So, how was it?" Whatever distance had been in Jenny's eyes before was gone now. She looked excited. "Lots of research?"

Katy couldn't lie, not again. Not when she'd all but made up her mind to take the part. "Jenny . . ." She felt her smile fade. "Can we talk when we get home? You and Jim and me?"

Concern colored Jenny's expression. "Is everything okay?"

"It will be. I think so, anyway." She bit the inside of her lip. "I just need to talk, okay?"

"Definitely." She looked at her watch.

"Let's talk in half an hour."

"Thanks, Jenny." Relief filled her voice.

Bailey and Connor were coming up behind them, walking fast and laughing about something. At the end of the hallway, behind them, Tim Reed jumped into view. "Hey, Bailey."

She turned around, her mannerisms all flirtatious sweetness. "Yes, Tom Sawyer?"

"How about you join me and Huck and Joe Harper on the island tomorrow?"

Just then Tim spotted Katy. She raised her brows at him and wagged a finger in the air. "I'll join you on the island if you don't have your lines down by tomorrow, Tim." She wanted to smile, but she resisted. "Got it?"

He straightened up, his goofy smile replaced by wide, worried eyes. "Yes, Katy. Got it."

Bailey muffled a giggle and gave a little wave to Tim before he turned around and darted out of sight. Katy hadn't seen Tim with Ashley Zarelli once today, and she was tempted to ask Bailey about it. Just for fun. She liked staying up to date on the small crushes and friendships that grew from the soil of CKT.

But she didn't say a word. She had too much to do before leaving the church. Instead she told the Flanigans good-bye, headed back to her classroom, and collected her things. The conversation with Jenny and Jim was getting closer with each passing minute.

By the time Katy got home, ten minutes late, and found the Flanigans in their living room, she was out of breath and her hair felt damp against her head. She rushed into the room and took the seat opposite them. She wasn't sure if her heart was beating fast because she'd raced so hard to get there or because of all she had to talk to them about.

"Hi. Sorry I'm late." She looked from Jenny to Jim. They were calm, their faces kind and open. Had she been wrong about them from the beginning? Was the tension she'd felt only something she'd dreamed up? She exhaled, catching her breath. She smiled. "Thanks for taking time for this."

"I had the kids go upstairs to do homework." Jenny crossed her legs and leaned comfortably against Jim. "What's on your mind?"

Katy closed her eyes for a few seconds. Where should she start? She knew the answer as soon as the question breezed through her mind. "First . . ." She blinked and looked at Jenny. "I need to tell you the truth about Los Angeles."

Jim leaned closer. "The truth?" He put his hands on his knees. "You were doing research, right?"

"No." Katy's breathing was back to normal. She slid to the edge of her seat, willing them to understand. "See . . . a few weeks ago I got a call from a casting director in Los Angeles."

"I remember." Jenny's eyes were narrow, curious. "You thought it had something to do with Sarah Jo Stryker."

"Right." Katy gave a nervous laugh. "I was wrong about that. It turned out they wanted me to come to LA for an audition. An audition for a romantic comedy."

Jim sat back. The expression on his face told her he was shocked at this information. "Why didn't you tell us before?"

"I thought nothing would come of it." She turned her palms up and shook her head. "Besides —" she shifted her attention to Jenny — "I thought you were mad at me. I wasn't sure how to get past that."

Jenny gave the slightest nod. "It was hard for a while there."

"You really were mad?" Katy looked down. If she could disappear through the crack in the sofa, she would.

"Mad about what?" Jim looked lost.

Jenny turned to him. "About Bailey not getting the part of Becky Thatcher in the play. She read for it, but Sarah Jo won the role." Jenny's tone was calm and understanding. If her voice was any indication, whatever frustrations she'd had about the situation were gone now.

"You were mad about that?" Surprise lined Jim's forehead. He was a big man, a former pro football player who was assisting Ryan Taylor coach at the high school. But sitting there he looked like a kid on his first day of school — lost and overwhelmed.

"Not really." Jenny crossed her arms. "I struggled with it at first." She met Katy's eyes. "If we're being honest, I should tell you that." She paused. "I'm sorry. I was wrong. I told you not to play favorites, and you didn't. It was my fault I was frustrated. Sarah Jo's doing a wonderful job."

"If we're being honest, then I'll disagree." Katy gave her friend a crooked smile. "Bailey would've done a better job. Sarah Jo's so uptight about her mother's constant coaching, she can't relax and have fun. That needs to happen before we'll see what she can bring to the part."

Jim tossed his hands in the air. "I'm in the dark." He glanced from his wife to

Katy. "I want to know more about this movie thing."

"Okay, but first —" Katy leaned over her knees — "the tension thing wasn't just you, Jenny. I knew you were disappointed, but then I kept my distance." She sat up again. "Stupid, I know. But I'm sorry. I just wanted to get that out."

Jenny stood and crossed the gap between them. "We love you, Katy Hart. You're like family to us. I might be disappointed, but it'd never be enough for you to stay away like you've been doing." She leaned down and hugged Katy. "Let's not do that again, okay?"

"Okay." Katy felt the sting of tears in her eyes. She should have done this two weeks ago.

Across the room, Jim had an amused look on his face. He held up his hand. "Waiting patiently over here."

Jenny and Katy laughed, and Jenny returned to her spot next to her husband.

Katy drew a deep breath. "Okay, well . . ." Excitement welled within her, and the next words came fast. "I figured it couldn't hurt to audition for a movie. It used to be my dream a few years ago, and — I probably never told you this — but I was in a TV series pilot back then."

"All right." Jim whistled. "I can hardly wait to hear what other things we don't know about our little mystery houseguest." He scratched his head and looked up at nothing in particular. "Let's see, maybe she's in training to be an astronaut, or she's in the government's witness protection program. I'll bet that's it."

Katy gave an embarrassed laugh and covered her face. "I know . . . I know. Don't be mad." She peered over the tips of her fingers and then let her hands fall back to her knees. "Okay, so anyway, I get there and the film's a major deal. A big picture starring Dayne Matthews."

Jenny gasped. "What?"

"Oh, good." Jim rolled his eyes in a teasing way. "Now I'm spending the evening with a couple of groupies."

This time Jenny and Katy both laughed. Jenny leaned closer. "Okay, so I'm dying here. What happened? I guess it went well, right?"

"It went great." Katy felt like dancing. Jenny's initial reaction was another sign that this was God's plan for her. It had to be. "Dayne asked me to come back, and that's what this second trip was about. I did an on-camera scene with Dayne."

"Wait!" Jenny held up both her hands.

"You mean it's not a small part? It's a speaking role?"

Katy clenched her fists and knocked them together a few times. She could barely stay seated. "It's the lead, Jenny. The female lead, starring opposite Dayne Matthews."

"No!"

"Yes!" Katy tapped her feet. "So I went back and did the scene on Tuesday and —" she squealed — "they offered me the part!"

There was the sound of something near the stairway, and Jim looked in that direction. "Kids? Who's up?"

"Sorry, Dad." It was Bailey's voice. "I need a glass of water; is that okay? I know you're talking."

"Sure, honey. Hurry."

Bailey walked down the stairs, and Katy could tell by her wide-eyed expression that the girl had heard their conversation. She'd have to talk to her later, explain that she wouldn't be leaving forever, just for a few months.

The whole time Bailey was getting her drink, Jenny gave a series of excited looks to Katy. At one point she grabbed Jim's knee and mouthed, *Dayne Matthews!*

Jim only chuckled and shook his head.

When Bailey was back upstairs, Jenny did a mock scream. "I can't believe it, Katy. So did you take it?"

"I have the contract. That's what I want to talk to you about. I've never done anything this big, and I don't have an agent. I need someone to look it over." She realized she'd been holding her breath, and she exhaled. Everything was so much better now that she'd told the truth. In fact, the idea of accepting the offer seemed better than ever.

For the first time, Jenny's excitement dimmed. "You wouldn't have to move there, would you?"

"No, of course not." Katy sat back and relaxed her fists. "The filming would last maybe a couple months. I'd have to miss the winter show, but then I'd be back."

"So what's the contract say?" Jim had experience with these types of things — not in the entertainment industry but in the world of professional sports.

Katy pulled it from her bag and handed it to him. "The price they'll pay me is amazing."

He skimmed down and nodded. "Not bad." He grinned at her. "A little more than you make as CKT director."

"A little."

Jenny looked over her husband's shoulder, and her eyes reacted as she reached the place halfway down the first page. "Katy, that's fantastic. Can you believe this is happening to you?"

"Not really." She was almost bursting she was so happy. Now that she had told the Flanigans, the whole experience felt more real. But it was still more than she could fully take in. The important thing was, the Flanigans were happy for her. Now she couldn't imagine a single reason why she wouldn't take the part.

Jim looked at her over the top of the contract. "Have you seen the script?"

"Yes." She nodded, more serious. "I have it in my room. I read through the whole thing. There's nothing objectionable, nothing I'd feel embarrassed about."

Jim pursed his lips. "No love scenes or language?"

"It's pretty clean, but there's a scene where we kiss on the porch step." Her cheeks grew hot. "That's the scene we did together for the second audition."

Jenny grinned at her, but Jim looked at the contract again, turning to the second page. "Just kissing?"

"Just kissing." She appreciated Jim's attitude and was glad she was getting his opinion. He was treating her the way her father would if he were here. She planned to call her parents before the weekend, and her dad was bound to have the same response. "I made sure."

"Well —" Jim lowered the contract to his lap — "it looks good. There is something I've heard about, something you might want to look into. It's a no-between-the-sheets clause. You can have them write it in. That way the director can't add a more detailed love scene once filming gets started."

"Great idea." Katy had heard of that type of clause, but she'd never needed it in a contract before. She couldn't imagine signing her name to a contract thinking the script was one thing, then getting halfway through the filming and being ordered to do something that would compromise her faith or her reputation.

They talked a little bit more about the story line and the possible cities where the movie might be filmed. Katy told them she'd recommended Bloomington, and they both thought the town would be perfect.

"What a blast!" Jenny gave Jim's arm a quick squeeze. "A Dayne Matthews movie filmed right here in Bloomington, starring our very own Katy Hart."

Eventually the excitement died down, and Katy thanked them both. "I need your support." Her eyes shifted from Jim to Jenny. "It means the world to me."

When she finally went to bed, it was too hot to fall asleep. She opened her window and kicked off all the blankets except the top sheet. Then she lay there, eyes open. Every dream she'd ever had about acting was about to come true. It was like something from a storybook, only it was real and true and it was happening to her.

God, You've made it clear so far that this is Your will. And I'm so grateful.

Daughter . . . wait on the Lord.

Katy made a face in the dark. *Wait on the Lord?* Why was that verse coming back again now? Unless maybe God was warning her not to get too excited. There were still nearly four months until the movie would be filmed. Maybe that's what the wait part meant.

That, or maybe she was just imagining things. She closed her eyes. *Thank You, God. Thanks that I got everything out in the open with the Flanigans. I'm so glad they're excited for me. It makes it more real. I can't wait to call Dayne and tell him —*

That's when it happened. Right in the middle of talking to God, the face of Tad Thompson flashed in her mind. His image was so clear and vivid that for a heartbeat it took her breath away.

After losing Tad, her dreams about acting had died. At least she'd thought so until these past few weeks. What would've happened if Tad hadn't died, if he would've found his way out of the maze of crazy partying? Would they be together now, acting in movies, working their way up? Would she have gotten a break as big as his had been?

Years had passed since she'd thought about Tad in detail, since she'd let herself go back to that time and remember once more what happened. But tonight, with a warm summer breeze dancing across the nighttime and with sleep a million miles away, Katy gave herself permission.

The friendship she had with Tad in high school had carried over to their college days. He was funny and confident, and he shared her dreams. They went to the same university, their goals of acting so similar that they thought it would be more fun to pursue them together.

From the beginning, Tad had been aggressive about getting starring roles. He didn't have leading-man good looks, but he was cute and quirky, and everything he said made her laugh. Katy never cared what role she received. She was happy playing a lead or a member of the ensemble. As long as she was onstage or in front of a camera and Tad was somewhere nearby, making her laugh.

It was at their fall audition their freshman year of college that Katy first heard Tad sing. His voice melted her insides and made her knees tremble. She fell for him that afternoon and never looked back, but she didn't know how to bring up the subject. Besides, she wasn't sure if Tad had the same feelings for her.

She remembered when things had changed between them. It was closing night of their first college production — *The Sound of Music.* They went with the cast to a local burger joint to celebrate a successful run, and afterwards Katy's car wouldn't start. Tad stayed with her while everyone else left, and since it was cold, they waited for the tow truck inside her car.

She had a bench seat in the front back then, and they sat side by side, laughing and reenacting scenes from the play. Katy had been the oldest daughter in the von

Trapp family, and Tad teased her that maybe she enjoyed the "Sixteen Going on Seventeen" song a little too much.

"Come on, admit it." Tad poked her in the ribs, tickling her even when she pushed his hand away. "You thought the guy was cute."

Then Tad launched into the song, sliding across the bench and singing in a voice that left Katy breathless. He was teasing, but as she joined in and sang along with him, the atmosphere between them changed. The song ended, and their faces were only inches apart.

"Katy, how come you never look at me like you looked at the guy in that scene?"

"Because —" she swallowed, her breaths coming fast and shallow — "because I'm afraid."

He searched her eyes. His voice was a whisper, his breath warm against her face. "Afraid of what?"

"Afraid that you wouldn't look at me like . . ."

"Like what?" He moved closer still.

She felt her heart swell within her. "Like you're looking at me right now."

Tad had kissed her then, kissed her until the tow truck arrived fifteen minutes later. After that there was no turning back. She'd often thought that if she and Tad ever found love together, they'd never break up. Because their friendship was already stronger than anything either of them knew.

Sure enough. By their second year of college they weren't only talking about getting through college and landing parts in movies one day — they were talking about marriage. The best time, they figured, would be the summer after they graduated. But they started going to auditions for films in their junior year, and that spring Tad got the break most actors only dream of.

It was a supporting role opposite a man who was not only very well-known but very wild. The movie would be shot overseas on an island.

Katy was concerned from the moment she heard the news. "Be yourself, Tad. Remember who you are."

He laughed at her. "Nothing could change me. I know who I am, Katy. You're worrying about nothing."

But during the six weeks on location with the film crew, his phone calls came less and less often. On one call, Katy was sure she could hear girls laughing in the background. When she asked him about it, he accused her of being jealous. Tensions built between them, and Katy spent every night praying for him to guard his heart.

When Tad came home, there were two weeks of shooting in Los Angeles, and by then he'd missed an entire semester of school. Also by then, she'd won the part in the series pilot, a TV movie that would film a few weeks later in downtown Chicago and neighboring communities. Tad was thrilled for her, and the night Katy's movie wrapped, he told her he'd celebrate on her behalf.

Something in his tone left her feeling cold and lonely. His film wrapped six days later, and that night the leading actor asked Tad to stick around for another film.

"They love me, Katy. Isn't that great?"

She had done everything she could to smile and cheer him on, but she wasn't happy. Something didn't seem right about him. When he would call, his words would come a little too quickly, and his throat would sound a little too dry. Word on the street was that the actor he was chumming around with had been arrested with cocaine before.

Finally Katy came out and asked him. "Just tell me, Tad. Are you using the stuff?

I mean, everyone you're with these days is into the night scene, so what about you?"

It was the first time he ever got angry at her. He accused her of being a wet rag, a killjoy, someone who couldn't be happy for him in his season of success. She denied that and eventually she began crying. Only then did he settle down and find a voice of reason once more.

She could still remember the last thing he had said to her. "Katy, I'm sorry. I know things are a little strange right now, but they won't always be this way. I'll come home, and we'll go back to being the way we were. I promise."

"It's hard being so far away." Her voice was a choked whisper. "I love you, Tad. I miss you."

"I love you too."

They hung up, and that was the last time she ever talked to him. He went out the next night with the movie crew from his second film, and over the course of the evening he ingested a ridiculous amount of cocaine. Sometime around ten o'clock he was returning to his table from the dance floor when he collapsed.

Several of the people with him tried CPR, but nothing revived him. He was pronounced dead of cardiac arrest at the hospital. Another casualty of the under-world of drugs.

Katy had wept and grieved and tried to make sense of Tad's death. The thing that troubled her most was that he hadn't told her the truth. If he would've been honest, she could've flown out to him, found him the help he needed. She talked to one of the other actors from the film, and he told her that Tad was always the life of the party, that he went from politely telling the crew no, he didn't do drugs to taking more than anyone else.

When the shock of losing him began to wear off, Katy did what she'd always done. She went to auditions. On her third one, she witnessed two casting directors whis-pering about something in the back of a studio soundstage. She asked the leading female actress about it.

The girl just laughed. "It's a drug buy. Happens all the time."

That was the end of it for Katy. She looked at the two men again; then she walked over to the one who had invited her to the audition. "Take my name off the list." She pointed to his clipboard. "I'm not interested."

She walked out before he had a chance to say anything. A few months later she stumbled upon Christian Kids Theater in her area, eventually moving to Bloomington, and never went on another audition again.

Not until Mitch Henry's call.

The memory lingered in her mind a few more minutes before dissolving on the gentle stirs of the nighttime breeze. She never liked to think of Tad dying in an LA nightclub. Rather she believed he had died shortly after he told her good-bye and boarded a plane for the island.

Because the entertainment industry had killed him.

At least that's what she'd always told herself, her way of making peace with what had happened to him.

But now . . . now that she was facing an even bigger break than the one that sucked him into the industry, she finally realized how wrong she was. The entertainment industry hadn't killed Tad. Not that or Hollywood or fame or any other such thing.

His own choices killed him.

He had made the choice to take drugs, to throw everything he knew to be good and true and right out the window and to become someone totally different from the guy he'd been raised to be.

All of it was his choice.

A sense of peace came over Katy, and she felt torn between sadness and the freedom this new understanding brought. Because if it was Tad's choice, then there was no reason to avoid taking a part in a movie simply because of what happened to him.

It was very simple, really. The wild life in Hollywood or New York or anywhere was a choice. And there wasn't a chance in the world that Katy would choose any of it. That's the reason she would be safe filming a movie with Dayne Matthews. It was the reason she would be safe no matter how many movies she might make. And it was the reason she was going to call him one day very soon and tell him she'd done the thing he was dying for her to do.

Sign the contract.

Chapter Twenty-two

Dayne was anxious for a night to himself.

He'd spent the last part of the week with Mitch Henry at the studio going over the *Dream On* cast list and discussing a handful of key scenes. They met with the main director, who shared his vision for the music and camera angles and emotions they needed to get from Dayne to make the film a hit.

Analyzing a script was the part of acting Dayne liked least of all. He'd rather memorize a script and shoot from the hip. Most of the time his knack for understanding people paid off, and he didn't need much coaching. But this was a big film, and his deal with the studio was long term. His agent had told him he needed to have as many conversations with the directors as they wanted.

While he worked through conversations and debates and informational meetings,

Dayne's cell phone never left his side, but Katy still hadn't called. Whenever his phone rang he checked, hoping to see her name, knowing he would see it. Dayne wasn't worried; she would call.

But Mitch was practically beside himself. "What's she waiting for?" He had been in the middle of breaking down a scene, and he suddenly paused and shouted out the question. "I mean, what on earth is she waiting for, Matthews? We gave her a great offer." He shook his head. "You know why she hasn't called?"

"Yes." Dayne used his most pious expression. "She's praying about her decision."

"Great." He tossed his hands in the air. "I'm telling you, she won't take it. I have a feeling. Especially if prayer is involved."

Dayne laughed. He knew a thing or two about prayer. His parents had been missionaries after all. Praying about something didn't mean you'd wind up pulling yourself out of the world. "Of course she'll take it." He patted the casting director on the back and grinned at him. "She'll take it."

"What makes you so sure?" His face was a mass of lines and worry. "There's a lot of money riding on this film, Matthews. We need a female lead."

"Relax. I saw the look in her eyes that day in my trailer. She wants the part, Mitch." Dayne smiled to help ease the situation. "If she needs to pray, then fine. When she's finished talking to God, she'll call. When she does, I guarantee she'll take it."

"I'd like that in writing."

"It will be."

Mitch had brought it up a few other times after that, and now that it was Friday night, Dayne was exhausted. In his younger days he would've called a group of friends and hit the town. After a week like this one, it was fun to swap war stories — who was getting which part, and what studio was handling the moviemaking process better than the others.

But that night he couldn't care less what his colleagues were doing.

He drove home, stopped at his familiar drugstore, and picked up the latest gossip magazines. He used to pick them up once in a while, but lately he'd been getting them every week. He couldn't bear conceding his interest and getting a subscription, so he still bought them when he was out.

As long as the drugstore wasn't busy.

The same old man who had been there

most of the other times was working. He recognized Dayne now, but not because of his celebrity status. Rather because Dayne was a valued customer.

"Dodgers let us down last week." The man shook his head while he rang up Dayne's sale. "You're a fan, right? Isn't that what you said?"

A fan? The term struck Dayne and made him feel whole somehow. Fans were always on the other side of his world. But in this context, yes, he was a fan. A big fan. He smiled at the man. "Yes, I am. And you're right. The Dodgers laid a big egg last week." He paid for his magazines and a few packs of gum and thanked the guy. "I bet they turn it around soon."

Again, photographers snapped pictures of him as he left the store, but the old man didn't notice. Dayne drove the rest of the way home with a smile on his face. His peers liked to complain that they couldn't go anywhere, couldn't have a single normal moment without it being interrupted by autograph seekers or paparazzi. But Dayne couldn't complain. At least he had the drugstore.

He was making stir-fry tonight. His housekeeper had been given a shopping list, and when he got home he found the groceries right where he wanted them. He sautéed the onion and garlic first, then added slivered bamboo shoots, shiitake mushrooms, snow peas, water chestnuts, and broccoli.

Out on his patio he started his grill and placed four fresh, seasoned chicken breasts on it. The fog was creeping back in along the coast, and even though it wasn't quite seven o'clock, the sky was dusky.

Dayne turned on a country music station and felt himself unwind as it filtered through his house. This was the part he loved — being home, making dinner, pretending for a while that he was maybe a lifeguard taking a break from his job down on the beach or a health-club trainer. Someone regular and normal, without the crazy life that came so easily for a guy in his position.

He was flipping the chicken when the phone rang. It wouldn't be Katy Hart. He'd given her his cell phone number, not the home phone. He went into the kitchen, grabbed the cordless receiver, and pushed the On button. "Hello?" His tone sounded lighter than it had been since Katy left.

"Mr. Matthews?" The man at the other end was all business.

"Yes?"

"This is Sergeant Halley from the police department. We've contacted you a few times before."

Dayne rolled his eyes and leaned against the bar that separated his dining area from his kitchen. He took a deep breath and closed his eyes. "How can I help you?"

"We received another of those letters, the ones we told you about before. This one's signed by an Anna Madden. First time the person's left a name." He paused. "Is that familiar to you?"

"Nope." Dayne grabbed a tray and headed back outside, the phone still to his ear. "Probably just an obsessed fan."

"Probably." The sergeant didn't sound convinced. "The problem is, she's threatening worse actions with every letter. This one is the most severe."

Dayne didn't want to ask, but his hesitation gave the sergeant a reason to continue.

"She tells us she's your wife and that she's tired of waiting for you to take your place by her side."

"Oh, brother." Dayne muttered the words under his breath as he moved the chicken to the tray.

"Right, but then she says if any other woman tries to get in her way, she'll have no choice but to kill her."

For a heartbeat, the threat sounded suddenly real. A quick burst of adrenaline flooded his veins and wound up as a small knot in his stomach. Dayne swallowed as he carried the chicken inside and to the kitchen counter. "That's all we've got to go on? Anna Madden thinks she's my wife, wants to kill the competition?" He forced a confident chuckle. "I appreciate the call, Sergeant, but I'm not worried. A lot of fans aren't dealing with a full deck."

"We do have one additional piece of information." The sound of rustling papers sounded over the phone line. "We have a report from someone at DreamFilms Studio, just came in yesterday. Apparently they've seen a woman in a yellow Honda Civic watching the place for quite some time. Figured it was paparazzi, but lately the studio thinks it's some sort of stalker."

A yellow Honda Civic? Dayne squeezed his eyes shut. Where had he heard that before? He drummed his fingers on the countertop, and then it hit him. He opened his eyes. "Kelly Parker saw a yellow Honda Civic outside her home not too long ago."

The sergeant hesitated. "Have the two of you been seeing each other?"

Dayne was used to being asked these

questions by reporters and fans, and he could always be evasive. But this was serious. "Off and on. We've spent some time together at her house recently."

"That's a concern."

The pieces were coming together. If the weird fan was threatening harm to any woman who would get in her way, then maybe she saw Kelly Parker as the competition. "So . . ." Dayne hated this. The phone call was ruining the atmosphere of the evening, changing it into a scene from some sort of horror flick. "You think this is the real thing?"

"We do." The sergeant's voice had been serious throughout the conversation. Now it was even more so. "Her language, the frequency of the notes, the idea of this yellow Honda . . . we don't want to take any chances." He paused. "Did Ms. Parker have any other details, a description of the driver, maybe?"

Dayne sighed and raked his fingers through his hair. "It was a woman and she . . ." Suddenly he could hear Kelly telling him the details. He felt his stomach fall to his knees. "Kelly thought the woman had a knife."

"We'll need to contact Ms. Parker and get a report on that, just so we have the information in the file." There was another sound of papers rustling. "It sounds like this woman's a threat, Mr. Matthews."

"Great." Dayne turned off the fire beneath his stir-fry. No point keeping it warm; he wasn't hungry anymore. "What am I supposed to do, sit here and wait for this crazy woman to show up?"

"Well, we'll have surveillance on your home and when you're at the studio. We'll also have an unmarked car follow you as you come and go from the studio."

Dayne paced to the refrigerator and back to the stove. "How long will you do that?"

"At least a few weeks. Until we catch her. If she's delusional — and it sounds like she is — then she won't be too worried about being caught. She'll think she has a right to stalk you. And a right to harm whoever gets in the way."

"Anything else?" Dayne's stomach was in knots now.

"Yeah." Worry colored the sergeant's warning. "Look out for a yellow Honda Civic."

Chapter Twenty-three

Dayne willed himself to let the warning go.

The sergeant was smart to contact him, keep him on his toes. And extra security couldn't hurt. But how often did a fan actually hurt someone? He thought the question over. There had been a young woman in a sitcom once who was shot by a stalker when she opened her door; that one was hard to forget. And a few other big names who'd had close calls with obsessed fans. But otherwise, police must get letters from crazy people all the time. That didn't mean they'd climb through his window or hunt down his friends and try to kill them.

The muscles at the base of his neck started to relax. He took one of the chicken breasts, cut it into little cubes, and tossed it into the pan with the stir-fried vegetables. Then he turned the heat back on and covered the pan. Two minutes later it was hot enough to dish onto his plate.

He grabbed the magazines he'd bought and took them and his dinner to the dining-room table, the small one that sat just inside his patio door. The sun was setting, and another bank of fog was moving in. Fog was typical for this time of year, especially on the coast. At least it had been burning off during the day.

The magazines were still in the bag. He took one of them out and stared at the cover. On the lower corner was something he hadn't noticed before. A small snapshot of Kelly Parker and him, their faces close together. The caption beneath it read "Back together again?"

Dayne groaned. He flipped to the inside cover, scanned the index, and turned to the story. The two-page spread was almost entirely photos — one of the photos showed the two of them sitting in his car talking; another showed them in a full liplock; a third had the two of them heading through the darkness into her house; and a final shot showed him slipping out through her back door the next morning.

The copy read: "Dayne Matthews, perennial playboy, spends a night with hotshot actress Kelly Parker. Sources say things are steamy between the two, but Matthews denies reports of a patchup."

"Don't you people ever let up?" he whispered. What if Katy Hart saw the article? She'd lose all respect for him. It might even influence her decision. He thought about that. Probably not. She wasn't the type to read the gossip rags. He tapped his fingers on the edge of the table. What about Kelly? She'd already had enough of the paparazzi. If she had feelings for him — and he thought she still might — this would be salt in her wounded heart, for sure.

He tossed the magazine onto the table and focused on his dinner. This was supposed to be an easy night, dinner and the privacy of his own home. Instead he was frustrated and tense, warned about a wacko in a yellow Honda and facing the reality of the pictures in the magazine.

If they'd caught him at any other time the pictures wouldn't matter — shots of him coming and going to Starbucks, spreads of him walking on the beach or leaving the studio. But early morning pictures of him leaving Kelly Parker's house? His blood boiled from the insanity of it.

Strange, really. But all he could think about were his parents. His parents dead these past eighteen years. They'd been so supportive of his interest in drama, so sure he could use his talents for the Lord.

Dayne managed a soft, sarcastic laugh.

The idea never even crossed his mind. The Lord had gotten enough of the important pieces of his life — his parents' time, their attention, and finally their lives. The last thing Dayne had ever considered was giving his acting talent to the Lord.

Still, the idea of his parents seeing photographs of him caught in the act of casual sex was something that grated on him. He took four quick bites of the stir-fry. Never mind his parents. Everything grated on him tonight, ever since the phone call from the sergeant. He stared at his plate. The vegetables were limp and the chicken was cold. Even his dinner wasn't working out.

He pushed his plate back and stared out the window. The fog was thicker now, settling in around the edges of his patio.

Once — not long after he visited Bloomington, Indiana — he had gone to a cupping expert, and a spiritualist in the next room had given him a free session on visualization, ways to clear his mind and find inner peace. The cupping was different. For hundreds of dollars a session, he would lie facedown on a table, and the therapist would push a heated drinking glass against his back, creating a vacuum.

The harder she pushed, the more muscle tissue would be sucked into the hollow space.

It was supposed to cleanse his system, something like that.

But the part that stayed with him was what the spiritualist had said. "If you're looking for inner peace, you need to find something holistic and centered. Something like Kabbalah."

Kabbalah had come up a few times.

Some of his friends in the industry were pretty taken by the idea. An older actress once explained that Kabbalah was better than Christianity because it allowed you to become your own god, to find a center in your being where spirituality and goodness could thrive, separate from the guilt and legalism normally associated with religion.

Sounded good.

At least it would if it weren't for his upbringing. Twelve years in a Christian boarding school for missionary kids had left him with the inability to think of religion separate from Jesus Christ. Right or wrong. Still, maybe there was something to this Kabbalah. If he could get over the guilt. Maybe the spiritualist was right, that finding his center, knowing his own nature better, would give him peace.

Especially on days like this.

He pushed away from the table and cleared his plate. Visualization would take too much time. He rinsed the dishes, dried his hands, and pulled his cell phone from his pocket. Nothing. No call from her. *Come on, Katy. Let me know what you're going to do.*

For a few seconds he stared at the phone, willing it to ring. Then an idea came to him. Maybe he could find the peace he needed by watching her TV movie, the pilot she'd starred in a few years ago. That would do it. He'd never finished it, and something about her — watching her, studying her — filled him with a sense that all was right with the world.

If he were a praying man, he'd be begging God for her to decide yes about the film. But prayer wouldn't change the mind of a woman two thousand miles away. Only she could do that. In the meantime, he could watch her movie.

He turned off the country music, found the video, and set it up in the family room. He wanted the view to the outside, even with the fog. Sitting in his theater room alone was no way to spend a Friday night. Not with some fanatic lurking outside. He clicked the remote, and his gas fireplace sprang to life. That was the nice thing about summers on Malibu Beach: the evenings were still cool enough for a fire.

The movie needed to be rewound, but after a few minutes it was ready to play. He took the most comfortable chair in the room and clicked the remote. The moment the credits and music started, he felt himself unwind again. Katy might not call, but he could still spend an evening with her.

He was fifteen minutes into the movie, right in the middle of a scene that featured Katy, when the doorbell rang. For the flickering of an instant Dayne hesitated. Was it the psycho fan? He thought about grabbing his pepper spray, but then he stopped himself.

She wouldn't walk up to the front door and ring the bell. Not if she'd been stalking him all this time.

He paused the movie and walked to the front door. He opened it, and there was Kelly Parker, a shy smile playing on the corners of her lips. "Hi."

"Hi." Dayne tried to hide his frustration. He didn't want to hang out with Kelly. Not tonight and not alone in his house. He leaned against the door. "What's up?"

"I was lonely. I thought I might find you here." She gave a delicate shrug of her shoulders. "Aren't you going to let me in?"

"Oh." He forced a chuckle and opened the door wider. "Sorry."

She stepped in and closed it behind her. Before he had time to say another word, she wove her hands around his waist, leaned up, and kissed him, a kiss that told him why she'd come. He returned the kiss, but he felt nothing stir within him. It was the way he sometimes felt when he did an on-screen kiss. Like a professional, good at what he was doing, but not even the least bit personally involved.

"Dayne?" She drew back, breathless, and searched his eyes. "You don't want to kiss me?"

He hooked his thumbs through her belt loops. "Of course I do." He hated lying, but what else could he say? He had a feeling honesty wouldn't go over real well right now. "But, hey, what's this all about?"

She lifted her chin, confident even in light of her doubts. Her voice held a smoldering desire. "I can't stop thinking about you, Dayne. How it was the other night."

"Oh yeah?" He let his eyes wander down the length of her. She was a knockout, no question. So what was his problem? How come he kept comparing her to —

"Anyway, I wanna know if I got the

part." She pulled him close again, keeping her head tilted back far enough to see his response. "It's mine, right?"

Dayne laughed. "You amaze me, Kelly Parker. Just when I'm most worried about you, here you are. More cocky and sure of yourself than ever."

"So . . . did I get it?" She giggled and kissed him again. But something in her eyes wasn't quite right. Her pupils maybe, just a little too dilated. Her words were fast and sticky, like she needed a glass of water. "Tell me, Dayne, tell me. I'm dying to know."

What was wrong with her? He resisted the urge to push her away. Instead he ran his tongue over his lower lip and studied her expression. "We're not sure yet. You did a great job, Kelly. We're just waiting to see what happens."

"Waiting?" Kelly frowned. "I'm in this business, remember, Dayne? What you mean is you offered it to the newcomer, right? Is that it?"

Dayne took a step back and leaned against the entryway wall. "Okay, yes. We offered it to her. Mitch loved her." He tossed up his hands. "We have no idea if she'll take it or not. If she doesn't, you're next in line."

Disappointment filled in the gentle curves of her cheeks and lips. She seemed calmer now, more herself. "Mitch loved her . . . or you did?"

"Come on, Kelly. Don't take it personally. You know the routine in this business. When it comes your way, take it. When it doesn't, don't take it seriously. The part fit her."

She grinned at him. "You're teasing me, right, Dayne? Is that it? Telling me this just to make it more exciting when I get the part, right?"

"If I said yes, I'd be lying." He winced. "Sorry, Kelly. It was nothing you did."

Her smile faded. "Well, that's lousy. What about my audition? What about — ?"

He held his finger to her lips. There it was again, the wild roller coaster of emotions. She hadn't stayed one way more than a minute since she arrived. "Shhhh." This time he leaned in and kissed her, more to change the subject than anything else. When he drew back he grinned at her, willing her to relax. "The new girl might turn us down."

"Thanks." She rolled her eyes, but the hurt from earlier was gone. "Keep me posted, okay?"

"Okay."

She moved past him, set her purse on a shelf near the entryway, and headed into his family room. Dayne followed her. For a moment she stared at the image frozen on the screen — a close-up of Katy still on pause from a few minutes earlier. Kelly's eyebrows came together in a puzzled look. "Who's the girl?"

Dayne moved between Kelly and the television screen. "Katy . . . Katy Hart." He grabbed the remote and turned off the set. "She's the newcomer." He pointed to the TV. "That was a pilot she filmed a few years ago, something that didn't pan out."

"So why'd you turn it off?" She flopped down on the sofa and patted the spot beside her. "Sit down and let's watch it."

Dayne wanted to tell her no, that the night was going to be just him and Katy, and so maybe she should just leave. But Kelly was his friend, so instead he dropped to the spot next to her and aimed the remote at the television. After pressing a couple of buttons, the film was back on again. "There, you happy?"

"Depends on how good she is." Kelly crossed her arms and smiled at him. Then she focused on the screen.

They watched the movie in silence. With Katy in living color before him, Dayne forgot he had someone sitting next to him. What was it about the Bloomington kids theater director that was so appealing, so fresh? He studied her, and he began to imagine. How new and wonderful it would be to make a film with her. She would be different from the Hollywood girls he knew, the ones who would agree to coffee and wind up in your bed a few hours later.

Katy was one of the real people. Maybe that was it.

He was still thinking about her, still mesmerized by her actions, her voice, her emotions on-screen, when beside him Kelly turned off the television.

"Hey . . ." He took the remote from her. "What's that all about?"

"Dayne Matthews, I can't believe you." She didn't look angry but rather amazed. As if something she couldn't quite understand had just occurred to her. Her mouth hung open for a few beats. "You're in love with her!"

"What?" Dayne slid to the far end of the sofa, putting distance between them. He angled himself so he was facing her. "What're you talking about?"

She pointed to the television. "That . . . that whatever her name is. Katy something." She laughed, but it sounded more like shock than humor. "I was watching you during the last scene, and I'd know that look in your eyes anywhere." She stood and looked down at him. "You're in love with her, aren't you?"

"Kelly, that's ridiculous." Dayne rose and stuffed his hands in his jeans pockets. "I don't even know her." He nodded toward the screen. "I was watching that more for research than anything else."

"Fine." She walked past him through the dining room and into the kitchen. "I won't stay, Dayne. I get the feeling you don't want me here."

He followed slowly behind her, and while she poured herself a glass of water he wondered again if she was on something — cocaine maybe or some mood-altering drug. He steadied himself, digging deep for the patience he didn't feel. "I thought we were friends, Kelly. Wasn't that what we decided? Things wouldn't work between us, right? That was you, wasn't it?"

She whirled around. "That wasn't how things were the other night at my house." Her voice was low, but it was filled with hurt. She spread her fingers on her chest. "I felt something, Dayne. Didn't that mean anything to you?"

"Yes." He went to her, took the glass of

water from her, set it on the counter, and caught her hand. "It means I care a lot about you, Kelly." He released her fingers. "I can't offer more than that."

Her shoulders eased a little, and she pulled him close, slipping her arms around him in a hug that was different from the first one. "I'm sorry." She peeked up at him. "I probably sound like a raving maniac."

He stroked her back. This was better, the Kelly Parker he knew and cared for — not the one demanding something he couldn't give. She couldn't be on drugs. Kelly wouldn't stoop that low, not even in her worst hour.

"Hey . . ." He remembered the call from the police. "Speaking of raving maniacs . . ." His voice was low and calm. He didn't want the news to scare her. "Remember the yellow Honda Civic and the lady with the knife?"

Kelly shuddered and leaned back enough to make eye contact with him. "Of course."

"Well —" he pursed his lips — "the police called today. This stalker person who's been sending them crazy letters about me — remember I told you?"

"Yes." Her eyes were wider now, her lips parted.

"The police think she drives a yellow Honda Civic."

"Wonderful." She lifted her hands above her head and let them fall. Then she snatched her glass and dumped the water into the sink. "Where's your wine?"

He took the cup from her again and set it back down. "Look, Kelly, no wine. I'm turning in early tonight. I just wanted to tell you about the Honda lady. You know, so if you see that car again you can call 911."

For a few seconds she stood silent, shocked. Fear and anger taking turns with her expression. Then she spotted something, and he followed her gaze. The magazines on the dining-room table. "I thought you said it was better not to read them." She passed him, walked to the table, and picked up the first one.

"I said *you* were better not to read them." He came up behind her and tried to take the magazine from her.

But she jerked it out of reach. "It's okay, Dayne. I can handle it." At that same instant she saw the photo of the two of them on the cover. "Great." She flipped the magazine open to the section where their photographs took up the two-page spread.

She muttered something under her breath and then turned to another story a few pages away. This one referred to the six worst-smelling people in Hollywood. She was number five. "What?" She made a sound that was more like a cry than a laugh. " 'Kelly Parker's penchant for Italian foods gets the best of her in this poll. Our advice: Lay off the garlic!' "

Dayne wasn't sure if she was going to drop to the floor in a heap or explode in rage. Then, with a burst of emotion, she ripped the page from the magazine. She tore the page apart the way he'd torn apart the magazine at Ruby's that day, only Kelly cried as she did it.

"Kelly, c'mere." He held his hands out to her. "I told you not to read that garbage. None of it's true."

"It's not true, is it? We're not getting back together!" In a frantic whir of motion she crumpled the pieces of paper into a ball. "Because you . . . don't . . . want me." She wiped at her tears, then stormed back to the kitchen and stuffed the paper in the trash beneath his sink.

As she turned around to face him, her eyes filled with desperation. "I hate this, Dayne." Her arms were shaking, but the anger left her. She crossed her arms and stared at the floor. "I hate everything."

"Kelly, you can't think like that. Everything's going to be okay."

"Forget it." She pulled her keys from her pocket and headed toward him. "The magazine thinks we're an item; isn't that a joke?" She choked on a sarcastic laugh, one that was part sob. Then she walked past him. "If they only knew."

Before she left she turned to face him once more. "I'm losing a starring role to a nobody, the guy I want doesn't want me, the public knows my private life, and if that's not enough, they think I smell like garlic. I haven't eaten Italian food in years. Too many carbs." She twisted her expression and lifted one hand in the air. "Go figure." She forced a smile. "But at least the fans are entertained. Especially the crazy one in the yellow Honda." She bit her lip. "Excuse me —" her voice fell to a whisper — "if I can't believe everything's going to be okay."

She marched back through the family room and grabbed her purse near the front door. But as she turned the handle, her purse slipped and fell on the floor, spilling an assortment of business cards and pens and coins and something else. Something that made sense of every strange thing Kelly Parker had said and done all evening.

A bottle of unmarked pills.

Chapter Twenty-four

The *Tom Sawyer* cast was working on the schoolroom scene, and Katy could feel things slowly coming together. The point of this part of the play was to show Tom's increasing interest in Becky and the fact that Tom's gang was not made up of stellar students.

They were attempting to do the scene with props — even though they wouldn't have all props in place until the week before opening night, when they would move into the Bloomington theater. But props were needed for this one. It included an apple and Tom's rowdy friends tossing it across the aisle to one another every time the teacher turned around.

In the midst of the chaos, Tom was supposed to slip from his side of the classroom and zip over to the other side to sit by Becky. Tim Reed knew his lines, and Sarah Jo had come into her own, showing the same striking ability to get in character that Katy had seen at the callback audition.

Relieved, Katy sat near the front of the sanctuary. At least that much was going right. She stood and made a circular motion with her hand. "Okay, let's run it again from the top."

Half the kids took seats in the mock classroom, while the others disappeared through a door into the hallway. The teenager playing the schoolteacher took her place at the front of the classroom and began talking in a whiny, nasally voice. "Now, class, today's lesson will be on mathematics." She turned toward the blackboard.

As she did, Tom and his gang came sneaking into the classroom and quickly took their seats.

The teacher spun around, her face beet red. "Tom Sawyer! Late again! I do say, Tom, you'll need a paddling before the day is through." She turned back to the board.

This time, Tom tossed an apple to Becky to get her attention. The way they'd blocked the scene, the apple was supposed to land nicely in Sarah Jo's hands. But Sarah Jo was whispering to the girl next to her, something about where they were supposed to be sitting by the looks of it. The apple flew across the aisle and hit Sarah Jo square on the head.

"Ouch!" Sarah Jo rubbed her temple. The apple rolled off to the side of the classroom, and more than half the kids started giggling.

"Okay." Katy wanted to laugh, but she kept her tone serious. She stood and made eye contact with the kids who were smirking. "If that happens during the show, what're we going to do? Sit here and snicker?" She kept a straight face so the kids would know she meant business.

One of the little girls in the front row raised her hand. "Maybe we should run after the apple if it gets away like that. Then we could give it to Sarah Jo."

"Good . . ."

The morning dragged on, but they managed to block three scenes, enough to get back on schedule. The group ran through two of the songs until Katy was satisfied. She glanced at the clock every few minutes. She'd finally made up her mind. She was going to call Dayne when practice was over and tell him the news.

She was taking the part.

Alice Stryker pulled her aside after the break and frowned. "Sarah Jo needs to be upstage more; don't you think? Everyone knows she has the prettiest voice. If you want your show to be a success people will need to hear her sing."

Katy only stared at the woman, baffled. How could the mother of such a sweet little girl be so awful? She cleared her throat. "I'll do the blocking, thank you. If I need your help I'll ask."

Mrs. Stryker smoothed out the wrinkles in her blouse and tossed her head. "I'll work with Sarah Jo when we get home. Maybe if she projects more you'll be able to hear her better. I've sat near the back of the room, and she simply isn't loud enough." She glared at Katy. "If you won't move her up, I'll get her to sing louder."

Never had Katy been tempted to ban a parent from practices, but Alice Stryker was pushing her. She ignored the woman's last comments and set to work on the second half of practice.

Krissy Schick, the program coordinator, found Katy a few minutes before it was over. "We're sold out for the first five performances!" She grinned. "Way to go, Katy. I don't know what we'd do without you. The whole community's talking about CKT."

Katy felt her heart sink. How upset would Krissy be when she found out Katy was taking a part in a major motion picture, that she'd miss the next show, and that her future with CKT was in limbo? She hesitated. "Thanks, Krissy. That's good to hear."

Krissy was a wonderful person, kind and warm, the mother of four kids. Whenever Katy had been discouraged about a certain play or a performance, Krissy was the one she went to. The woman had an innate ability to read Katy and offer just the right words to lift her mood.

This time was no different. She studied Katy. "Is everything okay? You look a little distant."

Katy leaned in and hugged her. "You're so good, Krissy. Always sensitive to what I'm feeling." She drew back and smiled. "I'm fine. Just a lot on my mind."

"Okay." Krissy didn't look sure. "I'm here if you need me, remember that. I'm always here."

Guilt stabbed pushpins at the center of Katy's conscience. Krissy had done everything to make Katy's time in Bloomington nothing but wonderful. She would have to tell the woman about her decision very soon. Otherwise it would feel like she'd been hiding things from her. Katy couldn't let that happen.

When practice was over, when she'd answered fifty-two questions about costumes and rehearsal times and made thirty-eight suggestions about how to improve a line or a scene, she looked at Al and Nancy Helmes and Rhonda Sanders and took a deep breath. "Well, how do we look?"

Nancy grinned. "Everything's shaping up great, Katy. You're working your magic again."

"I'm surprised, frankly." Al winked at her. "This one had me a little worried."

Rhonda pointed straight up. "God's on our side — don't forget that. Of course, it always comes together."

"God and Katy!" Al linked arms with his wife, and they headed for the door. "Off to get her a half cup of coffee. See you next week."

Rhonda waited until they were gone. Then she turned to Katy. "You're going to do it, aren't you?"

Katy couldn't lie to her friend. She could feel the way her eyes danced, even before she said a word. "The part?"

"Yes, you're taking it, right?"

"I am." Katy folded her hands and squealed. "I'm calling him right now."

"I can't believe it, Katy." Rhonda gave her a quick hug. Her eyes held as much uncertainty as they did joy. "I'm happy for you. Just don't forget to come back home."

"I won't." She squeezed Rhonda's hand, grabbed her bag, and together they walked out the door.

Not until Katy was alone in her Nissan did she make her decision. She wouldn't call Dayne, not yet. She'd call the studio and make travel arrangements. Then she'd call him Monday, as soon as she arrived in Los Angeles. That way they could talk about the contract details in person.

Katy's heart raced as she started her car and headed out of the church parking lot. She'd already told the Flanigans, and she had their blessing. Now she only had to make flight plans and pack her things. The mere idea of going to LA to sign a movie deal was enough to take her breath away.

She could hardly wait to get on the plane.

Dayne was tired of sitting home alone waiting for the phone call from Katy.

Tonight he called Marc David, his actor friend, the one who was suing one of the biggest gossip magazines for the story about his father. A night out would be a good way to catch up. They agreed to hit the Starleen Café, a three-story state-of-the-art dance club on the outskirts of Hollywood. It was another hot spot among the Hollywood elite, and this one — like the others — had a private area for the stars. The entire third floor was for members only.

Dayne and Marc knew the guard at the elevator door and were waiting for the ride up when a woman from the crowd grabbed Dayne's arm. "Dayne Matthews! I can't believe it — Dayne Matthews!" She screamed his name, and everyone in the downstairs section of the club who hadn't noticed the two actors breeze toward the elevator spotted them now.

"Hey." He jerked his arm free, and then he remembered the sergeant's warning about the possibly dangerous female fan. What if this was her? She might be armed. He glanced at the woman and saw that she had her hand in her pocket.

She lunged toward him again, and this time he shoved her back, making her lose her balance and fall onto her backside. The woman screamed and pointed at Dayne. "I'm contacting my attorney! You can't push me like that!"

The crowd grew restless, casting rude looks at Dayne and Marc. But before the scene could get too out of hand, Marc elbowed him. The elevator was ready. They slipped inside and fell against the back wall. "That was insane." Dayne's breathing was hard and fast. "I thought she had a knife."

"A knife?" Marc eyed him strangely; then a knowing look came into his eyes. "The stalker lady I've been reading about?"

"Yeah." Dayne raked his fingers through his hair. He was still trying to catch his breath. "The police told me to be careful of crazy women fans, and when she grabbed me . . ." He shook his head. "I can't believe I pushed her."

"You did everything right." Marc rolled his eyes. "If she calls her attorney, let me know. I'll be your witness."

The doors opened, and the atmosphere on the third floor was entirely different. The lighting wasn't quite so dark, and no one ran toward them as they made their way to a table in the back. Three of the city's leading men were sitting at the nearest table, and all of them nodded or waved at Dayne and Marc.

"What's up, boys?" One of them stood and grabbed first Dayne's hand, then Marc's. "You look a little lost."

Dayne ran his hand over his brow. "The natives are restless downstairs."

"I'm telling you, man —" one of the other actors chuckled — "take the back elevator. No one knows about it."

The guy was right. Dayne had forgotten about that entrance, but not after tonight. He'd never go through the main doors again. He gave an easy laugh. "Good plan."

The third guy at the table was a pillar in Hollywood, one with impeccable character even after two decades of starring in films. He was drinking what looked like iced tea. "So, crazy Dayne, no women tonight?"

"Not tonight." He shook his head. "Living a little cleaner these days."

The man smiled. "Good for you."

They talked a few more minutes, and then Dayne and Marc took seats at their table. They ordered drinks, and Marc updated him on his case against the magazine. "It looks pretty solid." He anchored his elbows on the table. "I'd like to see the suit put them out of business."

Dayne leaned back and raised one eyebrow. "Don't count on it. Those rags have more money than we know." He crossed his arms. "I think it's a national addiction, finding out the dirt on movie stars. They probably budget to lose a lawsuit or two now and then."

The waitress came with their drinks. She was a professional, paid to act unimpressed by the recognized faces on the private third floor.

Their conversation shifted to the projects they were working on. Marc was filming the sequel to a blockbuster hit, but he was worried that it wasn't as strong as the first one. "You have to be so careful." He drew a slow breath. "Take part in a lousy film and the fans hold it against you for a year."

"I know it." Dayne made a face. "Happened to me a few years ago. Could happen again if I don't get the girl I want for *Dream On*."

"New girl?"

"Yeah, an unknown." Dayne looked down. He didn't want to give away too much. Especially when he wasn't sure of his own feelings toward Katy. "I'll let you know if she comes through."

They talked awhile longer about *Dream On* and the scenes Dayne had worked through with Mitch Henry during the week.

Then Marc pulled out a flyer from the inside of his sport jacket. "Hey, Dayne . . . you ever heard of Kabbalah?"

Kabbalah? There it was again. "Lots of

people are talking about it." Dayne took a sip of his drink. "I don't really understand it."

"I'm going to give it a try. There's a center not far from here." The music was louder than before, so Marc had to raise his voice to be heard. "God is within you, a part of you. If you reach a high enough level of consciousness, you can become your own god. That sort of thing." He shrugged. "Beats any traditional religion I've ever heard of."

"Yeah, something I should look into." Dayne wanted to feel good about the possibility, but it still stirred up old guilt in his soul. The remains of a childhood of Christian doctrine.

"So tell me about the new girl." Marc lowered his chin and shot Dayne a curious look, one that implied Dayne might know more about the girl than how well she could act. "I don't know her, right?"

"No one knows her." Dayne felt warm at the thought of Katy. If only she'd call. He was about to say something more about her, how she was from Bloomington and didn't want anything to do with the wild life in Hollywood, but his phone rang first. He held it up and grinned. "Maybe this is her."

He slipped into a corridor where it was quieter and flipped his cell phone open without checking the caller ID. "Hello?"

"Dayne . . ." The voice was raspy and breathless, as if the caller was gasping for air. "Help me . . . Dayne, help me."

"Who is this?" Immediately Dayne thought about the wacko fan. Could she have gotten hold of his cell phone number?

"It's Kelly." Her words were slow and fading.

"Kelly?" Dayne paced from one end of the corridor to the other. Had the stalker found her? His stomach dropped to his feet. "Kelly, talk to me!"

"I'm . . . sick." She took two shaky breaths. "Help me . . . Dayne."

He felt himself relax. This wasn't about the stalker. Kelly must've had the flu, something like that. "What's wrong, honey? You sound awful."

"Pills . . . too many pills."

His heart did a flip-flop. "Did you try to . . . Kelly, you didn't do this on purpose, did you?"

"Help me . . . not . . . much time!"

Suddenly Dayne snapped into action. This wasn't a sympathy call — it was an emergency. "Kelly, hold on. I'm calling for help, honey. Stay awake. Don't go to sleep, okay?"

"Okay." There was a clicking sound.

"Kelly?" He checked the cell phone, but the call had ended. He dialed 911 and paced another time down the corridor.

"Nine-one-one, what's your emergency?"

"A friend of mine took a bottle of pills. She needs help."

"Okay, sir. Why don't you give us your name."

Two minutes passed while the operator got all the information — his name, Kelly's name, her address. It felt like forever.

When the call was over, Dayne tore back into the seating area and found Marc. "Come with me. Kelly Parker's in trouble." He nodded toward the door. "I think she overdosed."

Marc was on his feet instantly, and five minutes later — despite the fans that tried to circle them — they were in the car and on their way to Kelly's house. At least two photographers tailed them, and this time they made Dayne furious.

"Are you sure? Kelly Parker over-dosing?" Marc faced him, his expression tense. "Why on earth would she do that?"

"Because . . ." Dayne tapped on his rearview mirror and looked at the sedan following them. He gritted his teeth. "Because the photographers are driving her batty."

When they arrived at her house, the ambulance was already there, its lights flashing. The photographers were bound to get every gritty detail, but there was nothing Dayne could do about that now. He had to see how Kelly was doing. He and Marc raced from his Escalade up to her front door.

Paramedics had her on a stretcher, an IV bag hooked to one arm. "I'm Dayne Matthews. I'm the one who called." He took a few steps closer. Kelly's complexion was a scary gray, her body lifeless. "Is she . . . will she be okay?"

"Her heartbeat's slow but steady." The paramedic nearest him looked over his shoulder at Dayne. "We're taking her in, but I think we got here in time."

Dayne felt relief spread through his body. The paramedics were moving her out of the house, and suddenly Dayne realized what was about to happen. The photographers would capture the moment for the next gossip rag, and the whole world would know Kelly Parker had tried to kill herself. "Hey." He held his hand up to the lead paramedic. "Can you wait a minute, let me get rid of the paparazzi?"

The man gave a quick look at Kelly and nodded. "Hurry."

"Come on." Dayne grabbed Marc's elbow and jerked him out the front door. They ran out, Dayne in the lead, and darted into his car. "There's only two of them. Let's get 'em both."

"What're we gonna do?"

Dayne's mind rushed ahead. "Let's stage a fight." He pointed down the street. "See, they're both over there. Parked in those cars. You up?"

"Definitely." Marc looked at him, waiting for a sign.

When Dayne's SUV was just a few yards from the photographers, he suddenly slammed on his brakes, flew out the door, and stormed around the front of the vehicle. "Get out and do something about it!" he shouted at Marc, drawing on his best acting skills.

Marc jumped out of the SUV and shoved Dayne so hard he stumbled back five or six feet. From the corner of his eye, Dayne saw the photographers turn and aim their cameras straight at them. The plan was working.

The shouting continued for almost a

minute, while the paparazzi hounds took pictures. Finally Dayne pushed Marc back into the SUV, pretended to kick the door, and raced around to the driver's seat. When he sped off down the street, the two photographers were right behind him.

After a ten-minute chase, Dayne stopped the vehicle, and both he and Marc climbed out. As the paparazzi snapped pictures, no doubt certain they were about to see the second half of a rollicking fight, Dayne and Marc walked to the back of the SUV, leaned against the bumper, laughed, and shook hands.

"Good job." Dayne kept the smile on his face. "Kelly's halfway to the hospital by now."

Marc laughed to keep up the act. "Mission accomplished."

They waited three minutes until the photographers got bored of the happy scene. By then they must've realized they'd been tricked, because they both took off in the direction of Kelly's house.

As soon as they were gone, Dayne nodded to the SUV. "Let's get to the hospital."

Dayne's mind whirled as he drove. What had just happened? Kelly Parker was flying across town in an ambulance because life — the life she lived as a premier Hollywood actress — wasn't worth living. He'd had to stage a fight with one of his best friends just to give Kelly the privacy of being carried out on a stretcher from her own home.

Their lives were insane. And somewhere in Bloomington, Indiana, Katy Hart was trying to make up her mind about taking a leading role that would put her smack in the middle of it. As he drove to the hospital and considered what he'd say to Kelly Parker to give her hope again, all he could think about was that he'd done his best to get Katy to say yes.

But maybe if he cared about her that was the worst thing he could've done. Because everything she worried about regarding the life of fame and fortune wasn't exaggerated the way he'd told her.

It was right on.

Enough of the warnings. Chloe was ready to act.

She hadn't eaten in three days. Just an occasional cup of coffee and a smoothie or two from the ice-cream shop in Malibu Market. Otherwise she barely left her car. She and Anna, that is. But she was keeping Anna down, reminding her that she held control. She and no one else.

The knife was always with her, the knife and the camera — in case anyone asked questions. She'd even used the camera a time or two. Photographs that could go in their family album later on. But it was the knife that consumed her these days, the knife that filled her thoughts. She'd starved herself long enough. Finally she was ready to use it.

"You're loony," Anna had told her the day before when she sat in her private place on the hill watching Dayne's house. "You'll get caught, and then we'll both go down."

"I won't get caught!" Chloe had screamed at her sister. "Leave me alone!"

The thing was, something had to be keeping Dayne away from her. By now he should've come out and found her, introduced himself, and explained how sorry he was for neglecting their wedding vows.

Forever, right? Wasn't that what he'd promised her?

She'd told Anna that she kept Dayne in the glove box, but that was only half the truth. The glove box wasn't a real glove box. It was a private place in her mind, a place where no one else could enter, not even Anna. And that's where Dayne had lived since they were married. But now it was time for him to come home.

If she had to take him by force, so be it. She was ready.

And since something had to be keeping him, she was pretty sure it was another woman. That was Dayne's style, something she'd have to break him of. Other women all the time. He wouldn't be able to lie to her because she read the magazines. If Dayne was sleeping with someone, she knew it. In fact, she knew it first. Because she knew where he was every day, every waking hour.

That's more than the celebrity magazines could say.

Now it was Monday and she was parked outside the studio again. Who cared if the police came and asked her questions? She could always wield the knife on them, right?

"No, you can't wield a knife at a police officer, stupid." Anna appeared in the passenger seat and sneered at Chloe. "They'll pull a gun and shoot you dead."

Chloe thought about that. "Dead's better than being without Dayne. He's my husband, Anna. We have a right to be together."

"You're a nutcase."

Chloe glared at her. "Shut up or I'll stick the knife through you instead."

That quieted her down. It always quieted her.

She turned and stared at the driveway that led to the studio. If Dayne wanted to fool around with other women, that was his business. But it was her job to get rid of the cheap Hollywood trash who would dare sleep with her husband.

And so it had come to this: The next woman she saw with Dayne Matthews was as good as dead. She would follow him every hour until she saw who was taking his time, his heart. Then she would find a way to grab the woman and kill her. Kill her once and for all. It would be messy with a knife, but Chloe had no other choice. She would kill her and bury the body. She'd done it before.

Then Dayne would be free to take his place by her side, and one day very soon they could start planning the trip they'd put off for far too long.

Their honeymoon.

Chapter Twenty-five

Katy made the call Monday at five o'clock — two hours after landing in Los Angeles. It was her third trip in less than a month, and this time she didn't tell Dayne she was coming. She had his cell phone number, and as soon as she was settled in her hotel, she dialed it.

He answered on the first ring. "Katy?" His voice was so full of hope, she almost laughed.

"Hi." Her smile sounded in her voice. "Guess where I am?"

"Hannibal, Missouri?"

This time she did laugh. "No, I'm on vacation from there." She paused. "I talked to the studio travel department and booked a flight. I'm in LA."

"Really?" The hope doubled. "So . . . have you made your decision?"

"Yes." She didn't want to keep him waiting a minute longer. "I'm taking the

443

part. I have the contract with me."

Dayne let out a shout, but almost as quickly he recovered. "You won't be sorry. We'll have a blast making this movie."

"That's what I figured." She stared out her hotel room onto the busy boulevard below. "Have you had dinner?"

"Not yet. I'm still at the studio." He hesitated, but it sounded like his enthusiasm was still building. "How about you come pick me up and we'll go down to Paradise Cove — it's a private beach. They film a lot of movies there."

Katy felt a chill pass from her neck to her elbows. Was this how it would be? Together with him day after day, sharing meals and conversation? Building a friendship? Katy tried to gather her thoughts, but they were like fallen leaves in a windstorm. "That'd be great. What about dinner?"

"I'll get us box picnics from the commissary."

Katy was at the studio thirty minutes later. She stepped in through a back door and found Dayne where he'd been before — in the office down the hall. He beamed at her as he stood and held out his hand. She took it, and the resulting handshake made them both smile. "The car's outside."

He drove, but he kept the window up. "This is great. These rental cars throw off the paparazzi every time." He grinned at her. "Life feels almost normal."

Katy's smile faded. "Is it that bad? The fame and attention?"

"Depends on how you judge it." He adjusted his sunglasses and shrugged. "Day to day it isn't bad. You get used to it."

"They don't really follow you everywhere, do they?" She was surprised at how comfortable she felt, driving down Pacific Coast Highway with Dayne at the wheel. "The paparazzi, I mean."

He gave her a crooked frown. "Yeah, they do. Some of their high-powered lenses can see through windows into the darkest rooms of your house. You have to be on your guard all the time."

The thought cast a shadow on the sunny feeling in her heart. "But that's just for people like you and a few others. The biggest names, right?"

"Not really." He rolled the window down now and leaned his elbow on the frame of the door. "If you've got a name or a face the public might recognize, they'll follow you." He grinned at her. "You know, in case they catch you scratching yourself or with your hair less than perfect."

Her heart rate picked up, and she silently scolded herself. What was she worried about? God had led her to this decision, hadn't He? Certainly she wouldn't be of any interest to the paparazzi. "I guess it's better to stay away from the gossip magazines."

"Exactly." He leaned back against the headrest, the sunshine on his face. He gave her a quick look. "You don't read them, do you?"

"Rarely." She laughed and stared at the Pacific Ocean off to their left. The sun sprayed a million diamonds across the water. "I guess I wouldn't believe the garbage they print, anyway."

"That'a girl."

They reached a crest in the hilly highway, and Dayne slowed the car. The ocean was blocked from view at this point, and an exclusive tree-covered neighborhood lay spread out between the road and the beach beyond. A sign read Paradise Cove.

"This is it." Dayne turned. At the security box, he punched in a code and the gate opened. He drove down a narrow asphalt drive until it ended in a parking area and a beach no bigger than a football field, surrounded by natural rock that jutted out into the ocean on both sides.

"It's beautiful." Katy pointed to a short pier off to the left. "I recognize that."

He turned off the engine and leaned back. "It's been in too many movies and television shows to count. It's easy to get a film crew down here, and you can avoid the public almost entirely." He looked at her. "Not the paparazzi though. They'll use kayaks or hike in from the highway through a hole in the fence. Anything they can do to get the pictures."

Again the thought of such a constant interruption grated on Katy, but she changed the subject. No point borrowing from tomorrow's troubles. Besides, one film wouldn't make her a target. If she didn't want to do more than that, she didn't have to. She scanned the small beach and saw no sign of other people. Dayne was right. Good thing they had her rental car. At least this evening he wouldn't have to worry about photographers.

"All clear?" Dayne grabbed the two picnic boxes from the backseat.

"Looks like it." She chuckled as she climbed out and shut the door. "Now you've got me paranoid."

"That's the whole point; you can't be paranoid. You've gotta roll with it, not let

it bug you. Sometimes I smile for them —
takes the fun out of the chase." Dayne led
the way down toward the sand and
stopped at a picnic table on a small patch
of grass. "How's this?"

Katy took in a full breath and tilted her
head toward the sun. "Beautiful." She
looked at him. "Sunset on a private beach?
Are you kidding?"

She took her spot opposite him, and for
a moment she thought about praying for
the meal. But she didn't want to make him
uncomfortable. Instead she uttered a quick
silent prayer and opened her picnic at the
same time he did.

"Turkey sandwiches, chips, and fruit.
Nothing special." He smiled at her across
the table. "Okay, Miss Katy Hart, so tell
me about your decision. What swayed
you?"

"God." She met his eyes and held them.
"I couldn't have come if I didn't feel I had
His blessing."

Dayne still had the sunglasses on, but
she could see him studying her all the
same. "You're serious?"

"Very." She tried to see beyond the surface of him. "Haven't you ever had that
kind of faith?"

"Not really." He took a bite of his sandwich and gazed at the ocean for a few moments. Then he looked at her again. "My parents were missionaries."

Katy had to hold on to the bench to keep from falling off at the news. Dayne Matthews' parents were missionaries? "Are they overseas?"

"No." Dayne took a breath and sat up a little straighter. "They died in a single-engine plane crash over the jungles of Indonesia when I was eighteen." The muscles in his jaw flexed, and for a moment he didn't talk. "I was an only child."

A somberness hung in the air between them. "Where were you? When the plane crashed."

"I was a senior in high school. I grew up in a boarding facility for missionary kids." He let out a bitter chuckle. "In my life, God's always won out. Every time."

Understanding dawned in Katy's soul. No wonder Dayne didn't talk much about faith. She wanted to ask him more questions, how he felt about growing up away from his parents and how he managed without a family. But it didn't seem like the right time. Besides, the answers were as obvious as the tone in Dayne's voice. He felt terrible about it.

"It's okay." He grinned at her and

opened his bag of chips. "That was a long time ago. I'm fine."

"Good." She hesitated, then bit into her sandwich. There had to be other things they could talk about. "Thanks for bringing me here. It's wonderful."

"I wanted to look in your eyes and hear it from you." He pushed his sunglasses down the bridge of his nose and peered at her. "You're really gonna do it?"

"Yes." The happy feelings were back. Whatever Dayne held against God, she could talk to him about it later. They'd have almost two months together during filming. She'd simply pray for a chance to talk to Dayne, and maybe in the process he'd find his way back to the faith his parents had taught him. It was one more reason God must've allowed this opportunity.

They finished their sandwiches, talking about the beach and the films that had been made here.

When they were done eating, Katy pushed her box away and studied him. "Can I ask you a personal question?"

"Sure." Dayne folded his box and stuffed it into hers. "Ask."

"I might not read the gossip magazines, but everyone knows your reputation,

450

Dayne. Are you seeing anyone right now?"

"Nope." His answer was quick and sure. "I'm tired of ten-minute Hollywood relationships." He rested his forearms on the table. "I'd rather be alone." He angled his head. "What about you? I asked before, but any true loves back in Bloomington?"

Katy thought about Heath and smiled. "No. Nothing serious."

"That'll make it easier when we film." Dayne's voice was quieter than before, barely audible over the ocean breeze. "People outside the business have a hard time understanding the hours we put in."

Dayne stood and reached out across the table for her hand. "Come walk with me, Katy. Tell me more about yourself."

She stood and put her fingers in his. They tossed their trash in a nearby bin and walked slowly out onto the sand. Halfway to the shoreline, they stopped and stared at the water. Katy felt a chill run down her arms. She wasn't sure if it was from the cooling temperatures or Dayne's nearness.

The fact that they were holding hands was merely his way of being her friend; she was pretty sure. Still, she had to bite the inside of her lip to remind herself she was really standing here on the beach holding hands with one of Hollywood's leading men.

Dayne was telling her something about the movie, about a direction Mitch Henry wanted to take in a certain scene. But Katy couldn't focus. All she could think about was the statement he'd made earlier. About how being single would make it easier when they filmed. She was crazy to think this, but something wild and frightening told her his words held a double meaning, that being single might be easier not only because of the hours they put in.

But because of whatever the two of them might find together.

Chapter Twenty-six

Dayne had never felt this way before.

With Katy's hand tucked in his own, he felt like the recipient of a great and precious treasure, something rare and delicate that could be gone in a moment's time, a gift that could be taken from his life as quickly as it had been given.

It was almost eight o'clock, and the sun was setting. They talked about his rise to stardom, how quickly it had happened. "I never planned on being a star." He led her a little closer to the water and pulled her down beside him on the sand.

"I guess no one plans for it." She pulled her knees up to her chest with her free hand. "When did you know? I mean, that there was no turning back?"

He gazed up at the dusky sky. "I was maybe twenty-eight, twenty-nine years old. I'd been busy making one film after another, getting a bigger role each time. I went out to dinner with one of the biggest names in the industry, an older actor." He paused. "That night I must've signed two dozen autographs, and the old guy was recognized maybe three or four times. When the dinner was over he looked at me and said, 'Dayne, my boy, you've arrived.' " He glanced at Katy. "Nothing's been the same since."

She told him about her past, her dream of acting in the movies, and her relationship with Tad Thompson. "He was the only guy I've ever loved."

"What happened to him?" The last time they talked, the afternoon at Pepperdine University, Dayne had guessed that her departure from acting had something to do with a guy. "Was he in the business?"

Katy hesitated. Then she told him about Tad and her going off to college and Tad's success in film.

"Now that you mention it, I remember him. I think we met at a party once or twice."

She didn't look surprised. "So you knew about his death?"

Dayne squinted, trying to remember. Then the details came back to him. "Drug overdose, wasn't that it?"

Katy nodded. The sun had set now, and

darkness washed over the beach.

"The wild party life you talked about before."

"Yep." She rested her chin on her knee. "Poor Tad. He got in too deep and didn't know how to get out."

"I'm sorry." The pieces were all coming together. Of course Katy had walked away from acting. She associated the loss of her boyfriend with what she perceived to be the Hollywood lifestyle. "He got caught up with the wrong crowd; that's all." Dayne gave her hand a gentle squeeze. "Not all of us are like that."

"I know." Her eyes still held the memory of sadness, but the corners of her lips lifted some. "That was a long time ago."

The wind off the ocean was chillier now. Dayne stood and helped her to her feet. "We better get you back to your hotel." He wanted to ask her back to his house, sit beside her in his warm family room, and watch a movie. Maybe even her pilot. But she wouldn't go, not when they barely knew each other.

"This was nice." She looked at him as they walked. The moon was little more than a sliver, the parking lot and the houses a couple hundred yards beyond shrouded in darkness. Still, he could see that her eyes shone. "I'll come to the studio tomorrow, and we can go over the contract with Mitch."

"Sounds good." Dayne slowed his pace, and as they reached the grassy patch near the picnic table, he turned to her. Suddenly, with the steady sound of the waves and the whisper of a breeze in their hair, he couldn't resist. He took a step closer to her, leaned in, and kissed her. Not the passionate kiss he might share with Kelly Parker or a handful of his recent leading ladies. Rather, a kiss that spoke of uncertainty and interest all at the same time.

At first she kissed him back, her lips moving across his as they drew nearer to each other. But after only a few seconds she pulled back, her eyes wide, her breathing fast and irregular. "Dayne —" She released his hand and took another step back — "I can't."

He came to her again, frustrated at himself. "Katy, I'm sorry. It's just . . . I had such a good time tonight."

The hint of a smile returned to her lips. "Me too. But still . . . kissing has meaning for me. It's not something I just . . . you know, something I just do on a whim."

"That wasn't a whim." He looked to the deep places of her heart. "I can't describe the way you make me feel, Katy."

For a moment she said nothing, though she looked flustered even in the darkness. "I want to be your friend." She crossed her arms. "Nothing more, okay?"

"Okay." He held his hands out, palms up. "I'm sorry. We'll save it for rehearsals, fair enough?"

She tried not to laugh but lost the battle. Her giggling started quietly, but after a few seconds it took over, bending her at the waist and making her gasp for breath. When she straightened she gave him a sheepish look. "Sort of silly, I guess."

"No." He smiled at her and reached his hands out to hers again. "Not silly at all."

She took hold of his fingers and looked to a place in his soul few people found. "Thanks for understanding. I guess I'm still a little old —"

Katy's words were cut short by the sound of clicking coming from the distant bushes. Cameras.

"Here we go." Dayne took a few hurried steps toward the sound, Katy's hand still in his. He looked over his shoulder at her and whispered, "Watch this!"

She tiptoed across the grass behind him and took up her position near another set of bushes. "Be careful."

"We're fine." He led her closer to the sound, let go of her hand, and ran full force toward the bushes, yelling as he went. There was the sound of something crashing just a few yards in front of him and then the distinct sound of people running away, as if fleeing for their lives.

Dayne made a loud growling sound and took another few steps; then he turned around and broke into laughter. "That was the best one yet."

"Whoever they were probably thought you'd lost it." She covered her mouth and stifled a laugh. "You looked that way."

"At least I scared them away." He took a step toward her, his laughter fading. "The bad news is, I have no idea how many pictures they took before we heard them."

"In other words —" She made a face — "My picture might be in a magazine?"

"Right." He tossed his hands and grinned. " 'Dayne Matthews Meets Mystery Lover at the Beach'. . . that sort of thing."

"At least they don't know my —"

In a rush of motion, a yellow-haired woman jumped from the bushes behind Katy and grabbed her by the arms. Katy screamed, loud and shrill, but before Dayne could do anything to help her, the woman put a ten-inch knife blade to Katy's throat.

"Don't move or I'll kill you," the woman hissed at Katy. Her body trembled, and as Katy went stiff, the woman looked at Dayne. "Isn't it time you stopped this nonsense, Dayne?"

Dayne's heart was slamming against the wall of his chest. How had this happened? And where had she come from? "Hey." He slowly took a step closer, his voice a forced calm. "What nonsense?"

"Stay back!" The woman looked like a witch, her hair long and wild, her eyes evil, lifeless. "Don't come closer."

"This will never work, you idiot." It was the woman talking again, but this time the hiss was gone. In its place was a high-pitched voice. "You'll get us both caught."

"No!" The hiss was back. "Shut up. I told you to shut up or I'll kill you."

Dayne took another step closer. He had to get within range of the woman, close enough so he could snatch her arm or knock the knife from her hands.

Katy was breathing fast — too fast. Her eyes were wide and she shook her head. "Stay back, Dayne. She means it. I can . . . I can feel the knife on my throat."

"Hussy!" The hissing voice spat the word at Katy's cheek. "You'll feel the knife more than that in a few minutes." She relaxed some, though she kept the knife pressed against Katy's throat. "I have to talk to Dayne first. Then he can watch me get rid of you."

Dayne moved closer. "You said something about stopping the nonsense." He had never been so terrified in all his life. This had to be the stalker, the woman who had been sending the notes. He glanced at the parking lot. Sure enough, there in the space next to Katy's rental car was a yellow Honda Civic. He swallowed hard. "Let's talk about that."

"You don't even know my name." Her voice was loud again, angry.

"Of course he doesn't, idiot." The high voice cut in. "That's because he isn't your husband."

"Yes, he is, Anna!" She stiffened, bringing the knife harder against Katy's throat. "He's my husband, and he knows my name is Chloe."

Dayne jumped at the opportunity. "You're right, Chloe. It's all my fault." Dayne took another step. He saw Katy's eyes react, but he gave a subtle shake of his head. Her only chance was if he got close enough to help her. "I'm sorry about everything."

460

Chloe's shoulders relaxed a little. "See, Anna, I told you." She threw Dayne a disgusted look. "Anna's always telling me I'm not married to Dayne Matthews."

"You are, Chloe. It's all my fault."

"So then —" she tossed her matted, wild hair — "you're ready to come home with me?"

"I am." Another step. "But first I need you to let my friend go, okay?"

Rage filled Chloe's face and she jerked back a few feet, taking Katy with her. Katy tried to swallow, tried to talk, but the knife blade was too tight against her throat. "She's not your friend; she's a home wrecker, a Hollywood hussy. And hussies need to die, Dayne." Her voice sent chills through him. It was so evil it sounded otherworldly. "Do you understand that?"

Dayne reached out his hand, but she screamed at him. "Don't!" Then she took the knife and made a three-inch surface slice down the inside of Katy's upper arm.

Katy cried out, clenching her jaw to keep from screaming louder. Blood ran down her arm, dripping on the ground.

"See, Dayne. Pretty girls bleed easy." She pressed the knife to Katy's throat again. "Not me . . . nothing can make me bleed."

Dayne wanted to grab the knife and plunge it through her heart, test her theory. He gave Katy a look, one intended to calm her. Then he took a step back and focused on the lunatic. "I'm afraid I can't go home with you, Chloe. Not if you use that knife."

His statement caught her off guard. She lowered the blade a fraction of an inch. "What do you mean? We have a honeymoon to plan."

"Not with the knife, Chloe. I can't stay married to you unless you stop cutting my friend."

"It's a trick, Chloe!" It was the other voice, the high-pitched one. "Dayne doesn't care about you. He's not your husband!"

"He is too!" The hissing voice fought back. "If he's coming home with me, I need to hear him out." She twisted her face into a hateful glare and stared at Dayne. "If I cut her she'll be gone forever. She'll never be in our way again."

"Besides . . ." Dayne was desperate. One wrong move and Katy could have her throat sliced. He gulped. "You've got the wrong girl, Chloe. The one you want is Kelly Parker."

"Kelly Parker?" The hissing voice barely

whispered the name. "Yes! I want her more than this —" she gave Katy a disgusted shake — "this little tramp."

"Okay, good." Dayne didn't let up. If she read the magazines — and of course she did if she was this obsessed — then she knew about his recent photo spread with Kelly. "I have an idea."

"It's a trick, Chloe. We'll both go down." The shrill voice was more insistent.

"Shut up!" she hissed, looking over her shoulder this time at an empty clearing. "Leave me alone. I've finally found my husband, and you still can't be happy for me." She jerked her head and found Dayne's eyes. "You're right. I want Kelly more." But she continued to press the knife close to Katy's throat. "Maybe I should kill this one and then go find Kelly."

"No, Chloe, that won't work." Dayne was ready, tightly wound, looking for any sign of weakness in the woman. Any chance to jump at her. "Those aren't the rules."

"The rules?" She blinked. Her trembling had gone into a full-bodied shaking. "What rules?"

"You know, Chloe." Dayne did his best to sound at ease, relaxed. "The rules about knives. You can only use them on one person a day." He nodded to Katy. "You don't want to waste your chance on her."

Chloe lowered the knife a couple of feet. She had her mouth open, about to say something, but Dayne didn't wait. In a sudden burst, he kicked Chloe's hand with all his strength. The knife went flying and Dayne rushed in. He grabbed Chloe's arms and wrenched her away from Katy. Then he flung the woman onto the ground facedown and fell on top of her.

He looked over his shoulder and shouted at Katy, "You have a cell?"

"Yes!" Katy was frantic, her voice seized with fear.

"Call 911."

"Dayne, look out!" Katy screamed, pointing at Chloe.

The woman had stretched herself, squirming on the ground, and now she had her hand around the handle of the knife. Dayne brought his fist down full force on her forearm and heard a sickening crunch. Her hand went limp. She groaned, writhing and fighting him, trying everything in her power to get him off her back.

He pulled the knife from her grip and tossed it back toward the picnic table. "Stop moving or I'll suffocate you!" He shoved her face into the grass and slid up higher on her back. "You're lucky I don't kill you and call it self-defense."

Behind him, Dayne heard Katy on the phone with the emergency operator. She sounded breathless, in shock, and twice she had to repeat herself. Meanwhile Chloe was kicking, thrashing about, trying to buck him off her back.

"Anna, help me! Where are you?"

The high-pitched voice answered. "It's all your fault. You got us into this."

Dayne felt a chill run down his spine. The woman had at least two personalities fighting it out inside her. Both voices had dark and frightening undertones. No doubt she would've killed Katy and maybe him if she'd had a few more minutes to think about it.

Katy was off the phone. "Dayne, be careful!" She was still out of breath. He wanted to leave the psycho woman and comfort Katy, but he couldn't. Not when it was taking nearly all his strength to keep the maniac pinned.

"If this is how you treat your wife . . ." It was the hissing voice. Chloe. Her words were short and clipped from the struggle and the fact that her forearm was definitely broken. "If this is how you treat your wife . . . I'll have to kill you too, Dayne."

Dayne didn't say anything. He wasn't interested in the ramblings of a lunatic. All he cared about were the quiet whimpers coming from behind him. What would this do to Katy? Of all the times for the wacko to act on her threats, she had to do it when he was with Katy Hart. How terrible was that?

His knee was pinned against Chloe's arm, the one that wasn't hurt. She was still thrashing when the sirens came into earshot. "The game's almost over, Chloe."

"Don't talk to my sister like that!" The high voice ordered him. It was Anna this time. "I told her not to kill you, but now . . . you better watch your back, Matthews."

Dayne shoved her face closer to the ground again. "Shut up!" He hated that she was still fighting him, probably scaring Katy to death. He couldn't see Katy's eyes, but he could feel her terror from five yards away. His chest heaved from the adrenaline coursing through him. He heard the police now, heard them running from the parking lot toward them.

The one who arrived first drew his gun. "Police! Freeze." His eyes met Dayne's. "Mr. Matthews, we've got it from here."

Dayne rolled off the woman and ran to Katy. She was shaking, her eyes locked in terror. The gash on her arm had stopped bleeding, but a dried streak of blood ran halfway to her wrist. "Are you okay?" They were both out of breath, but even in the shadows beneath the trees he could see that Katy's face was worse than pale.

"I . . . I can't . . ." She was still shaking — almost convulsing — too scared to speak.

"Shhh." Dayne put his arm around her. "It's all right. The police have her."

Katy brought her hand to her throat. Ugly scratch marks ran along the area where the woman had held the knife to her. "She . . . she was going to kill me."

He tucked her head against his chest and smoothed her blonde hair. "It's over, Katy. It's all over."

One of the officers came up and looked at Dayne. "She admitted to stalking you and writing the letters." He shifted his attention back to his notepad. "We have your address. A couple officers will be by your house tonight for a statement. We'll need one from both of you." He looked at Katy. "Are you all right?"

She still had her hand on her throat. "Yes."

"Okay. You two can go." He gave a disgusted look at the woman in handcuffs still on the ground. Then he directed his attention back to Katy. "I'm sorry about this. I guess it's the price of fame."

Dayne nodded. He kept his arm around Katy and led her to the parking lot. The whole way he whispered to her, assuring her, promising her that the terror was behind them.

Katy looked up at him as they reached her car. "Are we going to your house?"

"Yeah." He opened the door for her and waited while she climbed in. The sound of the surf filled the air, but now it held an ominous sound, as if each wave were pounding out a rhythm of impending doom. "Is that okay?"

"We have to . . . the police said so."

"Right." He went around the other side and got in. "Katy, everything's okay."

But even the police officer had underlined the fact that it wasn't. What had he said at the end there? This was the price of fame? It was exactly what he didn't want Katy to think, but it was the truth. After tonight how could he tell Katy anything different?

They were halfway home when Katy turned to him. "That lady's been writing letters about you?"

He gave Katy a sideways glance. "Yeah, I guess so. The police told me about her a few days back."

"We never should've gone out there." Her tone wasn't angry or accusing but straightforward. "Why didn't you tell me?"

Dayne exhaled hard. "I didn't believe it. There're lots of crazy people out there, Katy. I didn't think she was serious."

They were mostly quiet the rest of the ride, but as they pulled into his garage he turned to her. "I'm sorry. I never meant for you to be in danger."

She looked calmer, the color returning to her cheeks. "I know." Her lips were shivering, and it made it hard to understand her. "You're right. The police will take care of her."

"Exactly." He reached out and touched her cheek. "She won't be a threat anymore."

But somehow he didn't sound convincing. Kelly Parker was still in the hospital, undergoing a mental evaluation; the magazines were still relentless and always would be. And with a star's every move chronicled in print, there would always be the possibility of freak fans like the one they'd encountered tonight.

Dayne could only guess how the rest of the evening would play out, but he had a feeling it wouldn't be good. And that come tomorrow he wouldn't be trying to convince Katy that everything was okay.

He'd be looking for someone else to fill her part.

Chapter Twenty-seven

Katy was still shaking.

She barely noticed the lush furnishings and expansive rooms as Dayne held her hand and they walked into the house. The beach was in his backyard, but it was too dark to notice anything other than the sound of the pounding waves. And right now that only served to remind her of what had just happened.

Dayne directed her to the family room, and they sat side by side on the sofa. "Want coffee? anything?"

She was numb, exhausted, drained from the fight for their lives. Her eyes met his. "I'm fine."

"I'll make some anyway." He stood and headed toward the kitchen. "Might make you feel better."

Katy doubted that, but she didn't say so. As he left the room she stared at her trembling hands. What sort of bizarre life was this, anyway? She'd been in town only a few hours, and already she'd been caught on camera kissing Dayne Matthews at a private beach and nearly killed by a maniac fan.

She closed her eyes, and the image of the woman came back again. Wild yellow hair, intensely evil expression on her face. And the knife. Dull black handle and a thick stainless-steel blade that caught the light of the moon and flashed in the darkness. She would remember the knife as long as she lived.

Her neck hurt, even though the woman hadn't drawn blood there. Only on her arm. She rose and followed the sounds of Dayne in the next room.

He was filling the coffeemaker with water, but he must've heard her behind him because he turned around. "Hi."

"Hi." She smiled. It wasn't Dayne's fault, and he was right: They were safe now. "Where's your bathroom?"

He directed her down a hallway, and she thanked him. Once she found it, she turned on the light and looked in the mirror. Her neck was worse than she'd thought. The knife blade had left three long horizontal lines across her neck. She looked closer. They wouldn't scar, but they'd be there for a few weeks at least.

Katy grabbed the edge of the sink, closed her eyes, and hung her head. *God . . . thank You for saving me.* Her throat felt thick, bruised. The remembered pressure of the knife against her skin made it hard to swallow even now. *Lord, what am I doing here? I thought You showed me that this was Your will.* She swallowed, resisting the tears that welled in her eyes. *But how can this be Your plan for me?*

Daughter . . . hear My voice . . . know Me.

She opened her eyes and gazed up. "God," she whispered, "is that You?"

There was no response, but the quiet words still echoed in her heart. *Hear My voice . . . know Me.* What did it mean? Hadn't God made His ways clear to her earlier? The Flanigans had given her their blessing, and Dayne had told her that the situation with Tad was a rarity, an exception. Wasn't this the dream come true she'd spent her childhood wanting?

She blinked and steadied herself. Dayne would be waiting, and tomorrow they were supposed to talk about the details of her contract. Only now nothing about it seemed as exciting as it had a few days ago, even a few hours ago. She left the bathroom and padded back down the hall.

All the while her heart pounded out an irregular beat.

Dayne was making a plate of cheese and fruit when she turned into the kitchen. "Hey." He smiled at her. "Sit at the table over there in the dining room. I'll be done in a minute; then we can talk."

She did as he said, but she wondered what they would talk about. The fact that stalkers were a rarity? that the life of a Hollywood actor really was pretty normal other than the paparazzi and stalkers and wild nightlife and autograph seekers? She checked her watch. It was late, and the police were still on their way. She wouldn't get to sleep until midnight.

Across from her was a magazine, one of the tabloids sold at supermarket checkout stands, the kind she rarely bought or looked at. But now, with Dayne busy in the kitchen, she slid it closer.

There on the cover was a picture of Dayne and actress Kelly Parker. The two were kissing, and the headline questioned whether they were back together again. Katy frowned and looked at the date. It was the current issue. Hadn't Dayne said he wasn't seeing anyone? She opened the magazine to the spread of Dayne and

Kelly. If the story the pictures told was true, Dayne might not be "seeing" Kelly, but he was definitely sleeping with her.

Katy felt her stomach turn. The strange feeling in her chest, the tightness and odd heartbeat, felt worse than before. Why had he lied to her? Did he think she wouldn't find out about Kelly? And what did he owe her, anyway? This was obviously the way of things among Dayne and his peers. He probably thought nothing of spending the night with someone.

She shuddered.

The words she'd felt God impress upon her heart a few minutes ago came back: *Daughter . . . hear My voice . . . know Me.* In light of all God would want for her life, everything about Dayne Matthews and his offer felt cheap and plastic.

She turned the pages, flipping past stories of two long-married couples, both now broken up, and one actress who had spent tens of thousands of dollars on Botox injections and chemical burns to keep her face looking young. "In this business," the actress was quoted as saying, "you're only as good as the skin on your face."

Nausea welled up in her. What was she doing here, anyway? She felt like Dorothy in *The Wizard of Oz*. If she could click her heels three times and be back at the Flanigans, she would.

"You okay out there?" Dayne called from the kitchen. "I'm almost done."

Katy struggled to find the words. "Yes. I'm . . . I'm fine." Another few pages and she saw photographs of movie stars caught in terrible moments — blowing their noses or adjusting their clothing. And near the back was a series of pictures of Dayne at a nightclub, a drink in one hand, a cigarette in the other.

Katy studied the picture, stunned. Hadn't Dayne said he avoided the night-life? So what did he mean? That he only partied on the town a few times a week? She felt like she was being shown an entirely new side of the man, and the view wasn't attractive.

It was Tad Thompson all over again.

Suddenly everything the Lord had laid on her heart made perfect sense. What had she felt before when she prayed about taking the part? That God would give her a sign, right? And now it was the same thing all over again. God wanted her to hear His voice, to know Him. And how better to know Him than by knowing what He wasn't, where He wasn't?

Dayne came up and stopped short, two

plates of food in his hands. "What are you reading?"

Katy shut the magazine and pushed it away. She turned and met Dayne's eyes. "Take me back to my hotel, please, Dayne."

"Katy . . . you can't believe what you read; I told you that." He set the food down and took the chair beside her. He was about to say something else when there was a knock at the door.

"The officers?" She sat back in her chair. They wanted a statement from her too. "We'll talk about this after they go."

Dayne opened the door, and two policemen came in. He showed them to the table, and for an hour they recounted the events of the night. With every passing minute, Katy became more certain, more sure of her decision. Her time in LA was almost over. She would go home and find her place in Bloomington where she belonged. God had been faithful, as always.

If the night's events weren't signs enough, she wasn't looking.

When the officers had everything they needed, they gathered their notes and promised to be in touch with Dayne. "With the threats she made in writing and the attempt on Ms. Hart's life, we're pretty sure she'll be locked up for a long time."

Katy wished the news brought with it some relief to the anxiety that strangled her soul, but it didn't.

When the police left, Dayne turned to her. "Did you hear what they said? She's gone, locked up. She won't be a problem." He sat down beside her, his eyes locked on hers. "Don't run, Katy. Please . . ."

His words were too little, too late.

"Dayne . . . you tried." She looked at the magazine and raised one shoulder. "I can't do it."

"Listen to me, Katy." He ran his fingers through his hair, looking desperate for the right words. "What happened today will never happen again. Obsessed fans jumping out of bushes with knives?" He tried to laugh, but it fell flat. "The photographers and magazines, yes." He ran his tongue over his lower lip. "There'll always be that side of the business. But what happened tonight won't happen again in a . . ."

His voice trailed off, and silence put up a wall between them.

What was he trying to do? Convince her that staying would be best for *her?* It would be best for him, yes, but not for her. She closed her eyes for a moment. *God . . .*

let him see what he's doing, please.
Dayne needed to release her rather than convince her to stay.

Another minute passed, and then he sucked in a strong breath and hung his head. "I'm sorry." He took her hands in his. "You don't belong here, do you?"

It was the first completely honest thing he'd said since the police left. She gave the slightest shake of her head, her eyes watery. "No, Dayne, I don't."

He ran his thumbs along the tops of her hands. "You know what's sad?" His eyes found hers.

"What?"

"That's why you're perfect for the part." He studied her, his heart transparent. "Perfect, and perfectly unable to take it at the same time."

She felt the loss, much as he must've been feeling it. There would be no friendship forged, no chance at love. The canyon between their worlds had proved greater than any bridge that might've spanned it.

The time had come for him to let her go, and after a minute he found the strength to do so. "I'll take you back now."

"Thank you, Dayne." She stood and slipped her purse over her shoulder. "Thanks for understanding."

He breathed out and his shoulders slumped. Dayne Matthews, golden boy of the silver screen, looked — for the first time in the brief period Katy had known him — utterly defeated. "Okay." His lips came together tight in a straight line. "I'm sorry, Katy. This isn't how I thought things would go."

She didn't want to cry, not until later. She gave him a sad smile. "Me either."

On the way back to her hotel, they said little. Katy remembered her conversation with Rhonda, the idea that maybe Dayne Matthews was the man God had planned for her. The idea was both sad and laughable now. Dayne might've played the role of a genuine, well-mannered guy. He'd convinced her that he wasn't only single but quite possibly interested in her.

She shivered at the thought of what might've happened if she'd taken the part: her picture in the magazines time and again, people guessing about whether they were in a relationship and whether Kelly Parker was upset by the fact. All the wondering and waiting and not knowing if Dayne was finding his way back to one of his former loves when he wasn't with her.

She stared out the side window at the heavy traffic on the Hollywood freeway.

God . . . You rescued me more than once today. I'm so glad I heard You.

"What are you thinking?" Dayne gave her a quick look but kept his eyes on the road. His tone was filled with compassion, one that Katy didn't doubt.

"I was praying."

Dayne hesitated. "That doesn't surprise me."

Katy felt sorry for him. Big-time actor with everything in the world going for him but with a grudge against God bigger than his mansion in Malibu. She bit her lip and looked at him. "Prayer helps me." She kept her tone soft. "You prayed when you were younger, right?"

"Right." Dayne gave her a casual look of disdain. "Whatever came of it? I grew up without my family and lost my parents in a plane crash." He tried to smile, but the corners of his mouth barely lifted. "Wasn't real encouraging, you know?"

Now that she was headed back home, she could take a fresh look at Dayne. He was lost, more than she'd realized at first. "Even though I'm not taking the part, I wish we could stay friends. I think . . . I think it would be good."

He chuckled, more relaxed. "You mean maybe you could help me?"

"No! Not like that." For the first time since the attack she felt her spirits lift. "I mean, maybe I'd be a safe person for you, someone you could talk to without worrying that the press was going to capture every minute."

"I know." His expression softened. "I'm just giving you a hard time." He pulled up in front of her hotel. For a long while he only looked at her, searching her eyes. Then he touched her cheek the way he had earlier. "You sure I can't change your mind?" He paused. "It's just one film."

The possibility wasn't even a little tempting. God had given her the answer she needed, and back in Bloomington there were a hundred CKT kids who wouldn't ever have to say good-bye to her. The prospect made her feel safe and warm and right inside. Bloomington was where God wanted her, and she would go back with no regrets.

He was waiting for her answer. She took hold of his hand and shook her head. "I can't, Dayne. I have no doubts."

"Okay." He leaned against the inside of his door and looked at her. "I'm sorry again." He pressed his knuckles to his lips, as if there was a lot more he wanted to say. Finally he dropped his hand. "Can I tell you something honestly?"

"Yes."

"Even though I don't like it —" his eyes shone a little more than before — "I have a feeling you're making the right decision." He shrugged. "Like I said earlier, you don't belong here."

They said their good-byes, and Katy made her way to her hotel room. When she shut the door behind her, she fell against it and breathed out. The whole thing — getting the call from Mitch Henry, auditioning with Dayne, thinking she could waltz into Hollywood and take a leading role without disrupting her real life — all of it felt like something from a dream.

But it was over, and that's what mattered.

She thought about Dayne's last statement. He must've cared about her somewhat; otherwise he wouldn't have told her what was in his heart. That though he wanted her to take the part, though he wanted to convince her that starring in one movie wouldn't change anything, the truth was he agreed with her decision.

Bloomington was better for her; anyone could see that.

An unfamiliar feeling began working its way through Katy, from her hands and feet through her limbs and all the way to her heart and soul. Only then did she realize what it was. It was peace. And with that, she pulled her cell phone from her purse and dialed Rhonda Sanders' phone number.

Her friend answered almost immediately. "Hello?"

"Rhonda . . . it's me." Katy felt a smile fill her face. "I have something to tell you. . . ."

Chapter Twenty-eight

The party tonight was at the Baxter house.

They had gathered to give Ashley and Landon a proper send-off on their much-delayed honeymoon, a barbecue compliments of Ashley's father and a full house with everyone except Luke and Reagan in New York City and Erin and Sam in Texas.

Ashley was in the kitchen with Brooke and Kari, the three of them peeling fruit for the ambrosia salad.

"So . . . you must be so excited." Brooke was working with the bananas. The sleeves of her pale blue blouse were rolled up. "You and Landon deserve this after all you've been through."

The anticipation had been building for the past week, and Ashley nodded. "I can't wait. A cruise for a whole week, Landon and I on the Caribbean seas?" She laughed and raised her brow. "I'm way beyond excited."

Kari dumped a pile of apple peelings into the trash and looked at Brooke. "Let's get the kids together a couple times while they're gone." She grabbed another few apples and moved back to her spot at the counter. "Cole's thrilled to hang out with Jessie, but I know he'd love to see Hayley and Maddie too."

"Okay. We can go to the park."

A strange feeling poked at Ashley's heart. "I'm going to miss my little guy."

"You haven't been away from him this long since he was born, right?" Kari took the peeling off another apple.

"Right." Ashley swallowed. "But it'll be good for all of us."

"It will." Brooke smiled at her. "You can't stay by their sides every minute."

The comment hung in the air among them for a few moments. Brooke had come so far since little Hayley's near drowning. She and Peter had been through counseling, and they understood that parents can only do so much to protect their children and that ultimately they belong to God first.

Kari put her arm around Brooke. "How's Hayley?"

"She's doing so well." Brooke's eyes glistened. She ran a handful of green grapes under the kitchen faucet. When she turned the water off she looked at Kari and then at Ashley. "She said a sentence the other day. She said, 'Mommy, see Maddie!'" Brooke gave an amazed shake of her head. "Every word she says, every step she makes, I'm reminded of the truth — that God still works miracles among us today."

Ashley felt her eyes get watery. "And all I have to do is look at the wedding picture of Landon and me."

"There were days when I really doubted you'd ever get together." Kari grabbed another apple and started peeling it. "I'm so glad Mom got to see you marry him. It was something she'd prayed about for so long."

"I know." Ashley felt her lip quiver. She hesitated, letting the moment pass. There were too many happy moments ahead for her to be sad now. "God was good to let us have that."

Landon came into the kitchen. "Sounds like a serious conversation." He came up behind Ashley, slipped his arm around her waist, and kissed the back of her neck. "Our plane leaves in twelve hours."

"Someone's eager." Kari giggled and raised her eyebrow at Ashley and Landon.

"Are you kidding?" Landon took a step back and smiled at the three of them. "I've been eager for a year."

The group laughed, and Ashley noticed Peter outside talking to her father near the barbecue. She loved this, having everyone together. They were setting the table when Cole came running in from outside. His face was tan from the recent warm days, his hair blonder than ever. "Papa says the chicken'll be done in three minutes."

"Okay." Kari tousled his hair and smiled at him. "Tell Papa we'll be ready."

The dinner came together in a way that would've made their mother proud. It had been a year since she died, but still they felt her loss as strongly as if she'd been gone only a few days. Times like this were especially hard. Ashley still caught herself looking over her shoulder, expecting to see her mother in the kitchen whipping up one of her famous salads or a pitcher of lemonade.

But in her absence, they were better off being together, celebrating life the way she would've celebrated it with them had she been there.

Dinner was upbeat and lively.

Cole told everyone he was learning to walk on his hands. "When I grow up" — he had a smear of barbecue sauce on his chin — "I wanna be in the circus and walk on my hands all day long."

Ashley gave a thoughtful nod, hiding the smirk on her face. "We'll definitely buy tickets for that."

"Hey, Cole." Peter held his fork in one hand and looked down the table. "I thought you were going to be a fireman like your daddy."

"I am." Cole chewed a bite of chicken and then grinned at Peter. "I'll fight all the fires at the circus, and when there's no fires I'll walk on my hands."

Ashley's heart was full. She loved Cole so much. If God was willing, she hoped she and Landon would have a child. The sooner the better if she had her way. Cole would make a wonderful big brother.

The conversation shifted to Kari and Ryan's baby. Ryan Junior was trying to pull himself up already.

"He'll be throwing touchdown passes any day now." Ryan chuckled. "At least that's the way it feels when I look at him."

"It's amazing, isn't it?" Their dad had been fairly quiet throughout the meal, but now he smiled at Ryan and the others. "There's nothing like watching your children grow up, watching them become the people God created them to be. Your mother and I . . ." He paused, and for a moment his voice was too thick to continue. "Your mother and I loved every minute of raising you kids."

Again the warmth of what they shared together worked its way through Ashley. She would never for a minute take for granted the love in the Baxter family. And never be anything but grateful for her place in it. Then she remembered the scrapbook her father had mentioned, the one with copies of their mother's letters.

"Hey, Dad —" Ashley rested her forearms on the table — "so what about those letters of Mom's? Are you really going to get some of them copied so we can have a set?"

Their dad's expression changed. He sat up a little straighter and blinked twice. "The letters?"

Ashley had the sudden feeling she'd said something she shouldn't have. But why would she feel that way? What was it about the letters that flustered her father so? It was the same feeling she'd had when her father had caught her in his closet that afternoon. As if she were doing something wrong, when all she wanted was to read some of the letters her mother had written through the years, letters that would give them an additional piece to remember her by.

Brooke looked from Ashley to their father. "Letters?"

"Yes." Ashley gave her sister a look. "Mom has a whole box of letters in her closet." She turned to her dad again. "You said you'd make a scrapbook of some of the better ones so we could see them, right?"

"Right." Their dad coughed and seemed unable to make eye contact with any of the girls. "I'll do it soon, Ashley. I . . . I haven't had time."

"No rush." Ashley hated pushing him. He looked so uncomfortable. If this was how he reacted every time she brought up the letters, then maybe she should wait a year and ask then. She stood, went to her father, and put her arm around him. "Hey, Dad, sorry."

The others were quiet, watching the scene.

"No, sweetheart." He looked up and covered her hand with his. "It's just . . . well, going through those letters will be tough. It might take a while."

She kissed his cheek and gave him a side hug. "Take your time, Dad. But when you do, just remember we'd like a scrapbook, okay?"

Brooke nodded. "That would be wonderful." She looked at Kari. "I didn't know she had a box like that in her closet."

"Me, either," Kari replied.

Ashley sat back down. Her father had gotten enough scrutiny. It was time to change the subject. She raised her eyebrows at Landon and smiled. "You're not finished packing, are you?"

"Not yet." He kissed the tip of her nose. "But that's okay." He winked at the others. "I like getting ready in a rush."

Ryan raised his glass. "Spoken like a true firefighter."

Everyone laughed, and the somber feeling from a minute ago lifted. Sometime after eight o'clock, the party broke up, and one at a time Ashley's family took turns saying their good-byes to Landon and her. Cole had his things with him, and he was going home with Kari and Ryan and their kids tonight.

Ashley and Landon wanted a private good-bye with Cole, so the others waited in the entryway. All along Cole had been thrilled about the idea of spending a week with his aunt and uncle and cousins. But when the moment finally came to say good-bye, his eyes welled up. He hugged Landon first, tight around the neck, long enough that Ashley was pretty sure he was crying.

"Hey, buddy, come on," Landon whispered against his face. "It'll be okay. You'll have so much fun with Aunt Kari and Uncle Ryan you won't even miss us."

Cole only nodded against Landon's shoulder. "A week . . . is a long time."

Landon looked at Ashley, his own eyes watery. He hugged Cole close again. "It'll be a long time for us too. But we'll call, all right?"

Cole nodded twice and pulled back. "Okay." Then he turned to Ashley, and a fresh batch of tears brimmed. "Mommy . . . are you sure you wanna go?"

"Coley." She held out her arms and he ran to her. The lump in her throat was too thick for her to say anything at first. Instead she held his little body against hers, memorizing the feel of him, six years old and not nearly her little baby anymore. How long would he still need her this way? How many short years before he would be blazing a trail into middle school and high school and off to college?

God, get me through this. Please. She closed her eyes and felt the Holy Spirit leading her away from thoughts of his high school graduation. Not when they still had half the summer ahead of him before he would enter first grade. She sniffed. *Thank*

You, Lord. You're here. I feel You here.

"It's like Daddy said, honey." She pulled back and searched his eyes, willing him to understand, to be brave the way he'd felt the day before. "You'll have so much fun you won't even miss us."

Cole dragged his fists across his cheeks. "I know." He took a few quick breaths. "Aunt Kari said we can make meat loaf one day."

His words caught Ashley off guard and she laughed. Next to them, Landon laughed too. Though neither of her men could've known what had made her lose composure.

"Why are you laughing, Mommy?" Cole giggled too, the sadness lifting. " 'Cause meat loaf is funny stuff?"

"No." She held him close and allowed another round of laughter. "Because I had the picture of you making meat loaf standing on your hands."

Cole tossed his head back this time, busting up and holding his stomach from laughing so hard. "You're funny, Mommy." His laughter faded to giggles. "I wouldn't make meat loaf standing on my hands, silly."

"Yes." Landon rubbed small circles into the low part of her back. "Mommy's very silly." He grinned at her.

"Okay." Ashley gave Cole a cheerful but pointed look. "You need to go, Coley. So say good-bye." She thought of something else. "Hey, wait. What should we bring you from our trip? A captain's hat or maybe a T-shirt?"

Cole thought for a minute and his eyes got shiny. "How about a baby?"

Ashley felt her mouth drop open. She looked at Landon. His smile took up his whole face. "Did you have something to do with this?" she whispered.

He shook his head, his face a mask of mock innocence. Then Ashley turned to Cole. "Honey, we can't bring a baby home from our trip. What made you think that?"

" 'Cause Daddy says babies take a long time, and then they come to live with you." He shrugged. "And you guys are gonna be gone a long time, so I thought maybe you could bring me home a baby." He thought for a second. "A baby brother."

"Honey, it takes a lot longer than a week for a baby to come."

Cole's smile let up a little. "Oh."

Landon stooped down to Cole's level. "But, hey, buddy, we'll keep that in mind, okay?" He gave Ashley a sly grin, one that Cole missed.

"Okay, Daddy." Cole seemed better now, not thrilled with the fact that they were leaving but much more content than he'd been a few minutes earlier. "Bye. Have fun with Mommy."

"I will." Landon stood and waited next to Ashley.

This time Cole turned to her and jumped into her arms. He was heavier now, almost too heavy. In a year she wouldn't be able to hold him this way. She rubbed noses with him. "You have a great time with Aunt Kari and Uncle Ryan, all right?"

"All right, Mommy. I love you."

"I love you too." She kissed him, fighting the lump in her throat. And with that she set him back down and watched him run into the next room. Ashley and Landon followed, and another quick round of good-byes took place before Kari and Ryan and the kids left.

Ashley and Landon were the last ones to go. Her father walked them to the door. "Your mother would be so happy you're taking this trip." He kissed Ashley on the cheek. "She never wanted her sickness to stop you from having a honeymoon."

Ashley hugged her father. "I wish I could tell her about it."

"I'm sure she knows." Her dad smiled,

but something in his eyes remained sad. He shook Landon's hand and then pulled him in for a hug. "We'll have another barbecue after you get back so we can hear all about it."

"Thanks." Landon took a step toward the door. "And thanks for dinner. It was great as always."

They were halfway home, the car quiet without Cole's constant chatter, when Ashley turned to Landon. "So what should we really get Cole? He'd like a captain's hat; don't you think?"

"I sort of like his first idea." Landon reached out and took her hand. "A baby brother."

John Baxter watched Ashley and Landon pull away, and for a long while he stood in the doorway, absorbed by the quiet. This was the time when he and Elizabeth would take a walk or make their way out onto the front porch. They would share a cup of coffee and rehash the conversation from dinner.

Together they would sift through the details of their children's lives, rejoicing over the positives and reflecting on the areas that needed more prayer. They would laugh at the funny things the grandchildren said and comment about how fast they were growing up. Elizabeth would remind him that all of life went far too fast, and John would agree. The evening would fade, the sun would set, and they'd have the night to share each other's company.

But here, in the setting sun, he was alone. More alone than he'd felt in a long time. He wandered out onto the porch and took his seat in the rocker next to hers. He gave a light push with his heels and set the chair in motion. These were their golden years, weren't they? The ones where they would watch their children raise families and have endless hours of laughter and conversation?

Elizabeth had been right about something she said in her final hours, the hours before cancer claimed her life. She had told him she wouldn't really be gone, that he'd see her in Hayley's determination and Ashley's paintings and Cole's laughter. It was true; he saw her in all of them.

But it didn't ease the loneliness of a moment like this, a moment when the house still echoed with the sounds of conversation and laughter, a night when the quiet was deafening without her.

He leaned his head back and gazed at the darkening sky. If she were here, he'd tell her that the letters were causing a problem. He didn't want to hide the whole box, but he wasn't ready to go through them yet either. And though he'd hidden the letter she'd written to their firstborn son and the letter he'd written to her when Luke was born, certainly there were other letters in the box that would give away their secret.

A long sigh drifted over his lips.

It would be a year next Monday, a year since she'd left them. More and more he found himself reliving her final weeks, that crazy emotional roller coaster when the best and worst of times came together in a kaleidoscope of dark shadows and brilliant colors. Ashley and Landon's wedding and the family reunion and Elizabeth's death, all within days of each other.

The more he remembered, the more he wondered about her last prayer to find their firstborn son. How sad that God hadn't granted her that last wish, even when she cared so much she'd convinced herself that in her final hours the boy had come. That he was tall, an actor named Dayne. Kind and forgiving with a face like Luke's.

Hallucinations, for sure. But the memory of her certainty made him wonder.

Was that what Elizabeth would've wanted from him? That he do everything in his power to locate their grown son, the one they'd never known, the one Elizabeth had held for only a few minutes before giving him up?

He let the thought rest for a while in the comfortable places of his mind. The idea sounded good until he played it out. What would he tell the other kids? And how would they handle the news about their parents' moral failure? No, the thought of finding their firstborn was too much, more than he could imagine. More than Elizabeth would've wanted them to know.

Once in a while since Elizabeth's death, he'd thought about telling Pastor Mark Atteberry at church, asking him for advice about what he should do and whether there was another option for finding the young man.

But he would get cold feet before he picked up the phone. Having that child was something so far in the past it seemed like another lifetime ago. And since Elizabeth was gone, it wasn't as important as it had been last year. Wherever he was, he would have his own life, his own family by now. He probably wouldn't appreciate the disruption in his life any more than Kari and Brooke and Ashley and Erin and Luke would appreciate the disruption into theirs.

The sky was darker now, and John stopped rocking. With a heavy heart he stood and made his way slowly to the front door. When Elizabeth was alive he had felt young and vibrant, perfectly intent on living another thirty years by her side. But these days he felt slow, tired, as if half his heart had stopped beating right along with hers.

He searched the sky for a little longer, then went into the house and turned off the lights. With heavy feet he trudged up the stairs to his bedroom — their bedroom. As he was falling asleep in their bed, he ran through his earlier thoughts. He would have to sort out the letters sooner rather than later. Otherwise one of the girls might get to them first, and if there was a letter in that box he didn't know about, something that might refer to their first-born son, then what?

John felt sick at the thought.

The last thing he could imagine was his precious children feeling that he and Elizabeth had lied to them. Especially when the truth about their older brother was never, ever supposed to get out. No, he couldn't let them know about the young man, not ever.

He'd have to take care of the letters tomorrow. Before anyone else got to them.

Sleep came slowly, the way it had for the past year. But when it caught him, it was with good thoughts, happy thoughts. Thoughts of a lifetime of love with the greatest woman he'd ever known.

Elizabeth Baxter.

It was the third day of their cruise, and Ashley couldn't have been happier. She and Landon had known each other so long — years while they took turns fighting the way they felt. But when they finally found each other, when it was clear that God was going to give them a lifetime together, they'd made a promise to Him and to each other.

They would wait until they were married.

Ever since saying their vows, their love had been something beyond Ashley's greatest imagination, beyond what she dared dream about married love. Their honeymoon was further proof — loving Landon was something that had started beautifully, something that would grow stronger with every passing year.

They ate well and danced every night, but they always turned in early. Their cabin had a private balcony. Sometimes they'd get up at two o'clock in the morning and sit outside in their terry-cloth bathrobes, admiring the silver moon on the water and the magic of love the way God — from the beginning of time — had designed it.

They slept in every morning and spent their days lounging in reclining chairs, facing the open sea. It was a magical experience, and Ashley could hardly believe it was half over.

This afternoon she turned to Landon and pressed her finger against his tanned stomach. "You're not burning, are you?"

"Not me." He rolled onto his side so he could see her better. "How 'bout you? Need more sunscreen on your back?"

She smiled. "I'm okay." For a while she looked at him, taking in the sight of him, storing away the memory for some far-off winter afternoon when she would find it again and re-create it on canvas. She drew a slow breath, squinting in the bright sun. "You know what I hope?"

"What?" He laced his fingertips with hers. "That we're bringing Cole home a baby brother?"

Her smile reached to the center of her heart. "Okay, that too." She waited a beat, and her tone grew more serious. "I hope God gives us windows in heaven."

Landon thought about that for a little while. The ocean breeze brushed against their faces, bringing just enough coolness to keep the heat manageable. Finally he turned to her. "I like that."

"Yeah." She brought his fingers to her lips and kissed them. "I'm not getting as sad as I used to, because that's what I believe." She looked at the deep blue above them. "That way Mom can look down at us anytime she wants." Another smile tugged at her lips. "Isn't that a nice thought?"

"It is."

"With a window in heaven, she could celebrate our good times with us and pray for us when things are tough."

"Hmmm." Landon bit his lip. "Sounds like the sort of thing God would give His people."

"I think so." She pressed the backs of her fingers against his ribs. "Hey, you're burning up, Landon Blake."

He let his eyes take in the length of her. "You too, Mrs. Blake."

"Let's swim."

"Another good idea." Landon's eyes sparkled even in the heat of midday. "But I like your other one better."

She gave him a happy sort of frown. "The one about windows in heaven?"

"No, that one was good, but I was thinking of the first one."

"The first one?"

"Yeah, you know, Ash . . . the one about bringing a baby brother home for Cole."

Chapter Twenty-nine

❧

Four weeks had passed since Katy left town, and Dayne could hardly believe how dramatically life had changed. Kelly Parker was given the part in *Dream On*, something that lifted her spirits and made her treatment from the overdose that much easier.

He, of course, was the other part of her recovery.

The two of them were together now. She'd moved in with him a few days after accepting the part, at first under the guise of friendship and recovery and her desire to not be alone in her house. But after a couple weeks, it went in the inevitable direction, the way both of them had known it would go. She wound up in his bed one night and never left.

Now they were in preproduction meetings almost every day, and Dayne was busier than he'd been in months. Only once in a while did he have time to wonder why he didn't feel happier.

It was ten o'clock at night, and Kelly was asleep inside. Summer was coming to an end; he could feel as much in the air. He stood on his deck, leaning on the railing and staring at the moon's reflection on the water. Everything should've been fantastic.

He was about to make a hit comedy movie with one of the brightest talents in Hollywood, and more than that, she was his current lover. If anyone asked her, she would've said they were serious. Very serious.

But there was something he couldn't quite figure out.

Why couldn't he get Katy Hart out of his mind?

It didn't matter, of course. He hadn't heard from her since she'd gone home. By now she was probably in the middle of the run of plays for *Tom Sawyer*, celebrating the kids and their ability to rise to her direction. He stared at the way the moon played across the surf. If he looked long enough the shimmery lights weren't a reflection at all, but Katy, her eyes shining as she laughed with him that day at Pepperdine.

Of course, there was no point thinking this way.

He straightened and let the breeze blow over him. He and Katy Hart were in two different worlds, worlds so far apart there could never be any passage between them. Fame was an island, a strange, isolated place where people bought eighty-thousand-dollar watches and spent thousands of dollars every week at fancy spas and department stores, a place where the so-called privileged changed wives the way people in Katy's world changed hairstyles.

Fame had cost him everything, and still he stayed, still he kept on, unable and unwilling to leave it. On the island, there would never be any connection with the Baxters and no relationship with Katy. But that was the way of things.

Even so his life wasn't without hope.

He liked Kelly enough. They had almost everything in common, especially now that they were working together. Also they'd talked about spiritual things, and though she wasn't as interested as he was, she was willing to explore the options. This week she had promised him they could go to a Kabbalah center together.

So life wasn't all bad.

It just wasn't all he had hoped for, the way he had thought — for a brief time — it might actually be. Back when he thought

Katy Hart might not only be his leading lady but the love of his life.

The thought was ridiculous, of course.

People on the island could never really mix with mainlanders. But tonight Katy's face haunted him, wouldn't leave him alone, and he wondered something that made him feel sad and old and trapped. He wondered whether one day soon he'd forget about Katy, whether he would compromise to the point that Kelly Parker would be enough for him.

Or whether he'd spend the rest of his life wondering about a girl from Bloomington, Indiana.

A girl he would've loved if given the chance.

A girl named Katy Hart.

It was opening night for *Tom Sawyer*, and Katy couldn't wait for the curtain to part. The play had come together, the way her plays always did. Never mind that it had gotten off to a rough start. As of dress rehearsal the night before, the show was so strong it brought tears to her eyes. Tears and one absolute truth.

She'd made the right decision by coming back to Bloomington.

In the weeks since she'd been home, the

kids had formed a bond as cast mates and friends. Sarah Jo was perfect in her part, and whatever her mother was telling her behind the scenes, it no longer dragged her down at rehearsals. Tim Reed and Ashley Zarelli were perfect as Tom and Aunt Polly, and a special friendship seemed to have formed between Tim and Bailey Flanigan.

The people of CKT were a family in many ways, and most of all they were her family. A group that brought richness to her life that could not have been gained by any acting part or by allowing herself to fall for Dayne Matthews.

Her one regret was that she'd kissed him so easily on the beach that night. Kissing meant more than that to her; it always had. But somehow alone with him at Paradise Cove it had seemed the most natural thing to kiss him back. Seconds had passed before she came to her senses, and for that she was ashamed.

Some nights she felt so bad about it she almost called him to clear things up.

But he would only think she was strange. He was used to girls giving in to his every whim. He probably saw her as just one more on a list of women he was mildly attracted to.

In the end, that was the reason she didn't call. By now he would've forgotten about her, anyway. Kelly Parker had gotten the part; Katy read about it in one of the gossip magazines. After a lifetime of not reading them, she'd bought one every week since she came home — mostly to stare at the stories in horror and thank God that she hadn't taken the part.

The pictures of her with Dayne ran a couple weeks after she returned home. The images were dark and shadowy, but the headline was just what Dayne had guessed it would be: "Mystery Woman Makes Out with Dayne Matthews on the Beach!" She figured no one had seen it until one day at practice when Rhonda Sanders unfolded it from her backpack.

"Why didn't you tell me?" Rhonda had wanted every detail when she came back, but Katy hadn't said much.

"I told you, we were almost killed." Katy gave Rhonda a half smile. "There isn't much more to it. God wanted me to come back, and here I am."

Rhonda raised an eyebrow. "Nothing much happened, huh?"

Katy didn't try to deny it. Instead she hung her head for a moment before meeting her friend's eyes. "It was only a kiss, but it was wrong."

Katy was downstairs in the greenroom now, trying to keep the kids from bursting at the seams from excitement. Tim and his gang of Tom Sawyer followers were being rubbed down with stage dirt, their hair teased and brushed so they would look unkempt.

Sarah Jo came up to her as she was making her rounds, checking on last-minute details. "Katy?"

She turned around and gasped. "Sarah Jo, you look beautiful. I don't remember that dress at the rehearsal yesterday."

"It wasn't there." Sarah Jo looked down, clearly embarrassed. "My mom bought it for me. She thought the dress she'd made me before was . . . well, a little too plain."

Katy gritted her teeth. Alice Stryker wasn't going to ruin her opening night. She smoothed the white blouse and silk scarf she was wearing and smiled at Sarah Jo. "Sweetheart, the dress is perfect. Tell your mother thank you."

A smile lit Sarah Jo's face. "Okay, Katy. Thanks."

They played to a full house tonight, and the show was amazing. The only mistake came during the fence-painting scene. When the actors moved their paintbrushes against the fence, a few girls on the back-stage crew were supposed to work from behind to make a white stripe appear on the fence for the audience.

Done right, the effect was fantastic, making it look as if the boys in Tom's gang were actually painting the fence. But tonight the actors were still talking about painting the fence when suddenly a white section moved magically up the center of one board. The problem remained until Tim anchored himself on the edge of the fence and between his lines whispered for the girls to change the fence back again.

The audience got a good laugh out of the mistake, and the cast worked through it. Katy didn't mind. This was the part of live theater she loved so much. It was unpredictable, and with children it was even more so.

When the play was over, the Flanigans found her. Jenny gave her a long-stem rose and her best smile. "It was wonderful, Katy. Another phenomenal job." She leaned in. "It was perfectly cast. You're the best."

When the Flanigans moved on, Katy felt a wave of emotion wash over her. Only with God at the center could a mom watch her daughter take a lesser role and know in the end that it was for the best.

The foyer of the theater was packed, the parents dressed to the nines the way Katy asked them to dress on opening night. She squeezed her way through, saying hello to one parent or student after another. Finally she reached the place where the actors were autographing the programs for starstruck kids.

For a moment Katy studied the scene.

This was the way it should be — a simple admiration, but one that would pass as soon as the next play got started up. She was about to move farther into the foyer when Ashley Baxter Blake approached her. She was still tanned and happy, glowing the way she had ever since she returned from her honeymoon cruise.

"The play was brilliant." Ashley's eyes grew wide as she took hold of Katy's shoulders. "I can't believe the magic you worked on these kids."

Katy pointed straight up. "I get a little help!"

"I know just what you mean." Ashley grinned. "Let's get together sometime for coffee."

"I'd like that." Katy smiled. "I think we'd have a lot to talk about."

The conversations continued, and finally

near the stairs back by the greenroom, Rhonda Sanders found her. The two rushed together in an embrace that put the coda on all their hard work. "We did it! It was beautiful, Katy. Perfect!"

They were going over the highlights of the play when Heath Hudson joined them. Beside him was a handsome guy, a friend of his named Doug Lake. Katy hugged Heath and thanked him for helping with the soundboard. Meanwhile, Doug started a conversation with Rhonda.

After a few minutes, Heath led Katy a little closer to Doug and Rhonda. "Hey." He nodded to his friend. "Doug and I wanna take you and Rhonda out for ice cream." He shrugged. "If you don't have anything else going on."

Rhonda gave her the slightest eyebrow raise, her way of saying yes, she'd like to go. Katy smiled at Heath. "That'd be great."

The trip to the ice-cream parlor was more fun than Katy had expected. Yes, once in a while she still wondered about Dayne Matthews. But only in a curious sort of way. What he might be doing and whether Kelly was playing the part the way Dayne wanted it played. That kind of thing.

Dayne was make-believe in her life, a moment that sometimes felt like it never happened at all. But Heath Hudson . . . Heath was real. Maybe it would take time to develop feelings for someone like Heath, but if that night was any indication, the feelings could come.

When Katy's head hit her pillow it was with a full heart. Things were good in her life — very good. God had spared her in more ways than one, and now she was exactly where she belonged. *Tom Sawyer* still had twelve more shows running, and then they would get ready for their fall production. The play would be *Annie*, and auditions would start in just three weeks.

Katy smiled into the dark night. She could hardly wait for auditions.

A Word from Karen Kingsbury

Dear Reader Friends,

I'm thrilled to be at the beginning of this new adventure — the Firstborn series. By now you understand the dynamic setup for Dayne Matthews, Katy Hart, and the Baxter family.

There are tenuous secrets that hang in the closets of Dayne Matthews and John Baxter. If they come to light, everyone around them will be changed forever. If not, then lifelong heartache will result.

As for this, the first book, it was obviously an exploration into the world of the famous. But not only that. It was a look at the people who desire fame, the mesmerizing allure of the wealth and power at the center of the world where America's most well-known people live out their lives.

Nearly everyone has — at one time or another — wanted to be famous. A famous singer or actor or dancer, a famous politician or astronaut. But what comes with that fame? What does our modern-day society do to those people? The cost is always high, much like it is for Dayne Matthews. He has family in Bloomington, people he might love and build a life with, but he's afraid to make the call. Certain their two worlds could never mix.

How many of you are in that situation? Maybe it isn't a secret you're keeping from the people you love. You might not be famous and afraid of paparazzi, but you have fears all the same. Fears that keep you from the ones you care about most.

Maybe you have something in your heart, deep feelings or compliments or admiration. But you're afraid to bring those thoughts to light. If that's where you're at, let me encourage you. Love must be in the light if it's to be love at all. Make the phone call, write the letter, offer forgiveness where it's needed.

The urgency of our days is one of the things I love talking about most when I have the chance to speak to groups around the country. There is no waiting until tomorrow when it comes to the people we care about, the people God has put in our lives. If you are a parent, then put down the newspaper. Get on the floor with your children while they're still little enough to want you down there.

Play and sing and laugh with abandon, for tomorrow will come soon enough.

My youngest son said something to me the other day, something I'll remember forever. The day was beautiful — crisp December air and a brilliant blue sky. But the sun sets early in the winter, and Austin knew that all too well. "Mommy —" he looked up at the fading afternoon — "why's the sun in such a hurry to go away?"

Time moves fast. The opportunities of today will be nothing but a memory tomorrow.

That said, I can tell you that I could hardly wait to pull Katy Hart back to Bloomington and away from the strange and bizarre world of Hollywood and fame. I studied the gossip magazines, appalled at the things written about these people. I found myself hurting for the megastars who are scrutinized so closely.

How could any sort of normalcy exist in that arena?

I can hardly wait to bring you the next pieces of Dayne's story, the next chapters involving Katy Hart, the Flanigans, and the Baxter family. So much lies ahead, so many triumphs and tough times, so much to learn, and so many ways in which these characters will be stretched and tested.

I have good news for you! As you remember, the Redemption series had a total of five books. Now the same is true for the Firstborn series and the books after that — the Sunrise series. They will release about every three months and will include the following:

Firstborn Series
Fame
Forgiven
Found
Family
Forever

Sunrise Series
Sunrise
Summer
Soldier
Someday
Sunset

These, I'm certain, will be some of the best books I've written, because I can feel God breathing life into the plotlines and characters, writing the stories on the pages of my heart even now.

On a personal note, our children are growing like weeds! This fall Donald is taking some time off work to homeschool our five boys. The goal is to take the same six hours that they used to be in a classroom and train them to excel in academics, athletics, and character. It's a once-in-a-lifetime opportunity, and we are seizing the chance. Kelsey remains involved in high school, theater, and dance — just like Tyler.

Our home continues to be a place where young people gather, a safe spot where they can learn about God and see love modeled in a dozen ways. We are humbly grateful that the Lord keeps using us in this way.

As always, I love hearing from you. Please write to me at my Web site, www.KarenKingsbury.com, or at my e-mail address: rtnbykk@aol.com. I appreciate all your prayers, comments, and feedback, and I will always lift you up to the Lord as I go back to my laptop, looking for what God would have me bring you next.

Until we meet again,
in His light and love,

Karen Kingsbury

Discussion Questions

Use these questions for individual reflection or for discussion with a book club or other small group. They will help you not only understand some of the issues in *Fame* but also integrate some of the book's messages into your own life.

1. What issues is Dayne struggling with in *Fame*?
2. What are some of the difficulties of living a celebrity life? Which of these were new to you after reading this book?
3. How do you think you would handle a celebrity life?
4. Why does our culture hold actors, actresses, etc., in such high esteem?
5. What are the dangers of this way of thinking?
6. Explain the connection between movies, media, and the desire by many people to be famous.
7. What are some of the ways we have been hurt as a society because of our fascination with celebrity and fame?
8. How do the celebrity life and the ad-

miration of the celebrity life conflict with living a life for God?

9. What does the Bible say about self-worship or celebrity? Use a concordance and search out three verses.

10. Based on Scripture, what are some cautions we should use while living in a society so taken by celebrity?

11. Explain how God was attempting to get Dayne's attention throughout *Fame*.

12. Why was Katy drawn to the audition in Hollywood and led to almost take the part in Dayne's movie?

13. Explain a time when something crept into your life that would've been harmful to you and your faith.

14. How did God get your attention?

15. How did God get Katy's attention? What were the turning points that convinced Katy to return to Bloomington?

16. Have you ever been tempted to be a "stage mom," the way Alice Stryker was with her daughter?

17. Why do you think parents fall into that mind-set?

18. In what ways did Alice Stryker's behavior damage her daughter?

19. Dayne begins to have a fascination

with Kabbalah, a cultlike religion currently popular in Hollywood. Why are
people drawn to false religions where
they can be their own god?

20. Do you think John Baxter should keep
the secret about his firstborn son?
Why or why not?